Coming Full Circle

About the Authors

A Professional Wetland Scientist (Emeritus) and Wildlife Biologist (MS), Budd Titlow is also an award-winning photographer and author. He has published four other natural history books, including *BIRD BRAINS — Inside the Strange Minds of Our Fine Feathered Friends*, and *SEASHELLS — Jewels from the Ocean*. He has also published five hundred magazine/newspaper photo-essays, five thousand photographs, and presented two hundred nature programs nationwide. Budd is currently using his writing and photography to focus public attention on the climate crisis and biodiversity loss — two of the most serious environmental threats our planet has ever faced. Budd's work is summarized on his web site at www.buddtitlow.com.

Mariah Tinger is an author and educator teaching sustainability at Boston University's Questrom School of Business. Additionally, she is pursuing her Ph.D. in climate communication at Otago University and applying her knowledge as a co-host on the podcast, *The Climate Minute*. When she is not chasing chickens or her children in her Massachusetts home, she is dreaming of new ways to tell the climate story. You can learn more about Mariah on her website www.mariahtinger.com.

As a father-daughter team, this is their second book; their first was the award-winning non-fiction book about climate heroes and their solutions, *PROTECTING THE PLANET — Environmental Champions from Conservation to Climate Change*.

Budd Titlow and Mariah Tinger

Coming Full Circle
A Sweeping Saga of Conservation Stewardship Across America

Olympia Publishers
London

www.olympiapublishers.com
OLYMPIA PAPERBACK EDITION

A CIP catalogue record for this title is available from the British Library.

ISBN: 978-1-80074-568-1

This is a work of fiction.
With the exception of historic figures and places, authors, and contemporary climate scientists, the names, characters, places and incidents originate from the writers' imaginations. Except as noted, any resemblance to actual persons, living or dead, is purely coincidental.

First Published in 2022

Olympia Publishers
Tallis House
2 Tallis Street
London
EC4Y 0AB

Printed in Great Britain

Dedication

I dedicate this book to my father, Franklin H. Titlow, Jr., who knew he wanted to be a newspaperman at age seven when he received a toy printing press for Christmas. Although I didn't appreciate it as much as I should have at the time, he passed along his love of the written word and life-long emphasis on having his words make a difference. I also dedicate this book to my wife, Debby Igleheart Titlow, whose life-long commitment to teaching music to children inspired me to make the world a better place by writing this book. Finally, I dedicate this book to my three children — Mariah, Merisa, and David — and five grandchildren — Harrison, Sierra, Max, Wylie and Coco. It is my profound hope that this book will help them all to continue knowing, loving, and protecting our natural world.

Acknowledgements

Budd Titlow

I owe my love of conservation and the natural world to several teachers and mentors, including William 'Bill' Hall, my high school biology teacher and cross-country coach, and Virginia Tech Wildlife Ecology Professor Robert T. Lackey who helped create a career for me where none had previously existed. Throughout my career as an ecologist and conservationist, I have also drawn continuous inspiration and dedication from the work of the landmark conservationists who came before me — most notably Harriett Lawrence Hemenway, John Muir, Robert 'Bob' Marshall, Rachel Carson, Roger Tory Peterson, Ding Darling, Howard Clinton Zahniser, Marjory Stoneman Douglas, Aldo Leopold, David Brower, and Edward O. Wilson.

Mariah Tinger

Just as the *circle of life* keeps the balance in nature, so, too, have my mentors and mentees kept the balance for me. My first conservation mentor is my father, Budd Titlow, and I owe a debt of gratitude to him for including me in his circle. My podcast co-host, Edward "Ted" McIntyre keeps me thinking, makes me laugh, and is an unwavering cheerleader for me." I would also like to thank the professors that have inspired me along the way, beginning with my biology professor and research advisor, Professor Michael O'Donnell who taught me the patience and courage to track raccoons through the woods overnight. Dr Craig Schneider is a consummate storyteller in addition to an influential botanist, as is Dr Nancy Longnecker. Dr Mark Leighton taught me, quite literally, to embrace trees (in transects, of course!). All have my deepest gratitude for their advice, support, and belief in me. My students at Boston University teach me new ways of looking at the world. They impress me year after year with their abilities and passion to make a difference in the world. Last but not least, I thank my husband and children for making do when I couldn't be there and making me smile when I could. To my children, especially, I extend a deep well of thanks; they make my heart swell with love and keep me marching on for the cause — I do this all for their future.

PROLOGUE

There is a lot that our U.S. biology and history books don't tell us. Tracking the triumphs and travails of a multi-generational American family, this book sets the record straight.

From a biological perspective, many American colonists didn't care about protecting our native wildlife or conserving our natural resources. Just think about the once abundant species that are no longer with us — the passenger pigeon, the eastern elk, the Carolina parakeet, the heath hen, the American bison (almost), and the black-footed ferret (almost). Then consider our native tallgrass and midgrass prairies — most of which were swallowed up by settlers' plows and then blown away during the Dust Bowl of the 1930s. Finally, look at our air and water quality — both poisoned by industrialization and still trying to recover.

On the history side of the ledger, no group of U.S. citizens has ever been more disrespected and abused than our Native American tribes. They respected all species as equals and managed their lands not just in sustainable ways, but in ways that enhanced the flourishing of the ecosystem. Yet they lost both their ancestral lands and their cultural societies to colonial *progress*.

But — in the end — this book carries a very positive, hopeful message. We can still extract ourselves from our past *faux pas*. By shedding our polarized viewpoints and working cooperatively, we can still save our planet before it's too late.

For both of us, this book is a career self-examination. For me (Budd) the text expresses many things I've learned about the natural world during my fifty years as a wildlife ecologist and resource conservationist. For me (Mariah), the book's content captures the joy of the natural world that my dad (Budd) taught me, how that joy has shaped my career as an educator and science communicator, and how I hope it influences my children's paths. We both see reflections of our past and visions of our future modeled in the multi-generations of families connected to nature.

Throughout this book, we also emphasize our lifelong beliefs in the sanctity and equality of all living things — both human and non-human. Our belief system encompasses all races, religions, cultures, and lifestyles — but especially those of the Indigenous (or Native) Peoples of the world.

As expressed in our main title, *Coming Full Circle,* our book's central theme revolves around two primary terms — *the circle of life* and *biodiversity.*

Many of us — especially those with kids or grandkids — know the first term, *the circle of life,* as the mega-hit song from the Broadway musical and blockbuster movie, *The Lion King.* In reality, *the circle of life* is a symbolic representation of birth, survival, and death — which leads back to birth. For example, an antelope may live for years — grazing peacefully on African grasslands and producing several healthy calves. But — as she nears the end of her life and thus her speediness — a hungry lioness captures and kills her. The antelope dies, but the lioness brings her body back for the nourishment of her hungry cubs. In this way, the antelope's death sustains the life of the lioness's pride — or family of lions.

Life is thus represented as a circle because it is a constant loop. The idea of life as a circle exists across multiple religions and philosophies. This belief was prevalent throughout the early Indigenous Peoples of Earth. Unfortunately — owing to what some may term '*progress*'— this fervent belief in *the circle of life* is much less common in today's world.

The second term — *biological diversity,* or *biodiversity* for short — is primarily used by biologists and ecologists. *Biodiversity* means the variety of life — the total number of species, both plants and animals — living on Earth. This includes everything from the tiniest microbial spores to the gargantuan blue whale. Generally speaking, the greater the *biodiversity* — the total number of species present — the healthier our planet.

As career environmental scientists, we believe that these two terms are very closely related. In fact, they build off of and intensify one another. Picture the diameter of *the circle of life* as the number of species that participate in that circle. In our antelope-lioness example above, the diameter would include the lioness and her pride, the antelope and her calves, the grass that the antelope eats, the vultures that feed upon the remainder of the antelope's carcass, the decomposers that help break down what the vultures leave behind — and so on. In this manner, *the circle of life* is always intricately populated with species and interdependencies. The larger the circle — in terms of its diameter — the greater Earth's *biodiversity* and vice versa. Because of this, we use these terms interchangeably throughout this text.

Unfortunately, *the circle of life* — or *biodiversity* — of the United States has decreased dramatically since the first European immigrants landed on our shores. By telling this fictional account — partially based on historical facts — of one multi-generational family of American immigrants, this book explores how and why this change has occurred and how we will — eventually — come back around to again achieve closure of *the circle of life*.

Our story begins with quite different — but keenly interrelated — anecdotes about two American heroes whose lives were separated by more than half a century.

BOOK ONE
Two Early American Heroes

Strong Bow Becomes a Mighty Chief

Young Strong Bow's fingers quivered as he aimed his arrow at the heart of the mule deer doe, placidly nursing her twin fawns in the woodland clearing. He drew back his bowstring, took a deep breath, sighed, and then — released the tension in his bow without firing his arrow. He just couldn't do it. He couldn't kill this beautiful, docile woodland creature — especially one that was so placidly nurturing her offspring.

The Year was 1767. Strong Bow was the only son of Chief True Arrow, the leader of the mighty Oglala Nation located in the heart of what is now the State of South Dakota. Like most tribes of Native Americans, the Oglala viewed the species around them as brothers and sisters; to be cherished and respected accordingly. But they were also completely dependent on the wild creatures of the land to provide their families with food, clothing, tools, and many other essentials.

After his failed hunt, Strong Bow sat down with his father in one of the tribe's traditional sweat lodge sessions. These sessions were intended as a time of purification and unity.

"Son, tell me what is bothering you," said Chief True Arrow.

Strong Bow looked at his father, surprised. How had he known?

"How can I ever become a tribal leader if I can't kill a deer?" lamented the young boy.

True Arrow looked at his son, his usually stern brown eyes softening. "My son, that feeling of hesitation you have is natural. The deep veneration and respect we have for Nature can lie in sharp contrast to the feeling you get when you are about to take the life of one of our animal brethren."

"You must understand that we are part of an important cycle for the deer," continued the chief. "We kill mercifully, quickly, and with reverence. If we do not, the deer population will grow to be too many. They will die of starvation when their numbers overwhelm the plants that nourish them. Their death will be drawn out — beginning with the youngest, weakest members of the population. When we hunt them, we help keep their system in balance."

Enheartened by the glistening spark of understanding he could now clearly see in Strong Bow's eyes, True Arrow pressed on, "Your heart told you not to kill a nursing mother. This was the right instinct. You knew that if you took that mother, her fawns would also die. While it may have felt cowardly to you, it is that spirit of compassion, that innate knowledge of when it is right to kill and right to let live, that sustains us within nature's *great circle of life*."

Strong Bow pondered these words for a moment. Finally, he said, "But Father, I don't think it was just because it was a doe with fawns that I couldn't shoot. I was afraid of the animal's pain."

Chief True Arrow nodded. "You will overcome this — my son — when the time is right."

As Strong Bow's adolescent growth gave him the strength of a bison, the speed of a puma, and the craftiness of a wolf, his place within the tribal hierarchy became bolder and bolder. He watched the ways that his elders planned their hunt — considering the many intricacies of the web of life in which they were but a tiny thread.

When Strong Bow swiftly and successfully shot his first buck — an older animal that had sired many offspring and was losing his speed — he now understood that the animal's pain was part of lessening the pain for the species as a whole. But — as he began to recognize his father's failing health — Strong Bow also knew there was much more to learn than just when it was imperative to hunt and when it was time to lower his bow. With this in mind, he sat down with his father as often as possible. During these intimate talks, he learned — and finally understood — much about his father's life and the tribal traditions he had so rigorously followed.

Starting as a young boy, True Arrow began earning his leadership role by honoring and splendidly succeeding at hunting and all the other traditions and rituals expected of an Oglala brave. He used his finely-honed hunting skills to feed not only his own family but also many other sick, infirm, and otherwise incapacitated tribal members.

Young True Arrow also instinctively knew how to use the wonderfully diverse native flora of the American wilderness to ward off and treat all sorts of different ailments and maladies — from the common cold to whooping cough and what we now know as tuberculosis, malaria, and pneumonia. True Arrow held great belief in the all-encompassing and pervasively effective medicinal healing qualities found in the plant world.

Like most Native American tribes, the Oglala believed that the natural landscape — Mother Earth — was sacred ground. True Arrow's elders taught him that they were just one strand in the delicate tapestry of creatures that worked in synchronicity to keep nature's system in balance. They viewed the creatures of the natural world as their equals — worldly connections to the Great Spirit that ruled the heavens above.

Because of this, the Oglala meticulously used every scrap from every animal they killed. The flesh was used for food; the skin for clothing, shelter, and warmth; the hooves for tools; and the bones for tooth and skin treatments. Young braves were taught at an early age that — along with the right to hunt — came a solemn duty to properly field dress, transport, and process each animal they killed. To do any less was considered the ultimate heresy — to both oneself and to the tribe — that would keep the offender away from entering the afterlife of the Great Spirit.

True Arrow learned his lessons well. He never failed to show his respect for all the wild creatures he saw and hunted. Plus, he had a fire in his heart and a light in his eyes that were unquenchable and beyond reproach. His every action was guided by the forces of nature — a wild wind blowing down the crests of the mountains, a sudden shaft of sunlight searing out from an overcast sky, the increased energy in a bubbling brook swollen by an unseen cloudburst several miles away. It was these intangible skills — these things that can't be taught — that soon made young True Arrow a natural leader of men.

Now, just a few years into his adolescence, Strong Bow was ready to accept the mantle of tribal leadership. The morning after his father passed on, Strong Bow vowed to continue emphasizing his father's belief that all living things were important. Since so many of the Mother Earth's creatures provided his tribal family with sustenance and security, it was his solemn duty to care for them as equals and protect the intricate web of life on which they depended.

This *one earth united* philosophy allowed North America's Indigenous peoples to live in a state of bliss with the natural world for thousands of years. But — as soon as the white European *settlers* began arriving *en masse* — everything in this delicately balanced equilibrium quickly — and permanently — changed forever.

Thaddeus Adams Proves His Survival Skills

Early one icy cold early spring morning in 1820, Thaddeus Adams was awakened from a sound sleep by the snapping of frozen branches. He had just grabbed the icy barrel of his loaded musket when he heard the spine-tingling snuffling and snorting of the wilderness creature he feared most. Yep, there was no doubt about it — a fierce mountain grizzly, most likely having just awakened from its winter slumber, was foraging for food right there in the middle of his campsite.

Thaddeus' first thoughts were about the safety of his trusty packhorse, Castor. He knew that if the grizzly injured or killed Castor, he would be stranded here high in the mountains, for several days — possibly even more than a week — from home. He would be forced to leave his load of beaver pelts and slog his way back down the mountains with only the supplies he could carry on his back. Fortunately — or unfortunately — depending how he looked at it, the grizzly seemed to be totally focused on the tent where Thaddeus was now lying, in anguished silence.

Afraid that any sudden movement — like getting out from under his sleeping blankets — would cause the great bear to charge, Thaddeus ever so gently raised his musket and tried to determine where the grizzly was in relation to his tent. He knew if he could figure this out, he would at least have a chance of taking a shot through the tent. Then — if he was really lucky — a hit, or a close miss, would scare the bear enough to make it flee his campsite and let him live.

But — having spent much of his young adulthood in the seemingly-endless wilderness of western Virginia — Thaddeus realized what would happen if he just wounded this feared monarch of the mountains. After all, the grizzly wasn't named *Ursus horribilis* because of its docile nature. There would most likely be hell to pay and he would be the one facing the vicious, grasping claws of the devil.

Quickly rethinking his hasty plan for a blind shot, Thaddeus knew what he had to do. It was a very risky idea — some might even say outrageously so — but he knew it was the only chance he had to save both the bear and himself.

While Thaddeus had little formal schooling, his life in the wild had taught him about the importance of the grizzly bear in the overall *circle of life*. He knew that without grizzlies, wolves, and mountain lions to keep them in check, large prey species — like deer and elk — could quickly overpopulate the land's ability to support them. So, he really did not want to kill this grizzly bear unless it was his last resort. Besides, he didn't much care for bear meat — it was way too dark and greasy for his taste and he was taught to always eat whatever he killed.

In one swift motion, Thaddeus ripped open the flaps of his tent and — with all his might — hurled his almost empty, metal canteen into the rocky outcrop behind his campsite. The canteen landed with a loud clatter — followed by rapid huffing, shuffling sounds as the bear loped over to investigate.

This was just the reaction Thaddeus had hoped for. He bolted from his tent in the opposite direction of the canteen and the bear, and — in five mighty leaps — was hugging the trunk of a huge pine tree.

Disregarding all manner of cuts and scrapes as he went, Thaddeus shinnied up the pine's thick trunk until he was a good fifty feet off the ground. Fortunately, another thing his wilderness days had taught him was how to tell a grizzly bear from a black bear. If you climb a tree, a black bear will climb up after you and pull you down. But grizzly bears will sit at the base of the tree and just wait until you come down or fall out from fatigue. (In actuality, he understood that grizzly bears can't climb trees because their claws are too long and bulky to grip the bark.)

Sure enough, as soon as Thaddeus knew he was high enough to avoid the grizzly's grasping, frightful claws, he looked down to see the bear furiously scratching, biting, and snarling — but thankfully not climbing — around the base of the tree. Now he knew he just had to hold on tight and wait long enough for the bear to get bored and leave.

In the meantime, Thaddeus prayed for God to keep him awake. He knew that one careless moment of dozing off would mean his head would end up in the gnashing jaws of this mighty omnivore. And because no one in the whole world really knew where he was, his grizzly-gnawed bones wouldn't be found for years — if ever! He also knew that by staying awake, he could continually yell at the bear. This was keeping the beast's attention focused on him and away from his horse, Castor — tethered to trees one hundred feet away.

Thaddeus's naked fingers and toes were half-frozen now and starting to ache from the tension of holding tight onto the mighty tree's trunk and branches. He considered climbing higher into the tree's upper boughs, just to get some circulation going again in his feet and hands. But he thought better of it since — in the dark — he wouldn't be able to tell for sure which branches would support his weight. He decided the best plan was to just sit tight where he was, concentrate on ignoring the creeping pain of the frigid mountain air, and wait until the bear moved on — which he knew it would do, sooner or later. Right now, he just wished with all his might that it would be sooner!

After what seemed more like days — rather than just a few hours — Thaddeus finally saw the faint glow of morning brightening the tops of the mountains on the eastern horizon. Looking down, he could still see the grizzly's hulk nestled against the base of the tree. The bear was no longer moving or making noise, so Thaddeus figured it must be asleep.

Reaching up above his head, he grabbed a rock-hard pinecone and suddenly another crazy idea came into his mind. The frozen pine cones were just like big musket balls. If he chucked a few down and hit the sleeping grizzly square in the head, the furry behemoth might just wake up and move off in anger. In an instant, he yanked several cones off their branches and threw them with all of his might straight down at the head of the sleeping grizzly.

Thaddeus' latest brainstorm worked like a charm — at least the part about waking the grizzly up. Letting out a ferocious sound that was a cross between a high-pitched yowl and a guttural roar, the great bear lunged to his feet and looked straight up to find the source of his annoyance. Summoning every ounce of strength left in his body, Thaddeus kept yanking and throwing pinecones down at the now fully-awake bear. Each cone that hit its mark elicited another fearsome roar from the extremely annoyed grizzly.

Past experience had taught Thaddeus that the most vulnerable and sensitive part of just about every large mammal is the soft-as-calves'-skin tissue of the nose. He knew that if he could just get a direct hit on the grizzly's muzzle, it might just hurt enough to persuade the bear to finally leave. Grabbing another cone, Thaddeus took careful aim at the flared, glistening nostrils perched above the gnashing teeth below his feet. He reached way back behind his ear and threw the cone as hard as he possibly could.

Thaddeus's aim was true and this final cone hit the bear square between the nostrils. With an otherworldly yowling scream, the massive bear spun around in a circle and grabbed its nose in its front paws. It then turned and ran back into the forest, letting loose with a painful stream of bleats and bellows as it went.

After waiting ten or so minutes to make sure the bear was gone for good, Thaddeus slid back down the tree to the ground. Mother Earth never felt so good — he thought to himself — as he jumped up and down and waved his arms to restore the feeling and circulation in his aching body.

Thaddeus felt both relieved and strangely satisfied that he had figured out how to handle this potentially deadly situation without hurting either one of the two most efficient meat-eaters in his wilderness home — the great grizzly bear and himself. Or at least, not hurting the bear — whose tender nose should regain its sensitivity within a few hours — too much.

Dead tired — but fortunately still alive — after his grizzly encounter, Thaddeus Adams crawled back into his tent and pulled his sleeping blankets tightly over his head just as the shafts of early morning sunlight started to filter through the needles of the oak-pine forest surrounding his campsite.

He wasn't sure how long he had slept when he awoke later that day, but he knew one thing for certain — spring was settling into the landscape of the Virginia Mountains in a hurry. It was so warm in his tent that his whole body was covered in sweat. He threw off his sleeping blankets with one arm and swished open the flaps to his tent with the other. The cool rush of early spring air turned the sweat beads all over his body into instant goose bumps, and he never felt so refreshed in his young life.

Thaddeus sprang out of his tent and gazed around the tranquil forest. The tops of the massive oak and pine trees rocked and creaked back and forth in a gentle warm breeze. Insects buzzed all around him and the first birds to arrive on their northward migration sang in a lively chorus.

It was as if winter had left along with the grizzly last night. The last vestiges of the snowpack — that still clung to the forest floor when he set up camp three days earlier — had disappeared completely. And, as if by magic, patches of wildflowers — tiny bluets and delicate spring beauties — were now blooming where the snow had been.

In that instant, Thaddeus believed that this was how he would live the rest of his life. But — as is the case with many human plans — such was not to be the case.

The Circle Begins Closing

While Oglala Chief Strong Bow and Trapper Thaddeus Adams lived more than five decades apart, they shared a strong common bond that was deeply rooted in their mutual love and respect for the natural world.

Chief Strong Bow always felt most spiritually alive while sitting on his horse on the top of a mountain — gazing at the vast wilderness beneath his feet. Similarly, Thaddeus Adams felt his ultimate contentment when the solar wind blew across his face as the first golden rays of the rising sun illuminated the steep valley walls surrounding his campsite.

Unfortunately, this natural kinship between Chief Strong Bow — a Native American leader — and Thaddeus Adams — a Colonial American white man — was an anomaly in what the legions of immigrating Europeans optimistically deemed their *New World*.

Imbued with dogmatic strictures, the first white settlers to arrive on the shorelines of colonial America immediately assumed their professed 'royal duties'. They preached the word of God — teaching the 'native infidels' and 'pagan peoples' about the way of Our Lord — indoctrinating them with 'true Christian faith and beliefs'. And the most harmful of these beliefs — which directly contradicted how Native Americans traditionally lived their lives — was that man was mandated by God to have 'dominion over nature'.

And so, it was with the beginning… now, for the rest of the story.

BOOK TWO
Thaddeus Adams Makes Big Changes

Colonial American Farmers

A strapping youth with a rugged square jaw offset by piercing blue eyes, Thaddeus Adams was the third of four sons born to a farming family eking out a meager existence in the southern end of Virginia's Shenandoah Valley. At the time — around 1800 — the Adams' family farm was still on the fringes of the vast untamed wilderness that was to become the continental United States.

Never one for regular household and farm chores, young Thaddeus — from the time he could move his legs fast enough to run — took off into the neighboring woodland whenever his parents turned their backs. After maybe the one hundredth time this happened, Thaddeus' parents stopped panicking that their upstart son was about to face sudden death in the evil woods and just let him go. They trusted that his now well-honed survival skills would serve him well and continue to bring him home unscathed.

As soon as he was big and strong enough to hold a steady aim with a musket and ride a horse with aplomb, Thaddeus took off for good or — at least — mostly so. He came back home whenever his craving for his mom's breakfast biscuits overcame his taste for his rustic campfire cooking. But mostly, he lived deep in the wilderness, where he felt whole and connected. He earned enough from running a beaver trap-line to pay for his camping supplies — with a little extra to help his family out every time he came back home.

In the Appalachian Mountains in the early 1800s, beaver were as thick as flies. Every mountain stream that maintained any sort of flow throughout the year had multiple beaver dams. As Thaddeus' mountaineering had taught him, a beaver family typically colonized the lower end of a stream first and then moved subsequently higher up the watershed by forcing their young to move out and build their own dams and lodges. Within a decade or less, a beaver family would typically colonize an entire drainage — from the headwaters down through a spider web of secondary and tertiary confluences — finally ending where the stream ran into a major river.

Thaddeus took great advantage of his plentiful and easily trapped quarry. If everything went just right and the weather was reasonably cooperative, he could pile up some two hundred beaver pelts on his horse-drawn sled within two full moons. These were the times that Thaddeus would surprise his parents and siblings by showing up at the family homestead — typically just in time for dinner. In the warmer months, dinner would be followed by a joyous night of drinking homemade wine and singing around the flames of a huge bonfire that roared throughout the night. The next morning — even if he was still groggy from the night of conviviality with his family — Thaddeus would always leave his load of pelts with his brothers to sell at the local trading post. Then — after raiding the family's food caches — he would jump on Castor and head back up into the mountains in search of more beaver.

The first few times Thaddeus showed up at home, his parents and brothers begged him to stay home and live a life of relative comfort and tranquility on the family farm. His life would be a lot less dangerous, they reasoned, and they could sure put his strong back and boundless energy to use in tilling the soil and raising the crops. In truth, they all knew they were just wasting their breath. No amount of logic or reasoning could keep Thaddeus Adams tethered to one place, day after day. His vagabond spirit and endless desire for new adventures were too much to overcome. His heart belonged to the rushing streams and wild winds of the Appalachian Mountain wilderness.

Understanding Nature's Web of Life

When he was trapping, Thaddeus Adams — before dozing off each night — kept busy documenting his thoughts and experiences in a journal. Next to Castor and his musket, his daily writings were his most valuable possession. His formal education was limited to the three years he spent in the one-room schoolhouse that was about two miles down the valley from his family farm. But he was fortunate to have parents who both learned how to read and write while growing up in a Quaker community that was close enough to Washington, DC to benefit from the colonial city's educational amenities.

Most evenings when Thaddeus was just an infant, until he was old enough to go to school, his parents would sit him and his three brothers down in a circle and read to them until they fell asleep. The family's cache of books — while limited to only a few dozen titles — was a treasure trove to all four brothers. No matter how many times they heard the same stories they could never get enough of hearing and seeing the wonderful words that were so carefully crafted on each page of every book. When they were each old enough, the brothers started reading on their own — curling up in a corner of the family home with a different book every night.

It was this love for books that kept Thaddeus writing in his tent by the glow of a candle-lantern, often until the wee hours of the morning and — on occasion — until sunrise the next day. In fact, while he would never have admitted it to anyone else — without his penchant for writing — Thaddeus knew he could have never made it alone through an Appalachian Mountain winter.

Never really fancying himself a serious writer, Thaddeus still took great pride in his detailed descriptions of the wonders of nature that filled all his waking hours in the Virginia Mountains. Scarcely a day went by that he didn't see something that he had not seen before. He had an appreciation for subtlety and a special knack for observing things that most people — especially the lowland 'tenderfeet' — would probably walk right by and never even notice.

Thaddeus also prided himself on his instinctive understanding about how everything in his wilderness world was connected to everything else. He thought of the world as one gigantic spider web — made of silk that was so tightly-spun that when something happened on one strand it shook everything else in the web. It was seeing and then writing about how all the strands of his personal *web* fit together that he really enjoyed.

Thaddeus also understood that when certain important wilderness animals died, this could also — over time — affect all the rest of a woodland community. For example, if a farmer — fearing for the safety of his livestock — wiped out all the adults and pups in a wolf pack, the other wild animals might suffer as well. Without the wolf pack to keep them in check, the large-hoofed, vegetarian animals — deer, elk, and moose — could overpopulate and consume most of local forage species, including grass, leaves, nuts, and berries. This, in turn, would leave minimal food for smaller plant-eating creatures like rabbits, groundhogs, and squirrels. The widespread loss of these prey species would then leave slim pickings for the ferocious, but smaller carnivores — the badgers, weasels, and martens — to eat and many would starve to death.

Even tiny animals that most people called 'vermin' — the field mice, voles, and woodrats — would soon run out of seeds to eat because most of the flowering plants were gone. It was all a vicious cycle of decreasing biodiversity that could — after just a few years — open huge ecological voids in the local forest communities that could take a long time to recover.

Thoughts of the spiraling loss of animals in his beloved forests often wore heavily on Thaddeus' mind. This was especially true after he had finished setting his trap-line and was passing the long hours until it was time to go see what he had caught.

It was during these reflective times that Thaddeus always comforted himself by remembering how the natural world of his youth tended to recover well from whatever man decided to do to it. He thought back to his parents' farm. When he was still living at home, he delighted in watching fallow agriculture fields return to nature during the spring months. First came the tall grasses, then the field mice, voles, and cottontail rabbits. Once the prey species had re-established, the coyotes, wolves, and hawks moved in to feed and the *circle of life* was soon restored.

Forest fires were another testament to nature's adaptability to change that Thaddeus often witnessed in his mountain world. On warm spring and summer afternoons, fierce lightning storms would well up deep in the cloudbanks that built up over the mountaintops and then rolled down into the valleys. Like fire from the front end of a muzzle-loader, lightning bolts would shoot out of the dark clouds and shatter the tallest trees below. The struck trees would often ignite into roaring fireballs — looking like massive candles with long wicks. Torrents of fire would then flare through the forest canopy and roll down the tree trunks to the ground where the insatiable flaming tongues would turn everything in their paths to red-hot embers.

Thaddeus was often amazed by how fast the forest floors recovered — even after the fiercest fires. Feeding off the sunlight blazing down — now without the dampening shade of the forest canopy — wildflower patches and stump sprouts popped up like weeds. Within a few short weeks of summer, areas of old-growth forest — devastated by the lightning strikes — turned lush with emerald-green grasses and colorful flowers.

When he returned to these same burned areas just a few years later, Thaddeus was awed by how rapidly the forest had re-grown. In each case — out of the death and destruction caused by wildfires — there suddenly were freshets of renewed life. Pine saplings — finally freed to grow by the fire's intense heat — were sprouting everywhere. It was like the old worn-out forests had given birth to brand-new growths that were now attacking life with all the enthusiasm and vigor of youth.

This ability of nature to bounce back from total devastation always filled Thaddeus with hope and the belief that the wilderness he treasured with all his heart would never disappear. No matter how mighty and pernicious it might be, no man-made force could ever be strong enough to overcome the indefatigable forces of nature. Because of this, Thaddeus believed — with all his heart — that man would never be able to tame and control his wilderness home.

During the early 1820s in the mostly unpopulated Appalachian Mountain wilderness, Thaddeus was absolutely right about nature's built-in ability to fend off sudden disruptions and thrive again. Unfortunately — as he would soon learn — such was not always to be the case.

Lessons of Life and Death in the Wilderness

The days after he had finished setting his trap-lines were always Thaddeus' favorite times in the mountains. He would spend hours either walking or riding Castor at a peaceful gait — following game trails that paralleled ridgelines or meandered through lush stands of wet meadow grasses and woodland shrubs. Whenever he heard a new sound or saw something different, he would stop to investigate. Always moving stealthily and silently upwind — just as he had learned from the Native American hunting parties he sometimes met in the woods — he was often able to approach woodland creatures close enough to study what they were doing.

Thaddeus especially enjoyed watching wild animals with their young. He was amazed at how often he saw woodland creatures doing the same sorts of things that human families do. Usually, it was something as simple as watching a female robin feed her young by dropping wriggling worms into the gaping mouths of the chicks that filled her cup-shaped nest of twigs, grasses, and leaves.

One spring — soon after the frost had left the ground — Thaddeus spent several days watching a family of red foxes at their den which was dug underneath a large rotting stump. He chuckled softly at the playful antics of the pups rolling and tumbling over and over one another as they fought to see who was the strongest of the lot. It reminded him of how he and his brothers used to toss each other around as they played King of the Mountain on the piles of corncobs stacked around the family barn. He could also relate when an adult male fox showed up at the den with a freshly-killed rabbit in his mouth. It was just the same as when the dinner bell rang at the family farm and four, hungry, growing boys all piled into the kitchen and dug in to heaping helpings of steaming vegetables, mashed potatoes, and barbecued beef.

On many occasions, Thaddeus had seen what he knew was the law of the wilderness in action. He once watched in awe and horror as a mountain lion leaped from the boughs of a pine tree onto a pair of cinnamon-and-white spotted fawns that were curled up in a grassy spot — some ten paces away from where their mother was placidly grazing. Seeing the big cat, the doe raised her white-flagged tail straight up in the air.

Thaddeus could see the dread in the doe's eyes as she cast one last look at her doomed fawns, before bounding away and disappearing into the woods. The cougar was mercifully quick in dispatching the fawns before they could even bleat, snapping their spinal cords with two quick slashes of his mighty jaws.

Surprisingly, the most fearsome battle Thaddeus had ever seen did not involve any of the supreme 'alpha' predators — the mountain lions, grizzly bears, and timber wolves — that ruled his wilderness world. That honor was reserved for a battle royal he once watched between — pound-for-pound — the two most ferocious and efficient predators in the Appalachian Mountains.

Working just after sunrise, Thaddeus had finished setting his traps along the lower reaches of a stream with a series of active beaver dams and ponds spaced about a half mile apart. The onset of winter was in the air. Most of the trees had dropped their autumn skirts of gold, purple, russet, and orange, exposing the clumps of mistletoe and leafy squirrel nests scattered amongst the stark black-gray skeletons of winnowing limbs. A glint of frost coated the needles of the evergreen trees and a scattering of snowflakes swirled through the air and drifted softly to the ground.

While sitting on a fallen log skinning out a freshly-caught beaver, Thaddeus heard an other-worldly commotion in the woods quite close to where he sat. He was so startled that he threw his skinning knife in one direction and the partially-skinned beaver pelt in the other.

Bolting upright, Thaddeus grabbed the barrel of his musket from the tree where he had propped it and prepared to face an attack from some sort of wild adversary he had never before encountered. He looked first to his right, then to his left. Seeing nothing, he quickly spun around to look behind him and there he saw the source of the commotion.

Not more than five paces away from where he now stood, a long-tailed weasel and a fisher cat faced off — nose-to-nose — each letting loose with cascades of ear-splitting yowls, screeches, and screams that sounded worse than the fury of the devil himself. Between the two snarling beasts lay the subject of their confrontation — a freshly-killed cottontail rabbit.

Thaddeus could not determine which one had actually made the kill, but it was obvious that neither was going to give it up without a fight. With claws slashing and teeth gnashing, two of the forest's most efficient carnivores went at it with all their might.

It was a remarkable battle — unlike anything Thaddeus had ever witnessed in his life. Neither animal would give an inch as they both furiously parried and jabbed, trying to get at each other's throats to inflict a fatal wound. The fur flew and the blood spattered for what Thaddeus estimated to be at least fifteen minutes.

In clear view of both animals the whole time, Thaddeus might as well have been invisible to these two valiant warriors. It occurred to him to raise his musket and end the blood bath by shooting one of the animals, but he just couldn't bring himself to do it. As painful as it was to watch these two splendid predators biting and clawing each other to pieces, he knew that he had to let nature take its course and decide the winner.

The fisher cat eventually prevailed, using its much larger size and longer claws to reach out and rip open the weasel's throat. With the weasel's chest heaving its final breaths and blood gushing from its mouth, the fisher claimed his rabbit prize and shakily waddled off into the forest leaving an unbroken trail of his own blood in the fresh snow.

Thaddeus knew that it was very possible that the fisher might not even survive the night because of the serious wounds inflicted by the weasel. But for now, the fisher was the king of the forest and he had his trophy to prove it.

The Long Winters Begin to Take Their Toll

Spring was by far Thaddeus' favorite season. He always felt gloriously elated and alive knowing that he had survived another Appalachian winter and he could now look forward to many days of easy living. At least — he always thought — as easy as life can get when you're alone in a mountain wilderness with only your own guile and gumption to provide sustenance and day-to-day survival. But — whenever spring finally rolled in — he knew he didn't have to worry about freezing to death in a blizzard for a while — maybe even six months — if he was lucky!

Inspired by spring's emergence, Thaddeus always renewed his beaver trapping in earnest. But the past few long, cold winters — with their unusually deep snowpacks — were gradually sapping both his energy and his typically unbridled enthusiasm for life. Thaddeus was especially concerned about the health of his beloved horse, Castor.

While Thaddeus was a teenager and still only dreaming about his life as a wilderness trapper, he could easily see the incredible strength and energy that Castor possessed. He instinctively knew that this was the horse he wanted to carry his supplies and beaver pelts on his mountain forays for the next decade or so. But even Castor had his limits when it came to plodding through knee-deep snowdrifts.

In truth, the last few winters had taken a severe toll on both Thaddeus and Castor. Castor had often gotten off his feed and Thaddeus was deathly afraid that his horse might just give up and freeze to death, or become so weak that a wolf pack or roaming mountain cougar could take him down without a fight.

Thaddeus was even worried that the same fates could befall him. He had to really concentrate on eating enough to keep his own internal furnace burning during the seemingly endless dark, cold nights inside his tent. Especially on days when it was just too cold and snowy to venture outside of his campsite, he often longed for home and civilization. Many times, the longest winter nights drove him to the breaking point.

More than once, Thaddeus had burst out of his tent, half-naked, running and screaming in frustration until he stumbled headfirst into a snowbank. There he would lie, shivering and crying frozen tears, until he had released all his pent-up tension and managed to regain his wits enough to return to his tent.

The Comforts of Home Harken

Thaddeus continued trapping and living in the Appalachian wilderness for the next five years. Only one thing changed slightly; he began going home on a more regular basis — at least once every couple of months. His family was delighted to see him whenever he showed up, and his brothers took advantage of each opportunity to razz him about going soft.

Of course, Thaddeus would never admit that this was the case. Each time he came home, he just made up excuses, about needing to re-supply more often. He said it was because his trapping was so successful that he was covering much more ground each time he went back out.

In reality, Thaddeus was developing a sort of homesickness. Each night that he spent in his tent, he thought more and more about the warmth and strong family bonds he shared with his parents and his brothers. He found it harder and harder to fill his nights with writing in his journal. His thoughts often drifted away to everything that he was missing on the family farm. Especially now since all three of his brothers had children of their own, and he had a passel of nieces and nephews.

Thaddeus liked nothing better than the greeting his gang of family young'uns gave him each time he and Castor rode out of the woods and onto the family farm. The kids always flocked around him — before he could even dismount from Castor — wanting to see what new mountain treasures he had brought them. And he never disappointed. Eagle and hawk feathers, raccoon and deer jaw bones, dried owl pellets full of field mice bones — he always had something new to capture their attention and fuel their imaginations. He was their hero — plain and simple — the wilderness adventurer returning home with incredible stories and wonderful gifts from an unknown and dangerous land.

While the harmony of home life was definitely tugging harder and harder on his heartstrings, nothing could really ever get Thaddeus to give up his life in the wilderness. Or, at least, so he thought. But — as it turned out — there was one thing that would make Thaddeus change his ways forever, and one sparklingly clear Sunday in late October, he found out exactly what that was.

Then Along Came Minerva

Minerva Graham was a flaxen-haired beauty with a proper upbringing and a finishing-school education. Her light-blue eyes and rosy complexion belied the strength of spirit and body that was packed into her tiny, five-foot-two-inch frame. She could outthink any man and out arm-wrestle most of them. Of course, owing to her prim and proper nature, she didn't display her sheer physical strength unless she absolutely had to — but woe to any man who mistreated her in any way. He would be lucky to come away with just a busted jaw and an aching backside after tangling with her.

Thaddeus was never one for organized religion and — what he considered — all its phony trappings. He found all the spiritual stimulation he needed sitting on a mountaintop in his wilderness world. But one Sunday morning — after he had been home for a few days longer than usual — his parents and brothers hitched up the team and insisted that he clamber up into the family wagon and join them on their weekly trip to the village church.

With a clucking gee-haw, Thaddeus' father, Franklin Adams, turned the wagon into the big gravel-packed circular pathway in front of the immaculate, white-steepled church. He stopped right in front of the door and let his sons help their mother, Louise, out of the wagon and into the sanctuary. After escorting their mother into her regular pew up near the front of the church, Thaddeus and his brothers went back outside to help their father tether and tend to the horse team.

Perfectly poised and self-confident, Minerva Graham immediately sashayed over to greet the Adams boys and — mainly — to introduce herself to Thaddeus, whose handsome, clean-cut features attracted her full interest at first glance. Thaddeus was also struck by Minerva's radiant elegance and way with words, but he was far too shy to do anything about it. He meekly extended his hand, and with downcast eyes mumbled a barely audible 'hello' while Minerva enthusiastically pumped his arm up and down like she was trying to draw water.

Although his face didn't show it, Thaddeus had already made up his mind — this woman with beautiful features, an incredible mind, and the unbridled energy of a month-old colt — was exactly what he needed at this point in his life. Maybe, just maybe, he could leave his rugged mountain life behind after all.

Back at home after the Sunday service, Thaddeus surprised his family by announcing that he intended to hang around through the holidays and not head back up into the mountains until sometime after the New Year. He told his family that he had experienced some physical discomfort during his last few weeks in the wilderness and he wanted to make sure that it wasn't something serious before he went back out again.

While this all sounded well and good and quite believable to his family — truth be told — Thaddeus was sick all right, but it didn't have anything to do with his physical condition. He was lovesick, and he just knew that Minerva Graham was the cure he needed.

Although Thaddeus had only seen Minerva that one time at church, he thought about her all day long. He just couldn't get her mesmerizing smile and energetic manner off his mind.

The next Sunday morning — much to the surprise and delight of his family — Thaddeus was the first one dressed and down at the barn, tending to the horses and getting them hitched to the wagon. By the time that his brothers and parents were up and dressed, he was chomping at the bit to get everyone into the wagon and off to church.

Everyone thought that Thaddeus somehow had found religion on his last foray into the mountains and just couldn't wait to get to church to talk more with God. But unless God was actually Minerva Graham — which, in Thaddeus's current mindset was entirely possible — the deity wasn't the one he was hoping to talk to. Trouble was — much to Thaddeus' deep consternation — Minerva and her family didn't come to church that Sunday.

The last thing in the world that Thaddeus wanted to admit to his family was that some girl had captured his fancy. He knew his three brothers would never let him hear the end of it — about how the mighty mountain man now couldn't get along without the care and nurturing of a woman.

But it was true, Thaddeus was beside himself to know where Minerva was and how he could get to talk to her again. His mind was filled with horrifying thoughts that she might have gone off to get married and when he saw her again, she would have a huge new ring on her finger.

If Thaddeus could have gotten up the courage to ask his parents about Minerva, they would have immediately put his mind at ease. Because of the Grahams' prominence, just about everyone in the area knew all about them — including where and when they went places.

In fact — during one of the church service's weekly meet-and-greet sessions, Reverend Josh Bacon told the congregation that the Grahams had traveled to Washington, DC for a few weeks, and led a short prayer for their comfortable travel and safe return home. Thaddeus would have heard all this if he hadn't been sitting outside in the family's wagon, pining away — worried that he wouldn't get a chance to talk to Minerva — maybe ever again!

True Love Settles In

Thaddeus had no way of knowing this, but Minerva wanted to see him again just as much as he wanted to see her. Minerva's parents wondered what was wrong with their normally outgoing, fun-loving daughter. She always enjoyed the holidays and she especially loved visiting her grandparents in their seaside estate on Maryland's Eastern Shore. But for the past week, Minerva had been unusually sulky and argumentative.

Minerva was even rude to the horde of younger cousins who adored her and couldn't wait to see her each year. She always brought them all sorts of wonderful gifts — that she had made especially for them — and played games with them from before breakfast until after the dinner dishes were scraped, washed, and put away.

But this visit was different. Minerva often told the children they were bothering her, and when she talked to them it was only to chastise them for doing something wrong. Instead of the happy-go-lucky friend they all knew and loved, the cousins thought that they now had just another parent in the house telling them what they could and could not do.

The holidays couldn't go by fast enough for either Thaddeus or Minerva. Thaddeus because he sincerely hoped that Minerva must only be away for the holidays and wanted her to come home, and Minerva because she just wanted to get back home and see Thaddeus. On a crystal clear — but frigid — mid-January Sunday morning, they both got their wishes.

When the Adams' family wagon first came into view, Minerva ran to the top step of the church and began waving frantically. As soon as Thaddeus caught sight of Minerva, his heart started fluttering and his hands began shaking. This was the moment he had been so eagerly anticipating — for more than a month now.

But Thaddeus wasn't sure what he should do. Should he act like he didn't see her waving and just casually say 'hi' when she came over to him? Or should he act like mister big-shot and walk right past her when she tried to talk to him? After all, he had a reputation for ruggedness that could be quickly ruined if he was seen fawning over some girl.

As it turned out, Thaddeus didn't have to worry about preserving his masculinity in front of his family and neighbors. Minerva immediately ran over to him and hugged him so tightly that it took his breath away and left him gasping for air.

Minerva grabbed Thaddeus by the hand and tugged on his arm until he ran off with her behind the church. When they were both out of sight and earshot of the rest of the congregation, Minerva hugged Thaddeus again and told him that he was all she had been thinking about the whole time she was away. As far as Thaddeus was concerned, that was all it took to permanently cement their relationship.

Married Life in the Shenandoah River Valley

Practically the whole town turned out two months later for the wedding of Minerva Graham and Thaddeus Adams. It had taken them only a few dates to realize they were both madly in love with each other. By spring planting time in early April, the bride and groom were living comfortably and very happily on the forty-acre homestead that her wealthy parents had given them as a wedding present.

For the next five years, Thaddeus and Minerva lived the typical lifestyle of a farming family in Virginia's Shenandoah River Valley. They raised corn, beans, squash, and tomatoes — all grown in the river valley's fertile floodplain. They pastured hay on the back twenty acres of their spread and used it to feed the herd of goats and milk cows they raised for food, and the beef cattle they raised for money. During this time, they also had three healthy and beautiful children — Caleb, Ethan, and Delilah.

Only one thing was wrong — Thaddeus was becoming bored and hankering for a change. Each day that went by, he talked more and more about the freedom and adventure of the years he spent alone in the Appalachian Mountains.

It often got so bad that Minerva, many times, started to tell Thaddeus that if he missed the mountains so much, why didn't he just leave and go back up there. But she loved him too much to tell him anything of the sort. She just learned to put up with his grousing and complaining, knowing that the next day he would be out working hard — as was his inherent nature — raising the crops and tending to the livestock on the farm.

As time went by, Thaddeus took up with a group of other young farmers who lived in the river valley. They started meeting every Wednesday night at the village church. There, they talked mostly about farming subjects — like how to raise the best corn and where they could get the best price for beef. And — on occasion — they also talked about their hopes for the future.

More often than not, these discussions involved leaving their Virginia farms and joining the ever-growing number of families who were moving westward in search of vast acreages of open ranchland and riches like gold and silver. These were talks of dreams and fortunes that could not be found in the broad river valley — nestled between the Appalachian and Blue Ridge Mountain Ranges — that they currently called home.

The letters that the stagecoach drivers brought back from the families who had already packed up their covered wagons and headed West were enough to make even the most set-in-their-ways valley farmers want to pull up stakes and go take a look for themselves. There were tales of herds of buffalo so vast that they filled the horizon for as far as the eye could see and flocks of birds so dense that they darkened the sun.

Many of the families who left just took over as much western land as they wanted. Their letters described cornfields that covered hundreds of acres and pastures of golden grain that stretched for miles. These messages were the same for anyone who was dedicated to hard work — the opportunities and rewards in the vast, uncharted western territories were without limits.

Planning the Westward Move

The more the group of young farmers met and talked, the quicker and more often their conversation turned to moving westward. Not all the men were in favor of uprooting their families to pursue promising — but uncertain — lives in the west. But many were seriously thinking of organizing a wagon train and taking off as soon as the next spring began to settle across the land.

Thaddeus Adams was not only in favor of moving west, but the rest of the men who were ready to go saw him as their leader. They fully believed his years of wilderness savvy and guile were exactly what they needed to get them and their families safely across the mountains to this new, western 'promised land'.

Soon, the weekly meetings at the town church turned into planning sessions for the westward move. The desire of the group of energetic young farmers to move west seemed to increase with the increasing hours of daylight as the winter months waxed into spring.

Each week, the men stayed at the church until well past midnight talking about how they could sell off or trade their farmsteads and livestock for enough money to buy a rugged, new, covered wagon and enough supplies to last them the four months they figured they would need to reach the vast prairielands that awaited them on the other side of the mountains.

Thaddeus wasn't sure how to tell Minerva about the westward move. He knew — or at least he thought — she would be dead set against it. For one thing, she wouldn't want to risk all the bad things that could happen to their three young children during such a risky trip. For another, he knew Minerva's parents would be furious with him for even bringing up such an idea. They had given him the farm, barn, house, and livestock knowing that they had provided a place for him to live with Minerva and raise their children in peace and comfort for the rest of their lives. They certainly had not given Thaddeus all this to throw away on some wild-eyed scheme that would — even if it was successful — take Minerva and their grandchildren away from them for good.

Despite all his misgivings about the reaction of Minerva and her parents, Thaddeus' enthusiasm could not be denied. During their last meeting at the church, the men — that were in favor of leaving — decided that they were now past the point of no return.

They all agreed that they were going to form a wagon train and head west, and they were going to do this around the vernal equinox. After the meeting, Thaddeus rode home, marched confidently into his house, asked Minerva to sit down, and told her exactly what they were going to do.

To Thaddeus' great surprise, Minerva didn't even bat an eye. In fact, she already knew what the men at the church had been planning for all these weeks. She was just waiting for Thaddeus to tell her about it.

As far as Minerva was concerned, if Thaddeus really believed — with all his heart — in what he was doing, she would trust his judgment completely. She just wanted to make sure that his commitment was genuine and grounded in reality, instead of some dream that he hoped might come true.

A few of the westward-bound men dropped out after discussing the wagon train plan with their families, but the majority — some twenty-six families in all — decided to stay the course. The wives of most of the men who wanted to move westward felt the same way as Minerva. They trusted and loved their husbands enough to believe in what they were doing.

One-by-one, the westward-bound families sold their farms and livestock, and used the cash to buy the covered wagons that would become their homes on wheels for the next few months. As the designated leader, Thaddeus kept busy helping each family stock up with the supplies they would need for the trip.

BOOK THREE
Westward Ho

Hitting the Trail

As several of the families had difficulty selling their homesteads, they had to push back the wagon train's departure date a week. But bright and early on the morning of March thirtieth, 1833, the families pulled their covered wagons into the circular drive, in front of the church.

Next, everyone clambered down out of their wagons and filed into the church's sanctuary where Reverend Bacon led them in prayer, bidding them all — with God's help — a safe journey and great success in their new homes on the midwestern frontier. Afterward, Reverend Bacon had tears in his eyes as he shook everyone's hand and gave them his blessing one last time. He was honestly happy for them and their prospects for exciting new lives — but lamented the loss of more than half his congregation and many dear friends.

Now, it was time to go. Thaddeus Adams gave a whoop from the lead wagon and all the others fell in line and traveled the two miles out to the Great Wagon Road.

This colonial road began in Philadelphia, Pennsylvania and extended to the southwest for eight hundred miles. Entering the Shenandoah River Valley near present-day Martinsburg, West Virginia, the well-marked path continued southwest through the valley's two-hundred-mile length to what is now the City of Roanoke, Virginia. Here, the Wilderness Road branched off from the Great Wagon Road and proceeded to the northwest through the Cumberland Gap into southeastern Kentucky.

Thaddeus knew that following the Great Wagon Road would be the easy part of their journey. This main trail was well traveled and — for the most part — wide and smooth. The first test of the courage and conviction of the families — especially the men and teenage boys — would come after they turned to the northwest on the Wilderness Road and crossed through the Appalachian Mountains at the Cumberland Gap.

From the letters he had read from families that had already made the journey, Thaddeus knew that the wagon trail through The Gap was very rugged, deeply rutted, and — in many places — washed away by heavy rains and winter snowmelt running down from the mountains above. There was always a chance of a wagon becoming 'high-centered' if a driver wasn't paying close enough attention to the height of the ruts in the trail.

Additionally, more precious time could be lost if they came to a wash-out. It could take days to haul in enough large rocks and timber planking to build a temporary bridge strong enough to support the heavy weight of the covered wagons. Then — if the bridge failed — that would mean the families who lost their wagons would have to spread out and double-up with the families in the remaining wagons.

Thaddeus didn't share all of these concerns with the other families. Instead, he remained very positive, continuously assuring everyone that they would all be just fine, as long as they were very careful and thoughtful about every move they made along each mile they traveled.

Seven days after they left the church, the wagon train arrived at the junction where the Wilderness Road split off from the Great Wagon Road. Although it was only mid-afternoon, Thaddeus gave a loud whistle which was his signal for everyone to circle the wagons for the night. He wanted to make sure they were all nice and fresh before they set out on the treacherous trail through The Gap.

Just after sunrise the next day, Thaddeus walked around to each wagon, clanking a cooking spoon against a metal plate as he went. Despite the many groans and moans that greeted this wake-up alarm, within thirty minutes, everyone was up, dressed, and eating breakfast around the cooking fire that was roaring away in the center of the circle of wagons. Thaddeus was pleased and comforted to hear the eagerness of anticipation in everyone's voices as they talked excitedly about the adventures that lay ahead.

After breakfast, the women and children cleaned up and re-packed all the supplies into the wagons while the men harnessed the teams. An hour later, Thaddeus let out another of his now characteristic whistles as he pulled his team out of the circle and onto the Wilderness Trail. The other wagons fell into line behind the Adams family's wagon. As far as Thaddeus was concerned, their great adventure was now just beginning.

Big Trouble on the Gap Trail

For the first two days, the wagon train had easy going as they moved along through the rolling Appalachian foothills. They were only slowed down a few times when they had to stop to clear away trees that had been blown down across the trail. Everyone remained in jovial moods — punctuated by lots of cheerful banter — as they guided their teams along the narrowing trail and toward the looming mountain ridges.

When the wagon train entered the higher mountains, Thaddeus turned over his wagon's reins to Minerva's strong hands and rode ahead on Castor to scout the trail conditions. After he had ridden no more than a mile, he came upon a Cherokee hunting party. The group of five young braves were riding bareback on their horses, with their bows slung across their chests and quivers full of granite-tipped arrows hanging from rawhide ties around their waists.

Thaddeus knew the Cherokee well from his years of living in the wilderness. He had never had any problems with them — always using a friendly smile and hand gestures to tell them what he was doing in their mountains. Using his rough sign language, he would very carefully explain how much he respected their land and that he was there only to trap beavers and then go back home.

Greeting the hunting party's leader with crossed arms to show friendship, Thaddeus next mimicked a wagon train by curling his fingers on both hands into open fists and then leap-frogging his fists over one another several times. When the young brave nodded in recognition, Thaddeus again crossed his arms and then waved his open hand to the horizon to say they came in peace and were just passing through.

With a broad smile that said he understood fully, the Cherokee brave reached into a rawhide pouch tied to his horse's reins and handed Thaddeus a handful of rocks. Looking closer at the objects in his hand, Thaddeus quickly realized that these were not just any old rocks. They were actually polished gemstones that the Cherokees traditionally used to signify friendship.

As he reined Castor around to head back down the trail, Thaddeus waved a goodbye to his new-found friends. His mind welled with pride in knowing that the wagon train could now pass through the mountains with the support of the native Cherokee tribesmen.

The next day, the wagon train began the steep ascent up to the pass through the mountains that formed the Cumberland Gap. The morning was unusually hot for mid-April, and Thaddeus watched with growing apprehension as thunderhead clouds piled up on top of one another as the afternoon progressed.

Then it happened. Just as the wagon train was moving slowly along a portion of the trail etched into the face of a steep, rock-strewn hillside, the clouds turned an eerie greenish-golden hue and torrents of rain started gushing from the sky. In all his days in the wilderness, Thaddeus had never seen it rain so hard. To make matters worse, the wind was whipping the rain sideways straight into the mountainside above the wagons. The rainwater bouncing off the steep slope quickly coalesced into raging torrents of foaming whitewater that raced back down the hillside and under the wheels of the wagons.

Fearful that the trail would give way under the wagons, Thaddeus rode along the outside of the wagon train yelling at the top of his lungs for all the women and children to get out and walk along on the inside of the trail beside their wagons. Thaddeus knew that this was risky, because the sheer force of the water coming off the slope could actually pick up and carry away some of the smaller children. But he reasoned that getting everyone out was a better option than having a wagon — or several wagons — tumble off the trail and down the slope with the families trapped inside.

Once again, Thaddeus' instincts proved to be accurate. In an instant, the trail gave way under the three wagons immediately in back of the Adams' family's lead wagon. Miraculously, the front wheels of the first wagon hung up on a clump of oak saplings just below the trail, but — with supplies and tools flying out in every direction — the other two wagons tumbled down the slope and came to rest against some granite outcrops next to the a now-raging stream.

While screaming at the other drivers to rein in their teams, Thaddeus barreled down the slope in giant leaps until he was next to the stricken wagons. He found Benjamin Travers — one of the drivers — splayed against the rocks with blood gushing from a deep cut in his head. Benjamin wasn't moving and his right leg was twisted in such an awkward manner that Thaddeus knew it must be broken.

Thaddeus quickly looked around for Samuel Johnson — the other driver — but didn't see him anywhere on the ground. Instinctively, Thaddeus crawled underneath Samuel's overturned wagon and found him lying in a heap on top of the canvas that used to form the wagon's roof.

Samuel was moaning in pain, so Thaddeus knew he was at least alive and probably in better shape than Benjamin. Employing the triage system that was used to treat soldiers injured in battle, Thaddeus hopped up and ran back to tend to Benjamin.

By this time, the heavy rain had subsided to a warm drizzle, and several other drivers had skidded down the slope to assist Thaddeus. Two of the men walked over to where Thaddeus was kneeling over Benjamin while the other three worked to push Samuel's wagon back upright. Samuel was now talking and said that he was all right except for a few bruises and scrapes on his head and arms.

Benjamin's injuries were severe; as his wagon tumbled down the hillside, he was thrown brutally against the rocks. Thaddeus motioned all the men over and told them to use the wood and canvas from the wrecked wagons to fashion a stretcher that could be used to carry Benjamin back up the slope to the trail.

Once the men got Benjamin back to the trail, Thaddeus was able to take a closer look at his injuries. As best Thaddeus could tell, Benjamin had suffered a nasty broken leg. The jagged end of his shin bone was protruding through the skin of his lower leg.

Plus — because of the intense pain Benjamin was experiencing around his upper right arm — he likely had broken his collarbone. The deep cut over his right eye also needed attention, which Minerva — using the nursing skills she learned from her mother — deftly sutured shut with four stitches made from fine spinning wheel thread.

Because of the severity of Benjamin's broken leg, Thaddeus volunteered to take him and his family back down into the valley to the nearest doctor. But Benjamin would have none of it. He knew that leaving the wagon train and all his friends at this point would mean giving up his dream to move west.

Benjamin told Thaddeus to give him a few shots of whiskey and a stick to bite down on, and he would endure the pain of forcing his broken shinbone back into place. Benjamin knew he might never walk right again, but he didn't care as long as he made it to the promised land of the Midwestern prairies with everyone else.

Under Minerva's watchful eyes, two of the other men held Benjamin steady while Thaddeus made an incision in Benjamin's lower leg and pushed his broken shinbone back into place. Benjamin's screams told everyone in the wagon train exactly how painful this was, but — after he was done — Thaddeus was cautiously optimistic that Benjamin's leg would heal well enough to allow him to at least walk again — albeit with a permanent limp.

After he had finished performing his wilderness surgery, Thaddeus turned to the matter of the fallen wagons. The impact on the rocks decimated Benjamin Traver's wagon, so it would have to be left behind. But the Johnson family wagon was still in reasonably good shape and could be salvaged if the team could get to it. But — after a lengthy discussion — the majority of the men voted not to try and fix the Johnsons' wagon. They reasoned that it could take them several days to haul everything back up the slope to the trail and then make the necessary repairs, and even then, it may not be sturdy enough to make the rest of the trip.

Since Benjamin Travers still needed some special care for his broken bones, Thaddeus said that Benjamin — along with his wife, Winfrey — should ride in his wagon where Minerva could keep an eye on him. Benjamin's son and daughter — aged eight and ten — enthusiastically accepted an offer to ride with their best friends in the Paulson family's wagon.

That left only the Johnson family in need of a ride and — in short order — they worked everything out with their former farming neighbors — the Smiths and the Owenbys. Samuel Johnson and his wife would ride with the Smiths and — in return — Clara Johnson would help Elizabeth Smith take care of her three young children, a two-year-old girl and four-year-old twin boys. Finally, the Johnson's three teenage children would travel with the Owenbys — alternating in shifts of walking along beside and riding inside their wagon.

After coordinating all the logistics of moving forward, Thaddeus decided it was best to give everyone a day off to recover from their harrowing bout with Mother Nature. First, he guided the wagons onto a relatively flat area above the now gently-flowing stream. Then he told everyone to secure their gear and scramble down to the stream for an afternoon of picnicking, swimming, fishing, and just relaxing on the rocks below.

Experiencing Nature's Bounty

The next day, Thaddeus used his spoon and plate alarm to roust all the families out of bed an hour before sunrise — while the pinkish-yellow glow of dawn was just barely visible on the eastern horizon. He wanted to get everyone on the trail as soon as possible to help erase any misgivings about their trip that may be still lingering from the mishaps of yesterday's downpour.

When they first moved out, Thaddeus took back the reins of the lead wagon from Minerva while she and Winfrey Johnson worked to make sure Benjamin Travers was resting comfortably on his stretcher in the back of the wagon.

As soon as he was convinced that Benjamin could endure the journey without severe pain, Thaddeus reined his team back onto the trail and the rest of the wagons followed suit. Thaddeus then asked Minerva to come back and take the reins because he wanted to continue his scouting duties ahead of the pack. He believed that his scouting was especially critical to their safe passage up through The Gap.

As soon as the wagon train was moving again, Thaddeus mounted Castor and galloped ahead. He let Castor have his head for a good while, firstly because his horse really needed the workout, and secondly because he wanted to check out the trail conditions near the top of the pass.

Several miles of steady riding brought Thaddeus to the crest of a ridgeline overlooking a narrow valley, that was sliced in two by one of the most beautiful mountain streams he had ever seen. Spring freshets of mountain snowmelt tumbled over a series of rocky cascades alternating with ice-blue pools that he knew were chockfull of native brook trout. A massive herd of hundreds of eastern elk grazed the lush, emerald green grasses that lined both sides of the bubbling brook.

Thaddeus didn't really want to stop the wagon train again, but the wealth of meat — both on the land and in the water — that he now saw before him was simply too much to resist. He knew that if he acted quickly, he could organize the men into a hunting party that could kill enough elk and catch enough fish to last them until they reached the Midwestern prairies. He also knew that — if he planned everything just right — he could have all the meat salt-cured and the wagon train back on the trail in no more than two days.

Taking one last look at the incredible natural bounty in the valley below, Thaddeus wheeled Castor around and spurred him on back down the trail. He could scarcely contain his excitement as he reached the wagon train and motioned for the drivers to stop and tether their teams.

Wondering what in the world could now be going on, everyone eagerly gathered in a circle around Thaddeus. Their eyes grew wide as Thaddeus described the incredible natural bounty he had witnessed, a few miles ahead. To a person, they agreed with Thaddeus' decision to stop and harvest enough elk and fish to sustain them and their families for at least the next few weeks.

Thaddeus knew everyone would agree with his plan. In fact, he had figured all the details out in his head during his ride back down the ridge. When the wagon train neared the crest of the ridge, he directed all the wagons to pull off the trail into a flat, grassy meadow on the opposite side of the ridgeline from the stream and the elk herd. The drivers then coaxed their teams into a circle that was just tight enough to fit inside the meadow without spilling over into the surrounding forest. Next, the adults and older children set off into the woods to collect enough fallen timbers to build several large racks for salt-curing meat.

Around that night's campfire, Thaddeus told everyone what he had in mind for tomorrow's hunt. Two hours before sunrise the next day, the men grabbed their muskets and climbed to the top of the ridge. They then fanned out along the escarpment, spread out at a distance of some fifty feet apart. When Thaddeus whistled like a bob-white quail, the line of men moved stealthily down the ridge and into the valley toward the herd of sleeping elk.

The morning dew soaked every inch of their clothing as the men strode down through waist-high stands of meadow grass. They held their muskets and powder horns high above their heads to keep them dry as they walked along.

When they were about twenty-five paces from the elk, Thaddeus held his hand up high, motioning for them to stop moving. Shivering in their wet clothes, the men stood stock-still and watched as hundreds of wisps of steam rising from the nostrils of the sleeping elk drifted across the sea of meadow grass in front of them.

Thaddeus raised his hand again, signaling for the men to shoulder their muskets. He then pumped his arm three times and clapped and whooped as loud as he could. The ground shook and the meadow seemed to rise up as the huge elk herd came to their feet all at once — snorting, huffing, and pawing the ground in mass confusion.

Following Thaddeus' instructions, the men sighted in on the biggest elk now standing in the meadow before them. Thaddeus figured that the largest elk would most likely be bulls — they had not yet re-grown their antlers — and by killing only the males, their hunt would have the least impact on the herd.

Thaddeus counted — one, two, three — and then fire and flashes of light cascaded from the ends of the men's muskets. Most of the men were dead-eye shots, having hunted with their fathers since the time they first started walking. Fifteen elk stood briefly in stunned silence and then toppled to the ground with musket balls in their hearts. Five more elk ran with the rest of the herd away from the gunfire for a few hundred paces, before falling over from blood loss through gaping wounds in their chests. The final tally was twenty dead elk—each of which weighed more than five hundred pounds.

Half of the men set to the tedious task of gutting and field dressing the elk carcasses while the other half pushed their way through the meadow grasses down to the edge of the stream. They dug earthworms and grubs out of the stream bank and skewered them onto the lines and hooks their wives had fashioned out of materials inside the sewing baskets brought from home.

The men deftly knotted small rocks to the lines just above the hooks to make them sink and then tied the other ends of the lines to stout twigs for use as poles. Within seconds of dropping their lines in the water, each man was battling with a plump trout. The trout fought to throw the hooks in their mouths by first boiling deep beneath the stream's surface and then blasting out of the water in strong, twisting leaps.

With their homemade gear, only a few of the men were able to keep trout on long enough to get them up onto the streambanks. The men who lost their fish quickly re-baited and cast out again, and had another fish as soon as their hooks hit the water. In less than an hour, the men had landed, gutted, and cleaned some one hundred trout — averaging more than a pound apiece.

The total haul from the morning's hunt was more than one thousand pounds of elk venison and almost one hundred pounds of pinkish-orange trout flesh. This success added to everyone's anticipation about the vast wealth of nature's bounty that awaited them on the other side of the mountains.

A joyous mood spread throughout the camp as the men, women, and children all pitched in to salt cure and store the meat as quickly as possible. From the oldest man to the youngest child, they were all now of one mind. Taking this journey to the 'promised land of milk and honey' was bound to be the best thing they had ever done.

Crossing the Eastern Divide and Their First Major River

For the next five days, the wagon train moved smoothly up toward the pass at the top of the Cumberland Gap. They officially crossed over the divide around mid-afternoon on a beautifully warm spring day. As they started their descent down the western slope of the Appalachian Mountain Range, Thaddeus reined his team off into a meadow dotted with an artist's palette of colorful wildflowers.

Motioning for the other drivers to circle the wagons, he mounted Castor and rode around to each wagon to tell the families that they were stopping for the night to celebrate their successful passage into the western wilderness. The night was filled with exuberant drinking of home-made wine, plus joyous singing and dancing around a huge bonfire, a welcome respite — just what the doctor ordered for this hearty band of travelers.

As happens quite often in the high mountains, the weather changed overnight. The previous evening's merry-makers woke up to see — many through bloodshot eyes — three inches of fresh snow blanketing the grassy meadow of their campsite. The air temperature had dropped a good thirty degrees from the previous night, and everyone mumbled good mornings through chattering teeth as they hurried over to the campfire for a fresh-made, steaming cup of coffee or hot cocoa. The day warmed quickly, and the snow soon disappeared as the wagons snaked back onto the trail for the descent into the Cumberland River Valley in the heart of Daniel Boone's Territory.

Shortly after noon, two days later, the wagon train came to the banks of the Cumberland River and the first test for one of their carefully-crafted covered wagons. With their large wheels and keel-shaped carriages, the wagons were designed to become boats and actually float across major rivers. But Thaddeus realized that if even a few of the wagons took on water and sank or —even worse — were carried away by the river's current, their journey might be over.

Thaddeus decided he needed some time to plan the crossing. He whistled for the wagons to circle and set up camp for the night. Next, he called all the men together and told them how critical it was to inspect their wagon beds and make sure that all the tar caulking was intact. Any cracks or gaps they found had to be repaired and completely sealed before they crossed the river the next morning.

The families immediately set to work inspecting their wagons. Thaddeus directed the men to move several large, flat rocks from the riverbank to the edges of the campfire. The men then moved the ten-gallon bucket of pitch-pine tar from the Adams family's wagon and straddled it across the rocks so that the bottom of the bucket was directly over the embers of the campfire.

Next, the women and older children ladled out tar into smaller buckets and took them to the men who were inspecting and repairing their wagons. The families worked well into the night, making sure that each wagon would be up to the challenge of a major river crossing.

The next morning, Thaddeus went to each wagon and carefully inspected all the work that had been done. He did not take any chances; if he saw even the slightest crack or gap in a wagon, he personally supervised the additional repair work that was needed. By the time Thaddeus finished with all the inspections, it was well past noon. He decided not to worry about making any progress for the day, and to just concentrate on getting all the wagons safely across the river.

Ever so carefully, the driver of the first wagon in line clucked to his team and pulled his bulky load down the steep riverbank and into the main channel of the Cumberland River. As soon as the wagon began to float, Thaddeus realized that there was another major problem he had not anticipated. The flatness of the water on the surface belied the power of the river's deep current. The sheer volume of water in the river created intense drag on the wagon box. The horse team fought to keep their footing, but it was no use.

The horses were quickly dragged off their feet by the wagon's weight as the powerful current pushed it downstream. All of the other men standing on the riverbank immediately crashed down into the river and grabbed onto the wagon's frame. Straining with all their might, the men were able to stop the wagon's downstream movement and create enough slack to allow the horses to regain their footing. The wagon driver then expertly turned his team back toward the shore and safely onto the riverbank from where he started.

Thaddeus now knew what he had to do to get the wagons and families safely across the river. He told everyone to unload everything from each wagon. He then told the men from the last twelve wagons in the train to un-tether their teams and bring them around to the front of the train. The extra horses were then tied in with the teams of the first twelve wagons. Thaddeus now had twelve empty wagons with doubled-up horsepower — eight horse teams instead of the usual four.

Thaddeus' plan worked like a charm. Within an hour, the first twelve wagons were safely across the river and up onto the opposite riverbank. The wagon drivers then unhitched their teams and — keeping them tethered together — rode back across the river. They then hitched the teams up to the remaining twelve wagons, and then drove them smoothly and safely across to the opposite riverbank.

The next problem for Thaddeus was how to get all the families, provisions, and supplies across the river now that the empty wagons were on the other side. His solution was to turn the wagon teams into packhorse groups.

First, the adults boosted the younger children up onto twenty of the horses. Then — in succession — an adult mounted each horse and tied ropes securely tethering their young passengers behind them. Once everyone was tightly mounted and ready to move, three groups of four men — with each man riding an individual mount — took their positions at the head, middle, and rear of the line of horses. These three pods of strategically-placed horsemen provided the extra stability and safety that was needed for successfully leading the string of horses into and across the swift-flowing current.

Once all the young children were safely across, the adults began the arduous task of transporting the huge stockpile of provisions and supplies across the river. They accomplished this by loading down and tethering groups of four horses together and then using a rider-mounted guide horse to lead each group of horses across the river.

While this whole process took the better part of a day, Thaddeus knew it represented two major accomplishments. First, it proved that — with enough foresight and determination — no problem is unsolvable. Secondly — and most importantly — it provided this intrepid group of western travelers with their first successful attempt at using group teamwork to overcome a very stressful and potentially disastrous situation.

Moving Through Kentucky's Bluegrass Hills

With the mountains, and now the Cumberland River, finally behind them, the wagon train moved at a steady pace — averaging ten miles a day — through the beautiful native bluegrass hills of central Kentucky. As May turned to June, the intense heat and humidity of the long late spring days began to take their toll on the families. To ease the tediousness of the trip, Thaddeus turned every Sunday into a day of rest and relaxation. He always tried to find a cool, shady spot beside a stream or a river to set up the wagon circle.

On Sunday morning, everyone sat around the campfire while each family read a selected passage from the family bible. Then they all joined in as Minerva Adams led them in singing a variety of sacred hymns that they all knew quite well. Each Sunday service always concluded with one of the adult family members telling a story about how their faith in God had pulled them through hard times.

After a hearty lunch, most of the men — a few stayed back to guard the campsite — grabbed their muskets and spread out into the hills to hunt for fresh game. While the men hunted, the women and children scouted the woodlands for mushrooms and edible plants that would balance their meat-heavy diets. They also took time to have fun — playing games like hopscotch, tag, and marbles and swimming in the cool, clear streams that adorned every hillside.

Thaddeus found that preserving the freshly-killed meat was easy because of the number of salt licks that dotted the Kentucky countryside. In fact, many of the settlements that had popped up in the area had the word 'lick' in their names. Typically, the name of the first family to settle a place had the honor of being the first word in each village's name — Mays Lick for the May family, Smiths Lick for the Smith family, and so on.

Late on one bright July afternoon, just before sunset, as the wagon train was moving across a broad river valley in western Kentucky, Thaddeus noticed the shadow of a massive, dark cloud moving rapidly across the sky. Fearing that the wagon train was about to be deluged by another sudden cloudburst, he wheeled around on Castor and headed back to circle the wagons and hunker down for the storm.

As Castor was galloping the half-mile back to the lead wagon, Thaddeus looked up again and saw a sight that he couldn't believe. The sky was being darkened not by a cloud, but by millions of feathered flapping wings. He then realized that he was looking at a massive migration of passenger pigeons on their way back to their roost trees along the river.

Reaching the wagon train, Thaddeus dismounted Castor, grabbed his musket and yelled for all the other men to do the same. Ordinarily — with the exception of turkeys — the men did not have much luck shooting down flying birds with their muskets. They found it to be pretty much a waste of time, gunpowder, and musket balls — but this time was a different story. Every musket ball they fired up brought down birds — often as not, three or four at a time. The men all whooped wildly as birds rained down from the sky all around their feet.

After they had knocked several hundred birds out of the sky, Thaddeus had the women and children collect the dead birds while the men circled the wagons and untethered the horse teams. That evening, everyone enjoyed the delicacy of freshly roasted pigeons for dinner.

The next morning, Thaddeus had all the wagons back on the trail well before sunrise. He knew they had another hundred miles still to go before they reached the Mississippi River ferry crossing between Hickman, Kentucky and Dorena, Missouri.

Thaddeus did not have any thoughts about pushing his families much further west after they crossed the Mississippi River. He fully intended for them all to establish their own settlement in the lush prairies of the Missouri Territory. He would leave it for later settlers to try and find a route across the impenetrable fortress of the mighty Rocky Mountains.

As far as Thaddeus was concerned, the endless tallgrass prairie with its deep and fertile soils that awaited them on the other side of the Mississippi River was the dream come true — the end of the rainbow — they had all been seeking for the past three months.

Bison Herds—to the Horizon and Beyond

As the wagon train moved steadily onward across Kentucky, the amount of forestland covering the landscape grew progressively less and less. Thaddeus knew that this was because the amount of yearly rainfall was decreasing steadily with their westward progress.

With every mile, the abundance of oak-hickory woodlands also seemed to decline proportionally to the increase in grazing bison. Thaddeus figured that this made sense — the more prairie grasses there were to munch on, the larger the herds of grazing animals there would be to do the munching.

Plus, Thaddeus also knew — just by common sense, really — that the grazing bison helped keep the prairie grassland from turning into forests. The huge herds of bison — coupled with the hundreds of lightning-sparked wildfires that roared across the prairie landscape each spring and summer — made it impossible for woody seedlings to gain a foothold and overtop the grassland vegetation.

Thaddeus was very familiar with these massive plant-eating creatures. He had learned a great deal about them from talking to his grandfather, 'Pop', who lived when the burly beasts could still be found grazing in woodland clearings — usually in clusters of five to ten animals — throughout the Appalachian Mountains.

With their huge, shaggy heads and broad shoulders, the bison were intimidating to the eye. But Thaddeus knew they were, in reality, quite docile creatures — provided they were left alone. He also knew that no predator — not wolves, not cougars, not even grizzly bears — would tangle with a healthy, adult bison.

The bison Thaddeus now saw grazing on these open prairies somehow looked different from the ones he remembered his Pop telling him about back in the forests of Virginia's mountains. Maybe they looked bigger and shaggier simply due to the sheer volume of their numbers. A few times when he took over the reins to give Minerva time to rest in the back of the wagon, Thaddeus would silently count to himself the number of bison he saw as they rolled along. He often counted hundreds of animals in each herd.

But Thaddeus' bison counting did not prepare him for the sight he saw as his wagon rounded a hillside bluff. Stretching before him, in a broad valley in western Kentucky, was a bison herd so thick and dense that it filled every inch of the landscape. The sight took his breath away, and he could only sit in stunned silence as the mass of black-and-brown bodies moved as one in front of him.

Slowly regaining his wits, Thaddeus jumped down off his wagon and motioned for all the trailing wagons to pull up in a straight line next to his wagon. As the other wagons pulled up, he could hear the gasps and mutterings of disbelief coming from each of the drivers and the other family members who had poked their heads out to see what was going on. Thaddeus had no way of knowing exactly how many animals there were, but he guessed it had to be in the thousands, maybe even more than a hundred thousand.

For the rest of the afternoon, the wagons sat perched in a line along the bluff several hundred feet above the flowing river of bison down below. Thaddeus knew that driving the wagons down off the bluff and into the herd would be fool-hardy — most likely triggering a stampede that would get them all killed.

There was nothing he and the other drivers could do but sit, watch, and wait for the bison herd to finally move through the valley. By the time the last animals had cleared out, it was almost dark. Thaddeus rode out on Castor to the front of the line of wagons and made a whirling motion with his right hand.

It was time to circle the wagons, set up camp, and settle in for the night. At least they would all get a good night's rest and be fresh to cross the sprawling valley at first light the next morning. Encouragingly, the massive bison herd was another sign of the vast resources that awaited them at the end of their journey.

At Long Last, The Mighty Mississippi

During the next week, the wagon train took full advantage of beautiful summer weather and long days, and arrived at the Mississippi River two days earlier than anticipated. It took one full day to ferry all of the wagons — one-by-one — across the broad river that everyone called the official gateway to the western prairies.

The general opinion was that once you were safely across the Mississippi River, your journey was a success. From there, it was just a matter of picking out the best location to start a new settlement.

The long day of the crossing gave all the families time to explore and marvel at the vast natural resources of the Mississippi River floodplain. Skein after skein of wild birds — geese, swans, and cranes — winged their way south down the broad, natural flyway created by the river's channel. Bison, elk, and deer grazed in large herds in the hardwood thickets — underlain by lush grasses along both riverbanks. The dappled rings of fish rising to feed on surface insects filled the still waters in the river's eddies and coves.

The next day, Thaddeus Adams took advantage of being ahead of schedule and called for an additional non-travel day for the families. During the morning, the women spent their extra free time washing and mending clothes and sprucing up their wagons, while the men went hunting. In the afternoon, everyone joined together and played their favorite games while also enjoying refreshing swims in a backwater oxbow lake.

Some of the men also tried their hand at fishing from the riverbank and were rewarded with several types of large fish — sturgeons, paddlefish, and carp — that they had never seen before. When they began to clean the fish, they quickly realized that the meat was far too bony and oily and probably not fit to eat. They left all the partially cleaned and dead fish on the riverbank to be eaten by the turkey buzzards that were circling high overhead and the bald eagles that sat perched in the tops of the cottonwood trees along the river's edge.

Attacked by Outlaws in the Hill Country

After they moved another one hundred and fifty miles into their travels on the western side of the Mississippi River — the families were all struck by how much the prairieland had now opened up before them. The woodlots were now few and far between, located mostly in the draws and stream bottoms of the eastern Missouri landscape.

Their horizon now consisted of two dominant colors, an endless ocean of gently waving greenish-gold grasslands topped by a brilliant-blue, cloudless sky. In many places, the prairie grasses were taller than a man standing on the ground. The wagon drivers were only able to see where they were going because the seats of their specially-crafted wagons were six feet above the ground.

As they passed through, the families gained great appreciation for the lush diversity of the prairie vegetation. Viewed from a distance, the density of the grasses masked the abundance of colorful wildflowers — coneflowers, asters, blazing stars, and lupines — that dotted the lush expanses like an artist's palette.

Every now and then, the wagon train passed through a large swath of land where the sea of prairie grasses had recently been parted by roaring wildfires. Bison and elk filled these natural pastures, grazing languidly on the green grass shoots that had quickly re-sprouted through the charred, but still fertile, soils.

Letters from families in previous wagon trains told horror stories about being held up and stripped of all their possessions by roving bands of masked bandits. Thaddeus felt fortunate that his wagon train had managed to avoid being robbed. Unfortunately, his luck was about to change.

The wagons were traveling through a low-slung valley of limestone hills that were honey-combed with caves and vegetated with stunted trees. With Minerva at the reins, the lead wagon rounded a wide curve bordering a dry creek bed. Thaddeus was riding Castor and working his

71

way along toward the rear of the train, checking the condition of each wagon and making sure each family was doing all right, when he heard Minerva shout, "Whoa, team" at the top of her lungs.

Thaddeus quickly wheeled Castor around and galloped back toward the front of the train to see several large rocks completely blocking the trail just a few paces in front of where Minerva had halted her team. Before Thaddeus could say anything to Minerva, the narrow creek channel seemed to sprout masked men coming up from all directions. Quick as a wink, the bandits surrounded the three lead wagons and — brandishing pistols and hunting knives — began yelling for everyone to get out of the wagons with their hands in the air.

Thaddeus moved his arm up and down slowly, warning the other drivers behind the lead wagons to stay put. He was afraid that if some of the other wagon drivers rushed up to the front, the bandits would start shooting and people — including his own family — would die.

Unfortunately, these masked men had used the element of surprise to perfect advantage. Forget all the tall tales about attacks from 'wild animals' and 'savage Indians'. The wagon train and all their possessions — and maybe even their lives — were now at the mercy of outlaw white men roaming this wild, untamed, western prairie.

It was all Thaddeus could do to contain his rage and urge to grab his musket from Castor's saddle and start busting heads. He kept reminding himself that trying to be a hero would only end up getting people shot. They were looking down the gun barrels and at the shiny knife blades of at least twenty bandits.

Thaddeus thought there were likely even more hiding behind the rough-hewn terrain that surrounded their wagons. He bit his tongue and held his temper while several groups of bandits moved along the wagon train, tying him, Minerva, and all the other men, women, and older children up to the large metal wheels of their covered wagons.

After they were finished tying everyone up, the bandit groups spread out to several wagons and started tossing goods and possessions out willy-nilly onto the ground. Whenever they found something valuable — a silver tea set or a jewelry chest — the masked men would holler with delight.

While this wagon-raiding was going on, one of the bandit guards walked over to Minerva and smiled, telling her that she sure was a 'purdy young thang'. He then made one of the biggest mistakes of his life — he bent over and grabbed Minerva's knees.

Before the masked misfit had a chance to go any further with his evil intentions, Minerva jerked her knees back up to her chest and kicked the thieving dolt right in the stomach with her boots. Minerva's vicious kick knocked the offending galoot so hard that he stumbled backward and toppled head-over-heels down the bank to the bottom of the creek bed. Casting stunned glances at Minerva — who was now grinning ear-to-ear — two of the other bandits walked over to check on their injured comrade.

One of the men slid down into the channel and — after a few minutes — crawled back up to the top, slowly shaking his head from side-to-side. He raised his fist and shook it at Minerva, but he didn't say anything. Minerva wasn't exactly sure what had happened, but she figured that the man she had kicked was either dead or too badly injured to be saved. Anyway, she never saw him again, and none of the other men even thought about trying to touch her.

The thieves continued raiding the wagons for another couple of hours. After they had finished cleaning out the wagons, they went back to the stuff they had tossed into piles and started pawing through — just to make sure they hadn't missed anything. After they had collected everything they wanted, the outlaws loaded all their stolen loot into one of the wagons.

Thaddeus had no idea what the outlaws intended to do with them now that they were finished with their robbery, but he was sure it wouldn't be good. The way he saw it, the thieves had two choices. They could either shoot them all dead on the spot or turn all their horses loose, take all their food and water, and leave them all there in the middle of nowhere to die a slow death.

Hopelessly mulling over which of these two awful outcomes would actually be the worst — sudden death or a languishing death — Thaddeus was suddenly startled back to reality by the thunder of horses and the war cries of Shawnee braves. Wheeling his head around from side-to-side, Thaddeus saw bands of Shawnee riding at a full gallop toward both ends of the wagon train. Aiming their bows and arrows and wielding tomahawks and spears, the braves were on top of the dumbfounded bandits before they could even raise and aim their pistols.

The outlaws had no chance against the mounted Shawnee. The masked men had fallen prey to their own element of surprise. In a matter of only seconds — or so it seemed to Thaddeus — all the masked men were lying in the dusty trail, either dead or badly injured. Once the dust had settled, the Shawnee braves dismounted, mercifully dispatched the outlaws who were still moving, and walked along the wagon train with their hunting knives freeing all the bound family members.

After one of the braves had cut the ropes off of his hands and feet, Thaddeus first crossed his arms and then placed his right hand over his heart, making his traditional Native American gestures of friendship. To Thaddeus' relief and amazement, the brave repeated the friendly gestures. With a broad smile, the Shawnee brave first crossed his arms and then touched his hand to his heart, then to his head, and back to his heart again.

Thaddeus knew immediately that the brave was telling him that they understood what had happened with the outlaws and that they had come to rescue them — not to cause them any harm. As soon as the Shawnee had freed all the family members, they re-mounted their horses and rode away almost as fast as they had come. The families all stood around Thaddeus in stunned silence, looking at the now dead outlaws lying all around their wagons and watching the dust of their rescuers' horses trailing off into the horizon.

Once they had regained their wits, the families started sorting through the jumbled piles of their possessions and re-packing their wagons. By the time they had finished deciding where everything should go, there were only a couple of hours of daylight left.

Wanting to get as far as possible from the bad memories of the crime scene, Thaddeus took the reins of his wagon and led everyone back onto the trail. They rode until well after sunset, finally pulling off into a stand of cottonwood and willow trees next to a gently flowing river. Most of the talk over the late dinner that night was about how topsy-turvy the world had become. How the native 'warriors' they had heard so much about had just saved them all from certain death at the hands of marauding, miscreant white men.

The near-tragedy with the bandits made Thaddeus realize they were pushing their luck. Relying on his almost always accurate instincts, he now sensed a pervasive uneasiness about his group's close call with death. He knew that everyone's thoughts were now often being invaded by fears about what other bandits — or worse — might be lying in wait for them as they moved farther and farther along into the increasingly wild, untamed landscape.

The Promised Land Beckons

For the next week, the wagons rolled steadily westward, leaving each day before sunrise and continuing onward until well past sunset. Thaddeus knew he was pushing everyone to their limits and yet no one complained — making it even clearer that they wanted their journey to end as soon as possible.

Early on the morning of the seventh day after the outlaw attack, Thaddeus reined in Castor at the top of a bluff overlooking a wide, slow-flowing river that had so many curves it looked like a sidewinder rattlesnake, curling its way across the prairie-scape.

The sprawling river was bracketed by cottonwood-willow stands growing along its banks and out into the meanders and islands of its broad floodplain. For as far as Thaddeus could see — on both sides of the river channel — there was nothing except raw, untouched tallgrass prairie.

Thaddeus knew in an instant that this was where they were meant to be. He took off his hat and waved it around his head — whooping as loud as he could as he and Castor galloped back to the wagon train.

When Minerva saw Thaddeus coming, she thought for sure he must have eaten some strange plant and gone plumb loco. She was worried what he might say until he was close enough to see the wide grin of sheer ecstasy on his face. Thaddeus rode past — right by Minerva's wagon — and moved along beside the wagon train exclaiming that he had just seen their promised land and it was right on the other side of the next hill.

An hour later when they had reached the east bank of the river, Thaddeus gave the signal for the drivers to circle the wagons one last time. They could all now see the fertile floodplain of the South Grand River — about five miles south of the present-day City of Harrisonville, Missouri — that was going to be their new home.

BOOK FOUR
A Pioneer Village Emerges

Finding the Next Best Place

After breakfast the next morning, Thaddeus Adams asked all the adults to join him around the campfire to discuss the plans for their new settlement. Their first order of business was deciding where to set up the center of their village.

Thaddeus suggested finding a wooded area that was within walking distance of the river, but up on one of the first breaks to protect themselves from floods. After everyone agreed that these criteria defined the best general location, he picked two men, Angus Robinson and Jacob Henderson, to ride out with him, after the group meeting was over, to find some sites that would fit his plan.

Next, Thaddeus asked his assemblage of townsfolk to vote on a name for their new village to be. By consensus — in appropriate honor of the river that would now be their lifeblood — the name of 'New South Grand' won the vote. He then asked everyone what type of buildings they would need to best serve the full community. He wanted to get some idea of how much land to look for to create the town center.

Right away, everyone agreed that the first building had to be a church — to serve as both a place of worship and a meeting hall. The next thing everyone thought of was a schoolhouse — so that their children could continue the formal education they had left behind in Virginia's Shenandoah Valley.

The discussion then moved on to include three other primary buildings, a mercantile store, a blacksmith shop, and a clinic for treating health problems and medical emergencies. Other buildings, including a canteen, a library, and a town barn, were also suggested. But after a round of discussion, everyone agreed that these were not needed right away. They could wait until later, after the settlement was firmly established.

Satisfied that the meeting had established the consensus he was hoping for, Thaddeus motioned for Angus and Jacob to follow him over to where the horses were tethered. The three of them then mounted up and headed off down river to scout for suitable settlement locations. When the three men returned to camp in the afternoon, Thaddeus walked around and told each family that they would meet again after supper to talk about the excellent location they had found.

The site the three men had picked was an upland terrace, directly abutting a forested river oxbow. This setting met all the criteria they were seeking. By virtue of being set off from the river's main channel, it provided protection from floods. And the oxbow lake provided everyone with direct access to both freshwater and fresh fish. Plus, the oxbow forest surrounding the lake harbored plenteous wild game.

The next morning, Thaddeus led the wagons and families into the middle of the river terrace that would be their new home. Once everyone had settled into their wagon train routine — for the final time — he again gathered everyone around the central campfire. He then told each family to go exploring and find a nearby piece of ground that would make a good homestead plot.

Thaddeus advised everyone to first look for level ground in the river's fertile floodplain where they could successfully grow corn, wheat, and pasture grasses. He emphasized that low-lying areas close to the river were fine — in fact, they would have the best soils for growing crops. And then — when these areas flooded during the spring — all the better. The spring floods would just enrich the soils more — making them even better for growing crops. But he also advised everyone to pick sites for their homes and barns on the upland river terrace, above the floodplain. This way the river's spring floods would not damage or destroy any of their prized family possessions.

Settling Into a New Community

Throughout the next two months, the families enjoyed beautiful weather with sun-drenched days and crisp autumn nights, as the cottonwood-willow river bottoms turned from summer green to brilliant hues of red, yellow, and gold. Under Thaddeus' leadership — as New South Grand's duly-elected mayor — the settlement grew quickly.

During the first week, everyone pitched in and had an old-fashioned 'church-raising'. When they had finished, they all agreed that the new church — with its white clapboard walls and classic steeple — was a thing of beauty; a fitting tribute to God who gave them safe passage to their wonderful new prairie home.

The steeple was topped off by an authentic church bell — a going away gift from Reverend Bacon. Samantha and William Robertson graciously agreed to haul the bell out in their wagon — since they didn't have any children to occupy the extra space.

The families next worked hard to finish the two-room schoolhouse. By the end of October, their children were all going to school five days a week. In fact, the kids hadn't missed any schooling at all. Their two teachers from back home — Naomi Watson and Blair Kitterly — were both members of the wagon train. They had been tutoring the children — in small groups — throughout their westward journey.

The men used the fabric from a few of the wagons to set up tents that served as a temporary blacksmith shop and mercantile store while the permanent buildings were being built. They also built a community livestock pen, connected to a five-acre pasture for keeping a herd of dairy cows and beef cattle that the families collectively purchased during trips into the frontier town and trading post of Independence, Missouri — located fifteen miles due north.

Due to the convergence of the Kansas River with the now mostly northward-flowing Missouri River approximately six miles west of New South Grand, Independence was the farthest westward point that steamboats or other cargo vessels could travel on the Missouri River. Because of this, Independence quickly became the primary jumping-off point for merchants and adventurers beginning their long westward treks on both the Oregon and the Santa Fe Trails.

The families shared everything they were able to grow in their autumn gardens — mostly meager crops of corn, potatoes, squash, root vegetables, and beans. Each family also had a flock of laying hens with a few extra roosters so that they had fresh eggs every day, plus a nice roast chicken for Sunday lunches and other special occasions.

The community livestock pen kept everyone supplied with fresh milk, butter, and cheese plus a butchered steer to treat everyone to a steak dinner at the church once a month. The protein for the families mostly came from the dried and cured buffalo meat — plus deer and elk venison — that the men accrued during their weekly hunting trips.

Befriending the Local Apache Tribe

As fall turned to winter and the frost began to settle into the ground, Thaddeus started thinking about ways to make life easier for his families. He knew that the local Native American tribes — the Shawnee, the Apaches, and the Sioux — depended on the local buffalo herds for their existence. They used every part of each buffalo they killed. The hides were used to make teepees for shelter, saddles for their horses, clothes for their bodies, and moccasins for their feet.

They used the hair from the shaggy beasts' heads and massive chests to stuff sleeping blankets and pillows. The bison hair was also twisted to make sturdy ropes. They even used the tongues of buffalo to make combs and the stomach linings as cooking vessels. Thaddeus had even heard that some white settlers were buying bison tongues at the Independence Trading Post to serve as a delicacy at suppertime.

Thaddeus knew life would be a lot easier for his families if he could figure out how to start regularly harvesting the buffalo that filled the virgin prairies all around their settlement. It was a shame to have to pay for their meat and clothes at the trading post when everything was right there all around them — free for the taking.

Early one morning, Thaddeus decided to try a different approach. He mounted Castor and rode off toward the nearest Apache tribal village — about ten miles northwest of New South Grand.

Thaddeus had heard that the Apache tribe was generally very peaceful, and often traded their furs and hand-made goods to white settlers for long rifles, tobacco, and home-brewed spirits. He also knew that the chief and many of the tribal elders understood enough English to carry on a basic conversation.

That's what Thaddeus was counting on — he wanted to pitch an idea he had conceived to the Apache chief. Thaddeus was hoping that the Apaches would lead his men in hunting the buffalo — getting close enough to them without spooking them into a stampede. In return, he would supply the Apaches with some Kentucky long rifles which would be much more efficient than the spears and lances they were now using for killing the massive animals.

Harboring these thoughts, Thaddeus confidently rode into the middle of the Apache encampment, bounded down off Castor, and walked over to the nearest brave. Thaddeus' bravado startled the tribesmen, and they all watched intently as the brave led him over to Chief Running Bull's teepee.

As he entered the teepee, Thaddeus doffed his hat and extended his right hand in greeting to the chief. As soon as he met him, Thaddeus could sense Chief Running Bull's remarkable charisma — exactly what he expected from one of the Apache tribal chiefs. He was both relieved and pleased when the great chief cordially greeted him and motioned for him to sit down next to the teepee's cooking fire.

While they passed a pipe back and forth, Thaddeus told Chief Running Bull about their westward journey, the harrowing robbery, their rescue by a Shawnee hunting party, and their new settlement on the river ten miles to the southeast. Chief Running Bull listened intently but did not comment as Thaddeus talked.

When Thaddeus finished explaining how they had come to settle in the land of the Apaches, Chief Running Bull smiled broadly and told Thaddeus that his tribe welcomed them as brothers and would be happy to help them adjust to their new home on the great prairie.

Hearing this as the opening he needed, Thaddeus began explaining his idea for the joint buffalo hunts. As he talked, he could see the chief's interest grow with every word he said. He obviously had hit on a subject that was critically important to the chief.

The tribe's health and well-being were totally dependent on harvesting the local buffalo herds. Anything that would make this easier for them to do was considered a gift from the Great Spirit. The Kentucky long rifles Thaddeus spoke of, were the greatest gift Chief Running Bull could imagine for his people. After their amiable discussion, Thaddeus and Chief Running Bull stood up, vigorously shook hands, and agreed that their hunting parties would meet for their first buffalo hunt at sunrise after the next full moon.

Learning to Hunt Buffalo

The day of the first buffalo hunt dawned clear and crisp, with a light frost covering the tall blades of the prairie grasses. Thaddeus rode out to the agreed upon rendezvous point — a bluff overlooking the South Grand River Valley — with eleven of his best riders, including the two teenage sons of Joshua Murphy.

The boys — Gregory and Josh, Jr. — were both not only terrific riders, but crack shots. They regularly brought home more deer and elk than anyone else during the monthly hunts that Thaddeus arranged to keep the families' pantries filled with pemmican and other cured beef.

When the settlers met the Apache hunting party, they immediately handed each brave a brand-new Kentucky long rifle. The braves talked excitedly in their native tongue as they admired the shiny blue-metal barrels and maple stocks, and decorative inlays of their new firearms. Since the tribe actually owned a few of these rifles, all of the men were already skilled in how to handle, load, and fire them accurately.

One of the oldest braves, Hunting Elk, rode over to the edge of the bluff and moved his arm over the large herd — easily several hundred — of still-sleeping buffalo scattered in the lush meadow below. Before he began to speak, Hunting Elk and all the other braves looked skyward and — again in their native tongue — prayed to the Great Spirit for a safe and successful hunt. In broken English punctuated by lots of hand gestures, Hunting Elk then described how the hunt would happen.

Exactly following Hunting Elk's directions, the mounted settlers and braves approached from downwind and formed a u-shape around the sleeping herd. They kept the open end, facing north — in the direction of a steep-walled wash.

Hunting Elk then gave the descending cry of a red-tailed hawk as a signal, and all the riders started methodically shouting and waving their horse blankets at the herd. Almost as one, the startled buffalo rose to their feet — snorting and pawing the ground as they curiously looked around for the source of the disturbing noises.

Seeing the activity on three sides, the dominant bulls began moving slowly to the north in the direction of the wash — leading the rest of the herd along with them. The plan was working just as Hunting Elk had said it would. The buffalo were moving together as a single group, but there was no panic in the herd.

Thaddeus understood how critical it was to avoid doing anything that might cause the herd to stampede. He knew that buffalo herds had only two speeds, slow and very fast.

Weighing seven hundred and fifty to one thousand pounds, a full-grown adult buffalo has no natural predator. But the burly beasts are — by their very nature — controlled by the actions of the herd. If several animals become spooked and start to run, all the other animals immediately follow suit. This creates a rolling thunder of hoof beats that can be heard for miles across the open prairie.

In less than an hour, the mixed-hunting party of Apache braves and white settlers successfully had the entire herd blockaded inside the dead-end wash. Now came the risky part of the hunt.

Each man had to shoot and kill a buffalo, and then immediately get out of the way by riding up the sides of the wash to higher ground before the rifle shots made the beasts turn around *en masse* and stampede back out of the wash. Any rider who didn't get out of the way fast enough was sure to get knocked down and trampled to death by the tight-knit mass of flying bison hooves.

Hunting Elk raised his arm high above his head, signaling all the mounted hunters to aim their rifles for what was to be their one and only shot at killing a buffalo. To bring down one of the massive beasts, each shot had to be perfectly placed — striking either the heart or the lungs.

A heart shot would drop an animal instantly — while a lung shot would mean trailing the injured animal for a few hundred paces until its body ran out of breath. Shooting a buffalo in the head was considered worthless, since the bullet usually just bounced harmlessly off the thick skull without inflicting any permanent damage.

When Hunting Elk hawk-whistled again, a barrage of rifle retorts rolled up and over the walls of the dry wash. Buffalo toppled like dominoes all along the leading edge of the herd as the flying hoofs of the hunters' horses made dozens of instant dust-trails up the sides of the surrounding bluffs.

Thaddeus reached the top of the bluff and breathed a deep sigh of relief when he looked around and saw that all of his men and the Apache braves had made it safely to the top of the ridges. Looking down, he saw an immense cloud of dust kicked up by hundreds of buffalo as they thundered back out of the wash and across the open prairie. He continued watching in awe for several minutes until the dust cloud finally stopped moving — some two miles away from where he sat mounted on Castor.

The hunting party of settlers and braves slowly rode back down the sides of the bluffs and around into the mouth of the wash. The shots of the men had been true as they counted the buffalo carcasses lying in the still-settling dust at the bottom of the wash. Eighteen buffalo lay right where they had been shot, while eight others were lying at the end of blood trails — just as Hunting Elk said they would be if they were shot in the lungs.

All of the Apache braves and most of the settlers set about the task of cleaning and butchering the slain beasts. Thaddeus took three of his men and rode back to get four wagons to haul the buffalo meat, hides, and bones back to the Apache village.

Just as Thaddeus and Chief Running Bull had agreed when they first met, the meat and hides were divided evenly. The Apache braves took all of the other parts — including the bones, skulls, horns, intestines, and hooves. When they were finished harvesting their bounty and loading all the buffalo parts into the wagons, scattered stains of dried blood in the prairie dust were the only signs that the hunt had ever taken place.

The settlers and the Apaches repeated their successful buffalo hunts each fall and spring. After each hunt, the New South Grand residents joined together and held a giant barbecue. The meat that they didn't consume right away was boiled and cured for pemmican, jerky, and sausages.

Thaddeus took pride in knowing that, during their communal hunts, the settlers and Apaches never killed more of the buffalo than they needed. He and some of the other settlers had heard horror stories from drivers and travelers on east-bound stage coaches about seeing huge piles of buffalo carcasses left rotting in the prairie sun.

In his mind, Thaddeus believed that it was terribly wrong to waste a resource like that — no matter how abundant it was. But he also figured that because there were so many buffalo — countless numbers just about everywhere he looked across the prairie-scape — that they would always be around. He had no way of knowing that his children would actually live to witness the great tragedy of the prairie-killing fields that almost eliminated the American bison from the face of the earth.

Weekly Trading Post Trips

As the days grew shorter and the nights became long and cold, the families in the settlement of New South Grand began to form tighter bonds of dependency on one another. They pooled their money and combined their shopping lists for the biweekly wagon trips into the Independence trading post. The day before the wagon left, they loaded everything they were going to trade — such as hand-made clothing, pickled preserves, and salt-cured beef. Then, the wives gave the men assigned to drive the wagon long lists of the dry goods, cooking tools, specialty foods, and decorative knickknacks they needed for their households.

On a rotating basis, three of the husbands drove a team and one of the wagons into the trading post. The men believed that it was too dangerous for just one or two men to make the trip. They figured that a second man was always needed to sit 'shotgun' on the wagon seat with his rifle close at hand — both to protect the driver and serve as an extra set of eyes — especially if the weather turned bad.

The third man's job was to hide inside the wagon with a pistol, guarding the provisions in case they were attacked by roving bandits. All three men could then switch off driving the wagon and — if necessary — stop and use the wagon as a barrier to fight off any potential threats.

Holiday Planning on the Prairie

When they first arrived in New South Grand, Thaddeus was worried about how being alone in a strange place would affect everyone when the weather turned cold and the holidays rolled around. After all — with the exception of himself — no one had ever been away from their families during the holidays.

The many years Thaddeus spent in the Appalachian Mountain wilderness gave him a certain sereneness and toughness about being alone, but he knew that no one else had anything like his experience to draw from in fighting off homesickness and missing loved ones during these special times of the year.

As Thanksgiving drew near, the families began talking about doing something special together, to offer their thanks to Almighty God for shepherding them safely to their new prairie homes. One Sunday after church — as a biting wind swirled snow around the windows — the women sat in the sanctuary and decided exactly what they wanted to do.

Back in Virginia, all of the families had a tradition of visiting their grandparents, aunts, uncles, and cousins during the holidays. Since they were too far away to do that this year, they decided to still follow the same practices with their neighbors. They would dress everyone up in fancy new clothes, bake special goodies, and then go around visiting each other from Thanksgiving through New Year's Day.

They figured that if each family visited each of the other families once, that would make a total of twenty-five visits for everyone. That would be just enough to fill the holiday period while giving everyone a few extra days to keep up with the cooking, baking, and cleaning in between. Then on Thanksgiving, Christmas, and New Year's Day all of the families would meet at the church for a community celebration of prayers, singing, dancing, and feasting.

With their plan in place, the women spent the next three weeks before Thanksgiving sewing everyone's new clothes and making special decorations to spruce up their homes for all the visits that would be coming soon. They also spent time trading old family recipes and thinking up new dishes that would inspire each other's palates. In fact, the preparations quickly became a friendly competition with each family enthusiastically looking forward to outdoing the other families when the visits actually happened.

As a final step, the planning committee officially agreed that — at the end of the holidays — they would all vote for which family hosted the best visits, and the winner would hold the title of 'Community Champion Host' until the next holiday season, when they would do it all again. Extremely happy with their planning results, everyone involved believed that they were embarking on a wonderful holiday tradition — something that their families could take pride in celebrating and passing down from generation to generation in New South Grand.

The week before Thanksgiving, the collective list of trading post items was so long that Thaddeus agreed to drive a second wagon in behind the regular wagon to handle hauling the whole load. He didn't mind doing this at all; in fact, he was quite pleased by the overwhelming sense of community pride and spirit that was developing among the families.

Thanksgiving Day finally arrived, ushered in by the first real snowfall of the season. Some three inches of fluffy, white flakes tumbled from the prairie sky all night long, delighting the children the next morning as they peered out at the wintry landscape. Many of them grabbed make-shift sleighs and excitedly dashed off to slide down the hill in front of the church.

By eleven o'clock — as the families gathered at the church for the worship service — the day had warmed enough to turn the snow into a slushy mess. Inside the church, everyone sat in reverent respect as the chosen family members — one-by-one — gave thanks to the Lord Above for all their special blessings.

Thaddeus then got up and gave a brief talk, thanking everyone for their diligence and hard work in making their new settlement such an overwhelming success. He said that he thanked God every day for giving him such a wonderful and wise group of people to lead on their journey to this — their 'Promised Land'. He concluded by asking God's continued blessings for them all to live and prosper in their new surroundings.

Next, Thaddeus beckoned Minerva to come forward to officially start the holiday visitation period by announcing a day of communal feasting and celebration. Sparkly as ever, Minerva didn't need any coaxing. She glided to the front of the sanctuary, and immediately started singing several hymns that everyone knew. As they sang, the women and children walked up to the front of the church and placed their special harvest dishes on the altar.

Several families brought up freshly-roasted wild geese and turkeys to serve as the main course, while many others delivered acorn squash, corn fritters, hominy, bundles of chard, baked sweet potatoes, and fresh bread. Then — of course — there were the desserts of all types; including rum and spice cakes, Christmas pudding, and pumpkin, apple, raisin, and persimmon pies. When they were finished, there was enough food piled on the altar to feed a small army.

Minerva then said a short blessing over all the food. after which she chided everyone to quit sitting around and get up to eat and begin the merriment. When Minerva spoke, everyone listened, so — in less time than it takes for a pin to drop — the sanctuary was filled with sounds of people laughing, joking, and feasting like never before.

After they ate, everyone moved over to the livestock barn where the animals had been moved outside and the dirt floor swept clean. The rest of the afternoon and into the late evening was filled with drinking, dancing, singing, and socializing.

At midnight, several women left to go back to their houses and soon returned with another round of goodies; including molasses and shortbread cookies, hot chocolate with cinnamon topping, and spicy mulled wine. The festivities continued to the wee hours of the morning, with many town folks staying until after sunrise when more food appeared including hard boiled eggs, fresh-baked bread, several rashers of smoked bacon, and stout roast coffee.

The next day — under the town planning committee's direction — the families started their round robin visiting schedule that would last until New Year's Day. Giving each round of visits a festive flavor, each visiting family always brought each child in the host family either a homemade gift or a goodie to eat.

To provide the main dishes for all the visitations, the men went bird-hunting early each morning. Even deep into the fall, there were always large skeins of both Canada and snow geese flying up and down the river channel — while flocks of wild turkeys browsed on mast and insects in the scattered floodplain woodlots.

Due to the sheer abundance of wildlife, the men easily bagged all the game birds they needed within an hour or two. They took the freshly-killed birds back into town where they cleaned and dressed them, then distributed a goose or turkey to each host family for roasting.

The visitation plan worked like a charm. When Christmas week arrived, everyone in the settlement had become almost as closely-knit as the families they had left far behind in Virginia. Thaddeus knew that this bonding would soon become especially important.

First Christmas in New South Grand

The families quickly realized that Christmas on the frontier would be unlike anything any of them had previously known. Many of the old country traditions — like an evergreen Christmas tree with sparkling, new, store-bought decorations — were a thing of the past.

Since there were very few trees —and almost no evergreens — growing on the prairie, the men cut bare-branched willow saplings from the river floodplain and put these up inside each house. Each family then decorated their tree with white tissue paper, popcorn and cranberries strung together with thread, apples, homemade cookies, and pieces of stick candy bought from the trading post. They also added ornaments — like pocket watches and pieces of jewelry — to give each tree a special, sparkly, family touch.

To add a festive flair to the town center, the men got together and dug up a fifteen-foot-tall cottonwood tree from the riverbank. They then filled one of the wagons with dirt and re-planted the tree right there in the wagon. Everyone in town came out to watch the strange sight of a tree seemingly floating along the prairie as several men hauled the soon-to-be community Christmas tree into town.

The men parked the wagon on the hill in front of the church, and everyone immediately got busy decorating their new holiday landmark with gourds, pumpkins, squash, and any other colorful items they could find. Some of the families even hung presents on the tree that would be handed out to the town's children on Christmas Day. As the final touch, the townsfolk scattered lanterns throughout the bare branches to show off the tree at night.

On Christmas Morning, each family built a roaring fire, sang carols, and exchanged hand-crafted gifts. The girls received dolls made of cornhusks, horsehair and cloth, while the boys received carved whistles, animals, or fighting soldiers. The children made simple drawings and finger-paintings for their parents. Around noon, all the families gathered for prayers, followed by another round of feasting, singing, and dancing into the wee hours of the morning.

By the end of the holiday season, the settlement behaved like one big, happy family whenever they got together at church or other organized events. The children all romped and rough-housed with each other like a group of first cousins, while the adults joshed and kidded together at will.

Both Thaddeus and Minerva took great pride in the camaraderie that had built up among the families in the three months since they officially founded their new prairie home. They both knew that these close-knit feelings were going to be severely tested for the first time by the long and bone-breaking cold winter they were about to face.

Winter Arrives

Thaddeus had read many letters from previous settlers describing day-after-day of below zero temperatures — often punctuated by fierce, two and three-day long blizzards. He also knew that the winter storms sometimes kept coming through March and even into April.

All the families in New South Grand were accustomed to the snowstorms that typically blanketed the Virginia mountains five or six times each winter. But none of them — including Thaddeus — had ever experienced the extreme conditions of a classic prairie blizzard. When one of these struck, the wind often whipped torrents of snowflakes sideways, so hard and fast that you couldn't even see your hand in front of your face.

Thaddeus knew the horror stories of children freezing to death less than a few hundred paces from their own front doors — because they couldn't see which way to go in the blinding snow. He had also read about how quickly a family's entire livestock herd could get buried up to their necks in massive snowdrifts and all perish before they could be rescued. Praying every night for guidance from above, Thaddeus always asked God to protect the New South Grand families from the travails of winter while getting them safely through to their first spring plantings.

Thankfully, the first two-and-a-half months of winter passed quietly and uneventfully for the twenty-six families in New South Grand. They continued to visit each other on a regular basis — forming an incredibly strong support system for the fledgling community. While they had to endure a few snowstorms, the winds remained relatively calm during each event.

So, despite being far more isolated than any of them had ever been in their lives, winter had not been anything that they weren't used to back in Virginia. But during the first week of March, 1834, everything changed — and in a big way.

Battling Through a Prairie Blizzard

The late winter morning dawned bright and calm — giving no hint of the intense cold weather front that was bearing down on New South Grand from the northwest. The gigantic storm arrived just after noon, beginning harmlessly enough with a band of gently falling snow that quickly coated the frozen ground in white. But the tiny size of the first snowflakes made many of the adults realize that this was going to be the storm they had feared would come. Most understood that the old axiom, '*big flakes, little snow — little flakes, big snow*,' was a truism ninety-five percent of the time.

Thaddeus — in particular — was a true believer in this time-tested method of predicting the severity of a snowstorm. During all the winters he spent living in the Virginia high country, he had never seen it fail. He immediately saddled up Castor and rode around to each log-and-stone home — all really just cabins — making sure everyone had plenty of firewood, food, and water and warning them to stay inside and ride out the storm, even if it lasted for several days.

Just as Thaddeus was finishing his rounds, the wind began to pick up — driving snowflakes horizontally across the village. By the time he arrived back home and put Castor back in his stall, it was snowing so hard that he couldn't see his house from where he was standing in his barn — a distance of less than one hundred feet!

The storm ravaged New South Grand for two full days. By the time it ended and the sun again emerged from the clouds, the blizzard had dumped more than forty inches of snow. Wind-whipped drifts towered up to twelve feet high against all immovable objects — including most of the homes and barns in the village.

The only structures visible after the storm, were the roof peaks and chimneys of the homes and the silos of the barns. Perched on the highest hill in town, even the church was buried up to its eaves with the steeple poking up above like a lighthouse set adrift in a sea of rolling, white waves.

Trapped inside their own cabin by the thousands of pounds of snow that blocked their door and had their sturdy roof trusses sagging, Thaddeus and Minerva knew they had to act quickly to save themselves as well as their neighbors. They had to figure out how to dig out of their home and into all the other houses before nightfall.

By looking up his chimney, Thaddeus could see a blue, sunny sky, so he knew that the snow should soon be starting to melt. He also knew that this was both good and bad news. The sun's warmth would certainly make digging out easier, but the melting snow would only freeze into a thick sheet of solid ice as the temperatures plummeted at night.

When this happened, the families could be entombed in their homes for several days without fresh air, food, or water. There was also the possibility that the extra weight of the ice could collapse the roofs of some of the cabins, crushing the helpless families inside.

Almost always thinking alike, Thaddeus and Minerva quickly agreed on what they had to do. They each grabbed the makeshift snow shovels that Thaddeus had fashioned out of the two halves of a metal washtub with stout tree branches for handles.

Thaddeus opened the cabin door and started furiously digging a tunnel toward the barn where the horses were — hopefully — still alive and ready to be saddled. As he dug, he passed each scoop of snow-back to Minerva who then used her shovel to toss the snow toward the rear of their cabin. The three Adams children — Caleb, Ethan, and Delilah — stood in a line in back of Minerva, using two brooms and a rake to push the snow all the way back against their cabin's rear wall.

Thaddeus and Minerva knew this was dangerous — since they ran the risk of burying themselves and their children alive inside their own cabin — but they didn't have any choice. They figured that there was enough room in the cabin to handle all the snow that it would take to tunnel out to their barn. Then — once they reached the barn — they could move all the dug-out snow from the cabin into the larger barn where it could melt without causing any permanent damage.

But moving the snow from their cabin to the barn was a secondary concern for Thaddeus and Minerva at the moment. Their primary goal right now was just making it to the barn where Thaddeus could saddle up

Castor and one of the other draft horses and harness them to the heavy metal plow that he had used back in the fall to turn large chunks of tallgrass prairie into community cropland.

After tunneling some forty feet away from his cabin's door, Thaddeus broke free from the massive snowdrift and into the startlingly white landscape. Just as he expected, the storm clouds had completely cleared, and the sun was shining down brightly from a crystal-blue sky.

The air was extremely cold — much colder than when the snow had first started falling two days ago. Looking around at the icicles that had started to form along the edge of the barn's roof, Thaddeus figured that the temperature couldn't be much above zero and that the intense rays of the sun were only melting and re-freezing the surface of the snow. Plus, all of the snowpack below the surface was only getting more and more compacted as the ice built up above.

Thaddeus knew time was now of the essence. They now had less than eight hours of daylight left to dig into the barn and get the horses and plow out. Then they had to make it around to dig each family out of their snow-bound homes.

Thaddeus called back to Minerva to let her know that he had broken through the drifts next to their cabin. Minerva scrambled up next to Thaddeus with her shovel and they both started digging as fast as they could, tossing the snow up over their shoulders and into the open air.

As Thaddeus and Minerva dug closer and closer to the barn, the snow kept getting deeper and deeper. When he got to where the snow was piled higher than his shoulder, Thaddeus told Minerva that he was going to start tunneling again. He ducked down and starting digging and passing each shovelful back to Minerva who then piled the white stuff back in the freshly dug path behind them.

After Thaddeus and Minerva had tunneled to the barn door, they realized they had a major problem. The barn doors swung outward, which meant they had to clear enough snow from around the doors to be able to get them open. The only choice was to stuff the snow from around the doors back into the tunnel they had just finished digging, completely blocking their pathway back into their cabin. But Thaddeus wasn't concerned about blocking their way back to the house, because he knew he could quickly push it all back out of the way once he got the horses hooked up to his plow.

As soon as they had the barn doors opened wide enough for the horse team and plow to pass through, Thaddeus and Minerva bounded over to the horses. Thaddeus saddled Castor and one of the wagon horses while Minerva reversed the frame for the plow so that the horses could push it instead of pulling like they did when they worked the fields. As soon as they were all hitched up, Thaddeus jumped on Castor and gave Minerva a boost up onto the wagon horse.

Thaddeus clucked a giddy-up to Castor, and the makeshift snowplow moved through the barn door and out into the path of the tunnel they had dug to get into the barn. As soon as they had pushed their way back out to where their dug path day-lighted into the open air, Thaddeus again clucked to Castor and the horse team pushed the plow blade directly into the snow bank on the right-hand side of the path. Thaddeus plowed out his house, and then he and Minerva quickly removed the snow from the inside of the cabin. Thaddeus then headed his team in the direction of the church, knowing that this would give the families a place to go if they needed to get out of their cabins.

Thaddeus and Minerva were fortunate that the blade of their plow was just high enough to push the snow up and over the snow banks that they were creating as they moved slowly along. As soon as Minerva saw that Thaddeus had the team well under control by himself, she leapfrogged up off her saddle over the head of her horse and landed, standing up with her feet straddling the frame of the plow.

Staring at Minerva, Thaddeus just shook his head in amazement at his wife's daring athleticism. Without even thinking about it, she had just done something that even the best-trained carnival acrobat wouldn't attempt.

Now that she was standing on the plow's frame and could clearly see all around, Minerva began yelling directions back at Thaddeus. Within minutes, they arrived at the drift blocking the door to Thelma and Julius Johnson's cabin — the couple that lived closest to them.

Once they had pushed as close to the cabin door as they could, Thaddeus and Minerva jumped down, grabbed their shovels off of the plow frame, and began tunneling toward the Johnson's door. Thaddeus had dug only about ten feet when he got a big — but pleasant — surprise.

The wall of snow in front of him suddenly collapsed and he looked up to see Julius Johnson standing there, looking just as surprised as he was. They sheepishly laughed as they stood there staring at each other, realizing that they had somehow managed to tunnel right into each other's paths.

Thaddeus walked behind Julius into his house, put his arm around Thelma, and checked to make sure that all four of their children were all right. He then walked back out to Minerva and the team with Julius now trailing behind — shovel in hand — to help in digging everyone else out.

They repeated this same process twenty-four more times — picking up new digging recruits at every cabin they tunneled into. Amazingly, by just after sunset, the entire village was connected by a maze of dug paths and tunnels all leading up to the front door of the church sanctuary.

One-by-one, the rescued families walked out of their cabins and up to the church where they embraced each other — often tearfully — and talked about their experiences during the storm. Dead tired but feeling as proud and satisfied as he ever had in his life, Thaddeus grabbed Minerva up in his arms and bear-hugged her with all the energy he had left in his body. They then grabbed each other's hands and walked up to the front of the sanctuary, where they led everyone in a prayer of thanks for helping them all survive the worst storm any of them had ever lived through.

While it didn't seem possible with this already tightly-knit community, the blizzard's trauma brought New South Grand's citizen-settlers even closer together. As the blessing of an early spring melted the frost away from the prairie soils, they all joyfully pitched in to help each other with spring cleaning, farm field plowing, and preparing for spring planting.

A Very Welcome Vernal Equinox

Three weeks past the vernal equinox — around the middle of April 1834 — all of the tallgrass prairie that the settlers had plowed back in the fall had been planted to crops — primarily wheat, cotton, tobacco, corn, and vegetables. The way Thaddeus figured it, the settlement of New South Grand now collectively owned around five hundred acres of cropland — averaging out at about twenty acres per family.

While some of the crops were used to feed each family, much of the produce was hauled to the trading post in Independence where it was exchanged for household goods, clothing and shoes, plus fanciful and luxury items like store-made toys, jewelry, liquor, smoking pipes, candy, and assorted other edible treats.

The New South Grand settlers also used another two hundred acres up on one of the river bluffs as summer pasture for their beef cattle and sheep herds. The idea was to fatten the cattle up so they could be driven to the stockyards in the trading post and sold at the end of the summer.

Money from selling the cattle — plus the wool shorn from the sheep — was pooled for buying building materials. The goal was to both expand the village and fix up the past winter's damage to the cabins and farmsteads of each of the families.

The calves and lambs produced by the community's herd were also periodically butchered, and the meat was evenly distributed for special family dinners. For basic daily consumption, each family also maintained a vegetable garden and kept a flock of chickens, a milk cow, and a small goatherd in the barnyard next to their cabin.

Growth Begets Growth

As the years went by, more and more wagon trains decided that this was where their journeys should end. The steady influx of newcomers brought increased security and economic stability to New South Grand.

The community now had a sheriff and several deputies — plus a justice of the peace and a jail. They finally felt secure from the gangs of bandits that still roamed the surrounding wild and wooly frontier. Plus, formal legal services — for weddings, funerals, and all other matters of the heart and mind — were available to anyone who needed them. Along with the addition of these protective and legal services came a small trading post — that was managed and stocked by a merchandiser at the much larger trading post in Independence — plus a canteen, barbershop, library, and community center.

Having direct access to all these goods and services that used to require a two-day round trip into Independence made life significantly easier for everyone in New South Grand. The more services the town added, the more desirable it became as a place to settle.

Many of the townsfolk likened New South Grand's growth to a snowball rolling downhill. The farther it rolled, the larger it got and the faster it moved. In less than a decade, the tiny prairie village of New South Grand had become a bustling — and mostly self-sufficient — frontier town.

As the children of the original families grew into teenagers, they began to help their parents plow more prairie and raise more crops. In time, they became strong young men and women — ready to start their own families and care for their own farms. Honoring a long-standing farming tradition, each new generation of original settlers created their separate lives by plowing new acreage and building a new home right next to their parent's farmstead.

Fourteen years after leading the original settlement, Thaddeus had no idea how many people now called New South Grand home — but he knew for certain that everything had changed forever. In some ways, he felt a sense of pride that the town he founded had grown into one of the largest settlements on the Missouri frontier.

In other ways, Thaddeus was saddened when he thought about just how much had been sacrificed along the way. For almost as far as he could see, the virgin tallgrass prairie had vanished — replaced by the new farmsteads and their adjacent croplands.

Thaddeus no longer saw the uncountable herds of buffalo and endless flights of geese that were always around when he first arrived. While there were still small herds of deer and antelope living in the river breaks and floodplain backwaters that weren't suitable for farming, the jaw-dropping abundance of wildlife had disappeared. And — in his heart — he knew that he would never, ever see anything like it again during his lifetime.

When he was alone, Thaddeus' thoughts often drifted back to the years he spent living off the land in the mountains of Virginia. He wondered if the trade-off he now saw in his new home was really worth it.

Were the original twenty-six families really better off now that the native tallgrass prairie had all been plowed under to support the endless flood of newcomers? Could they really justify sacrificing nature's bounty for their own personal and financial gains? While he never actually asked them, Thaddeus strongly suspected that each and every one of the original settlers would likely answer 'yes' to these questions.

After all, wasn't this why they had all given up their comfortable lives back East, enduring the many hardships it took to come all this way and settle this new land? Thaddeus was sure they all felt entitled — and rightfully so when he really thought about it — to the good life the deep and fertile prairie soils were now providing them all. He knew that — in their minds — these vast natural resources were put there by God for them to use and that everything they did was to serve Him.

But still, Thaddeus wasn't really certain he felt like all the rest.

BOOK FIVE
The Next Generation Heads West

Ethan and Caleb Get Happy Feet

Thaddeus Adams had another problem to deal with that he hadn't quite expected — at least not so soon. Both of his boys — Caleb and Ethan — had inherited his penchant for change. Now that they were both teenagers, scarcely a day went by that he didn't overhear them talking passionately about heading out on their own to find 'adventure, romance, and untold wealth'.

They mostly talked about joining the groups of prairie settlers who were loading up their wagons and heading further west. This time, they were all seeking a totally different way of life that didn't have anything to do with plowing ground or raising crops. They were all after the vast riches of gold and silver that awaited the first pioneers to settle in the great mountain ranges of the far western territories — from the foothills of the Rockies to the Pacific coastal ranges.

Every chance he got; Thaddeus tried to encourage the boys to embrace the opportunities they had in New South Grand but — in his heart — he knew it was hopeless. First, he realized he probably wasn't very convincing — since he fully understood and sympathized with how his sons felt. Second, he realized — from his own boyhood — that anything he said wouldn't make any difference to a willful teen with his mind made up.

He knew Caleb and Ethan had decided that the farming life simply wasn't for them. They were determined to be off — seeking their future lives and fortunes in the placer and silver mining camps of America's Wild West.

Caleb Adams was nineteen, and Ethan Adams had just turned eighteen one warm late winter morning in 1847 when the brothers walked into the family kitchen, pulled up chairs, and sat down with Thaddeus and Minerva to tell them about their plans. They had joined a group of ten other adventure-seeking lads and — using three covered wagons to haul their provisions — would soon be heading west.

Minerva was so shocked that she couldn't speak. She looked at Thaddeus who was slowly moving his head from side-to-side. In truth, Thaddeus had been expecting to hear this announcement much sooner. He was actually surprised that his boys had waited so long to announce their plans.

Thaddeus knew Caleb and Ethan were both big and strong enough to handle the journey. Plus, he had taught them all the frontier skills they would need to survive. They could both ride like the wind, shoot with dead aim, and — when they had to — fight like caged animals.

With his square jaw, thickly-muscled body, and chiseled good looks, Caleb took after his father. He stood more than six feet tall and weighed upwards of two hundred and twenty pounds. In short, Caleb was a solid rock of a young man.

Ethan was built more like Minerva, with thin features and musculature attached to a small frame. He was only five-feet-seven and maybe weighed one hundred and sixty pounds soaking wet. But — just like his mother — Ethan was sinewy, supple, and determined that he could do anything much larger men could do.

In fact, Ethan more often than not held his own whenever he and Caleb got into impromptu wrestling matches. On many occasions, Ethan ended a match by grabbing Caleb around the neck and body-slamming him to the ground so hard that Caleb had to limp around for the next several days.

Ethan also had Minerva's softer side. He was an excellent cook, sewed his own clothes, and kept everything he owned well-organized and neat as a pin. When they were growing up, Caleb and his buddies constantly razzed Ethan about being prissy.

For the most part, Ethan was good-natured about the ribbing and took it in stride. But he always let everyone know when he had heard enough, and it was time to shut up or face the consequences — which could mean ending up in New South Grand's infirmary.

As both boys soon found out, Ethan's domestic skills would serve them quite well during their journey west.

Moving On Again

The group of boys that Caleb and Ethan were joining had all known each other for many years. Most of them were sons of the original twenty-six New South Grand families, while a few moved in from the later wagon trains. They were led by Samuel Johnson Jr., the only one among them who — at age twenty-two — was older than a teenager.

Samuel Johnson carried his maturity well. He had all the attributes of a natural leader, and the other boys respected him and — for the most part — followed his direction without question. Caleb was the only one who disagreed with Samuel from time-to-time, but — when he did — it was always for a very good reason.

Caleb challenged Samuel to think through every angle and outcome of a decision he was making. For this, the other boys also deferred to Caleb and considered him to be the group's second-in-command.

Unbeknownst to their parents — or anyone else for that matter — the boys had been secretly meeting in the hayloft of Samuel's barn once a week since the turn of the new year. They had everything very carefully planned.

They were going to pick up the local wagon train trail and follow it to the ferry crossing of the Kansas River. There they would hit the broader — and better known — Oregon Trail, and stay on it for almost a thousand miles through what was to become the Kansas and Nebraska Territories, and on into the foothills of the Rocky Mountains. Once they got to the mountains, they would keep their ears to the ground to find out where, when, and how to best cross through the series of ranges that they knew would confront them during the rest of their westward trek.

The boys had read many letters written by other adventurous folks who had crossed the Rockies before them. Some told of finding passes between the high peaks that made their journeys relatively easy. But others described the horrors of blinding blizzards, frost-bitten feet and hands, deaths, and even cannibalism when things went really wrong.

Young as they were, the boys were all fully aware that they had to treat the mountains with the utmost caution and respect if they wanted to make it through alive. They realized that while they may be embarking on the journey of a lifetime, it wouldn't be any walk in the park.

The way they all had it figured, as soon as they got into the mountains, they would start looking for opportunities to pan for gold, mine silver, or — hopefully — both. If this meant staying put for a year or two, so much the better.

They hoped that things would be so good they could settle in and start their own mining camp or even — in the best of all worlds — a full-fledged boomtown. Then — if things didn't work out like they wanted — they would just pack up, move on, and try their luck again at the next place they found with a potential mother lode. The sky was the limit, and all of the boys had their eyes locked solidly into the rainbows they envisioned floating amid the puffy white-and-gray clouds of the future.

The boys planned on spending most nights camping out under the big, starry western skies. On the few nights that it rained — or worse — they would sleep under the protective canvas coverings of their wagons. They would just move their provisions out onto the ground and pitch their bedrolls inside the wagon beds. They had laid-in enough salt-cured venison and fish — plus wheat and corn meal — to last them a good six weeks on the trail.

They were also certain that they could easily kill enough game along the way to re-stock their food supplies every few weeks or so. All of the boys were masterful hunters and crack shots, plus they had several drying racks and barrels of salt for curing the meat.

Since they would be traveling through untamed land — still teeming with countless herds of buffalo, deer, elk, and antelope — they figured there was no way they could ever run out of food. But the one thing they hadn't considered — at least, not carefully enough — was how difficult it would be to just find game animals when the deep snows of winter came to the high mountains. This lesson they were all going to learn the hard way.

Since the western territories were still a lawless land, the boys knew that — as they traveled — they would all have to be constantly vigilant for bandits. This would be especially important when they traveled through tight canyons — where the landscape folded in on them — providing plenty of places for masked hoodlums to hide and attack. The boys knew they would have to close ranks in such country to protect their provisions if evil-doers decided to strike.

Understanding Native Americans

From their father Thaddeus' experience, both Caleb and Ethan Adams also knew the importance of staying on the good side of the local Native American tribes. After all — in many places — they would be constantly crossing through their ancestral lands.

Thaddeus had taught his boys to always make peaceful contacts with any tribal villages or hunting parties they came across. He told them to even go so far as asking the tribesmen to give them a scout to serve as a local guide along each part of their route.

It was in the best interest of each Native American tribe to provide white men with safe passage through their tribal lands. This way, the invaders wouldn't be tempted to stop and become squatters on tribal land — settling in to farm and start their own villages.

Plus, the local Native American tribes were often unjustly blamed whenever something happened to a group of white men traveling across the high plains. This sometimes meant having to fight off a flurry of federal cavalrymen — sent out from the nearest fort — to retaliate for any lost white lives.

Most U.S. history books don't tell the real story about how most of the early conflicts between Native American tribes and the colonizing white men could have been easily avoided. The local tribes just wanted to protect their native lands and maintain their way of life. They didn't hate the white man — at least, not at first.

Most tribes only wanted to establish peaceful bonds and friendly trading relationships with the frontiersmen and settlers. The white man brought with them many things — hunting rifles, cooking utensils, and smoking tobacco — that could make life easier and more enjoyable for the Native Americans.

In turn, the Indigenous people offered many valuable items — furs, precious gemstones, hand-made jewelry — that would fetch a pretty penny in frontier trading posts. For a while, happenstance meetings between white men and Native Americans were peaceful and productive, with both parties typically departing with smiles on their faces.

The real trouble didn't start until the newly-formed federal government decided to forcefully start taking land away from the Native American tribes. Federal cavalrymen — armed with high-powered rifles and fancy pistols — began attacking hundreds of tribal villages all across the western territories. With only horse-mounted braves — mainly fighting with bow and arrows and hatchets — the tribesmen could offer little resistance.

Thousands of Native American men, women, and children were massacred. In many cases, entire villages were wiped out — the teepees burned, and the bodies piled in shallow graves. As word of these atrocities circulated, the Tribal Nations of the West mobilized — and, in some cases, joined forces — to go to war against the white man. Their homeland, pride, and way of life were now all being threatened and it was not in their nature to go down without a fight.

Leaving New South Grand

Finally, the agreed-upon departure date for Samuel Johnson's team — March twenty-second, 1847 — was at hand. The early morning air was bright and crystal clear with just a hint of early spring frost. As planned, the intrepid troop of young fortune seekers rallied together in front of the church. Each boy had his own packhorse and the three covered wagons — locally known as prairie schooners — were each pulled by a team of four oxen.

Samuel Johnson sat astride the lead oxen team, handling the reins of the first wagon while Festus Parker occupied the same position on the second wagon. Jeremiah Highsmith sat in the buckboard seat of the first wagon, ready to take over the reins if something happened to Samuel.

Smiling like the cat that caught the canary, Ethan Adams sat perched on top of the third wagon's buckboard seat. He did this for two reasons. He wanted to sit as tall as possible so he could see everything that was going on ahead of his wagon's oxen team. Plus — as was obvious from the mischievous glint in his eyes — he planned on using his high seat to tease and taunt his big brother as they rolled along the trail.

In fact, a jaunty, festive atmosphere filled all the boys as they hugged their parents and siblings one final time. They all knew full well that the journey they were undertaking would be arduous and fraught with danger. But they were also all strong, hearty, and full of 'spit and vinegar' — as their parents always liked to say — and they were ready to hit the trail for their sure-to-be-grand adventure.

After Thaddeus Adams finished saying a prayer and wishing them all Godspeed, a safe journey, and everlasting happiness, Samuel Johnson geed his team off to the right — followed closely by the other two wagons — and the rest of the boys riding on their mounts in single file. As soon as they were on the trail and headed west, the boys all took off their hats and turned back as one toward the church — yelling and waving as they rode off across the brightening prairie landscape.

Everything worked like a charm during the first three days that the boys were on the trail. They made their ferry crossing of the Kansas River just before sunset on the second night out and two days later they hit the Oregon Trail just before noon.

Physical Trials on the Oregon Trail

Tying into the Oregon Trail, or 'OT' as everyone called it, was a landmark event for all westward bound travelers. Since it was heavily used, the OT was wide and mostly smooth — or at least not as bumpy — as all the other, lesser-traveled wagon trails. Plus, being on the OT meant that you were now traveling on a well-known and proven route that went almost all the way to the Pacific Ocean.

The boys were all so excited about finally being underway that they decided to give themselves an early travel holiday to celebrate their first major accomplishment. And celebrate they did — in a manner befitting the wild and wooly westward territories they were about to enter.

The day of rest and relaxation started after a leisurely, filling breakfast. First on the agenda was a frontier decathlon, including boxing, wrestling, musket shooting, weightlifting, swimming, cliff diving, log-hurling, distance running, sprinting, and discus throwing. The boys made up their own scoring system for each event — consisting of three points for first place, two points for second place, and one point for third place.

Many of the events required quite different body sizes and physical skills. For instance, slender James Hertzburg used his slick-as-silk jack-knife to take first place in the cliff diving event. Eagle-eyed William Wordsmith scored an impressive eight-out-of-ten bullseyes to win the musket shooting.

Meanwhile, Nathan Cromwell used his lightning-quick reflexes — honed from his days of catching pumpkins on the family farm during fall harvest — to take the boxing event. Next, Horatio Cornbluth featured his long arms and huge hands in winning the discus throwing — which actually consisted of hurling the cover of a cooking pot further than anyone else.

When it came down to the early afternoon, only two events — distance running and sprinting — remained. While the competition leader changed throughout the day, after eight events, only five remained in the chase.

As expected, the three oldest boys — Samuel Johnson, Caleb Adams, and Jeremiah Highsmith were still in the running. But they were being seriously challenged by two of the younger boys — Christian Lardner and Thomas Stringfellow — who were succeeding because of their impressive upper body musculature. In fact — between them — Christian and Thomas had either won or placed second in three of the events that emphasized pure strength — log hurling, weight lifting, and wrestling.

First up was the distance running, a ten-mile out and ten-mile back endeavor. As previously agreed, the five top finishers at the end of eight events were given a two-minute head-start on the rest of the boys in the distance event. An hour before the race started, Caleb Adams rode Snowflake out and tied a stake with a red bandana to mark the ten-mile turnaround point.

When the twenty-mile distance event started on Ethan Adams' count of *'ready-set-go'*, Caleb, Samuel Johnson, and Jeremiah Highsmith all took off like startled jackrabbits. Their strategy was to jump way out in front and — in so doing — demoralize the rest of the boys into giving up.

But — as anyone who has ever run a marathon will tell you — fast starts are generally not a good idea. Successful long-distance running is typically based on a combination of endurance and strategy. The keys are knowing when and where to coast and then when to put the hammer down. Such was the case in this race.

With their long, loping strides, both Christian Lardner and Thomas Stringfellow came across the finish line — demarcated by a strand of yellow ribbon — neck-and-neck. Christian beat Thomas by just a half stride, which was remarkable considering the twenty-mile distance of the race.

After they crossed the finish line, both boys enthusiastically hugged and cajoled each other. They admitted that competing so closely over that many miles was the most arduous thing either had ever attempted.

Caleb, Jeremiah, and Samuel eventually finished the race, but they were barely moving, and a good mile behind the other boys when they did. Thus, the old adage that 'the race is not always to the swift' had been proven once again.

Because of the intensity and competition of the distance run, the concluding sprint event became an afterthought. Caleb marked the course by walking about two hundred paces — six hundred feet — on a relatively flat portion of the Oregon Trail. As all the boys knew, sixteen-year-old Josiah Sumner was — by far — the fastest runner among them. Back home, he had even been known to chase down a gut-shot white-tailed deer before it toppled over from exhaustion.

Sure enough, Josiah won the sprint with ease — finishing three strides ahead of Thomas Stringfellow. But the final results had already been determined before the sprint was run. By virtue of his win in the distance event, Christian Lardner claimed the decathlon title with a total of fourteen points.

That night, the boys celebrated the decathlon by staging a formal — or least as formal as you can get on the open tallgrass prairie — presentation to all the event winners. Courtesy of the dedicated handiwork of Ethan Adams, each winner was presented with a flower-bedecked wreath woven from prairie grasses.

As the decathlon champion, Christian Lardner was crowned with a festoon of cut-stem flowers embedded in a dried pile of buffalo dung held together by saddle reins. Playing along with the gag, Christian buried his head in his hands and pretended to sob at the immense honor that had been bestowed upon him.

As soon as Christian placed the crown of dung on his head, all the other boys grabbed him, hoisted him onto a saddle, and paraded him around the campground as if he were a conquering hero just recently returned from the battlefield. With this as a starting point, the makeshift festivities roared and soared throughout the night until a combination of drunkenness and exhaustion finally overtook them all.

The next day, Samuel and Caleb decided to let everyone sleep it off until noon. Then, they pumped all the boys full of coffee and hot grub and told them to get ready to hit the trail. The party was over, and it was now time to start making serious progress on their westward trek.

Following the Platte

During the next week, the boys made great progress — sometimes traveling as much as twelve miles a day. Late in the afternoon — on what had been a blustery and difficult travel day — they rode up to the southern edge of the floodplain of the Platte River and were immediately awestruck.

There before them lay a sight that was almost impossible to fathom. The river appeared to be several thousand feet across. In fact, not one of them could tell where the opposite bank was, but the river channel was as much land as it was water.

The Platte's flow braided around, over, and through a mosaic of wooded islands of all shapes and sizes. Some of the boys who rode out into the channel were amazed to see that the water barely covered the tops of their horses' hooves — even several hundred feet from shore. Perhaps skeptical of its value, early plains explorers wrote of the Platte River: "It flows a mile wide, an inch deep, and sometimes not at all."

Equally as startling as the river's broad, shallow channel were the giant flocks of strange, large birds that were now flying in from all directions. Loudly trumpeting their arrival, skein after skein of these gangly, long-necked and long-legged birds swooped down into the middle of the river channel.

Soon the entire floodplain was covered by a mass of bobbing heads and fluttering wings, emitting a cacophony of sound that made it impossible for the boys to hear each other talking. They figured these large gray birds had to be at least four or five feet tall, with wingspans of six feet or more.

The Platte River provides ideal habitat for the masses of sandhill cranes — up to five hundred thousand birds — that stop and refuel before taking off again on the second leg of their thousand-mile migration, between wintering habitat in the southern United States and nesting grounds in Canada's high Arctic. The world's oldest surviving bird species, the sandhill appears curiously archaic. With legs dangling and bent in an awkward landing posture, and neck and wings extended, it is reminiscent of the ancient pterodactyl — the extinct flying reptile.

It's no wonder that the boys were so astonished to find thousands of these odd-looking birds filling the Platte River channel from bank-to-bank. During a typical spring day on the Platte, the sandhills leave the broad floodplain just after sunrise and head out into the adjacent wetlands and prairies to gorge themselves on tubers, insect larvae, and earthworms.

While feeding, the cranes put on quite a show — demonstrating their now famous courtship routine known as 'crane dancing.' During the dance, male sandhills do everything possible to impress the females — including leaping, bowing, and swirling in pirouettes in midair like ballet dancers. Then — just before sunset — they return to roost for the night in the middle of the Platte's broad river channel.

As they watched in dumbfounded disbelief, curiosity got the better of several of the boys. They pulled out their rifles and simultaneously fired off several shots into the quivering avian masses that were now bathed in the golden light of sunset.

Instantaneously, the entire river channel appeared to rise up. Thousands of frightened birds took to the air as one — filling the sky with flapping wings and fluttering calls. With the flushed birds noisily swooping around overhead — like a massive swarm of giant bees — several boys rode out into the middle of the channel to pick up their kills.

That night, the boys roasted the giant cranes over their campfire and — while they agreed that the meat wasn't as tasty as chicken or goose — it was still mighty good, compared to the beef jerky and salt-cured fish they had been eating for the past few weeks. Plus, there was plenty enough to go around — even though they had only killed ten of the giant fowl. They decided to make a regular evening hunt and meal of these strange, new birds for as long as they could, which — as it turned out — lasted for several more weeks.

After awakening the next morning, the young travelers were again treated to a visual feast by the nearby masses of sandhill cranes. Almost at the exact moment that the sun's orange-pink orb first appeared over the horizon, dawn's quiet hush was replaced by a thunderous flapping of thousands of giant wings.

Lifting off in the gathering dawn light, skein after skein of sandhills arose from their watery perches and used a variety of trilling calls — *kar-r-r-r-o-o-o, kar-r-r-r-o-o-o, kar-r-r-r-o-o-o* — coaxing their earthbound brethren to join them in the air. As the boys watched in rapt amazement, chevron after chevron of these massive birds crisscrossed the sky, practically blocking out the sun and creating an unparalleled blending of sight and sound.

The route of the Oregon Trail followed along the channel of the Platte River for the next five hundred miles through land that is now the States of Nebraska and Wyoming. The broad, flat floodplain of the Platte made for easy travel on mostly smooth surfaces. Plus, the shallow, braided river channel produced an abundance of lush, green grass for grazing the horses and oxen and firewood for making campfires.

Since they were now well into the western frontier, the boys were traveling through land that had — for the most part — not yet been impacted by white men. Vast acreages of mixed tall and mid-grass prairies were still intact and intense with fresh spring growth.

Buffalo herds grazed for as far as the eye could see along both sides of the river. Caleb Adams and Samuel Johnson and some of the other boys — who were among the first to settle in New South Grand — agreed that the buffalo herds they were now seeing were even larger than those they remembered from their youths.

In fact, the overall abundance of wild game — including large mixed herds of white-tailed and mule deer, elk, and pronghorn 'antelope' — plus vast flocks of geese and ducks, in addition to the sandhill cranes, was simply jaw-dropping. Nature's bounty appeared to be so great that the boys truly believed it was enough to last forever, no matter how many settlers came after them to plow the prairies and plant their crops.

Little did they realize that their perception of nature's endless bounty would soon change dramatically… and forever.

Two Groups Join Forces

On the tenth day of their ride along the Platte River, the boys met up with another group of twelve young men headed west to find their fortunes in the western mountains. The two groups rode along together all day and got to know each other.

The New South Grand boys were delighted to find out that their new friends had pretty much the same plans and ideas as they did. The newcomers had started their journey near the frontier village of Warrensburg, Missouri — about fifty miles southeast of Independence — the official start of the Oregon Trail.

Since the Warrensburg group had been traveling for the past month, they were able to pass along several pearls of frontier wisdom to the New South Grand group. For one thing, they pointed out that buffalo chips — which littered practically every square inch of land in the Platte River's floodplain — were a much better way to keep campfires going than firewood.

While the buffalo chips burned much faster and didn't especially smell good, they were much easier to find and collect. Plus, using them saved all the time involved with cutting, hauling, and — as was often needed when it rained — drying out firewood.

That night over dinner of roasted goose from a successful late afternoon hunt, baked potatoes, and a special stash of home-brewed sour-mash from New South Grand, the two groups of fortune seekers toasted one another and agreed to travel together for the remainder of their westward journey. They all agreed that there was safety in numbers — especially when they reached the foothills of the mountains — where there were many places for bandits to hide and swoop in unseen. The more men and rifles they had, they reasoned, the less likely they were to be attacked.

After dinner most of the boys moved off to tend to the oxen and horses while Ezekiel Hermadiah and Joseph Budd — the two leaders of the Warrensburg group — stayed around to talk to Samuel Johnson and Caleb Adams about leadership of the combined group. After a lively round of debating about who had the best leadership qualities, the four agreed to keep Samuel and Caleb as the overall group leaders, with Joseph and Ezekiel as the second-in-command lieutenants.

The newly combined groups were an impressive-looking entourage when they headed back out on the Oregon Trail the next day. Altogether the New South Grand and the Warrensburg groups totaled twenty-four young men plus six prairie schooner wagons, each pulled by a team of four oxen.

Samuel Johnson and his horse Biscuit rode out in front of the group while Joseph Budd brought up the rear on his trusty steed, Lightning. Meanwhile, Caleb Adams and Ezekiel Hermadiah rode on their horses Snowflake and Morning Glory — astride the two middle wagons — to keep a watchful eye on both flanks of the group.

Three or four times each day, Samuel would whistle for Joseph to ride up to the front and the two of them would take off to scout the trail ahead. Each time this happened, Caleb would move up to the head of the train and Ezekiel would fall back to the rear until Samuel and Joseph returned from scouting.

For the next several days, the combined wagon train and riders moved along swiftly without any incidents or problems. When they were scouting river breaks and floodplain terraces below the wagon train, Samuel and Joseph often chuckled to each other when they looked up and saw what appeared to be five white sails floating like clouds across the blue sky of the open prairie. The sight always made them realize why the smaller wagons of the west were known as 'prairie schooners'.

Buffalo Killing Fields

Early one morning, Caleb Adams was surprised to see Samuel Johnson and Joseph Budd riding like the wind back toward the wagon train. Since they had been out scouting less than an hour and — based on how fast they were riding — Caleb felt certain that they had run into some sort of hostile ne're-do-wells.

Caleb immediately turned around on Snowflake, whistled loudly, and held up his hand to halt the wagons and other riders. Almost simultaneously, Samuel reined Biscuit in to a stop beside Caleb and Snowflake. In a high-pitched panicky voice that was totally out-of-character, Samuel began to tell Caleb what he and Joseph had just seen up ahead.

As Samuel kept talking a mile-a-minute, Caleb soon realized why he was so excited. As Samuel described it — yelled it, actually — he had just seen the largest herd of buffalo 'that ever existed'. But that wasn't all, the buffalo were being attacked by hundreds of men who were wielding both long rifles and lances.

The buffalo were dropping like giant flies all across the prairie. And, instead of stopping to finish off, gut, and clean their kills, the men just kept moving on; shooting and lancing more buffalo, as they left the ones they had just slaughtered lying either dead, or writhing in pain in the prairie dust.

According to Samuel, the scene the hunters left behind was surreal — unlike anything even the most talented horror storyteller could conjure. In the aftermath, a cloud of dust billowed several thousand feet into the air — obscuring the sun before filtering back down to earth, and covering the untold number of buffalo carcasses in a blanket of ochre.

After hearing all this, Caleb just sat dumbfounded, staring quizzically at Samuel and waiting for him to finish his story. But Samuel was so traumatized and emotionally drained by this point, he could no longer speak.

Realizing that Samuel was waiting for some direction, Caleb rode over to him and Joseph and placed his arms around both of them. In a voice that was as quiet and calm as he could muster, Caleb told Joseph to turn the wagons around, move them back down into the stream bottom they had just passed through, and set up camp for the night.

As both Joseph and Samuel nodded in agreement, Caleb reasoned that they would be better off hunkering down, waiting until the next day, and then scouting the buffalo hunters again. While the four leaders all knew their hearty band of young men was as tough and brave as they come, they also didn't want to be foolish.

Caleb and Samuel both strongly suspected that the buffalo hunters were fully consumed by their killing spree. But there was no use risking danger. If for some reason the buffalo hunters decided to turn on them, they wouldn't stand a chance. They were certain that — within a matter of minutes — their young charges would all be lying as dead as doornails next to the rotting buffalo carcasses.

Just after dawn the next day, Samuel, Joseph, and Caleb left camp and rode back up the trail to see what — if anything — was still going on with the buffalo hunters. As they crested the last rise on the trail above the broad valley where the hunt had taken place, they again saw a sight that took their breath away.

There were at least ten large campsites, each with twenty-five to thirty over-sized wagons circled around huge bonfires that were still blazing away. They couldn't see anyone moving around — most likely the wanton murderers were all still asleep snuggled down inside their bedrolls in the chilly early morning air. But they could see that there were two huge piles — small mountains, really — of something stacked in the center of each encampment.

Joseph pulled a spyglass out of his saddle and took a closer look at two of the piles. After about thirty seconds, he let out a low whistle and passed his spyglass over to Caleb and Samuel so that they could both have a look. All three of them sat in stunned silence for several minutes.

They all now knew that they were looking at what was — most likely — the largest mass slaughter of buffalo in the history of their young country. The two stacks in each encampment were all the same, one was made up of thousands of freshly skinned buffalo hides. The other contained the naked carcasses of thousands of dead buffalo — all left to rot and stink in the searing heat of the open prairie.

Altogether, Samuel, Joseph, and Caleb figured they were looking at maybe as many as ten thousand buffalo skins and carcasses. They also reckoned that the men left in the camps were all skinners, tanners, and wagon drivers, hired to process and haul the hides. Meanwhile, the buffalo hunters had moved on to their next mass killing field, most likely in some valley further west.

Satisfied that they could now move their young riders safely past the encampment without worrying about an attack from any rifle-wielding buffalo hunters, Samuel, Caleb, and Joseph rode the mile or so back to their camp in thoughtful silence.

Caleb suspected the two others were thinking the same thing, but — in his own mind — he knew that he was dead wrong about the vast natural resources of the west enduring forever. Based on what he had just witnessed, he now realized that the white man had both the ability and the thoughtlessness to wipe out everything — and do so in a very short period of time.

If men on horseback can kill ten thousand buffalo in just a day, Caleb could only imagine what a troop of highly-trained soldiers — armed with repeating rifles and Gatling guns — could do in a week. His thoughts about what future senseless misuse of earth's precious natural resources might mean for mankind both sickened and saddened him deeply as he rode back into camp.

Pulling at all his inner strength to put on a positive face, Caleb walked around the camp and talked privately with each of the young men to explain to them what he had just seen. While he didn't try to hide his dismay, he also didn't let on about the deep despair he was feeling.

Instead, Caleb emphasized how they must now keep moving along the trail without worrying about attacks by the nefarious bison hunting parties. He also explained that they were likely to see much more evidence of the massive buffalo hunts during the remainder of their ride across the plains.

Caleb didn't actually know how prophetic his words would be. During the next two weeks on the Oregon Trail, his young riders passed one buffalo massacre site after another. He figured the buffalo hunters had stopped about every ten miles to start another slaughter.

The sickening stench of the rotting buffalo carcasses wafted across the open prairie on the prevailing west wind for such great distances that Caleb could tell when another killing field was approaching well before he could see any physical evidence of the actual hunt. When they first approached close enough to see the putrid mounds of rotting flesh, many of the boys became physically ill and had to dismount and run into the grassland to disgorge their stomachs.

Dealing with Trail Hazards

Encounters with Native American hunting parties were a regular occurrence for the young riders as they moved steadily westward toward the foothills of the Rocky Mountains. Whenever this happened, Samuel Johnson always whistled for Caleb Adams to come up to the front of the wagon train and serve as interpreter.

Well taught by his father, Caleb had a natural knack for befriending the local tribesmen and letting them know that they were only passing through their territories in peace, and intended no harm to the land or the native tribes. Caleb's easy relationships with all the Native Americans he met was another testament to the fact that they were — by their very nature and way of life — not destined to be mortal enemies of the white man.

From the stagecoach drivers and other groups of travelers the boys ran into on the trail, they heard many stories about being held up and robbed at gunpoint by roving bands of bandits. But they never had any trouble with the feared 'masked men' during their journey, probably because the bandits could see that — even with the element of surprise in their favor — they would be quickly outnumbered and outgunned by this intrepid group of hale and hearty young men.

Moving into the heat of summer, the group did, however, encounter their fair share of severe weather, as they moved steadily along the Oregon Trail. Many times, they watched in awe as a line of cyclonic winds — usually including a few twisters — ripped through the prairie-scape ahead of them. But their early years of growing up with the constant threat of tornadoes and torrential rains in the flatlands of their Missouri homeland had taught them well.

They always made sure to wait until each storm front had passed through before they pitched camp — even if it meant waiting until very late at night to eat dinner. Then — whenever they decided to stop — they kept all their wagons and camping gear out of any washes and draws that could quickly become deadly raging torrents fed by unseen distant cloudbursts.

The long days of summer passed quickly for the young riders, as they made their way through the Nebraska Territory and into what is now the State of Wyoming. They lived off the fat of the land — killing fresh deer and antelope every night for dinner and harvesting nuts and fresh berries from the trees growing in the Platte River's broad floodplain.

Frontier Games in Fort Laramie

Three weeks past where the Platte River split into separate north-flowing and south-flowing channels, the boys arrived at Fort Laramie, which — at the time — was the last frontier outpost on the east side of the Rocky Mountains. It was also a well-known place for groups of travelers to stop and blow off steam before moving into the foothills of the mountains.

Days in Fort Laramie were serious business with westward travelers. They carefully restocked their food caches, and repaired and replaced their gear for the arduous travel that lay ahead. But the nights were a different story.

After sunset, the streets and saloons of Fort Laramie quickly filled with wild and raucous men — taunting, screaming, gambling, and fighting with each other. The fights often became wild melees with bodies flying through windows and crashing over railings and hitching posts all along the fort's main street.

Afterwards, the inside of the fort looked like a battlefield. Drunken men were lying all over the place, alternately moaning in agony as they nursed their cuts and bruises, and laughing out loud at the fun they were having.

Most nights, no one was really seriously hurt and after sleeping it off, the men were typically all set to mount up and get back on the trail. Fort Laramie was primarily a 'male thing', which was just as well, since there were few women around for hundreds of miles in all directions.

After arriving inside the fort, Samuel and Caleb quickly agreed that their young charges had earned a few days of unsupervised recreation. When they got everyone together and told them they were staying for a few days, they realized it was the right decision. The boys all ripped their hats off, and with wild whoops and bellows, tossed them high into the air. A few even drew out their rifles and pistols and started shooting straight up into the sky — much to the dismay and anger of the soldiers on duty at the time.

For the next few days, all the boys ran around foot-loose and fancy-free. Caleb and Samuel would have loved to join right in with them, but they mostly sat back and watched and chuckled at the antics of their young men.

After nearly five months of having to be serious adults on the trail, the boys finally had the opportunity to let their hair down and act like the rough-and-tumble youngsters they really were. Caleb and Samuel's only concern was making sure that the grizzled assortment of mountain men who rolled in and out of Fort Laramie on a daily basis didn't take advantage — either physically or financially — of any of their charges.

One night after the boys arrived, a few of the local vagrants and conmen teamed up and organized what they called the 'monthly frontier games'. Caleb and Samuel kept a watchful eye on the proceedings while sipping beers on the front porch of the saloon. They knew full well what was going to happen.

The mountain men gathered the boys around in a big circle and told them about the schedule for the games. They clearly saw the lads as easy marks — who would readily fall prey to their expertise and end up losing all their money and valuables by the end of the night.

As the mountain men described it, the night's activities would begin right after supper with arm-wrestling, tomahawk and knife throwing matches, plus archery, quick-draw, and muzzle-loading competitions in the fort's hay barn. The games would then end the next morning with a full out-for-blood, winner-take-all match of Native American lacrosse on the fort's parade ground.

The boys all stayed in character — slyly displaying awe-struck gaping mouths and bulging eyes — as they listened to the mountain men lay out their plans. In truth, it was all they could do to keep from guffawing, since they knew the slovenly older men would be no match for their superior brain power, strength, and athleticism. The boys were also all excellent marksmen — handling rifles, pistols, tomahawks, bow-and-arrows, and knives with equal aplomb.

That evening, the fort's hay barn was packed with competitors milling around the open wood floor, and spectators perched on haybales all around the sides. All the props had been set up ahead of time. A line of targets hung from the rafters at the far end of the barn with three tea boxes positioned near the front doors for the arm wrestling.

Each group appointed a referee to oversee the activities and determine the winners in each event. Zachary 'Toad' Tyler — a bear of a man with a burly belly that hung way over his britches, and a beard that looked like it hadn't been trimmed in years — represented the mountain men. Joseph Budd was chosen as team leader for the boys.

To start things off, the arm-wrestling opponents moved forward and took their places on each side of the tea boxes. The boys picked Jedediah Johnson, Thackery Thomas, and Ethan Adams while the mountain men countered with three very large men who were clad head-to-toe in buckskin. They all looked — and smelled — like they hadn't seen a washtub in months. Based on the hoots, cheers, and catcalls coming from the rest of the mountain men, these three odiferous fellows were known only by their nicknames — Sawdust, Skunk, and Scruffy.

The first two matches were no contest, with Sawdust and Scruffy pinning Jedediah Johnson and Thackery Thomas in less time than it takes to shake a coon's tail. Now it was up to Ethan Adams to save some face for the boys' team.

Ethan sat down next to Skunk, who was rolling up his sleeve to show off his muscle. Ethan immediately wanted to pinch his nose shut to close off the smell wafting from the big man's now exposed armpit. Instead, he took a deep, cleansing breath and clasped Skunk's meaty right hand — which was at least a third larger than his own.

Joseph patted Ethan on the back and then loosely held a red handkerchief over the two clenched fists. When he whipped the handkerchief away, the battle was on.

Skunk gained an immediate advantage, bending Ethan's wrist back until it was no more than three inches from the top of the tea box. Just then Caleb saw an expression come over his little brother's face that he had seen more times than he cared to recall.

At that very moment, Caleb knew exactly what was going to happen. Letting out a roar so guttural and strong that it literally shook the rafters of the old barn, Ethan summoned every ounce of strength that he had in his wiry body and slammed the back of Skunk's wrist down against the tea box so hard that wood mixed with blood flew up in all directions.

The crowd gasped as Skunk bolted upright, grabbed his mangled wrist in agony, and stared at Ethan in sheer disbelief. He then kicked what remained of the tea box to the back of the barn and stomped over to teammates for comfort and medical attention. Meanwhile, the crowd regained their wits and roared their approval at Ethan's superhuman display of strength.

After the match, both Sawdust and Scruffy sidled over and grabbed Ethan's arms and raised them over his head in a victory salute. They both realized that — even though they won their matches — they didn't want anything to do with challenging Ethan. So, while their hands were still attached to their arms, they were both conceding the overall match.

The next two events both involved target practice. First up was tomahawk tossing, or — as it was more commonly called — 'hawk throwing' — followed by hunting-knife flinging. Caleb and Samuel knew that their young charges were at a disadvantage since these were basic survival skills for the mountain men. They had to save their precious bullets and black powder for self-defense against wild predators and roving bands of bandits, so the mountain men used tomahawks and knives to take most of the game they killed and ate.

Taylor Jenkins and Rhett Baumgardner, two of the younger boys from the Warrensburg Group, walked forward to face off against Bear Pole and Coyote from the mountain men's side. While Taylor tossed his hawks with skill, he was no competition for Bear Pole who never missed the target's bulls-eye with his tosses. The match was supposed to last three rounds, but by the end of the second round, Taylor was so far behind that he was forced to concede.

The knife throw was a different story. Rhett beat the pants off Coyote, both figuratively and literally. Near the end of the second round, Coyote became so upset by Rhett's consistently besting his throws by a matter of just inches that he missed when he went to jam his knife back down into its sheath. Instead, he ended up cutting right through the rawhide rope that was holding up his pants, sending them tumbling down around his ankles. He was left standing stock-still with a beet-red face that perfectly matched the crimson color of his now exposed long-johns. Finally regaining his wits, Coyote was quite a sight to see as he scuffled off across the barn floor with his hands covering his groin.

The next skills were musket loading and firing, archery, and quick-draw six-shooter handling and accuracy. Caleb and Samuel figured that their boys had these three in the bag, since they all grew up handling bows, guns, and rifles and could shoot an acorn off an oak branch at one hundred paces.

True to form, Joshua Hill bested the mountain man Eagle Eye Jack taking the first two out of three of the musket matches. Ethan Adams had a more difficult time with his foe — Quick Silver Slim — losing the quick-draw contest in three matches. So, the tiebreaker for the night's activities came down to archery, with William Wordsmith pitted against a mountain man who called himself 'Kemosabe' and bragged that he was a full-blooded Apache.

The match started with William and Kemosabe standing side-by-side, while firing arrow after arrow into the haybale-backed targets that were more than fifty paces away. William first fired an arrow into a target's bulls-eye and then Kemosabe put one of his own less than an inch away from William's.

Next Kemosabe shot first and William matched his shot by an inch or less. They went at it like this, back-and-forth, back-and-forth, matching each other's shots for the better part of an hour. After about the twentieth matching shots with no clear winner, Joseph Budd stepped in and announced that William and Kemosabe would each take just one last shot to determine the winner.

Kemosabe went first and sent his arrow on as precision a path as possible, straight into the center point of the bulls-eye. His perfect shot brought 'oohs' and 'aahs' from all the spectators. They knew that Kemosabe's shot was so true — square in the very dead center of the bulls-eye — that there was no way for William to win.

Undeterred, William walked forward, notched up an arrow, took a deep breath, drew back his bow, and let his arrow fly. The disbelieving gasp from the crowd told Caleb and Samuel what had happened before they could actually see it with their own eyes.

William's arrow had directly hit the feathered tip of Kemosabe's arrow, shearing the shaft into two pieces that were now hanging down from both sides of the arrow's head like shavings in a sawmill. The shaft of William's arrow was still quivering from the impact when Joseph walked over and raised William's arm, declaring him the winner as

Kemosabe sulked away in stunned silence.

After a few minutes had passed, Joseph walked to the center of the barn and asked all of his boys to form a circle around him. He then told them to all raise both arms in celebration of their hard-won victory.

Next — as the crowd of spectators held their collective breath — the mountain men formed a circle around the outside of the boys' circle. Absolutely no one in the place could have predicted what happened next. Eschewing a raunchy, pugilistic response, the mountain men all raised their hands above their heads and clapped in unison for the valiant effort the lads had all displayed in achieving their victory.

According to the local lore, this was the first time that the mountain men had ever been bested by another group traveling through Fort Laramie. To cap the occasion off, everyone moved on to the saloon where they alternated buying each other rounds for the next several hours.

With all the participants still very much hungover, the next morning's highly vaunted 'lacrosse challenge' was completely anticlimactic. The younger boys easily out-quicked and out-maneuvered their opponents in every facet of the playing field, leading 24-2 when the mountain men finally conceded defeat.

Moving Through the Shortgrass Prairie

Around noon the day after the 'macho showdown' at Fort Laramie, Caleb and Samuel decided that — since the clouds were building over the distant foothills and it was spitting snow — they needed to get on the trail as soon as possible. Both men knew how essential it was to make it through the mountain passes before the snow really started to fly and build heavy drifts that blocked their trail.

If this happened, they could be stranded in a makeshift tent village on the east side of the Rocky Mountains until the following spring. In fact, Caleb and Samuel both realized that — if the winter months brought especially heavy snow to the high country — they wouldn't be able to continue their journey until well into the summer months.

After lunch, Caleb and Samuel gathered all the boys around the cooking fire in Fort Laramie's courtyard and told them their concerns about the coming winter. They emphasized the need for pushing westward as fast as they could for the next few weeks. This meant riding hard from before sunrise until after sunset — then setting up a quick camp, wolfing down a hasty supper, grabbing a few hours of shut-eye, and getting back on the trail to do it all over again.

Caleb and Samuel knew that such a tightly-wound routine would be tough on their young charges. But they also knew it would prepare them well for the rigors of traveling through rugged mountain terrain for the next few months. While they hadn't experienced it themselves, Caleb and Samuel were well aware of the horrors that could befall mentally unprepared travelers when the air became thin and depleted the flow of oxygen to the brain — especially to young brains.

After the boys set out again on their westward trek, the cottonwood willow river bottoms had begun changing from summer-green to autumn-gold. Every night, the first light frosts of fall settled across the prairie landscape.

When each morning rolled around, the crispness in the air seemed to invigorate the lads. As soon as they unwound themselves from their bedrolls, they began bouncing around to stay warm while they hurled jokes and — for the most part — good-natured barbs back and forth across the breakfast campfire. Occasionally some of the ribbing would get a little out-of-hand and lead to impromptu wrestling matches among a few of the more vocal participants.

Caleb and Samuel didn't see this as a bad thing — the boys needed to get their energy out — but they cut the sessions off almost as soon as they started. There was no time for distractions — it was mandatory for the team to hit the trail at full tilt each day.

The intrepid group of young westward travelers was now crossing a prairie landscape that was filled with a vast array of natural resources. The dense mats of buffalo and blue grama grasses that festooned the shortgrass prairies were turning pleasing shades of russet in the cool early autumn air.

Here and there — on both sides of the trail — the ground was littered by thousands of burrows, each about four inches across. Back-and-forth between and in-and-out of these burrows skittered hundreds — maybe even thousands — of little tan animals that were not much bigger than good-sized rats with bushy-brown tails.

As they moved about, these rather cute little ground scurriers seemed to stop and talk with each other at every opportunity — both one-on-one and in groups of three, four, five, and more. The boys thought it looked almost like the Sunday 'go-to-meetings' in the villages where they grew up — when everyone came to town to visit and share stories about what had happened on the farms and ranches during the past week.

Every so often, the boys noticed that other animals also lived in these bustling rodent towns. They would occasionally see families of tiny owls perched comically in rows along the edges of the burrows they had usurped for their own residences. While the boys watched, these small birds of prey would swoop down on unsuspecting field mice, meadow voles, and dragonflies that skittered about everywhere.

Especially just after sunrise and just before sunset, the boys also saw strange-looking, weasel-like animals wearing black masks around their eyes — like bank robbers — and dashing about between and into the burrows. More often than not, one would emerge with a squealing rodent hanging from its mouth.

SAVING BLACK-FOOTED FERRETS

As a result of the widespread destruction of prairie dog towns — mainly for the creation of ranchland — the black-footed ferret was listed as 'extinct in the wild' in 1987. Fortunately, a captive breeding program — launched by the U.S. Fish and Wildlife Service — ended up saving the species. Today, more than one thousand wild-born ferrets exist in five self-sustaining populations in South Dakota, Arizona, and Wyoming. This saving of the black-footed ferret from the brink of extinction is one of the greatest success stories in the history of North American wildlife management.

The young travelers didn't yet know prairie-dog 'towns' by name — of course — but they were certainly impressed with how much of this flat prairieland they occupied. They would have no doubt been dismayed to know that the number of prairie dog towns would be greatly reduced during their lifetimes. And — accordingly — the tiny burrowing owls and mercurial black-footed ferrets that they were now watching would both become endangered species.

Much of the 'dog-town' action the boys were watching was taking place around and between the feet of lumbering bison and fleet pronghorn 'antelope' as they grazed languidly in vast herds — collectively numbering in the hundreds of thousands. Both of these native large-hoofed animals of the American shortgrass prairies had common names that were more typically associated with wildlife found on other continents.

The American bison were more commonly called 'buffalo', even though the true buffaloes are only found in Asia and Africa. Similarly — despite their strong resemblance to many species of African antelopes — the pronghorns of North America are not a true antelope.

However — as the boys often noticed — the one thing the prairie pronghorns do have in common with their African namesakes, is the ability to move at great speed when necessary to escape predators. In fact — with a top running speed of more than sixty miles per hour—the North American pronghorn is faster than any of the African antelopes. The only land animal that can run faster over short distances than the pronghorn is the cheetah.

Fortunately, the buffalo 'killing fields' — that the lads routinely observed farther back in the Nebraska territory — were absent here. Caleb reasoned that this was only because the throngs of hunters, butchers, and hide haulers simply hadn't made it this far west yet. He could only have guessed how right he was. In fact, the vast bison herds he was now seeing would be almost wiped off the face of the earth in less than forty years.

As they rolled along, the boys witnessed much about how the great American prairies were created and maintained by both animals and the resident tribes of Native Americans. In places, they saw herds of thousands of buffalo wallowing and rolling around in the muck of shallow, isolated depressions in the landscape.

These behemoths did this because the rich, dark mud was cooling to their parched skin. Plus, these mud baths also helped them get rid of the myriad of biting insects that chomped away mercilessly on their nostrils, eyes, and mouths.

Each time a migratory buffalo herd moved on to greener pastures, they left behind their scattered 'wallows' that quickly filled with lush growths of prairie grasses and wildflowers during the onset of spring growth. After months of bearing the weight of thousands of pounds of buffalo hooves, the soils in these wallows were too tightly compacted for shrub and tree roots to penetrate which meant they would be grasslands forever.

Prairie dogs also played a primary role in the long-term maintenance of grasslands. By constantly gnawing away and digging out any green sprouts that poked their way through the earth, the vast legions of 'dogs' made sure that no woody plants could ever gain a foothold in their prairie homes.

In other places, the boys saw massive wildfires roaring like blast furnaces across the mostly pancake-flat landscape. These fires — which were caused by both lightning strikes and intentionally set by local Native American tribes — also kept the prairie grasslands from succeeding to woody shrublands and forested habitats.

Pockets of land that were slightly lower in elevation formed large, shallow lakes — now known as 'prairie potholes' — which attracted tens

of thousands of ducks and geese, plus large flocks of wading birds —
herons, egrets, and cranes. Each time the young adventurers came across
one of these feathered oases, they stopped and blasted away with their
pistols and rifles — quickly and easily killing plenty of fresh fowl for
that night's roasting.

The result of all these disturbances was a shifting mosaic of
distinctive wildlife habitats scattered across the rolling prairie landscape.
Since it was unlike anything they had ever seen or known back in their
youths, the boys were continuously awestruck by the wealth and
abundance of natural resources — especially the wildlife — they were
passing by every hour. Each night after they had set up camp, eaten
supper, and crawled into their bedrolls, they were often serenaded to
sleep by the combined choruses of coyotes and gray wolves.

BOOK SIX
The Rocky Mountains Loom

Into the Badlands

Four weeks out from Fort Laramie, the boys left the open prairie and entered the puzzle-like topography of the badlands that marked the start of their ascent up the eastern slope of the Rocky Mountains. The badlands landscape was remarkable, both for its tortured patterns of jagged gulches topped by steeply-eroding hills and almost complete lack of vegetation. The prairie short grasses had mostly disappeared from the bone-dry surface soils and were replaced in the draws by widely scattered clumps of lime-green sagebrush, greasewood with its strange lenticular leaves, and rabbitbrush tinted with dainty yellow flowers.

This strange, other-worldly terrain raised many concerns for the trip leaders — Caleb Adams and Samuel Johnson. First and foremost, they had to stay especially vigilant for attacks from roving bands of masked robbers. The disjointed, close-quartered landscape provided perfect hiding places for men with evil intent to spring up and quickly overwhelm them all.

Another major problem was lack of water — most of the streams and potholes had either disappeared or dried up as the boys headed into the foothills. Plus, fresh meat was also now a concern. Because there were no longer any grasses or other low-growing forage plants to provide them sustenance, the bison herds were now gone.

The primary large game animals the boys now saw were widely scattered bands of pronghorns roaming across the flattop hills, and occasional small mixed herds of mule and white-tailed deer. Plus, they occasionally noticed another unfamiliar large animal — family groups of bighorn sheep grazing in shrubbery in the shelter of the dry washes.

Caleb and Samuel realized that the lack of water and game would only be temporary and that — in a few weeks' time — they would be moving out of the arid badlands, and into the higher elevation foothills where springs and freshets should again make water and animals plentiful. In the meantime, their badlands strategy involved stopping and setting out buckets, washtubs, pots, pans, and every other water catching device they had whenever it started to rain. In an ironic twist, they also now often stopped to hunt every time they saw a small group of deer or antelope when — just a few weeks ago — they had been riding by herds of thousands of large, hoofed animals without giving them so much as a second glance.

To minimize the potential for surprise attacks, Caleb and Samuel asked Joseph Budd and Ethan Adams to serve as advance scouts. Accordingly, Joseph and Ethan rode out front and stayed fifteen minutes ahead of the wagon train, taking turns galloping back to report anything they saw that seemed the slightest bit suspicious.

Early one morning — after they had been on the trail for less than an hour — Caleb looked up and saw Joseph riding straight toward him like a bolt out of the blue. This can't possibly be good news, Caleb thought, as Joseph reined Lightning up beside him. It was all Caleb could do to keep from laughing out loud as he listened to Joseph explain why he was so excited.

In a quivering voice, Joseph told Caleb they must be getting back into civilization because he had just seen several flocks of chickens, and this meant there had to be a farming village nearby. Of course, Caleb knew that there couldn't possibly be any farms or villages in this wild, untamed land and that the 'chickens' Joseph had seen had to be wild. Nevertheless, he rode ahead with Joseph to check the situation out for himself.

Sure enough — as soon as they topped a draw — Joseph started yelling and waggling a finger back and forth at Caleb. Joseph was pointing at a flock of strange, chicken-like birds skittering in and around the sagebrush flats immediately in front of them.

Acknowledging Joseph's excitement, Caleb moved on ahead for a closer look. He had to admit that what he first saw looked for all the world like a flock of laying hens and roosters, running around in a family farmyard.

On closer inspection, Caleb realized that these were some type of wild fowl, living free on the open prairie. Perhaps, he thought, they had escaped from flocks kept by the local Native American tribes. Caleb quickly called Joseph over and explained to him that these were likely wild chickens, since there couldn't possibly be any farming villages within hundreds of miles of the terrain they were now riding through.

In reality, Caleb was exactly right — the birds they were watching were indeed wild. The largest grouse in North America, sage grouse live on the high plains of the American West. They are named in honor of the high plains shrub that typically dominates their habitat.

Caleb reasoned that these strange, plump birds would make for a tasty dinner. So, he told Joseph and Ethan to shoot a passel of the skittering fowl and haul them back to the cook's wagon when they were finished.

Encountering the Romani

In addition to experiencing strange, wild animals, Joseph and Ethan — still acting as advance scouts — had a bizarre encounter with a diverse human element that had taken up residence among the convoluted river breaks. Cresting a ridge just after sunset, they saw a strange sight in the wide draw down below — a ring of small wagons surrounding a blazing campfire.

All around — in the shadows cast by the wagons — were men, women, and children dressed in brightly-colored, flowing clothing. They were all singing, dancing, and clapping in rhythmic motion.

Meanwhile, the group's horses — plus their small herds of sheep and goats — grazed languidly on the sparse grasses bordering the mostly dry streambed beside their wagons. Tight flocks of chickens and geese skittered about everywhere, jumping up and squawking every time a pair of dancing feet came too close to their pecking heads.

Joseph and Ethan sat watching in bemused silence for several minutes, before turning their horses around and trotting back to the wagon train to tell Caleb and Samuel what they had seen. Samuel had heard tales about nomadic Romani sheep and goat herders living in the West. They moved their livestock back and forth between summer pastures in the high mountains and grassland prairies during the winters.

Based on everything Samuel could remember, these people were friendly, fun-loving, and welcomed opportunities to interact with westward-trekking pioneers. Since it was now after dark, Samuel thought — and Caleb agreed — that it might be fun for the boys if they rode over and set up camp next to the Romanies. Samuel figured that both groups would enjoy each other's company in a night of reverie.

To first be certain that their idea for a night of fun was a good one, Samuel and Caleb told everyone of their plans, and then rode off to talk to the Romanies. They crested the ridge and then dropped down quietly into the gulch so as not to startle them into thinking they were marauding bandits.

As soon as Samuel and Caleb were within fifty feet of the campfire, one of the gyrating male dancers suddenly stopped and shouted a loud command. All of the dancing ceased instantly as every head turned toward Caleb and Samuel as they rode into the light of the campfire.

Raising his hand in a peaceful greeting, Caleb spoke confidently but respectfully to the first man he encountered. He asked if anyone spoke English to which the man immediately shook his head. Then — suddenly from the withering shadows of one of the wagons — a deep growling voice bellowed out, "I speak English — who are you and what do you want from us?"

Caleb and Samuel looked up to see a burly mountain of a man walking toward them with a stiff-legged gait. He had shaggy hair and a bushy black beard that covered nearly all of his face, except for his eyes. He was wearing a sleeveless red shirt that showed off his blacksmith-like, tattoo-covered arms. He was brandishing a pistol in one hand and a large dagger in the other. His skin was not as dark as the others and his voice showed no hint of a Spanish accent.

Caleb again extended his outstretched arm in a palm open, friendly greeting and said in a tempered voice, "We mean no harm to you or your people, my friend. We come in peace, and just want to know if we can share your campsite for the night."

For several uneasy minutes, the husky man just stared evilly at Caleb and Samuel, looking for all the world as if he wanted nothing more than to kill them both on the spot. The rest of the Romanies just held their places around the campfire — no one moved, talked or seemingly even breathed. Suddenly, the man broke into a broad smile and started guffawing with laughter that echoed up and down the gulch walls. In seconds, all of the other Romanies resumed their merriment — acting as if they had never stopped in the first place.

Dropping his weapons, the jolly brute extended his gigantic right hand toward Caleb and said, "Welcome to our carnival my friends. I just wanted to make sure you had no evil intentions. We are more than happy to share our food, drink, and laughter with you and your men."

Caleb grabbed the man's hand — or at least a few of the ends of his fingers, since that was all he could hold — and shook them vigorously, saying that he and Samuel would return soon with the rest of their party. With that, Caleb and Samuel wheeled their horses around and rode back toward their wagon train.

When they got back to the rest of the boys, Caleb and Samuel rode along telling everyone about all the fun they were about to have. Eager with anticipation, all of the boys hitched the wagons and saddled up quickly, anxious to go and see what Caleb and Samuel had found.

As soon as they crested the ridge and saw all of the frivolity down below, the boys broke ranks, and charged willy-nilly down the gently-sloping gulch walls. They quickly circled the wagons, hastily set up camp, and then ambled over to the Romanies' campfire.

After they had walked only a few steps, the boys were startled by what happened next. The Romanies all suddenly stopped dancing and ran toward them. The men grabbed the boys in bear hugs, while the women and children tugged at their arms, legs, and clothes.

Samuel and Caleb sat back, chuckling at the looks of amazement on the faces of their young charges. They knew that the last thing the boys ever expected to find in the middle of such desolate badlands terrain was a group of friendly and loving families.

As soon as the Romanies had finished excitedly dragging all of the boys back to their campfire circle, the music started up again. The Romani women and children immediately grabbed the hands of the boys, and started skipping and high-stepping with them to the rhythmic beat. The boys started off awkwardly — but after a few minutes of missteps — most of them found the beat and started moving in tandem with their twirling, whirling partners.

After more than an hour of this riotous exercise, the exhausted boys collapsed almost in unison on the assorted rocks and logs that had been placed next to the now-roaring campfire. As soon as their backsides touched the ground, the Romanies handed each of the boys a mug of steaming mulled cider and a bowl of hearty goulash.

The boys ate and drank with great relish while their hosts looked on in bemused wonder. The boys and the Romanies tried to talk to each other but with the language difference, no one made much headway, except for heartily punctuated laughter.

Meanwhile, Caleb and Samuel sat off to the side, talking with the gigantic leader of the group — who they now knew as Big Juan — about who his people were and how they came to be here in such a remote location. Big Juan explained that for a great number of years — far more than he could really remember — he was known as John Johansen and roamed through the Rocky Mountains as a solitary hunter and trapper.

Then one day — maybe five years ago — he came across this intrepid band of Romani sheep and goat herders. They were eking out a living by selling their wool and goat cheese to the wagon trains that were passing through.

Winter was fast approaching and — as he learned from a few of the men who could speak a little broken English — the group was worried that they would all perish when the deep cold settled in and the snow really started flying. As Big Juan now explained it, "They were lost, had almost run out of provisions, and most of their animals were sick with diseases, and weren't producing much wool or milk."

Since he had grown quite weary of living with no human contact, he decided to join the fun-loving group and help them cope with life in the rugged mountain wilderness. The desperate Romanies immediately anointed him 'Big Juan', and accepted him as their omniscient wilderness leader.

Big Juan then guided his band of Romanies back east to Fort Laramie where they — along with their livestock — could rest and recover during the winter months. The following spring — with refreshed bodies and now healthy herds of sheep and goats — the fifty-something members of the group followed Big Juan up into the lush high mountain meadows which then served as summer pastures for their livestock.

Ever since, Big Juan moved his merry band of herders twice a year, from the high summer pastures of May through September to the prairie winter range during October through April. Since it was now early October — or at least close to that, as he figured it — they were headed for their winter grazing land which lay about two more weeks travel time to the south and east.

The revelry around the campfire continued until the wee hours of the morning, as the boys — all woozy from way too much mulled cider and lamb goulash — stumbled one-by-one back to their bedrolls. The next morning — peering through reddened and hung-over eyes while holding their queasy stomachs — they all agreed that the night was one to remember. It was the first night they had been able to relax and enjoy themselves since they left Fort Laramie and began their race against the snow.

Now, it was back to the daily ardors of the long, steep, and dusty trail. They remained fully committed to their lofty goal of passing over the looming Continental Divide, before a treacherous snowpack settled into the high country and made their crossing impossible until the spring.

Exploring the Rocky Mountain Foothills

Around the middle of October 1847, the westward trekkers arrived at the base of the foothills leading up into the Front Range of the Rocky Mountains. Both Caleb and Samuel knew that this marked the start of what would be — by far — the most arduous, dangerous, and trying part of their journey.

Even though they remained concerned about crossing the Rockies before the deep snows of winter descended on the passes, Caleb and Joseph decided to give their young charges three days off to rest and reconnoiter before starting their ascent into the high mountains. They knew that once they acclimatized and gained some momentum on their upward trek, it would be difficult to stop and restart again.

That night after supper, Caleb and Samuel gathered the boys around the campfire and laid out the plans for the next few days. They told them they were free to explore but to travel in groups of no less than three, stay within ten miles of camp, and always keep their weapons and wits close at hand.

Throughout their welcome respite, the boys were captivated by the new plants and animals they saw living on the eastern flank of the Rocky Mountains. While they did not have the benefit of formal schooling on their trip, they all felt fortunate to have both Adams brothers — Caleb and Ethan — along to help them understand what they were seeing.

Growing up under the vast outdoor intuition and appreciation of their parents — Thaddeus and Minerva — Caleb and Ethan were highly skilled 'naturalists' decades before such a title was a real thing. Even though the Adams boys had not seen the Rocky Mountains before, their uncanny ability to relate what they were seeing to the vegetation and wildlife they remembered from their eastern forests and Midwestern grasslands allowed them to figure out the western mountain ecology. Eager to learn everything they could, the rest of the boys sat in rapt silence around each evening's campfire, listening to Caleb and Ethan explain the landscape, plants, and animals they had just observed.

On the first morning of their three days of discovery, the boys rode off in groups of three, four, and five and were immediately awestruck. These were mountains to be sure, but they were unlike anything they had ever seen before.

The terrain was mostly rolling but supported very little ground cover. Pockets of thinly yellowed cottonwoods and willows nestled in the dry creek beds that snaked down the hillsides like side-winding rattlesnakes.

Forests of widely-spaced, long-needled ponderosa pines decorated the hillside and ridgelines. The evergreen's fragrant, orangish-brown plated bark smelled like everything from vanilla to butterscotch. Several shrub species — including the bitterbrush with its three-lobed foliage, the feather-seeded mountain mahogany, the reddish-gray barked currant, the shrubby cinquefoil with its succulent leaves, and several varieties of spicy sagebrush — grew in scattered clusters underneath the sparse ponderosa canopy.

Like multi-colored jewels, a variety of songbirds flitted around and through this sparse habitat. Richly-luminescent, mountain bluebirds flew in lilting flight, back and forth between their cavities in dead or dying pines. Western tanagers — featuring their yellow bodies and coal-black wings — also caught the eyes of the boys as they rode into and out of the succession of draws and erosion gullies that sliced eastward swaths through the tumbling foothills landscape.

Closer looks revealed other birds, including the tiny, stubby-tailed pygmy nuthatch descending a pine headfirst in a continual assault on insects, while uttering its distinctively soft 'pip-pip-pip' calls. With their trilling flight — that often made them seen before they were heard — tiny broad-tailed hummingbirds boldly flew right up to the boys and their horses, as if asking "Why are you here in the middle of our territory?"

Here and there, small herds of antelope nibbled on browning tufts of grasses while ground squirrels, jackrabbits, and chipmunks skittered hither and yon. Overhead, a variety of broad-winged hawks and narrow-winged falcons soared high on thermals and scanned the ground below for easy prey pickings.

Every now and then, the boys noticed the furtive figures of small rodents moving like black ghosts through the branches of the ponderosa pines. While these critters looked a lot like the gray squirrels they knew from their prairie homes, they were not the same. They sported tufted ears that looked like horns, and sheeny coats ranging in color from solid black to metallic silver. The boys didn't know it, of course, but they were looking at a very rare rodent — the 'habitat specific' Abert's squirrel — which now lives only in the ponderosa pine forests of the lower eastern slopes of the Rocky Mountains.

Little could the boys have imagined that in less than two lifetimes, much of this seemingly endless ponderosa pine habitat would give way to massive, horizon-stretching subdivisions with large houses on tiny 'play pen' lots, that blended into shopping centers and office parks. As the high-tech building boom of the late 1970s and early 1980s skipped over much of the great plains and landed squarely on the American West, the relatively mild winters made the ponderosa pine forests of these Rocky Mountain foothills prime targets for land developers.

Ponderosa forests are also home to striking black-and-white, plank-tailed birds that seem to delight in outsmarting everything — especially humans who enter their territories. These are the 'thieving magpies' of Shakespearean fame, and a few minutes of watching their pilfering ways will prove how they live up to their name.

Another raucous thief that the boys frequently saw in the ponderosa woodland, was the Steller's jay. With their pompadour-type crests and cobalt-blue and black plumage accentuated by white facial stripes; these gregarious birds always look as if they're dressed for a night on the town.

The boys found out the hard way about the penchant for petty larceny, exhibited by both the magpie and the Steller's jay. One brilliantly sunny October afternoon, all of the boys decided to hike up into a patch of boulder-strewn hillside underneath some large ponderosas for a picnic. They took a large piece of clean white cloth with them to use as a ground cover.

Next, the boys carefully laid out their pieces of hardtack, chunks of cheddar cheese, and strips of jerky on the cloth. In the middle of the cloth, they placed several pieces of freshly-baked apple fritters for dessert. Since they only had enough apple fritters for five, Josh McCown suggested that they all race up to the top of the ridge and back down. The first five boys to make it back to the picnic site would then lay claim to the fritters.

The boys all lined up and toed a rough line that Josh made by dragging his foot across the ground. One his count of three, all of them took off — arms flailing wildly and legs churning madly up the steep, rocky hillside.

Watching from below at the campsite, Caleb and Samuel roared with laughter while they watched the boys stumbling and tumbling over one another as they raced upward. The race was really more of a wrestling match than a run, as the boys started grabbing and flinging each other downslope. The result was that — every few seconds or so — one of the boys would go cartwheeling head-over-teakettle back down the hill until he lodged against a tree trunk or boulder.

As soon as he stopped rolling, each boy sprang back to his feet and charged back up the hill again to find someone to grab onto and throw to the ground. In reality, this had suddenly turned into much more than a simple race up a hillside. It had evolved into a supreme test of manhood — with each boy doing everything in his power to prove he belonged in the fritter-winning group of the five strongest men.

Because of the tug-of-war mentality that had now broken out, the entire race took about three times as long as it should have. When the five battered and bruised — but winning — boys finally made it back to the picnic cloth, they had the shock of their lives. Most of their carefully laid-out food — including all five of the fritters — had disappeared, seemingly into thin air. As the rest of the boys came stumbling back down into the picnic site, they all stood staring in stunned silence at the remains of their picnic.

Suddenly, all of the boys turned in unison toward a raucous ruckus that was coming from the canopy of the closest ponderosa. Looking up, the boys saw throngs of flashing black, white, and dark blue feathers flitting through and around the thick pine boughs. Then, looking down, they saw hundreds of pieces of bread, cheese, meat — and yes, the hotly-contested fritters — scattered all around on the ground underneath the tree.

The boys all now realized that they had been seriously outsmarted by a band of thieving bandits, cleverly disguised as jaybirds. They sheepishly rolled up their ground cloth and headed back down to the campsite where they were met by Caleb and Samuel who were trying very hard — but without much success — to control their guffawing at the whole incident. The boys all knew that they were now in for a few days of merciless — if justly deserved — ribbing from their two 'adult' leaders.

When they stopped to rest and eat in other places amid the ponderosa-covered hillsides, the boys were often surprised to see a pair of round chocolate-brown ears bordering a cream-colored face peeking up from behind a nearby rock. This diminutive but elongated creature would then quickly disappear, only to pop up for another look a few seconds later. Their curious visitor was a long-tailed weasel — also called the ermine when he turns pure-white during the winter months.

As the late afternoon sun lengthened the shadows of the ponderosa pine branches into the crests of the nearby ridges, the boys often saw western mule deer browsing languidly among the shrubs growing on sun-soaked, south-facing hillsides. Looking closely, the boys noticed that the mule deer sported a different look from the white-tailed deer that they were used to hunting back in their prairie homes in New South Grand.

The mule deer had very large ears and antlers that branched equally instead of as prongs from a main beam. As they rode toward them, the boys also saw that the 'mulies' were very curious — tending to stop and turn around to peek at their pursuers whenever they were spooked.

This curiosity made mule deer much easier for the boys to approach closely and knock down with well-placed rifle shots — something that most of them did with great relish and delight. This easy hunting also meant that the campfire was kept snapping and crackling with fresh, roasted venison throughout their three-day respite in the Rocky Mountain foothills.

Finding Familiar Terrain

As they rode along, exploring in their separate groups, the boys found many broad, open, grassy areas that reminded them of the tallgrass prairie in their native Missouri Territory. These meadow-like areas — known as 'montane parks' — were created by glacial activity — during the last Ice Age — some ten thousand years ago. The rocky, forested ridges the boys saw bordering the edges of these parks were actually glacial features — known as moraines — left by the melting glaciers as they retreated in response to a warming climate.

In each of these parks, the boys saw both western elk — called 'wapiti' by Native Americans — and Rocky Mountain bighorn sheep. The massive elk — typically more than twice as large as a mule deer — grazed together in large herds on luxuriant, late-season growths of grasses. Meanwhile, the scattered groups of bighorn sheep seemed to cling perilously to the rocky slopes above, while they munched away on any remaining vegetation they could find.

Throughout a Rocky Mountain summer, bull elk grow their antlers which will then be shed the following spring. With regard to the elk, the boys' October arrival in the foothills was especially fortuitous. They were present for one of the most magnificent sounds in the natural world — the 'bugling' of the bull elk. Bull elk bugle for two primary reasons — to let other males know that 'this is my territory' and to let female elk know that they are 'here and available'.

Around the campfires each night, the groups of boys talked excitedly about the different wild animals they had seen during their explorations. They all reported seeing a variety of predators, including solitary coyotes and marauding packs of gray wolves.

They laughed heartily when Ethan Adams talked about watching a grayish-yellow, stumpy-legged critter using his shovelnose and long fore-claws to frenetically dig up the den of a family of golden-mantled ground squirrels. With dirt flying in all directions — in a matter of less

ALPHA PREDATORS

The badger and its even larger cousin — the wolverine — are both fierce and fearless predators. Often called the 'devil dog' by terrified pioneers traveling through the western mountains, the wolverine looks like a cross between a wolf and a small bear.

Sadly, the wolverine — along with the grizzly bear and the gray wolf — were all extirpated from the Rocky Mountains before the end of the nineteenth century. The many unfounded myths and legends about these three 'horrible beasts' made them the subject of widespread fear and loathing, and prime candidates for being shot on sight. Fortunately, the badger has fared much better than the wolverine since it is more adaptable to a variety of habitats, including grassland prairies and the montane woodlands the boys were now traveling through.

Today — thanks to the diligent efforts of a consortium of conservation groups — the gray wolf and the grizzly bear have been restored to Glacier National Park in Montana and Yellowstone National Park in Wyoming. We now understand the value and need for keeping such 'alpha animals' — also known as 'top carnivores' — in our ecosystems. They help keep the populations of deer and elk under control and maintain a good 'ecological balance'.

But — in non-park areas — this understanding came too late for the grizzly, wolf, and wolverine. Even if we could now accept them back into our crowded mountain communities, they are the kindred spirits of the true wilderness and — as such — simply couldn't abide the widespread presence of human activities.

than a minute — this master excavator grabbed a succession of eight squealing ground squirrels by the nape of the neck.

Using one slashing bite to sever each of their spinal cords, this skilled predator next tossed them one-by-one into the air — like cloth ragdolls — where they landed in a heap some ten feet away. After listening to Ethan's description, the lads all agreed that while they all were skilled hunters, their proficiencies paled in comparison to the killing ability of the American badger.

The hauntingly comfortable yip-yapping of a family of coyotes serenaded the boys as they sat talking and warming their hands over campfires on these still and cold autumnal nights. They gradually drifted off to sleep under a stage-full of stars that spread from horizon to horizon.

But — on the last night of their three-day respite — this clear and calm setting changed quite quickly. And the intrepid group of westward travelers had another unforgettable encounter with the forces of nature.

Mother Nature Changes Everything

As directed by Samuel and Caleb, the boys found sleeping sites along one of the many narrow-sided, east-facing canyons that striated the foothills region. For extra protection, the wagons were circled on a rocky outcrop — perched some fifty feet above the stream channel that bisected the canyon.

With the weather being unusually warm — almost balmy, especially for mid-October — most of the boys decided to pitch their bedrolls out in the open, down next to the lullaby sounds of the stream's gently flowing waters. Caleb and Samuel and several of the other boys stayed up above to guard the wagons.

Just after midnight, all of the boys were startled awake by intense bolts of lightning, and simultaneous clashes of thunder unlike anything any of them had ever experienced — even during the spring tornado-spawning storms that frequented their tallgrass homeland. Like prairie dogs in burrows, the boys popped up out of their bedrolls one by one and stood gazing transfixed at the amazing light show taking place right above their heads.

It didn't take long for them to also realize that the night air that had started out so balmy when they first bedded down was now near freezing. Within a few minutes, they all had wrapped blankets around their shoulders to ward off the chill. While they all stood agape looking up at the sky, one of the boys turned suddenly, gasped loudly, and pointed due west at what appeared to be a curtain of sheer-white hung from both sides of the canyon and billowing rapidly down over their heads.

Within seconds, the boys were all enveloped in a cloud of snow so thick and dense that they couldn't even see their hands in front of their faces. They were now trapped in the middle of what the Native American tribes reverently called 'the Devil's thunder-snow'. Almost as fast as it had descended, the snow fog turned to pelting sleet and then to solid rain, coming down in such heavy torrents that it was all they could do to remain standing in the downpour.

Next, they heard a sound rumbling up from the earth beneath their feet like a giant grizzly bear growling at the top of its lungs. Then — through the relentless drumming of the rain — they heard Caleb and Joshua screaming as loud as they could for them all to run uphill. The sound of their leaders' voices broke through their mesmerized lethargy as all of the boys scrambled and clawed their way up the slope just in time to avoid a fifteen-foot-high wall of water that came slamming down through the canyon, burying the stream — and most of the boys' bedrolls — in vicious swirls of foaming white.

Watching the raging torrent from above, the boys heard and saw everything imaginable — from huge boulders to towering trees and even mule deer and mountain sheep — being swept along by the rampaging water below their feet. Several hours later at dawn's first light, nature's fury finally subsided and the stream flow in the canyon went back to almost normal — confined within the banks of its main channel.

But the canyon itself was anything but back to normal. What had been a beautiful cascading mountain stream, bordered on both sides by mature growths of ponderosa pines thickets and aspen groves, was now just a scarified wash of rocky debris and broken tree trunks.

Just about everything the boys had seen when they pitched their bedrolls the night before now looked completely different. Mother Nature had scoured the canyon clean — wiping out her artistic creation of decades past and providing a brand-new canvas for her next work of inspiration.

When the lads all gathered safely back on the rocky promontory that had protected their wagons and supplies, they immediately clasped hands and knelt in a circle around the warming breakfast bonfire. They gave thanks to God that they all had emerged unscathed from the previous night of nature's fury.

As they prayed, the young travelers also reflected on what forces of nature may await them ahead during the onset of winter in the higher mountains. After several moments of silence, Caleb stood up and announced that he believed last night's storm was a sign for them to get back on the trail as soon as possible. In response, they all quickly got to work preparing the horses, wagons, and provisions to move out before noon.

BOOK SEVEN
Rocky Mountain High

Heading Up the Eastern Slope

As they made their way up the arduously steep trail connecting the foothills to the higher mountains, Caleb Adams noticed that a dense forest of Douglas fir trees now covered many of the north-facing slopes in the lower elevations of the Rocky Mountains. Instinctively he understood that Douglas firs form a forest type that is the antithesis of the open, sprawling ponderosa pine woodland they had just left. In fact, the spindly-branched fir trees typically grow together in such a foreboding mass that they block out the sun and severely limit the growth of understory plants. The tightly compacted, inch-long fir needles can stifle even the slightest breeze, often giving a Douglas fir forest an uncomfortable feeling of foreboding.

Gazing up into such a monotonous canopy, the boys quickly understood why they seldom saw any wild animals moving around in these dense fir forests. It's like living in a town where every home is exactly the same. Who wants to live in such a place with no diversity and no character? The saying 'variety is the spice of life' applies equally to humans and wildlife. But for wildlife, the rationale is simply survival instead of a constant quest for newness and stimulation.

In nature, biodiversity is the keynote to maintaining a healthy and productive ecosystem. A monotypic vegetative community — such as a Douglas fir forest — yields an equally non-diverse wildlife population. Because of this, the only thing the boys saw in the Douglas fir stands was the chickaree — a ubiquitous tree squirrel — chattering away while chomping on an unending supply of fir cones.

As they moved further upslope, the group stopped for lunch beside the tepid, lily pad-covered water of a small mountain lake. There, the boys were surprised to find frogs swimming in the cool water and salamanders hiding under rocks. These observations initiated a vehement, back-and-forth discussion about the types and numbers of snakes they might find living in this high mountain terrain. Most of the boys said they were surprised that they had not yet seen any snakes in the mountains. They were convinced that snakes had to be around — especially venomous rattlesnakes and copperheads — like the ones they often found around their prairie homes.

In truth, the leopard frog and tiger salamander — which the boys were seeing — are two of only a handful of cold-blooded animals that can endure the frosty climate of the Rocky Mountains. In fact, any stories about poisonous snakes in the Rockies simply aren't true. The only snake known to occur in these towering peaks is the harmless gray garter snake. In reality, there are no rattlers or other poisonous species anywhere to be found.

The boys also found that the many waterfalls scattered throughout the Rockies were a delight to explore. The mist and damp ground surrounding these water features produce unique communities of plants that would not otherwise have enough moisture to survive.

Early one morning, for invigoration before they headed back out on the trail, a small group of the boys, led by the always-adventurous Ethan Adams, hiked along a rugged deer trail about five feet above a rushing cascade of crystal-clear water. The roiling white stream bounced tumultuously through a channel lined with large boulders and craggy rocks that had been washed down from the mountaintops soaring above on all sides.

About a half-mile in, the boys saw a nondescript, stocky, dark-gray little bird dive headfirst from the top of a rock into the icy-cold stream. Their brains told them this couldn't possibly be true, as diving into the frigid stream would surely be a death wish for such a small creature.

Convinced that it must have been an apparition — maybe just a rock rolling down into the water — the lads kept walking slowly with their eyes glued to the spot where the movement had occurred. Then — to their utter astonishment— about thirty seconds later, the same small gray bird popped back out of the water and jumped on top of the same rock.

As the hiking group stood puzzling at what they had just seen, the little bird dived in again. This time — when it popped back up — it had the body of a large insect hanging from its beak. Now the boys finally understood what was going on. This brazen little bird was not crazy at all — it was just going for a swim to catch its lunch.

The little bird the boys were watching was the 'water ouzel'. Also called the American dipper, the ouzel often dives into and feeds off the bottom of high mountain streams throughout the western United States. In fact, the ouzel is the only songbird in North America that gets all its food by 'flying' along stream bottoms. The more common 'dipper' name comes from the bird's habit of bobbing its head up and down as it stands on rocks above a waterway.

After arriving at a crystal-clear glacial lake near the crest of the deer trail, the boys sat back and propped their feet up on several convenient boulders and soaked in the magnificent mountain vista that surrounded them. While certainly restful, the views they were taking in provided the boys with a daunting perspective of what they were about to do. Towering above them were the massive peaks of the mountains they must now challenge to head further west.

The Moose and the Grizzly

The most remarkable thing the young travelers saw during their progress up the east side of the Continental Divide involved a massive bull moose standing belly deep in a shallow, rocky pond. Since this was the first moose many of them had ever seen, Caleb and Samuel halted the wagon train to let the boys take a break and watch this impressive animal feed.

Samuel also thought that it might be a good idea to take down and butcher the thickly-antlered beast to augment their supply of jerky before they moved up into the treeless mountain peaks above. He reasoned that this might be their last chance for fresh meat before crossing over the Divide and — from the looks of it — this animal weighed close to a ton.

While the boys watched from the trail about one hundred feet away, the moose submerged his massive head and came up with a large wad of vegetation dripping out of both sides of his mouth. Every time the big bull came up with a stuffed mouthful, he stood and chewed for several minutes until all the dank plant material slowly disappeared down his gullet. As soon as the last morsel of dark green had disappeared, the moose submerged his head again and proceeded to pull up another bite.

The lads thought the sight of such a gigantic beast feasting on delicate water plants was quite ironic. They chortled with laughter every time the moose's head came up with sheets of water cascading down from his antlers and plants hanging down from his jowls — looking like some kind of scraggly, green beard.

Suddenly, they heard snarfing and snuffling sounds coming from a dense stand of tall willow shrubs that bordered the shoreline of the pond behind the moose. They all quickly turned toward the direction of the sounds and gasped in unison as a honey-colored bear — with a massive shoulder hump — reared up on its hind feet and bellowed out a deep guttural growl that reverberated through the mountain valley where they sat.

While the boys had seen plenty of bears back in their prairie homes, most of them were black bears and were nowhere near the size of this massive beast. Many of the boys instinctively grabbed and cocked their rifles in case the bear decided to charge up the gently sloping ground toward their wagon train. But — instead of moving toward them — the grizzly immediately turned toward the feeding moose and let out another ear-rattling roar.

Demonstrating only fearless curiosity, the moose slowly moved his head in the direction of the grizzly bear, stared for a few seconds, and turned back and submerged his head for another bite of fresh greens. Perhaps angered that the moose showed him so little respect, and being hungry for a fresh kill, the bear took several bounds out into the water toward the moose and let out another roar. The bear was now only about five paces away from where the moose was standing with his head still submerged.

The boys thought for sure that they were about to witness a fight to the death between two of the largest creatures living in the high Rockies. But to their great surprise, the anticipated battle of the beasts never happened.

Before the bear's last roar had totally subsided, the moose yanked his dripping head up and wheeled around again, this time facing the bear square on. The moose then lowered his head like a battering ram and — with water splashing in all directions — charged directly at the bear.

Startled by the moose's quick, forceful action, the grizzly bear turned around and rumbled through the water back toward the shoreline. Just before the bear made it back to the shore, the moose hooked the bear's rear end with his antlers and tossed him sideways onto the pond's bank.

Tucking his stubby tail between his legs, the now humiliated grizzly scrambled to his feet and — with long, loping, strides — headed upslope with the moose still in hot pursuit of his hindquarters. Now back on dry land, the grizzly bear — which can run as fast as a racehorse over short spurts — easily outdistanced the moose in just a few seconds. But the moose's victory was deeply etched in the boys' brains. They now knew which was the fiercest animal in all of the Rocky Mountains — and it certainly wasn't the grizzly bear!

After what they had just witnessed, Samuel told Caleb that maybe it would be best if they didn't mess with the moose. So, he whistled for the boys to grab the reins of their oxen and turn them back onto the trail, leaving the victorious moose to graze in peace and live to fight another day.

High Mountain Ecology

Day after day — as the wagon train crawled up the steep and often arduous trail — Caleb and Samuel were careful to balance the fine line between making reasonable progress and keeping their young group's spirits high. Nearing the end of each day, they began looking for campsites that would give their charges some time to relax and explore the exquisite mountain terrain. They typically picked either flat areas next to fast-flowing streams or open boulder fields next to crystal clear lakes.

Since their icy waters supported abundant populations of fish with multi-colored polka dots on their backs and brilliant crimson slashes on their gill covers, the lakes always provided the boys with special treats. Anything they threw into the water immediately attracted swarms of these colorful cutthroat trout — all fighting and battling to be the first ones to hit the lures. This ensured that plenty of freshly-caught fish would be popping and crackling over the evening campfire — providing a sumptuous change-of-pace from usual dinners of salt-cured meat, dried beans, and hardtack.

As the small wagon train passed higher and higher into the mountains, the boys noticed that two types of trees — quaking aspen and lodgepole pine — became more and more common. Fingering down into the spruce-fir forests below, the stringers of aspen and lodgepole pines both served the vital function of revegetating and stabilizing the soil after a forest fire or other major disturbance.

Riding ever so slowly upward, the lads had ample time to notice that aspen and lodgepole pine forests are — literally — as different as night and day. The sun-dappled interior and breezy, refreshing atmosphere make an aspen grove one of the most inviting places to spend a sunny afternoon. Because the delicately attached aspen leaves tremble and rustle with the slightest breeze, aspen trees are endearingly called 'quakies' by the Rocky Mountain locals.

EXTIRPATED SPECIES

The Colorado River cutthroat trout that the boys were catching provides an excellent example of a species that was extirpated from its native range. The word 'endangered' is applied to a species whose population has become so limited that its very existence on the face of the earth is in jeopardy. When this happens on a local scale, it's called 'extirpation' — meaning that although the species in question may be thriving elsewhere, it has been locally eliminated from a state or region.

When a species is extirpated, it leaves an unfilled niche or void in the area's wildlife community which presents several problems. It can cause the entire ecosystem to tilt out of balance; just as the absence of wolves and other alpha carnivores usually leads to an overpopulation of deer, elk, or moose. Also, an unfilled niche is a beckoning toehold to undesirable exotic or non-native species that can outcompete native species and cause ecological chaos: witness the European starling, the Chinese carp, and the Norway rat.

Every extirpated species is still an integral part of an ecosystem's heritage — a pristine link to 'the way things used to be'. This is why more than forty years ago the staff of Rocky Mountain National Park worked so diligently to restore extirpated wildlife species. The efforts of the park's staff included restoring native Colorado River cutthroat trout — as well as the greenback cutthroat trout — to lakes scattered throughout the park's high country. Teams of park biologists and rangers also worked together to restore river otter populations to the park's broad subalpine valleys and peregrine falcons to historic nesting aeries in the park's high country.

In contrast, a lodgepole pine forest is generally as dark and stuffy as a root cellar. Lodgepole trees are named for their flawlessly straight trunks which were perfect for building Native American teepees or 'lodges'. The trees usually grow so close together that they stunt each other's growth — creating what locals call 'dog-hair stands'. As the group soon discovered, a lodgepole forest can be so littered with spindly, fallen timber that it's a chore just to walk through.

Always astute observers of the landscape they were passing through, the boys noted the unequal contribution that aspen and lodgepole trees make to a colorful environment. With a flourish of broad down-sweeping strokes, the aspen tree is the brush that paints the autumnal landscapes of the high mountains. Seemingly overnight, the mountainsides are transformed into a striking mosaic of deep forest greens and cascading yellows, golds, pinks, and oranges. Meanwhile — with the onset of shorter days — most of the interior needles of the lodgepole pine turn a dull bronzy-brown and fall silently to the ground.

When it comes to living conditions, lodgepole pines generally take the high road while aspen prefer the low. Typically, lodgepoles grow in broad patches on dry, rocky hillsides while aspen inhabit the narrow, well-drained swales on lower slopes. Quaking aspen and lodgepole pine also reproduce in dramatically different ways.

Aspen trees tend to 'sucker out', sending up wild leafy sprouts all over the place. Typically, all of the trees in an aspen grove share the same rootstock. This means that an aspen grove is — in reality — a circular clone of interrelated trees. Because of this, all of the trees in an individual aspen grove will turn the same pastel shade in the fall, drop their leaves on virtually the same day, and leaf out simultaneously in the spring. It's not unusual for a clone of aspen trees on one hillside to have lost almost all of its leaves while an adjacent clone is just starting to turn color.

While the aspen grove is a beehive of activity, the monoculture of a lodgepole pine forest supports very little life. As their mounts clip-clopped up the trail through the torpid lodgepole forests, the young riders occasionally saw a snowshoe hare scurrying through patches of early snowfall or heard a chickaree chattering a warning from on high, but that was about it. To a man, they remarked that they were glad they didn't have to depend on lodgepole stands for their food supplies.

Early one afternoon, when it appeared that a vicious thunderstorm was rolling out of the mountaintops and straight at them, Samuel and Caleb ordered their charges to circle the wagons in the middle of a grove of mature aspens that was in peak autumn color. Before they had finished setting up camp, the storm rolled through but — other than a few mighty flashes of lightning and blasts of thunder — the rain missed them completely. Since they were now ensconced in the middle of a pristine and placid setting, Samuel and Caleb told the boys to just rest up and prepare to hit the trail hard again at sunrise the next day.

CONTROLLED BURNS MAINTAIN HEALTHY FORESTS

Lodgepole pines are also known as a 'fire species'. Their reproduction takes place when a forest fire sweeps through a stand and causes the cones of the mature trees to pop open and release their seeds to the ground below. It follows then that if we don't have forest fires, we don't have young lodgepole pines.

Natural, lightning-caused forest fires are vital to many types of healthy forest ecosystems. Forest fires are nature's brooms — sweeping away the debris and litter and opening up the forest to a fresh growth of grasses, shrubs, and wildflowers. An ecosystem that is allowed to go too long without burning can become too mature — thus lacking the dynamic growth and vegetative diversity so essential for wildlife.

Fortunately, the 'Smokey the Bear' philosophy that deemed every forest fire 'bad and destructive' for so long has been largely replaced by the use of controlled burns throughout most state and federal lands in the United States. Today, controlled burns — during which fire-lines are intentionally set and carefully managed by highly trained personnel — are commonly used to clear forest understory that has become too dense.

Most of the group decided to heed the advice of their leaders. Some nestled into comfortable niches in the granite boulders that covered the ground under the aspens while other perched on dead logs and stumps. Then they just sat back, relaxed, and watched.

By simply sitting and observing for a couple of hours, the boys saw signs of the many different wildlife species that can be found in an aspen grove. They saw several holes in tree trunks belonging to the delightfully named yellow-bellied sapsucker. This striking bird features bold black-and-white facial markings, a yellowish-buffy breast, and a red cap and throat. Actually, midsized woodpeckers, sapsuckers get their name from their habit of drilling sapwells — arranged rows of shallow holes — in the aspen trunks. They then feed on the sap that oozes from these holes as well as any insects that become entrapped in the sticky bark.

Each spring, adult sapsuckers exhibit nesting behavior that would make any equal rights advocate proud. The male and female sapsuckers work together to find and prepare a nesting cavity — often in a mature aspen grove. Once the time is right, the female lays the eggs while the male dutifully guards the entrance to the nest.

Next — after the eggs have hatched — the male takes turns with the female in bringing mouthfuls of insects to the squawking chicks. The male even tends the brood inside the tree nursery — allowing the female to get some air and stretch her wings. Such 'trading places' feeding behavior is exhibited by many bird species and ensures that — should something happen to one of the adults — the nestlings would still have a source of nourishment and parental care.

Another thing the boys noticed was a cup-shaped conglomeration of materials hanging down from a forked elbow of an aspen branch. Though barely still holding together after being used during the spring, this was the nest of a warbling vireo. This wren-sized bird — with its tiny, upturned beak and sparkling, dark eyes — is an excellent example of an 'indicator species'. An indicator species is a plant or animal that is always associated with a particular ecosystem. Today, wherever people travel in the Rocky Mountain West — if they happen to see this nondescript bird or hear its languid warble — it's a good bet that there's an aspen grove somewhere nearby.

As the lads reveled in their new-found mountain kingdom, the sighting of a patch of mushrooms — sprouting across the forest floor — was almost the unravelling of the crew. Mushrooms are the visible fruiting bodies of a group of organisms known as fungi — underground masses of threadlike material that serve as nature's chief decomposers.

The brightly-colored and funny-shaped fungi intrigued Thomas Stringfellow and Rhett Baumgardner so much that they decided to pick a few and see how they tasted. What could be the harm, they said to each other. The mushrooms didn't have any thorns or sharp edges, and they sure looked soft enough to chew. But — by the time they hiked back to camp — Thomas and Rhett were both so sick that they were moaning and groaning like crazed gut-shot animals.

Caleb immediately ran over to Thomas, jerked his head upright, and yelled in his face for him to say what happened. Unable to speak, Thomas pointed at some nearby mushrooms and then put his fingers up to his mouth. Fortunately, Caleb understood what they had done right away, and he knew just how to fix the problem. He dashed back to his wagon, grabbed two cups, and filled them both with a mixture of baking soda and cod liver oil. He then ran back to the sick boys and yelled for some of the other boys to give him a hand.

Caleb then forced both Thomas and Rhett to swallow his foul-tasting concoction — while some of the other boys held Thomas and Rhett's hands behind their backs. Five minutes later, both sick boys were standing in the forest with their hands on their knees heaving their guts out which was — of course — exactly what Caleb wanted to happen.

That night, while the rest of the boys ate a hearty dinner, Thomas and Rhett — who were still feeling pretty woozy — were just glad to be alive. As they laid by the campfire, they listened to Caleb's stern lecture about never putting anything in your mouth without first being sure exactly what it was and whether it was safe to eat. Caleb emphasized that the use of such caution was even more important up here in the wilderness — where they had no access to doctors and were completely dependent on each other for survival.

Nearing the Continental Divide

During the next few days, the wagon train moved laboriously up the now rough-hewn trail that seemed to get steeper and steeper with each new roll of a wheel. The lodgepole pine and aspen forests that had dominated the slopes below had now given way to a verdant green cover of solid evergreens. In many places—especially on the north-facing slopes—patches of last winter's ice alternated with pockets of freshly fallen snow. This setting was a forbearance of the brutality of weather in the high mountains — a situation the intrepid travelers were about to encounter in all its ferocity.

As anyone who has ever lived in a high mountain environment can attest, the threat of a whiteout blizzard persists throughout the entire year. Even summer snow squalls can descend quickly and powerfully — leaving up to a foot or more of fresh snow in their wake. In fact, the power of these quick-hitting storms is often most ferocious during the transitional 'shoulder seasons' of spring and fall.

Such was the case for the boys during a fateful night in late October. Caleb and Samuel knew that their young charges would soon cross over the high mountain pass that was the Continental Divide. They understood that — after crossing this landmark — they would officially be in the 'western half' of this bounteous new land.

They also knew that this would be — by far — the most difficult part of their journey. The already tightly-carved trail was about to become an even thinner thread — clinging to the sides of peaks — much steeper than anything they had encountered to date. Successfully negotiating the next ten or so miles — including both sides of the divide — demanded that all the boys be at their strongest with their senses at their keenest.

Because of this — despite being a gloriously warm late autumn day — Caleb and Samuel called a halt to the procession around noon. They told the boys to circle the wagons next to a rushing rivulet that was still nearly brim-full of water from the vestiges of last winter's snowpack runoff.

While many of the lads at first scoffed about wasting perfect traveling weather, they understood the situation when Samuel and Caleb talked to them after a hearty lunch of jerky, beans, and bullion. They dutifully turned to setting up camp and relaxing next to the calming waters of the fast-flowing stream. Many of them also spent a few hours hunting and fishing around the campsite. By suppertime, they had caught enough fresh cutthroat trout, and shot enough spruce grouse to provide a fresh meal for them all.

Because it was such a crisp, clear night, the boys decided to roll out their bedrolls on the ground instead of sleeping inside the wagons or under their canvas tent covers. At this elevation, the starry skies above seemed immense — chockfull of glittering celestial objects. They each fell asleep dreaming about the great beyond, and fantasizing about the perfect world awaiting them on the western side of these mighty mountains.

Just after midnight, the boys' heavenly visions became instant nightmares when a full-on, northwest-wind driven blizzard blasted into their campsite. It was all the boys could do to keep their sleeping gear from becoming kites and soaring away in the raging white-out. Miraculously, they all made it into the prairie schooners with most of their possessions. There they sat for the next six hours — wide awake and shivering together in huddled masses — while they listened to and felt the mighty storm as it pummeled the surrounding mountain landscape.

As is usually the case after a blizzard in the high mountains, the morning broke frosty clear and achingly cold. Since they were running low on provisions — especially meat — Samuel and Caleb decided to try and stock up before they tackled the trail again. They asked half the boys to form a hunting party while the rest stayed in camp and prepared the wagons and horses for getting back on the trail the next day at sunrise.

Since they had all decided to rest their horses for the day, the hunting party strapped shovel blades to their feet to keep them from sinking down into the fresh snowpack. With their makeshift snowshoes in place, the lads grabbed their rifles and set off in search of some game that they could shoot. They had no idea what — if anything — they might find in these conditions, but they decided to take a look just in case some animals were out and about. They knew that even a few freshly grilled rabbits would taste mighty good to everyone right about now.

The boys walked — or more aptly crow-hopped — for about an hour through a stand of old-growth spruce-fir forest. The freshly fallen snow was so soft and deep that even their wide snow shovel blades sank down a foot or more with each step they took.

About a mile from camp, the boys came to the timberline. Here the spruce-fir trees gave way to a scattering of gnarled, *krummholz* thickets where trees grew horizontally to survive in the bitter, unyielding winds that always swept across these exposed mountain peaks.

The hunting party decided to walk up to several of these curious, stunted tree thickets — hoping to scare some game out into the open snowfields where they could easily be shot. They split up into three groups — one group heading cross slope to the left, another taking off to the right, and the third heading straight up the slope. They agreed to meet at the nearest ridgeline and — if they didn't have any luck finding game — they would give up and head back down to camp.

Josh McCown took Jacob Lester and Henry Brown with him and — as planned — headed straight up the slope. After they had walked some fifty paces away from the forest edge, they stopped abruptly. Something seemed to be stirring under the snow right in the middle of a patch of small, rusty-brown twigs with tiny buds that were poking up through the snow all around their feet.

Suddenly, the peaceful white world all around them exploded upward in a blast of icy flakes and flapping wings. The boys looked on in awestruck silence as a flock of snowball-shaped birds skittered off in all directions. Most of the chicken-like fowl ran only a few feet before they stopped and looked back to see what had just invaded their frozen solitude.

The boys had no way of knowing what these strange birds were. Since they lived year-round on the always frozen tundra of the highest peaks, they had likely been seen by only a few — if any — white men before this.

One of the mountain tundra's most common residents — the white-tailed ptarmigan — is a master of camouflage. As the weather turns cold and snow begins to fly, ptarmigan undergo one of the most remarkable transformations in the avian world. Instead of flying south for the winter — like most 'normal' birds — these fowl prove that they are anything but normal. Almost overnight, their feathers start to molt and change from summer gray-brown to pure white. As a result — during the winter — ptarmigan become all but invisible to the coyotes and foxes that roam this frigid high country looking for easy meals.

Ptarmigan also have an uncanny ability to survive brutal mountain winters by burrowing down deep into the snowpack for warmth. Then — whenever a storm subsides — they pop back up to the surface and use their feathered feet as miniature snowshoes. This allows them to tread nimbly across soft snowdrifts while nibbling away on the buds of stunted arctic willows. The willows provide the ptarmigan's only sustenance throughout the more than eight months of high mountain winter.

This typical 'lifestyle' of the white-tailed ptarmigan explains exactly how they came to meet the boys on their rough-shod hunting expedition. Since the snow had only stopped falling a few hours before, the boys caught the ptarmigan while they were still entrenched in their blizzard hibernacula. The sounds of the group's shovel shoes spooked the birds enough that they burst up to the surface in order to flee from the approaching danger.

Unfortunately for most of the birds in this particular flock, making their presence known proved to be the last things they did in life. Crack shots that they were, the boys quickly and precisely dropped more than half the ptarmigan in their tracks. They then pursued and killed another ten birds before they could fly away to safety. All told, the boys concluded their very successful winter hunting foray by carrying twenty of the plump birds back to camp where they plucked, roasted, and gleefully ate them for dinner that night.

With their bellies full of fresh meat, the boys slept soundly under a clear but extremely cold night. The next morning, they found that everything in camp that had any water content — including sweat-soaked clothing — was frozen solid.

Still shivering under three layers of clothes, Caleb and Samuel stood off to the side of the roaring campfire and figured the air temperature had to be well below zero. They quickly agreed that — no matter how badly they wanted to keep moving — it was too risky to head out onto the trail in this extreme cold. So, they called their crew together and told them to just hunker down around the campfire and stay warm for the time being. Later in the day, Caleb and Samuel divided the gang up into five rotating wood-gathering and fire-stoking teams. To successfully fend off the cold, they knew they had to keep the campfire blazing throughout the day and into the night.

Full of the spunk of youth, several of the boys at first complained that Samuel and Caleb were babying them too much. But as the day drew on, the bone-breaking cold began to turn toes and fingers into miniature icicles — even underneath heavy gloves and thick leather boots. As a result, most of the lads now realized that venturing out onto the trail would likely mean severe frostbite and possibly even emergency amputations.

A Mega-Blizzard Wreaks Havoc

A thick cloud cover moved in overnight, bringing in much warmer temperatures. The next morning, while Caleb and Samuel realized the temperature was still below freezing, they knew it was at least thirty degrees warmer than it had been the previous day. Figuring the boys were plenty well-rested, they rousted them from their bedrolls well before sunrise and got everyone back on the trail just as the first shielded shafts of sunlight began filtering through the heavy overcast.

Just before noon — after the wagon train had traveled a few miles up the ever-steepening mountain trail leading to the crest of the divide — the weather suddenly closed in again. Within minutes, the group was trapped in a white-out of swirling snow so severe that they could just barely make out the trail ahead of them.

Realizing the descending desperation of their situation, Caleb and Samuel began yelling at the top of their lungs for the boys to circle the wagons off to the side of the trail. They knew it was futile to try and find a relatively flat camping site, so they just told their young charges to dismount and take cover inside the wagons and wait the storm out.

The wind howled and the blizzard raged all the rest of the day and into the night. The boys remained safe and warm by swaddling themselves in blankets and bedrolls inside their wagon covers. Since they had the foresight to outfit each wagon with a box of emergency provisions before they set off up into the mountains, they also had plenty of beef jerky and hardtack to eat and water to drink.

At first light the next morning, when the boys realized that the wind had subsided some, but the heavy snow was still continuing to pile up, they began to worry about the survival of their horses and oxen. They had tethered each oxen team to their respective wagons and individually hitched all the horses to nearby shrub clusters. But — because of the unrelenting blizzard conditions — they had not been able to feed any of the oxen or horses since the storm began. Now they looked out to see that the horses were buried up to their necks in fresh snow while the oxen were all buried under the snow.

Caleb and Samuel yelled to their charges to dig their way out of their wagons and try and find the oxen and feed the horses. When they did this, the boys found that the oxen had all frozen to death. Plus, most of the horses were barely alive. A few had even crumpled to their knees and were now completely buried in snow and most likely dead. Those that were still standing were barely breathing and were certainly in no shape to eat.

This situation saddled Caleb and Samuel with a very difficult decision. Do they let the still living horses suffer through freezing to death or should they tell the boys to put them out of their misery with single shots to their heads? Since they had no way of knowing how long this prolonged blizzard would continue, they decided to wait things out and pray that the snow would stop falling soon and perhaps a few of the horses could be saved.

As the heavy snow continued throughout the rest of the day and into the night, Caleb and Samuel realized that their survival concern now extended beyond the horses to the boys themselves. By the next morning, the snow level extended above the buckboards of their wagons, and was now pressing in on the sides of the canvas tops. Huddled together in their respective wagons, the boys stared out into the blinding white and wondered if they would ever see the green earth again.

Mercifully, the snow finally stopped falling around noon the next day — two full days after it had first started. Almost like magic, the snow clouds quickly blew away to the east and the full sun shone brightly on the glistening-white landscape.

The boys dug their way out of their wagons and then started shoveling pathways between the wagons. Much to their chagrin — but not unexpected — they found that most of the horses now lay dead under the five-and-a-half feet of fresh snow that had fallen during the storm. With tears streaming down their cheeks, Caleb and Samuel mercifully dispatched the few horses that were still barely breathing.

After they had finished digging a series of interconnecting snow trenches between the wagons and a central meeting area, the group collected all the nonessential materials they could find in each wagon and got a campfire going. As they stood somberly warming their hands and faces around the fire, Caleb and Samuel fretted about the future of their journey. Losing their livestock was a devastating blow logistically — how could they move the wagons forward without their power? But it also took a heavy emotional toll on the boys, many of whom had been caring for their horses since they were just youngsters.

Samuel and Caleb realized that they were in a tough spot, indeed.

Choosing the Best Bad Option

As the next few hours passed, Samuel and Caleb talked about several options with their group. First, they talked about just hunkering down and waiting things out — hoping that the snowpack would somehow melt down enough to allow them to manually pull the wagons up and over the Great Divide.

They all quickly agreed that this would not work. First of all, winter was just beginning to settle in. They had — in fact — just experienced the season's first two major storms. So, the snow was only going to continue piling up, not melt down. And — even with the robust strength of twenty-four hearty young men — there was no way they were going to be able to pull wagons uphill at this altitude. Plus — with no livestock left — what would they do even if they managed to make it over the divide?

Next, they considered forcing the wagons back down the trail — by laboriously digging them out and then successively clearing spaces ahead to push them into as they descended. They all immediately nixed this idea as being too labor intensive and slow-going. Plus — at least for the short-term — it would mean giving up on their journey, and none of them were quite ready to admit defeat.

The third option they discussed was abandoning the wagons and trying to make their way over the pass carrying only what they could on their backs. They knew this would be extremely risky, since the heavy snow made it impossible to see where the trail went. But they all agreed that this was the best plan. At least they would still be making progress — not just sitting around waiting to die.

In truth, they all had to know — in the backs of their minds — that trying to cross the crest of the High Rockies on foot in the dead of winter was sheer lunacy. But — in this time of ultimate tribulation — the exuberance and infallibility of their youthful brains took over. Each young man still had the mental fortitude to think of himself as indestructible. Once they made the decision to continue moving westward, thoughts of death barely crossed their minds. They were certain that — if they could just somehow manage to make it across the divide — everything would fall into place.

Realizing that trying to power their way through chest-deep snow would be impossible — even for the tallest and strongest boys — Caleb and Samuel decided that each boy needed to have some sort of wide foot support to keep themselves up on top of the snow. They took a reconnaissance of the wagons and found that they had three pairs of actual snowshoes that some of them had brought along from home. The rest of the snow-going footwear would have to be handcrafted out of shovels, wooden strips, flexible twigs, patches of rawhide, and the strong cord many of the boys brought along for fishing.

That afternoon, the lads set to work fashioning crude snowshoes and sewing backpacks out of the wagons' canvas tops. Next, they sorted out the gear they would carry on their backs up the mountain. The things they decided to take were limited to bedrolls, food supplies, water, hunting knives — plus their rifles and ammunition. They knew that — without the wagons — there was no room for such luxuries as extra clothes, cooking and eating utensils, and the assorted knick-knacks they each brought with them as reminders of home.

As night fell, the group crawled back into their wagons, knowing full well that this was the last night of warm, protected sleep they were going to have for a while. Yet, the spirit of adventure still burned bright in their dreams, and they saw this as just one more challenge — albeit quite a big one — that they had to overcome along their way to the 'Promised Land'.

They were all still convinced that once they crested the divide, they would find the land of gold, silver, and jewels that would make them wealthy men and render the hardships of their journey worth every minute.

Trekking Over the Divide

The next morning, Caleb and Samuel waited until a few hours after sunrise to roust the boys and get them out onto the trail. They felt it was better to wait a while for the sun to warm the blinding white landscape before getting everyone out of the last relatively warm conditions they would know for quite a while.

Samuel and Caleb also decided against building a breakfast campfire, reasoning that the boys would adjust better to the extreme cold on the trail without warming up first. After they woke everyone up, the two leaders told their charges to make a quick morning meal of hardtack and jerky, then gather up their belongings, and meet in the center of the circled wagons.

The first order of business for Caleb and Samuel was to inspect each young man's load. They wanted to weed out any nonessential gear, plus make sure that each boy was not overburdening himself. As soon as the inspection was complete, Caleb whistled for the group to line up behind him in one of the trenches that they had dug yesterday.

Next Caleb told the boys to put on their snowshoes and then he climbed out of the trench. Balancing himself on top of the snowfield — wearing his own makeshift snowshoes — he turned and headed due west. Scrambling out of the trench, the rest of the boys fell in line behind Caleb with Samuel bringing up the rear of the hiking party.

Their first day of snow-trekking was mostly trial and error. About every fifteen minutes, Caleb took westward compass headings and then turned around to watch how the gang was doing behind him.

Watching the boys plow their way through the fresh powder snow was almost comical had the circumstances not been so unfortunate and dire. While the handcrafted snowshoes kept the boys from sinking out of sight, they didn't work very well at keeping them perched on the top of the immense snowpack.

With each clumsy step, the boys flung their arms around in all directions — looking like a bunch of drunks on Saturday night in the town saloon — fighting to keep their balance and prevent themselves from tumbling head-over-heels down into the deep snow. Graceful they were not — but all the boys were so strong and in such good shape that they were able to stay upright and keep charging forward.

Every now and then someone would take a header and end up floundering around wildly — only succeeding in digging himself deeper and deeper — as he vainly struggled to regain his footing. Each time this happened, after dishing out the appropriate amount of good-natured ribbing to their fallen comrade, several boys would form a human chain and literally yank the embarrassed boy back to his feet on top of the snow. The whole group would them continue on until the next boy took a tumble and had to be similarly rescued.

While this process provided some comic relief and lots of exercise for the boys, Caleb and Samuel knew that their journey from this point on had become deadly serious. They were moving along at a literal 'snail's pace' — less than a half-mile an hour, as Samuel figured it — plus they only had less than eight hours of daylight each day during which to travel.

Caleb guessed that they had at least five more miles to go before they reached the top of the pass. He and Samuel both realized that if they were caught in another blizzard before they were able to cross the divide and descend into the shelter of a western-slope forest, there was a strong likelihood they would all perish.

The intrepid group also always had to keep in mind that they were trekking high above timberline. A place where even the horizontal-growing krummholz tree thickets were completely buried in the deep, drifting snow. A second blizzard would most likely trap them out in the open — in wind-driven air temperatures that could easily exceed thirty degrees below zero.

The Ultimate Horror—A Second Blizzard Arrives

Three days later, when they were less than a half-mile below the summit of the divide, the worst fears of Caleb and Samuel were realized. A fresh storm system descended and — within a matter of minutes — a blizzard was again raging all around them.

Caleb and Samuel understood that they had no choice about what to do next. They stopped and ordered their charges to begin digging a snow cave for shelter in the deep drifts that had built up below the crest of the ridge. They knew that the shelter of the deep snowpack offered their only hope of surviving the fierce wind and brutal cold of this new blizzard in which they were now ensnared.

Using the mighty strength of their young bodies — now honed to near-perfection by nearly eight months of rugged travel — it took the boys just a few hours to dig out a snow cave large enough to fit all twenty-four of them. Once they were all inside, the group tried to regain some of their spent energy by eating a quick meal of jerky and hardtack.

Caleb began the meal by blessing the food and then warning the boys not to eat too much. While they each had roughly two weeks of food left, Caleb emphasized the obvious by telling them that they would be better off rationing their food supplies — and staying a little hungry now — as opposed to completely running out of food before they reached the relative safety of the western side of the divide.

While Caleb outwardly showed strength and confidence in speaking to the group, deep inside he knew full well that this was likely the beginning of the end of their journey — and most likely of their lives. He knew that if this new blizzard dumped more than three feet of fresh snow on top of the more than four feet that already covered the landscape, the snowpack would be above all their heads.

After they finished eating, the boys sat sullenly — some dozing on and off while others prayed quietly — and just listened to the roaring blizzard a few feet above their heads. As the minutes became hours and the hours grew into days, Caleb and Samuel noticed that the combination of lack of food and water and the continued exposure to the extreme cold — was beginning to take its toll on some of their charges.

Several of them were continuously coughing, hacking, and sneezing — plus shivering so incessantly that it was obvious they were also running a fever. Caleb and Samuel knew that losing several of the boys to the dreaded disease called 'consumption' was now a very real possibility.

Awakening from a light slumber early on the morning of the third day after the boys had crawled into their snow cave, Caleb awakened to a strange sound — dead silence. He lay perfectly still and listened for the next few minutes just to make sure his ears weren't playing tricks on him. Yes, he was absolutely sure of it now. The howling wind had completely subsided, which likely meant that the snow had mercifully stopped falling.

Scratching and clawing his way up through the top of the snow cave, Caleb poked his head out like a pocket gopher, squinting into the billowing brightness of the full morning sun. The high mountain sky was as azure blue as blue can get, without a single cloud visible anywhere. The air itself felt almost warm and — if it weren't for the four feet of fresh snow glistening on the ground — it would almost seem as if the latest blizzard had never happened. But it had, and now Caleb knew that he was down to his last chance to save not only the expedition, but the lives of the twenty-three other boys in his care.

Caleb summoned Samuel to push his way up into the hole he had carved in the snow cave's roof. As they stood transfixed, gazing into the most wondrous world of white either one of them had ever witnessed, Caleb told Samuel what he was thinking.

Caleb knew that they had to abandon hope of making it to the summit on foot. With many of the boys sick and weakened, and the depth of snow surrounding them, their only hope was to be rescued. His idea was to gather together anything that would burn into one big pile on the surface of the snow and then soak everything with the coal oil some of the lads kept for running their lanterns. Caleb knew that the coal oil would produce a fire with thick black smoke that would be visible for miles in the clear, cold mountain air.

Next, he planned on using a blanket from his bedroll to alternately cover and then uncover the fire — thereby producing puffs instead of a steady cloud of smoke. He knew it was a long shot, but maybe — just maybe — someone would see the puffs of smoke and realize that it was a distress signal.

Immediately after hearing about Caleb's plan, Samuel dropped back down into the snow cave and began collecting everything he could find to build the fire. Understanding that this was their last chance to be found and saved, many of the boys even gave Samuel portions of their bedrolls to burn.

Forming a human chain, the boys passed the materials to be burned up to Caleb at the surface of the snow. Caleb then stacked the materials high on top of a slight depression in the snow that he had pounded hard and flat with the bottom of a shovel. When he had finished stacking everything he was given, Caleb had a burn pile that was more than five feet high. Next, he soaked the bottom edge of the pile with the coal oil the group had left.

Caleb then asked Samuel to come back up through the hole and stand next to him, so they could start the fire and then fan the flames with a blanket. When they were ready, one of the boys handed two flaming pieces of fire-starting kindling up to Caleb and Samuel. Within seconds, the fire roared up through the pile of dry materials and into the frigid mountain air. The acrid, black smoke was exactly what Caleb had hoped for, and he and Samuel began immediately using the blanket to create thick puffs spaced about ten feet apart.

For the next three hours, Caleb and Samuel continued to send their smoke signals straight up toward the towering mountain peaks that surrounded them on all sides. With the air as still as the mirrored surface of a reflecting pond, the puffs of smoke continued upward for hundreds of feet until they finally vanished from view.

After the fire had dwindled down to just smoldering embers, Caleb and Samuel knew that they had done all they could do. Now it was just a matter of time to wait and see if their smoke signals had been seen by someone — anyone — who might be able to come to their aid.

Native Americans to the Rescue

About twenty minutes after Caleb and Samuel had sent up the last puff of smoke they could muster, they got their answer. The sound of three flaming arrows thwapping into the snow behind them quickly caught their attention. They whirled around in astonishment to see a party of twelve horseback-mounted Native Americans, clad in buckskin from head-to-toe.

Caleb and Samuel both immediately crossed their arms in front of their chests and then extended their open palms upward toward the braves in their now well used expression of peace. To their relief, the brave at the head of the group smiled and returned the friendship gesture.

Using a mixture of rudimentary English and sign language, Caleb explained to the brave — whose name he determined to be Runs With Wolves — that they numbered twenty-four in total and were in desperate need of food, water, and shelter. In turn, Runs With Wolves told Caleb and Samuel that they were a Shoshone hunting party — out tracking mountain goats and bighorn sheep into their high-country lairs. In fact, they had already succeeded in killing both a large male goat and a full-curl bighorn ram.

Wasting little time, Runs With Wolves motioned for Caleb to climb up behind him onto the back of his horse. Runs With Wolves then clucked a command and his steed immediately turned and began plowing its way through the deep snow straight uphill toward the ridgeline.

Some three hundred yards later, Caleb and Runs With Wolves reached the top of the ridge where they dismounted and stood looking back down the slope at Samuel and the other Shoshone braves. Samuel was astonished to see that the snow on the ridgeline was no more than two feet deep and he suddenly realized that Runs With Wolves was showing him how they could escape the deep snow by simply walking along the windswept crest of the ridge.

Caleb and Runs With Wolves remounted and loped back down

through the deep snow to the snow cave's entrance. Once there, Runs With Wolves motioned for Caleb and Samuel to bring the other boys up to the surface and put them on the backs of the other horses in his hunting party.

In less than two hours' time, all of the boys now stood with their remaining gear — in less than knee-deep snow — lined up along the ridgeline of what was the Great Continental Divide. Once all the boys were safely assembled on the ridge, Runs With Wolves motioned for Caleb to have ten of the boys climb back up on the Shoshone horses which were not bearing the killed goat and bighorn sheep.

Caleb picked the seven boys who were most seriously ill — plus three others who were showing signs of becoming sick — to ride behind the Shoshone braves. Caleb, Samuel, and the twelve other boys then fell into line behind the horses and began slowly following them on foot down the ridgeline. They were headed toward the edge of another spruce-fir forest that lay several thousand feet below on the western side of the divide.

As they descended lower and lower, the snow got deeper and deeper — making for very slow going. Once they got back into waist deep snow, Runs With Wolves motioned for Caleb, Samuel, and the other twelve boys who were on foot to stay put while they rode on ahead to their encampment. With no option except to trust Runs With Wolves, Caleb and Samuel told the boys to dig themselves into a snow bank for warmth, and hunker down for a few hours until the Shoshone braves returned with fresh horses for them all to ride down to safety.

As the bright sunlight began to fade into the twilight of early evening, Caleb and Samuel grew more and more anxious since there was still no sign of Runs With Wolves and the other braves. After the full onset of darkness — as they sat shivering in the icy cold — the group looked up to see a most welcoming sight. A string of glowing torches was moving up the ridgeline in their direction. Within an hour, they were all mounted on horses — each sitting behind a Shoshone brave — and heading down through the deep snow toward the tribal encampment.

After a few hours of slow slogging through the deep snow, the fourteen horses — each bearing a Shoshone brave and one of the boys — finally arrived at a collection of about one hundred teepees scattered around several roaring campfires. The flames were casting eerie flickering shadows on the thick trunks of the old-growth spruce-fir forest into which the encampment was nestled. Off to one side, the boys could hear the burbling roar of a large stream that was cascading madly downslope beneath a surface veneer of ice and snow.

Eager to warm their chilled bones, Caleb, Samuel, and the other boys immediately jumped off their mounts and made a collective dash to the nearest campfire which was now spewing towering flames and hot ashes more than one hundred feet straight up into the inky black, star-laden sky. Soon after the fire's warmth had taken the three-day old chill out of their bodies, the boys — in unison — crossed their arms over their hearts and then extended their outstretched palms toward the Shoshone braves. These proud Native Americans had just risked their own lives in rescuing a raggedy band of white travelers from the horror of freezing to death.

For this, Samuel, Caleb and all the boys were eternally grateful. The Shoshone braves all smiled knowingly back at the lads as they returned their kind gestures of peace and friendship. Caleb looked at Samuel and winked — knowing that they were not only incredibly lucky to be alive, but now would be able to continue their journey once the sick boys were well again, and spring temperatures had melted some of the snowpack.

As Caleb stood warming his half-frozen hands and feet, he thought back to the many lessons his father — Thaddeus — had taught him about Native Americans. About how they had an understanding about the workings of Nature that far exceeded any knowledge the newcomer 'white man' had about this strange and wonderful land where they all now lived.

The Native Americans instinctively knew that they had to treat the land and all its inhabitants — including those they killed for food — with the utmost honesty and respect. In return, the land provided the tribes with all the shelter and sustenance they needed to survive — even during the worst winters when the snow seemed to never stop falling, and the temperatures stayed well below zero for months at a time.

Living with the Shoshones

Bright and early the next morning, Caleb and Samuel awakened all the healthy boys and took them over to meet with Runs With Wolves to find out how they could make themselves useful to the Shoshone village. Caleb knew that they would be dependent on the tribe's braves for guiding them to the nearest large trading post — Fort Robidoux — located in what is now the State of Utah. After arriving in Fort Robidoux, the group could then work to re-provision their expedition with both supplies and horses.

For the next several months, the lads fit right into the Shoshone Village. The healthy boys joined in doing all the work of the braves — including daily wood-gathering treks to keep the campfires stoked and hunting parties to keep everyone's bellies full.

As they worked together, the Shoshone braves and the boys developed a deep-seated respect and admiration for one another. Every day, the braves gave the boys invaluable lessons about how to read the land and track game.

Most of the boys — who considered themselves to be expert outdoorsmen — were astonished by how much they actually did not know. The Shoshone braves taught them how to see invisible bobcats nestled deep in spruce boughs, and how to tell where a bear was likely hibernating in places where there were no signs of life in the deep snow.

In return, the boys taught the Shoshone braves how to shoot their long rifles — which could take down an elk at three hundred feet — how to skin hides with their Bowie knives, and, perhaps most valuably, how to use a needle and thread to darn ripped and worn clothing.

Each night, the boys and the braves blended their youth and vitality — often whooping it up around the campfires. The braves also shared their special alcoholic concoction — a delightful and tasty blend of fermented berries —while the boys taught them a variety of dances involved in a good old country hoedown.

As to be expected with a group of healthy and handsome young men, quite a few romances developed between the white boys and the young Shoshone women. Fortunately, none of this ever got out of hand, since the boys — who remained steadfastly thankful to the Shoshone braves for saving their lives — always made sure that they weren't interfering with any ongoing relationships among the Shoshone braves and young women.

On a few occasions, Caleb passed along messages from Runs With Wolves to the boys about certain young women who were 'off limits' since they were already betrothed to some of the Shoshone braves. Without fail, the boys always accepted and heeded this advice — making sure that the Shoshone-Caucasian intermixing in the village always remained peaceful and restrained.

Within a few weeks, all of the sick boys were nursed back to health in delightful fashion by the kind and doting Shoshone women, and had joined the rest of the group in the daily camp chores. To say that Caleb and Samuel were relieved that they had not lost a single boy — considering how close they all were to death — was a vast understatement. They were thrilled beyond belief to know that they would soon be continuing their journey down the western side of the Great Continental Divide with everyone they had started out with almost one year ago.

After nearly six months of living with the Shoshones, Caleb watched with anticipated joy as the sunlight lingered on the landscape longer and longer each day. He noticed that much of the snow and ice covering the stream had melted — revealing pockets of glistening cascades — and that the depth of snow on the spruce and fir trunks was dropping by a few inches each day. Based on the way spring was making its presence felt, Caleb figured that — if no more big snows came — it would soon be time for them to reluctantly leave their now good friends and wonderful hosts.

Preparing for a Bittersweet Departure

Early one especially warm spring morning, Caleb and Samuel made their way to Runs With Wolves' teepee to talk to him about guiding them down the western slope to the nearest trading post. True to his peaceful nature, Runs With Wolves quickly agreed to provide two of his best braves to lead the group down the mountain. He then took a giant step further by saying that he would also supply them all with horses to make the long southwestward trek down to Fort Robidoux.

Being so overjoyed by Runs With Wolves generosity, both Caleb and Samuel simultaneously grabbed the chief in a big bear hug and started bouncing uncontrollably up and down. Their quick, bold actions startled Runs With Wolves so much that he let loose with a loud yell and pushed himself away from the cloistering arms of the two white men.

After they had all finished laughing about the Shoshone leader's shocked response, Caleb and Samuel sat back down with Runs With Wolves to decide on a date to begin their journey down to Fort Robidoux. Relying on his traditional method of keeping track of the days and months with assorted small, rounded river pebbles, Runs With Wolves showed Caleb and Samuel that it was now more than twenty days after the start of spring — typically the time when the rate of snowmelt began to exceed the amount of new snow that fell from the sky.

Using a combination of hand gestures and some of the vocabulary words they had learned from each other, Runs With Wolves, Caleb and Samuel agreed that — unless they had another major snowfall — the trip to Fort Robidoux would begin after the passage of another fortnight or fourteen days. As Caleb and Samuel figured it, this would put them leaving the Shoshone village near the middle of April 1848.

After again respectfully shaking hands with Runs With Wolves — no more bear hugs this time — Caleb and Samuel excitedly walked back to their teepees to pass the good news along to their young charges. Upon hearing the news about their departure date, the boys showed a bittersweet mix of enthusiasm and sadness. While they were — of course — glad to be able to resume their dream journey, they were also melancholy about having to leave their new-found friends for what would — in all likelihood — be forever.

Owing again to the exuberance of their youth, the boys quickly overcame their lingering sad feelings, and began counting down — with unbridled enthusiasm — the days until their departure. In addition to continuing their daily chores in the village, they began readying their gear — patching clothes, resoling boots, sharpening knives, cleaning rifles, reloading ammunition, and the like — for the trip ahead.

The boys also began smoking much of the game they had recently killed to build a supply of valuable protein for both themselves and their Shoshone guides on the upcoming trek to Fort Robidoux. They also continued their nightly campfire revelry with their Shoshone friends — enjoying the fun even more now that the daylight hours were longer, and their long-awaited return to the trail was growing closer and closer.

The gradual unfolding of winter into spring also served to enliven the overall attitudes of the boys as well as the tribal villagers living in the encampment. For people living in 'four-season' climates, there is perhaps no greater *joie de vivre* than that associated with the onset of spring.

So it was with the boys. They delighted in watching delicate purple pasqueflowers pop up through the middle of still frozen patches of snow that lingered in the shadows of the spruce-fir forest.

Their daily hunting trips were always very successful now that the deep snowpack had melted back to levels that their horses could easily move through. The snow that remained made it incredibly easy to track, find, and kill elk and mule deer, most of which were still 'yarded up' in evergreen thickets. The extra game that the Shoshone braves and the boys brought into camp each day ensured that they would have plenty of smoked meat for their pending long journey to Fort Robidoux.

With the exception of a few ephemeral skiffs and flurries, the next twelve days were virtually snow-free. On the day before their scheduled departure, the boys started talking about having one final grand celebration with their Shoshone saviors and now fast friends. Although Caleb and Samuel would have preferred that the boys go to bed early — so they could leave with the sunrise — they knew that it would be unfair to prevent them from having a farewell party with the Shoshone braves who were responsible for them all still being alive.

The boys and the Shoshone villagers spent most of the day before their scheduled departure preparing for the evening's fete. They gathered several cords of firewood from the forest floor and stacked it all in an immense, thirty-foot high pile right in the middle of the village.

Then — to provide plenty of room for dancing and carousing — they used shovels and brooms to clear away all of the snow remnants around the edges of the firepit. Next, they set out several vats of the village's special fruit wine in strategic locations around the giant bonfire.

Finally, they grilled up vast platefuls of food — including elk and deer venison and hominy grits. They also prepared hundreds of baked potatoes in the glowing embers of the cooking campfires. They then topped off the feast preparations by soaking fresh-baked bread in a sugarcane and honey concoction — creating the Shoshones' favorite sweet-tooth dessert known as 'fry breads'.

As soon as the last vestiges of alpenglow left the western sky, the festivities began. With ceremonial aplomb, several Shoshone braves ignited piles of kindling set at ten-foot intervals around the edge of the big central bonfire. Within minutes, the mountainous mass of wood was roaring up to the heavens — sending sparks into the night sky that outshone the brightest of the stars beyond. For a while, everyone just stood around admiring the immense blaze and drawing deeply from their cups and mugs of fermented libation. Then — just as soon as everyone was sufficiently lubricated with homemade brew — the fun and feasting began in earnest. The boys and the Shoshone villagers all joined in with each group, featuring their own brand of dancing and reverie.

As village guests, the boys first led everyone in holding hands and doing country line dancing. Then the hosts took over, bouncing and prancing around the campfire in traditional Shoshone ceremonial prayer dances that beseeched the Great Spirit for good luck and safe travels for everyone on the trail ahead. The gaiety continued until the wee hours when most everyone had passed out around the campfire.

Sunrise the next morning found all of the boys groggy, but fulfilled — feeling that they had appropriately said goodbye to their generous, new-found friends. Caleb and Samuel knew that they probably should let the boys sleep it off, but the day had broken bright and clear, and they wanted to take full advantage of all of the daylight traveling hours they could get. Both men knew full well that springtime in the mountain high country still held the threat of major blizzards which — when they struck — could produce even more snow than storms during the winter months. The major difference was that the spring storms were often followed by warm, Chinook winds that literally 'ate the snow' off the ground — almost as fast as it had fallen from the sky. Still, Caleb and Samuel were extremely wary of getting stranded again in a blizzard — even if it was for only a couple of days. So, they walked around, shaking each boy awake and gently telling them to get themselves up and ready to hit the trail.

While they were rousting their young charges from their groggy sleep, Caleb and Samuel found Runs With Wolves walking next to them, along with two Shoshone braves named Little Bearcat and Shining Otter. Runs With Wolves explained that the two braves were among the best scouts in the village, and would serve as their guides in leading them down to Fort Robidoux.

This was great news to both Caleb and Samuel because they knew that — among all of the Shoshone braves in the village — Little Bearcat and Shining Otter were among the most liked and respected by their group. Both Samuel and Caleb immediately stood up and profusely thanked Runs With Wolves for his judicious and wise leadership choices.

Runs With Wolves next motioned for Samuel and Caleb to follow him and the two braves to a clearing at the edge of the village. There stood twenty-four horses — all bridled up, saddled with provisions, and ready to ride. At first, Caleb and Samuel just stared in disbelief at the long line of mounts ready to carry their charges down into the first valley of the many they would encounter along their long, convoluted journey to Fort Robidoux. They were astonished by the effort Runs With Wolves had expended in getting everything ready to go — while they were all drinking and feasting the night away.

After getting over his delighted shock, Caleb stuck two fingers in his mouth and cut loose with a piercing whistle that his group knew was the rallying cry for them to gather around. Within minutes, the boys had secured their gear to their assigned horses and sat waiting for Shining

Otter to motion them forward and on down the trail. As their horses fell into line — one after the other — each boy smiled broadly and waved goodbye to all the Shoshone villagers who now lined both sides of the trail leading down into the valley. While they tried their best to hide it, most of the boys had tears streaming down their cheeks as they waved their last goodbyes to their Shoshone friends who had so successfully helped them through the unrelenting cold and snows of the past winter.

BOOK EIGHT
Traveling to Fort Robidoux

Tangled Up with Trappers

For the first few days, the downhill traverse was slow-going. The Shoshone horses and their mounts wove their way in long, winding switchbacks down the western slope of the Rocky Mountains. Although the calendar said spring, it was still the dead of winter across the high mountain valleys and plateaus.

Many days brought fresh snow to the landscape. It usually amounted from only a dusting to a few inches, but both Little Bearcat and Shining Otter knew that the 'Great Spirit in the Sky' could cut loose and bury them in a furious whiteout at any moment.

In the still deep snow, the Shoshone guides didn't bother trying to find and follow the many trails that they knew would lead them down into the sheltering canyonlands, dry gulches, and barren riverbeds scattered throughout the mountain foothills. Instead, they concentrated on going downhill as directly and as fast as possible to avoid the possibility of being trapped in another blizzard.

They stopped early enough each night to clear away snow for a campsite and fire pit. After this, the boys would break up into two groups — one led by Shining Otter and the other by Little Bearcat — and take off into the dense woodlands in search of fresh meat for dinner. Since game was plentiful and the snowpack was melting — even in the forested shadows — they always returned with fresh kills.

Outside of some good-natured banter, dinners around the campfire were quiet affairs with the boys and their Shoshone guides. They were all anxious for the task at hand, which was to reach the safety of Fort Robidoux as soon as possible. Within an hour after sunset, every man was snugged up in the warmth of his bedroll and then back up and ready to get on the trail well before sunrise the next day.

The only exception to their routine happened late one bright afternoon when they came upon a rowdy group of white trappers. The mountain men were sitting around swilling freshly-brewed moonshine and field-dressing their booty of beaver pelts from the morning's trap runs.

When the boys were close enough to be seen, one of the trappers stood up, waved his arms in the air, and let out a liquor-soaked whoop. "Well would ya lookee at what we got here. A bunch of wet-neck youngins being led around by a coupla savages. Ain't that just the durndest thang you ever saw!"

Caleb, Samuel, Shining Otter, and Little Bearcat conferred. While the trapper's language was offensive, Shining Otter and Little Bearcat shook it off. They could clearly see that the trappers were not a threat — they were so drunk they could hardly stand up — let alone fight anybody. Besides, they were close to the trading post at this point and seemed out of harm's reach should a storm blow in. The four leaders decided that a night of relaxing around the fire with the trappers would be good for morale, and would allow the men to let off some steam before they reached Fort Robidoux. Caleb rode up slowly and greeted the men with a glad-to-see-you. "Well, howdy there, boys—mind if we set up camp here and join in your fun?"

"Shoot no," the drunken trapper bellowed back at Caleb, "pull up some stumps and join our party!" They didn't need to be asked twice. Within thirty minutes, the twenty-four boys and two Shoshone braves were seated around the trappers' campfire — sharing their moonshine and listening to tall tales.

Turns out for eleven months of the year, these trappers lived, hunted, and ran their trap lines up here in the high country. Then — come first of every December — they loaded up their wares and headed down to Fort Robidoux where they traded their take for provisions plus profits that would see them through to the next year. Spending the month of December in Fort Robidoux also gave them time to unwind, romance the local 'ladies-of-the-night', and enjoy this new-fangled tradition of Christmas that had just spread into the western territories from the eastern cities.

All-in-all, the trappers agreed that it was a good and exciting way to live. But — to a man — they claimed that they planned on keeping at it for 'only a few' more years. They figured that by then, they would have saved up enough money to go back home, start families, and live out the rest of their lives as 'gentleman ranchers'.

If the boys questioned whether the trappers' rather idealistic view of life was really a possibility, they didn't let on. They just sat back, drank themselves into fuzzy numbness, and laughed at the all the lies they knew the trappers were telling.

Some of the trappers told stories that were so outlandish the boys knew there couldn't be an iota of truth to them. The story they told most often — over and over again, in fact — was about their encounters with a creature they called the 'Great GrizRam'.

The way they told it, this animal stood about ten feet tall on its hindquarters, and had the massive shoulders and head of a grizzly bear topped by the fearsome full-curl horns of a bighorn sheep. The trappers all claimed that each time they met up with this beast, they emptied their carbines and pistols into its hide. But nothing seemed to faze it. It always just reared up, roared ferociously, shook its horns at them menacingly, and then turned tail and loped off back into the woods from which it had first appeared.

The trappers honestly believed — or at least so it seemed to their audience — that the Great GrizRam was — in reality — the spiritual presence of the High Rocky Mountains. As such, it still regularly appeared to them. Its purpose was to keep them mindful that they were always subject to a higher power that reigned over these majestic peaks from which they took their bounties each year. In fact, Old One-Eye Jack — the trapper's chief storyteller — told the boys that because it had been more than three months since they had last seen the Great GrizRam, it was near time for it to make another appearance. Following Old Jack's pronouncement, the boys — all of whom were by now quite well liquored-up — stumbled off to bed. As the lads crawled into their bedrolls, many of them were still chuckling to themselves about the Great GrizRam.

Sometime later — well after midnight — Caleb, Samuel, and the other boys were startled awake by the most God-awful sound any of them had ever heard. It was a cross between the deafening rumble of thunder that follows the crack of lightning when it is directly overhead, and the high-pitched snarling squeal of a doomed prey being attacked by an alpha predator.

In unison, the boys all sat bolt upright in their bedrolls and looked downslope toward the source of the sound. What they saw coming toward them was completely beyond belief.

A hulking shadow — half-again taller and wider than a full-grown man — was clomping toward them in bounding giant steps across the forest floor. The next thing the startled group noticed made them think they were surely experiencing a collective nightmare. The massive shadow — that was now racing up the slope at full speed — was topped off by a set of huge curling horns.

Could this really be the Great GrizRam they had heard about around the campfire a few hours earlier? Caleb hollered for all the boys to jump up and grab their rifles.

Caleb next gave the order for them to shoulder their rifles and take aim. But before he could say fire, he stopped short — interrupted by the guffaws and bellows of laughter coming from the direction of the trappers' sleeping circle. In an instant, Caleb and all the boys knew they'd been had by one of the oldest tricks in the woodman's book — a campfire ghost story that comes to life and scares the bejabbers out of the guileless listeners.

By now, the Great GrizRam had walked into the light of the glowing embers of the boys' sleeping circle. There they saw that the fearsome creature was actually one of the smaller trappers perched on the shoulders of the largest trapper.

The trapper on top was holding the full-curl horns of a bighorn ram over his head, and they were both wrapped in the massive hide of a grizzly bear. Next, three other trappers emerged from the darkness, holding the skinned and tanned hide of a bull elk that they had been shaking to create the sound of exploding thunder. A fourth trapper held a large, wooden flute-like device that he had used to make the high-pitched squealing sound of a frightened prey animal.

"Works like a charm every time," spouted Old-One-Eye Jack in between breaths as he was still doubled-over in laughter. "Don't really matter if it's other trappers or young cowpokes — just like you'uns trying to find their way west. They always fall for our tall tales. Reckon, we should just quit trappin', find a traveling circus, and get ourselves on the road. Be a dang lot easier than fightin' Mother Nature up here in the mountains all year long!"

Soon as they had gathered their wits about them again, the boys — feigning indignity — swore good-naturedly at the still-guffawing trappers, and claimed that they knew all along what was going on and that they were just playing along to humor their hosts. After a solid hour of back-and-forth banter about whether or not they were really scared out of their wits — which, of course, they most certainly were — the lads drifted back to their bedrolls and fell back into a groggy, but strangely comfortable sleep.

Fooling the Ferrymen

The next morning — just after sunrise — the boys crawled, bleary-eyed out of their bedrolls. Caleb and Samuel were dashing around, imploring each of them to shake the cobwebs out of their heads so they could get back on the trail post-haste. After a quick breakfast of hot coffee, beef jerky and hardtack — which the trappers had whipped up for them — they were back on their way down into a mountain valley that now lay just several hundred below.

Shortly after leaving the trappers' camp, Shining Otter and Little Bearcat had the boys following a now well-defined trail. The lush-green of the spruce-fir forests, soon gave way to much drier forests of lodgepole pine interspersed with copses of fragile-leaved aspens.

Other than a few scattered patches, all of the snow had now disappeared. The boys could see gaily-colored pockets of spring wildflowers popping up all around — both under the sheltering trees and in the patchwork quilt of mountain meadows that bordered the aspen groves.

Day after day — as Shining Otter and Little Bearcat led the group lower and lower down the western slope — the terrain became progressively drier. Finally, the trail began to level out, and the boys noticed that they were now passing through a landscape that was more desolate than anything they had ever seen in their lives. In every direction, parched rolling hills supported only widely scattered shrubs — greasewood, rabbitbrush, and sagebrush — most no more than three feet high.

Here and there, terraced arroyos — bordered by lime-green freshets of cottonwoods and willows — broke the visual monotony of the dry hillsides. Despite the paucity of vegetation, game was still plentiful, and the lads never had any trouble finding and shooting fresh meat — jackrabbits, pronghorns, and mule deer — for dinner each night.

Once they broke out into the open western prairie land, the boys and their two Shoshone guides were able to travel quickly — some days covering as much as twenty miles. The rivers and streams they encountered were either broad dry washes or had minimal flows, since the majority of the spring snowmelt was still locked up in the high country snowpacks. The one exception came when they arrived at the Yampa River in what is now Colorado's Dinosaur National Park. Once they were within a mile of the river's edge, Shining Otter and Little Bearcat motioned for Caleb and Samuel to come forward to the front of the line.

Caleb and Samuel were surprised to see fear in the faces of the two Shoshone braves. After traveling with them for what was now more than a month, Caleb and Samuel were certain fear was an emotion that Shining Otter and Little Bearcat seldom experienced. They had slept right through the whole Great GrizRam antics with the trappers. In fact, Caleb and Samuel never even thought to ask them whether they knew it had happened.

Both Shining Otter and Little Bearcat were now gesturing emphatically — first with their hands toward the river crossing ahead, and then in a slashing motion across their throats. Caleb and Samuel finally realized that the Shoshone braves were trying to tell them that the crossing was unsafe — at least for Native Americans. They now understood that the ferry operators didn't take kindly to men of any tribe, and that if they all rode up to the crossing together somebody may get killed — most likely the racist white men who operated the ferry.

Caleb and Samuel knew that they could easily overtake the white men and commandeer the ferry for a safe crossing for them all. But they did not want to get a reputation for fighting with white men — especially not while they were being guided by Native Americans. As already evidenced on their journey, the Shoshone men were fighting unfair stereotypes — Caleb and Samuel didn't want to add fuel to that fire. So, they hatched a most ingenious scheme. They took over the lead and told Shining Otter and Little Bearcat to move to the back of the pack train. There, several of the boys carefully disguised Shining Otter and Little Bearcat as freshly-killed mule deer. They first wrapped the braves up in the deer hides they used for curing meat. Then, they carefully tied mule deer antlers to their heads and slung their guides sideways across the backs of the last two horses.

When Caleb and Samuel rode to the back of the line to inspect the group's handiwork, they were most impressed. It was nearly impossible to tell that the two Shoshone braves were anything except freshly-killed venison. Now it was up to Shining Otter and Little Bearcat to remain perfectly still throughout the river crossing — something that would be easy for two men who had been taught how to always move stealthily since the first days they could walk.

With everything now set, the thin line of Shoshone horses descended down toward the cottonwood-willow river bottom where the ferry was moored. When they were within fifty paces, one of the white men shouted out, "Well howdy there, boys. I hope you h'ain't had no Injun troubles. Them heathens can be downright nasty around these here parts."

Stifling an urge to pull out his rifle and just shoot these racist curs where they stood, Caleb just smiled and replied, "No siree, I reckon we've been pretty lucky so far!"

"Where you boys traveling to?" the first white man asked. He was standing in the prow of the ferryboat with the mooring line in his hand and a big fat stogie smoldering in his mouth. He was a tall, heavyset man—weighing more than three hundred pounds — with a round moon-face, framed by thick, graying sideburns and a bushy beard that ended in a long-tangled mess that looked like an unkempt coon's tail. He was wearing coveralls that no doubt hid an assortment of weapons — most likely a set of pistols and a knife or two.

His sidekick was the opposite in just about every way. He was short and thin as a rail, with a long-angular face that was shaved as close and smooth as a peach skin. He had a haughty expression and was leaning on a Sharp's rifle that he was holding in his left hand.

Caleb immediately hated both men intensely, but he kept his anger in check by telling himself that they were just necessary evils for the continuation of their journey. He knew the river was flowing far too deep and fast to be crossed on horseback.

"How much you boys gonna charge us for taking us across to the other side?" Caleb asked the big man. But the skinny fellow answered first, "Oh, we got a special rate going on today. Just for you boys, it'll be ten bucks apiece."

Caleb could no longer contain his anger. "Why that's just plain old highway robbery!" he bellowed in reply.

"Well, you can take it, or you can leave it and just turn yourselves around and go back where you come from," replied the skinny man. "Or we might just could make you a cheaper deal, if you was to throw in two of your horses — plus them two deer you got trussed up on 'em."

Now Caleb knew he was really in a fix. How could he get out of this without killing the two men and then using their ferry to get safely across the river?

Thinking back to their recent evening spent with the trappers, a solution suddenly came to Caleb, and he summoned Samuel over to tell him about his plan. Figuring these two river men were far from the sharpest knives in the drawer, he told Samuel that they should tell them that they could have the horses and the deer after they all were safely on the other side of the river. It would be risky, but — if they could make Shining Otter and Little Bearcat understand what to do — it just might work.

Even if it didn't work, they could just capture the river men and truss them up. Then they could all ride away before the bigoted morons could get themselves loose.

Caleb and Samuel told some of the other boys to keep the river men occupied with questions about the best places to find game. Meanwhile, they sauntered slowly back to the horses bearing Shining Otter and Little Bearcat.

Several minutes later, Caleb and Samuel walked back to the circle of boys surrounding the river men, and announced that they were now all ready to proceed with the river crossing. It took a total of four trips, but — about an hour later — all of the boys plus the horses bearing Shining Otter and Little Bearcat were safely on the southwestern side of the river.

Now it was time for the fun. First Caleb led the horses bearing Shining Otter and Little Bearcat over to where the river men were standing. Then he said to them, "You men should know that these two horses have been acting very strange ever since we tied these mule deer carcasses to their backs. At night, they let out high-pitched squeals that aren't like anything I've ever heard coming out of a horse before. It's almost like they're possessed by demons or something".

As soon as words 'possessed by demons' left Caleb's mouth, Shining Bull and Little Bearcat sat bolt upright under their deer hides and — with their racks of antlers pointed straight ahead — kicked their mounts in the sides so that they reared straight up in front of the two small-minded river men. The last the boys saw of the ferry operators, they were high-tailing it back through the cottonwood-willow flats, running in the other direction as fast as they could go.

Just as quickly, Shining Otter, Little Bearcat, and the twenty-four boys turned their horses westward and galloped away in a cloud of dust. As they rode off laughing and hollering, Caleb turned to Samuel and yelled, "Well, I guess we really owe that bunch of trappers we met a huge 'thank you' now. If we run into them at Fort Robidoux, we'll buy them a round of drinks!"

Fort Robidoux Arrival

After crossing the Yampa River, Shining Otter and Little Bearcat led the group south through pinon-juniper dotted mesas, bluffs, and gulches. While the undulating landscape supported little in the way of green vegetation, it still sheltered an abundance of game animals.

Since the impact of white pioneers was still fairly minimal in this remote location, the top carnivores — including mountain lions, gray wolves, and grizzly bears — were also still present. In fact, the boys were actually quite privileged to be passing through intact, complex ecosystems of the American West — something that, within fifty years, would be a thing of the past.

Three days later, the intrepid train of young adventurers finally arrived at the gates of the Fort Robidoux Trading Post. The arrival at the trading post was bittersweet for Caleb, Samuel, and the other boys. They were — of course — ecstatic to have finally made it to one of their primary westward destinations. But they also knew this would be the final parting with their Shoshone guides who were now their highly trusted friends.

On their first night at the trading post, the boys sat in the saloon feting Shining Otter and Little Bearcat — buying them round after round of drinks until the braves passed out. They then carried their heroic guides up to their second-floor rooms, and tucked them into wonderfully soft feather beds for a long night of much-needed rest. The next morning, the boys served Shining Otter and Little Bearcat a full breakfast in bed, which embarrassed the proud braves to no end.

After regaining their dignity, Shining Otter and Little Bearcat reined twenty-two of the horses into a long pack train loaded with provisions for the return trip to their village. Then — in a wonderfully kind gesture — the Shoshone braves gave Caleb and Samuel the horses they had ridden on the journey to Fort Robidoux. The braves explained that this was their gift of good wishes and best fortune to all of the boys — helping them start their new travels from Fort Robidoux to their 'Promised Land' destinations. Overwhelmed by this gesture of kindness, the lads gave Little Bearcat and Shining Otter a final farewell gesture by forming a human corral for them to move through on their way out of the gates of the trading post.

As they watched Shining Otter and Little Bearcat ride away until they were no longer visible in the rising heat waves of the late spring afternoon, the boys realized that they were truly back on their own. Because of this, there were now many critical decisions that had to be made.

The Group Splits

Caleb and Samuel asked the boys to all meet that night after dinner in the saloon of the trading post to discuss future plans. When the group was all assembled, Caleb walked to the front and asked for a show of hands: who wanted to stay and seek their fortunes in and around Fort Robidoux and who wanted to continue on to the California Territory?

Eight of the boys — including Samuel and Ethan — voted to end their arduous journeys and stay in the Fort Robidoux area. They were anxious to start putting down roots and raising families. The other sixteen boys — with Caleb as their leader — voted to hit the trail again as soon as they had the financial wherewithal to buy new horses and the necessary gear they needed to proceed.

The population of the trading post was growing by leaps and bounds, with tens and sometimes hundreds of new westward-bound travelers arriving each month. The arrival of so many new folks meant that the demand for jobs was everywhere. Since all twenty-four of the boys had a myriad of skills to offer, within a few days each of them had several job offers from which to choose.

The difference was this; the sixteen boys who were continuing westward with Caleb took short-term jobs — like blacksmiths, store clerks, barkeeps, cooks, and street laborers — which didn't require any long-term contracts or commitments. Meanwhile, the other eight boys — who had chosen to stay in the area — were only interested in permanent jobs. So, they rented horses and made their way out to the ranches scattered around Fort Robidoux. The job offers they had there — like wrangling horses and branding cattle — would, hopefully, lead to setting up their own spreads with the families that hired them. Meanwhile — under Caleb's direction — all twenty-four of the boys agreed to meet every Wednesday night in the trading post's saloon to report on how things were going.

Not surprisingly given their friendly nature and prairie work ethic, the eight boys — including Samuel — who had started working at neighboring ranches all reported very positive results. Most said they already 'felt like a member of the family' within just a few weeks. Many even hinted at budding romances — involving young ladies who were the daughters, nieces, and cousins of the ranch owners.

Meanwhile in town, things were also going quite well. Caleb was riding herd over the boys to make sure they put as much money aside as they could each week. He wanted to get everyone ready and able to get back on the westward trail as soon as possible.

There was still much treacherous country — desolate sandstone canyons, seemingly-endless deserts, and soaring mountain passes — to pass through before they reached the goldfields of the California Territory. From everything they had heard from other travelers in and around Fort Robidoux, the boys knew that their ultimate destination was a sleepy Spanish village named Yerba Buena that — within just a few wild and crazy months — would become the burgeoning 'gold rush' boomtown of San Francisco.

Caleb wanted to leave during the middle of the summer so they could complete their journey before the onset of the snows of late September and early October. The last thing he wanted was to be trapped in another blizzard and risk losing everything again. Plus, he knew full well that the High Sierra Mountains — which they would have to cross soon after they entered the California Territory — posed the greatest travel challenge of all.

Over the next few weeks, the sixteen westward-heading boys in the trading post all applied extra 'elbow grease' to their jobs. In fact, most of them either worked double shifts or two jobs. During the last weekly meeting in June, Caleb talked to all of them privately and was satisfied that they would each have enough money to buy a horse — plus the necessary provisions — by the second week in July. In Caleb's mind, this was the perfect departure date.

The plan was for each boy to pack enough gear and provisions for his own needs. They would all again augment their food supplies by hunting and fishing as they traveled.

Caleb also reported that he had worked out a deal to buy four covered wagons with one to serve as a cook wagon. The other three would transport hardware like picks and shovels — plus emergency gear — that they might need during their travels.

To replace Samuel and his leadership skills, Caleb selected Joshua Hill — the oldest boy who would be continuing on to California. Joshua had most of the same leadership skills that Samuel possessed, plus his maturity level had shown remarkable growth throughout their rigorous journey to Fort Robidoux. So much so that Caleb had no qualms whatsoever about turning the position of deputy leader over to him. In fact, when he announced his choice during their weekly meeting, all of the other boys stood up, turned toward Joshua, and gave him a rousing round of applause.

In closing the meeting, Caleb announced that he, Joshua, and the fourteen other California-bound boys would be leaving the trading post bright and early on the morning of July 15th, 1848. The setting of an actual departure date made the California group even more enthusiastic about getting everything ready before they left.

The boys all wanted to set aside enough funds to give themselves extra spending money at the pioneering outposts they might encounter along the way. They were so dedicated to their jobs, in fact, that many of the townsfolk in the trading post asked Caleb if they did anything else but work. Many single young women seemed especially chagrined that they could never find any of the hearty lads just hanging around when they weren't working.

BOOK NINE
California Here We Come

Canyonland Wonders

The morning of July 15th, 1848, was overcast, cold, and rainy — a very unusual occurrence for the semi-arid, summer climate of northeastern Utah. Because of this, Caleb Adams and Joshua Hill had a more difficult time than normal rousting the boys out of their warm bedrolls in the trading post's bunkroom. But as soon as they had downed a hot breakfast and a couple of cups of coffee in the saloon's mess hall, they were all raring to go.

The group said their final good-byes to their employers, co-workers, and various friends they had made during their stay at Fort Robidoux. Caleb hugged Ethan so long and hard that he almost smothered him. Caleb only released Ethan after his younger brother promised to come join him, once he was settled in the California Territory.

Their final departure — through the trading post's front gate — was punctuated by a lot of 'yippees' and 'hoorays'. They were finally on their way to the long-dreamed about gold fields of the great California Territory. Preceding Horace Greeley's now well-known slogan of 'Go West, Young Man' by a few years, the boys' adopted new mantra of 'Westward Ho, We Go' now burned deeply within their collective hearts and minds.

Two days after leaving Fort Robidoux, the group found themselves riding through some incredibly beautiful country that was beyond their wildest imaginations. The landscape was all slickrock sandstone that had been hand-painted by Mother Nature in just about every pastel hue imaginable. Everywhere they looked, they saw convoluted rock formations of every size and shape — including arches, bridges, and windows. Far below the trail, rivers sliced and sluiced their way through the sandstone, carving deep majestic canyons linked by spectacular waterfalls.

Whenever they stopped for a break, the boys talked about how they did not understand how this country could ever be settled and put to any productive use by men. They had no way of knowing — of course — that their assumptions were entirely accurate, and that less than one hundred years after their journey, ninety-five percent of the present State of Utah would still be virtually untouched and permanently protected as national parks, federal forests, and open rangeland.

As they rode along during the daylight, the bright sun in the cloudless sky parched and dried their skin to a leathery texture. But as soon as the sun went down, the air chilled almost immediately and the lads were glad to have several blankets to keep them warm under the brilliantly black, star-filled skies of this 'canyon country' landscape.

On the days when they stopped early to hunt some fresh meat for dinner, some of the group spent time poking around this beautifully inhospitable terrain. When they did, they never failed to find many things that amazed them — sights they had no idea even existed on the face of God's green earth.

For one thing, they found that what appeared — at first glance — to be just barren land, actually supported an impressive assortment of very strange-looking plants. For the most part, the plants appeared to be hiding from the intense heat of the sun. The boys always found them tucked away in some sort of shade — either under a rocky overhang or in small drainageways notched into the sandstone slabs by thousands of years of trickling water.

Close examination of these canyon plants told the young men about the harshness of the climate in this part of the world. The plants had very leathery exteriors and thin, sharp needles instead of leaves. Many also had very fleshy appendages that oozed freshwater when the boys broke them off and squeezed them. The lads quickly realized that this was how the plants had enough water to last them through prolonged dry periods. The fleshy nodules soaked up water when it rained, then stored it for the plant's use when it didn't rain for weeks — even months — at a time. It was as if the plants were taking water along with them for the ride — just as the boys did with their canteens.

Also amusing to the group, were the number of slinky little lizards they always saw skittering about during the cool, 'crepuscular' hours just before sunrise and right after sunset. But they were especially intrigued by the frightening creatures they often found in their bedrolls at night.

These odd beasts looked a lot like the crawdads they caught with regularity in the creeks back home when they were just youngsters. But these critters had one big very painful difference from crawdads. Their hind ends turned upward into venomous stingers — which as a few of the boys unfortunately experienced — gave out painful lashes when the animals were disturbed. While not deadly, the boys' scorpion bites turned bright red and welled up to the size of a grapefruit. Plus, they hurt like the devil until the swelling subsided a few days later.

The young travelers did have one unfortunate run-in with a venomous denizen of the high canyon country — the sidewinder rattlesnake. They were following a dry gulch one morning when a pocket of red sand literally came to life directly under the hooves of Joshua's horse.

Joshua had just moved into place at the head of the pack train — relieving Caleb who had moved to the rear. Through no fault of the snake — it was just trying to avoid being stepped on and crushed to death by the horse's hooves — the sidewinder suddenly raised up and sunk both of its fangs into the horse's right foreleg, just below the kneecap.

The horse immediately reared straight up so violently that it tossed Joshua backwards twenty-five feet so that his backside became fully impaled on the thick, three-inch long spines of a large cholla cactus. Once the boys realized that Joshua wasn't seriously hurt, they started laughing uncontrollably. It was difficult to tell who was making the most noise, Joshua writhing in pain and screaming at the top of his lungs or his horse whinnying in sheer terror.

Fortunately, the snake's fangs only gave Joshua's horse a glancing blow, and the animal survived. As did Joshua — although it was a very painful process. He spent the next three days standing whenever he could and — every so often — pulling another one of the cholla's spines out of his backside. For the rest of the westward trek, Joshua was careful never to get within six feet of any sort of cactus — erroneously fearing that the puffy plants might actually throw their spines into his still quite fragile behind.

Welcome to the Salt Lake Valley

Now traveling steadily westward, the group made good time as they passed through even more of the Utah Territory's spectacular but desolate canyon country. They eased through the last leg of their journey by picking up a wagon train spur road in the Salt Lake Valley that would lead them directly onto the California Trail.

After a week of hard riding with few breaks, Caleb and Joshua decided to give the boys a day of rest and relaxation in one of the valley's frontier outposts that offered bunkhouse lodging and sun-heated showers. While the boys cooled their heels and washed the dust off their bodies, Caleb visited the local surveyor's office and purchased some rudimentary mapping that was now available for the trails that headed west. He wanted to present the different travel options to his group and find a consensus mix of interesting landscapes coupled with judicious passage.

Caleb asked his charges to meet him in the local rough-hewn saloon where he showed them the maps he just bought. When the boys first looked at the brown parchment drawings with neatly blue-etched topographic lines, their eyes were immediately drawn to the gigantic body of water located to the northwest of where they now sat.

Jacob Lester was the first to speak up, "Wow, would ya look at that lake. That's almost as big as a dadgum ocean — yet it's right here smack in the middle of all these mountains!"

"Yeah", added Taylor Jenkins, "where in God's sweet world did that much water come from with all this desert that's around us?"

All the other boys chimed in with similar comments, and Caleb and Joshua had to admit that they didn't really have a good answer for their questions.

"So, I guess that settles it", concluded Caleb, "we're going to head out tomorrow toward that lake and find out what in the heck is going on. Maybe we can even get in some good fishing, before we head out on the trail again!" With that, the group swigged down the last of their beers and sauntered back to the bunkhouse to get a good night's sleep and an early start in the morning.

The next day, traveling northwest through barren terrain that can best be described as oppressively hot and mind-numbingly boring — the little wagon train reached the eastern shore of the Great Salt Lake around four o'clock in the afternoon. Eager — almost desperate — to cool their burnt bodies and assuage their parched throats with fresh cool water, the boys bolted from their horses and started stripping down to their skivvies while running pell-mell toward the water.

Being the fleetest of foot, Josiah Sumner was the first one to reach the lake's edge. Without hesitating, he bounced across the shallows like a skipping stone until he was immersed up to his waist. He then flung himself head-long down into the gently rippling waters.

As soon as he submerged, Josiah roared straight back up into the sky as if shot out of a cannon. Sputtering and stammering, he shouted at the top of his lungs, "Jesus Pete, there's something terribly wrong with this water. It's thick as molasses and tastes like donkey dung!" Watching Josiah's violent reaction, the other boys immediately stopped running into the water.

A few of them reached down, cupped a handful of liquid, and held it up to their lips. "Josiah's right", shouted Thackery Thomas, "this water is just plumb putrid. It tastes just like the toe of a dirty old sock smells!"

"Yeah, plus it's all hot and sticky — kinda like soup broth," added Rhett Baumgardner. "It doesn't cool you off at all. It just makes you even hotter — maybe we shouldn't even be in it!"

Eager to solve the mystery of the lake water and ease the lads' minds, Caleb stripped off his dungarees and shirt. He walked out into the lake up to his waist, dipped a finger into the water, and took a taste.

Then — to the amazement of the boys who were watching his every move — Caleb suddenly flung himself backward and spread-eagled flat onto the surface of the water. And there he stayed, with his head, arms, torso, and legs only partially submerged — splashing around and laughing out loud like he'd gone stark-raving mad.

Convinced that the strange water had somehow made Caleb lose his mind, the group began wading toward him in unison figuring they now had to save him. As soon as they were about ten feet away, Caleb sprang back up to his feet with his arms raised over his head like some long-lost spirit rising from a grave.

This so startled the boys that they wheeled around backward and tried to run away through the water. Several lost their balance and pitched head-first into the lake, screaming like banshees as they went down below the surface.

Sporting a smile as wide as the prairie sky, Caleb hooted at his charges and applauded as they stumbled and bumbled their way through the shallows. "Hey now, you boys are the ones acting just plain crazy. There isn't anything really dangerous about this water — it's just salty as all get out. Try plopping yourselves down into it and you'll see what I mean."

One-by-one, the boys screwed up their courage and flung themselves backward into the water just like Caleb had done. To their amazement, they all floated perfectly — like corks in a bathtub. Even the boys who couldn't swim — and were afraid of going in more than waist-deep — were all thrashing about and splashing each other like children playing in a schoolyard pond.

After they had spent all their pent-up energy in this strange liquid playground, the boys floated lazily and talked about what to do with the rest of the afternoon — since it was now too late to get back on the trail before dark. "Well, there for sure can't be any kind of fish living in this water," mused Josh McCown, "so I guess fishing is out!"

Staring off into the distance across the shimmering water, Jedediah Johnson suddenly bolted upright shouting, "Whoa now, would ya look at all those ducks — must be pert close to a thousand of 'em!"

Turning in unison toward where Jedediah was wildly waving his index finger, the boys all saw a flock of fast wing-beating birds swooping low across the path of the late afternoon sun. The flock was so dense that it practically blocked out the sun's rays — like some sort of avian eclipse.

"Well, there's our answer about what to do next", shouted Horatio Cornbluth, "let's grab our rifles and go shoot us some fresh duck meat for supper!"

The birds had no reason to fear the boys since most of them had never before faced white men with powerful rifles that could blast them

THE GREAT SALT LAKE — A MAJOR BIRD REFUGE

Even though its salinity is typically more than five times greater than sea water, Utah's Great Salt Lake has always provided a critical oasis for millions of migratory birds — including hundreds of thousands of shorebirds, wading birds, and — most notably — ducks and geese. While exploring some of the wetlands and shorelines of the Great Salt Lake in 1843, John C. Fremont wrote that the waterfowl were so abundant that they made a noise like thunder when they flew.

Today — even though its habitat quantity and quality have been significantly diminished since Fremont's day — the Great Salt Lake is one of the most important birding hotspots in the Intermountain West. More than thirty species of waterfowl — numbering between three to four million birds — annually use the lake's extensive and diverse bordering wetland ecosystems for migration stopovers and nesting. The lake's watery habitat complexes are especially critical for western populations of green-winged and cinnamon teal, northern pintails, gadwalls, eared grebes, mallards, ruddy ducks, redhead ducks, common goldeneyes, Canada geese, white pelicans, and tundra swans.

A variety of local state and federal waterfowl refuges — most notably the federal Bear River Migratory Bird Refuge and the state's Farmington Bay Waterfowl Management Area — preserve valuable habitat for two to five million shorebirds and wading birds. Wilson's and red-necked phalaropes, American avocets, black-necked stilts, marbled godwits, western sandpipers, long-billed dowitchers, and snowy plovers are among the more common species that visit the lake's wetland preserves on an annual basis.

The birds are attracted to these refuges by abundant food resources, including a combination of macroinvertebrates — most notably billions of brine shrimp and flies. Because of its importance to migratory birds, the Great Salt Lake and its surrounding wetlands were designated as part of the Western Hemisphere Shorebird Reserve Network in 1992.

out of the air. So, as the eagle-eyed group of boys blasted away, the ducks rained down from the skies.

Within two hours of running out of the water, dressing, and grabbing their rifles, the lads had killed some two hundred waterfowl of all different sizes and feather colors. It was quite literally as easy as 'shooting fish in a barrel'.

The freshly killed ducks provided the boys with multiple benefits.

First, they tasted fantastic grilled to a toasty brown over that night's campfire. Next, the leftover bones and flesh were simmered overnight into a sumptuous broth for the next few meals along the trail. Finally, the rest of the ducks were plucked, washed, and then packed in salt — which the group was delighted to find in abundance along the vast lake's shoreline.

With bellies full of duck meat and muscles tired from swimming — actually more like groping through the Great Salt Lake's viscous water — the boys slept very soundly. In fact, Caleb and Joshua had an especially difficult time rousting them the next morning. The two leaders treated their charges' groaning and moaning with insistence and gentle humor until everyone was all packed and settled in on their mounts.

Caleb and Joshua were quite anxious to get their troops back on the trail. They knew from studying their rudimentary mapping — plus talking with other westward travelers — that the way west from here on would be especially arduous and fraught with danger.

Crossing the Great Basin Plateau

The Great Basin terrain of northern Nevada is as close as you can get to a moonscape on earth. The greasewood-sagebrush-saltbush flats stretch out for seemingly endless miles. Shimmering heat waves rise up above the bare, sun-parched ground.

Treeless mountains are stacked high on all sides — like piles of dirt, haphazardly placed by a drunken giant wielding a colossal shovel. Viewing this, it's easy to understand why so many people stranded in this arid environment began to hallucinate about oases on the horizon. To the thirst-addled brain, the desert heat waves look exactly like the rippling waters of a cool refreshing lake.

Crossing this desolate terrain on horseback along a rudimentary wagon trail meant passing through wide playas, meandering arroyos, and shallow canyons fraught with perils — both wild and human. This is what the group faced as they made their way westward toward the border of the California Territory and the looming Sierra Nevada Mountains.

Caleb and Joshua both knew all too well that if they ran into trouble, they would be totally on their own. From this point until they reached the western side of the mountains, there were no outposts to run to for shelter. There were also no sheriffs — or even civilian posses — that could be summoned for help.

If they encountered any hostile parties, they would have to either fight or talk their way through. This meant that they could die with their bodies left to rot in the desert heat, or be eaten at night by scavenging animals. While the dangers were many, Caleb and Joshua firmly believed that the potential rewards outweighed the risks.

The sparse desert vegetation still supported scattered populations of meaty animals like mule deer, elk, and bighorn sheep. But the canyons and arroyos provided dusty hide-outs for skulking alpha predators — most notably, mountain lions, grizzly bears, and wolves. These carnivores could quickly dispatch unsuspecting horses tied off at their overnight hitching posts.

The three primary Native American tribes of the Great Basin — the Paiute, the Shoshone, and the Washoe — all lived peacefully and often shared common boundaries. Owing to the extremely dry climate of the desert terrain, these tribes were — of necessity — very nomadic, often freely intermingling with each other.

They were predominantly hunter-gatherers, and moved frequently during the year to take advantage of seasonal vegetative growth patterns and movement of wildlife herds. They had no permanent settlements — although winter encampments were often used again and again.

Despite their concerns about predatory animals and human bandits, the group's journey through the Great Basin was — while arduous — essentially uneventful. The California Trail that they were now on, followed a series of small streams until it met the Humboldt River near the present-day town of Wells, Nevada.

Following the Humboldt and Truckee Rivers

Reuben Cole Shaw once described the Humboldt River as 'not good for man nor beast... there is not enough timber in three hundred miles of its desolate valley to make a snuff-box, or sufficient vegetation along its banks to shade a rabbit, while its waters contain enough alkali to make soap for a nation.'

During the first part of their journey along the Humboldt's wildly meandering valley, the river provided the young adventurers with welcome access to much-needed water, grass, and wood. But — as they made their way further westward — the river's flow became increasingly alkaline, meaning that the flood zones supported less and less vegetation until there was no wood available at all for firewood. The lads were often forced to make do with sparse dried grasses and broken 'tumbleweed' brush.

Under such extremely difficult traveling conditions, the boys' patience and nerves became quite strained. Problems of internal strife became increasingly common. Nightfall invariably brought fisticuffs or wrestling matches sparked by continuous bickering or mean-tempered chiding all day long under the unforgiving blast furnace-like sun.

Caleb and Joshua didn't pay any serious attention to these flare-ups. They realized that they actually served useful purposes by letting their young charges blow off their pent-up anger about the unpleasant travel conditions.

In fact, at the conclusion of just about every battle around the campfire, the combatants shook hands — no matter who won — and shared a hearty laugh about the petty issues that caused the fight in the first place. The next morning — after everyone had finished breakfast and saddled up — it was always as if nothing untoward had happened the night before.

In reality, the only really good thing about following the California Trail along the Humboldt River was that it was the easiest way west —

passing through repeated gaps in north-south trending mountain chains. The old adage about 'water always seeking and finding the path of least resistance' was certainly serving the boys well along this leg of their journey.

In less than a week's time, the group's wagon train arrived at the burgeoning frontier outpost known as Lakeville. Knowing that the looming Sierra Nevada Mountains posed the most formidable obstacle yet to their westward push, Caleb and Joshua decided to give the boys a few days off.

Lakeville was founded when an enterprising young fellow named Charlie Lake decided to build a log toll bridge across the Humboldt River. In doing so, Lake provided a direct connection between the California Trail and the scattered gold-mining hotspots of the far western Nevada Territory.

Almost overnight, Lakeville became a full-blown gold-seeker's paradise — featuring an array of traveler's services. The town included a gristmill, livery stable, kiln, hotel, and grub hall. Plus — just like any boomtown during the early days of the 'Wild West' — Lakeville was also full of gambling casinos and bustling brothels that had few restrictions on human behavior.

A TYPICAL BOOMTOWM

While fictitious, Lakeville is based on the real boomtown named Lake's Crossing which was founded in 1859 and became Reno, Nevada.

The town was exactly what Joshua and Caleb felt the boys needed; a place where they could rip-and-roar to their hearts' content. They trusted their troop to make good decisions, and knew that healthy doses of flowing testosterone on the trail were always good. They served to spur male egos to prove they could conquer any hardships on the way to achieving their ultimate goals — self-made fortunes in the California gold fields that now lay just a few weeks ahead.

But Caleb and Joshua were also cautiously aware that too much vim and vigor could prove harmful to the critical cooperative functioning of the traveling group as a whole. As they rode into Lakeville on a sunny but brisk afternoon on October fifteenth, 1848, Caleb and Joshua strongly believed that this tipping point was close at hand and — because accordingly — a good testosterone release was exactly what the doctor ordered.

During the next three days, Caleb and Joshua let the boys run wild, with all the group adhering to a policy of 'Don't ask, don't tell!' The leaders just hoped that the group would have enough common sense to avoid the dangers that abounded in this wild-and-wooly setting. These threats included venereal diseases — that the village's 'ladies-of-the-night' might have — and getting thrown into the local hoosegow for public drunkenness, or picking fights with the local sheepherders who often came to town from the surrounding mountains to pick up supplies.

While the boys alternately rested and partied, they were lucky — or unlucky, depending on your point of view — to experience the beginning of the annual end-of-season, 'High Sierra Rendezvous'. This event typically lasted a few weeks and was known to be joyous and lively fun.

Everyone was welcome to either join in or just watch the games and festivities. Participants always included local ranchers and farmers, trappers plus the assorted mountain men they might drag along with them, local Native Americans, and California Trail travelers.

After three days of Rendezvous revelry, Joshua and Caleb sensed that all the boys were chomping at the bit to get back on the trail and pursue their individual dreams of untold riches awaiting them in the California goldfields. On the fourth morning, they all arose early and splashed the cobwebs out of their brains with ice-cold water from the river that ran through the town.

Hunkering down over local surveyor maps in the beer hall for most of the previous day, Joshua and Caleb had decided that their best bet for crossing the Sierra Nevada Mountains was the Carson Route. While this was not the shortest way across the looming mountain fortress, it was the most traveled and therefore the safest.

Considering they were venturing forth just as cold weather was beginning to settle in, the Carson Route also made the most sense. While still extremely rugged, this trail entered California smack in the middle of the central goldfields — a fact that Joshua and Caleb knew would delight all the boys. But as it turned out, only eight of the boys in Caleb and Joshua's pack train were counted among the group that made it across the High Sierras.

The story of what happened to the other six boys is a sad tale indeed.

Ascending the High Sierras

As soon as they began their ascent up the Carson Route — which was steeply-hewn out of the granite monoliths that comprised the east-facing slopes of the foothills — the boys were smitten by the awesome ruggedness and unyielding beauty of the Sierra Nevada peaks that towered overhead. Even during their crossing of the Rocky Mountains, they had never seen a mountain range lying so deeply chiseled and formidable across the landscape. In their minds, there was no doubt that they were entering the true 'Hall of the Mountain King'.

After a week of relatively balmy weather and uneventful riding, the sky to the west suddenly turned frightfully dark and foreboding early one afternoon. In less than thirty minutes, the air temperature had plummeted at least thirty degrees as Joshua figured it, and the wind had increased from calm to gale force just as quickly.

Sensing a fierce blizzard was about to overtake them, Caleb and Joshua signaled their troops to tether the wagons and horses and make camp for the night. As he talked, Caleb made a sweeping motion toward a small clearing on a narrow plateau that lay between steep granite escarpments.

In less time than the boys could tie up their horses and pitch their tents, the full force of the weather closed in. The snow came barreling down on them from the west, driven sideways so thick and strong that none of them could even stand against it. After they had all scurried for cover inside their tents, it was all they could do to hold onto the rope tethers for dear life to prevent the heavy canvas shrouds from ripping loose and blowing off down the mountainside like so many pieces of tissue paper.

Anyone who has spent a winter in the High Sierra Mountains can testify to the ferocity and intensity of its blizzards. The young adventurers were again about to be trapped by another snowstorm of biblical proportions.

For the next two days, the group remained hunkered down in their tents. They emerged only sporadically to attend to human necessities, warm up around the central campfire, and carry out their appointed tasks.

These included, gathering firewood to keep the fire going, tending to their horses, and shoveling snow from around the sides and off the tops of the tents. By the morning of the third day, the snowfall had slowed to light flurries. The snow depth had reached more than three feet on the level where it wasn't wind-blown. In areas where the snow had drifted up against rocky outcrops, it was more than ten feet deep.

Calamity Strikes at Timberline

The lads emerged from their tents showing symptoms of severe restlessness and nausea — sure signs that they were suffering from the high mountain malady known as 'altitude sickness'. Through chattering teeth and dripping hot coffee, they talked about a plan for getting back on the trail as soon as possible.

They also agreed that seven of the boys would form a hunting party to restock the stores of provisions consumed during the blizzard. Meanwhile, the other seven would stay back and dig out the supplies as directed by Caleb and Joshua.

Joshua suggested that it was Wilson Brock's turn to be in charge of a hunting group. Within an hour, the hunting party was off plowing through the deep snow on their steeds, with Wilson on the lead horse. Little did they know — at the time — that the designation of this headstrong young man as group leader would soon spell their doom.

After two hours of plowing at an up-slope angle through snow almost as deep as the bellies of their horses, the hunting party emerged from the tree line just below a wind-blown-ridge crest. Suddenly, Wilson stopped and began animatedly pointing at the ground below his feet. The other boys quickly circled around to see what he had found.

"Just look at those tracks", Wilson exclaimed, "we got us something really big and it's a whole family of 'em. Plus, they must have just come right through here!"

The other boys stared down at the fresh tracks and then looked around at each other in bewilderment. The lead two sets of tracks were quite large — about six inches across — while the following three sets of tracks were less than half that size. Whistling softly under his breath, Travis Jackson recognized the tracks instantly from the many times he had hunted deer and elk with his father along the river breaks near his prairie home. The rounded tracks had five toes, but the claw marks were not visible in the fresh snow — a fact that set these tracks apart from the typical canine tracks of a wolf or coyote. Travis knew that wild felines always withdrew their claws when they walked. Based on their size, these had to be the tracks of cougars or — as they were more commonly called, here in the west — mountain lions.

As soon as Travis said, "These are mountain lion tracks", Wilson unflinchingly retorted, "Well, big cats should eat just about as good as anything else we might find up here. I say we just keep on following them!"

While some of the other boys must have felt keenly uncertain about Wilson's decision, they didn't express it. They realized that they desperately needed meat of some kind if they were to successfully continue their daunting journey up, over, and through the High Sierras. Their unplanned blizzard stop had severely depleted their food supplies and they certainly had not seen any signs of traditional game animals moving around in the deep snow. With Wilson in the lead, the other six boys followed the lions' tracks up and over the ridgeline and then down along the leeward slope where the snow — due to windward side drifting — was barely more than a foot deep.

Travis wasn't sure what these lions were hunting, but he figured it had to be something that made its living among the high mountain peaks. He did remember one of his uncles from back home — who had traveled out west — telling stories about often seeing wild sheep and goats feeding up high above timberline. Maybe that was what these lions were pursuing. Whatever the case, Travis felt sure they had to be really hungry and were looking for anything that would provide fresh meat for their young.

The mountain lion tracks kept gradually moving lower and lower — west of the ridgeline — before entering a copse of spindly aspen trees growing amid a sprawl of granite boulders. Here the lion tracks became dispersed in all directions but didn't exit the sheltering tree stand.

"OK boys," shouted Wilson, "we've got 'em cornered. They've got to be in here somewhere! Let's dismount and find 'em."

Once again, if the other boys had any trepidation about dismounting — smack in the domain of a family of hungry mountain lions — nobody brought it up. They all dismounted, tethered their horses to nearby trees, grabbed their rifles, and started poking in and around the scattered boulders.

Suddenly, a piercing human scream shot up from behind one of the boulders and reverberated through the aspen grove. Travis Jackson and Luke Waller — the two boys nearest the source of the scream — scrambled behind the boulder and saw a sight that made them both freeze in horror. Sam Evers was sprawled face first in the snow with an adult mountain lion perched on his back, biting and ripping at his shoulders and neck.

Based on the blood that was flying everywhere and splattering across the snow, Travis and Luke knew that Sam was already severely injured. In the next instant, Travis raised his rifle and knocked the mountain lion off Sam's back with a single shot to its mid-section. He quickly reloaded and fired again, dispatching the still-quivering big cat with a shot to the head.

Rushing to Sam's side, Travis and Luke soon understood what had happened. Sam must have stumbled onto the entrance to the lions' den under the edge of a boulder. He was probably poking around in the hole with his rifle, trying to flush the cats out, when the adult lion jumped on his back from a boulder above. Instinctively, Travis and Luke also understood that the big cat was not hunting Sam. She was just defending her young brood from a dangerous human intruder. No matter the intent of the attack, it was now clear that they needed to hightail it back to camp to save Sam, who was moaning in pain and bleeding profusely from both shoulders.

While Travis sat comforting Sam, Luke rode around to the front of the boulder to let Wilson know what had happened. As soon as Wilson saw how badly Sam was injured, he yelled for the other boys to immediately mount up. Since Sam was in no shape to hold his horse's reins, Wilson and Luke used ropes to tie Sam's arms and waist to the neck of his horse. With Luke riding alongside Sam and his horse, Wilson then shouted for everyone to hit the trail back towards camp.

Panicked over Sam's massive injuries, Wilson no longer showed any concern for the safety of their route in the fresh, heavy snow. He first led the boys out of the aspen grove directly parallel to the fall line of the slope. Next — realizing that they needed to cross the mountain ridge to get back to their campsite — Wilson turned his charges and led them directly up the slope. After crossing the ridge, Wilson's final mistake came in guiding the group straight down the fall line — into the heavy snow cornice that had piled up right under the eastern side of the ridge.

"C'mon boys, just pretend like you're out sledding and let your horses just glide you down through all this fluffy white stuff!" yelled Wilson. These were his last words and — so it seemed — the last words the other six boys behind him would hear in their short lives.

With a deafening crack, the entire snowy slab above the boys gave way and came crashing down on them like a solid-white tidal wave. Within seconds, all the boys and their horses were picked up and swept downhill, disappearing into a massive whirlpool of snow and ice.

The Rescue Party's Grim Findings

As the day turned to dusk and then to darkness back in camp, the snow began to fall in earnest again — picking up in intensity as the air temperature dropped dramatically. Standing in the driving snow beside the warmth of the campfire, Caleb and Joshua were beside themselves with worry.

They kept hoping that they would look up at any moment and see the group riding back into camp. But in their deepest fear of fears, they both knew that some tragedy had befallen their intrepid hunting party.

The real problem was — neither Caleb nor Joshua had any idea what to do about it. They knew it would be foolhardy to send out a search party at night in a driving snowstorm. Besides, they had no idea which way the boys had decided to travel, and the new snowfall obliterated any hope of following their tracks. But they also knew that if they waited until dawn, it would probably be too late to save the missing boys and their horses from the freezing cold temperatures.

Joshua and Caleb agreed that the only prudent course of action was to wait out the night until dawn and then organize a search party. They gathered the rest of their charges around them in the fire circle, and told them to pray for a miracle, beseeching God that somehow, some way the lost hunting party would suddenly come riding out of the all-encompassing snowy darkness into the glimmering light of the campfire. But such was not to be the case.

The night passed slowly and fitfully for everyone. Sleep was impossible with the burden of worrying about the fate of their friends. At first light, Caleb and Joshua divided the remaining boys into two search parties. They set tracks out of camp, both heading north — the direction the hunting party had taken when they left camp the previous day.

The plan was for the two parties to branch off about a mile out of camp. Caleb would swing off to the northwest — leading his boys up and over the ridge and then angling down along the western slope. Joshua's group would remain on the east side of the minor divide — staying high to avoid the cornices of wind-blown snow. If either party found anything, they would fire rifle shots into the air to signal the other party to join them immediately.

About two hours after leaving camp, Caleb waved his arm up-and-down off to the side of his horse. After the other boys had reined in their horses and stopped near a wind-whipped escarpment, Caleb turned on his mount and said, "I'm pretty sure I just heard the crack of rifle shots from over behind the ridge."

The other boys calmed their mounts from whinnying and cocked their ears intently in the direction Caleb was pointing. "There it is again," exclaimed Josh McCown, "there's no doubt about it — the other group has found something!" The rifle shots were now reverberating throughout the rock-strewn landscape.

Caleb quickly turned his mount due east, and led the rest of his boys back up and over the ridgeline. As soon as they crossed to the eastern slope, Caleb's party could now clearly hear the sharp whistles and shouts of the boys in Joshua's party. They were sitting on their horses just a few hundred yards away — strangely huddled beside a dense stand of spruce-fir forest.

As Caleb's party approached, Joshua's group fell forebodingly still and silent. Caleb now suspected that the news was not going to be good. As his boys approached Joshua's hushed group, they saw a sight that shook them all to the core. They quickly realized that the boys in Joshua's group were all in shock. A broad, tousled jumble of snow, ice, trees, and rocks, lay just below where they were all sitting on their mounts.

Caleb rode up next to Joshua and saw that he had been crying. "I think they're all gone, Caleb," said Joshua in a barely audible whisper. "This big slide must have caught them all off guard and carried them downhill — buried beneath tons of rock and snow. We found some of their gear scattered around, but there isn't any sign of life anywhere. I believe it's for certain that they're all up in heaven now with their Maker."

Understanding that nothing further could be done, the remaining boys all spread out and rode gingerly and silently through the avalanche zone — being extremely careful not to trigger any further activity. They picked up salvageable gear — a rifle here, a saddlebag there — all the while, hoping upon hope that they might hear signs of life from beneath the mountainside of jumbled white.

After they had finished scouring the area, several of the boys dismounted and fashioned rough crosses out of rope and evergreen branches. They then plunged the crosses deep into the snow near the bottom of the slide zone where they figured most of the bodies of their lost friends must have come to rest.

Then suddenly — just as they were queuing up for the solemn ride back to camp — Joshua raised his hand for silence. Instantaneously, the other boys let out a collective gasp. In unison, they all wheeled around to look behind them and slightly upslope — toward the source of a gentle scraping sound.

Given the context of their situation, what the lads saw next was beyond belief. Three human fingers were scratching on the snow slide's granular surface. Reacting as one, the boys bounded off their horses and clawed their way up the ten yards of slope that separated them from this miraculous sight.

A few minutes of furious digging revealed Travis Jackson — badly injured and barely breathing — but remarkably still alive. Reacting instinctively and applying their best survival skills, the group kept Travis prone while wrapping him in several sleeping blankets and fashioning a makeshift stretcher out of spruce boughs. They then connected the stretcher to Joshua's horse for the trip back down to camp.

Once they were safely ensconced back in camp, Caleb examined Travis thoroughly and was very relieved to find that — save for a severe concussion and a few spots of frostbite — he was in remarkably good shape. He didn't have any broken bones or internal injuries that would require a prolonged time to heal.

In fact, Caleb told Joshua that Travis only needed a couple of days of rest and then he would be all set to get back on the trail. This was — of course — a relief for the other boys, but they were still heartbroken over the loss of six of their fellow travelers in the avalanche. They took the next two days — while Travis recovered — to reflect, mourn, and pray around the camp.

BOOK TEN
At Last, the Promised Land

A Gold Rush Boom Town

Two full days after the tragedy — with heavy hearts, but now renewed enthusiasm — Caleb Adams and Joshua Hill led the eight remaining boys back onto the Carson Route. Since they were now short a horse, Travis Jackson shared rides with the other boys, switching mounts every few miles.

Thankfully, it had not snowed, and Caleb and Joshua knew they had to push onward — harder now than ever — to outpace the fast-closing winter. Their supplies were severely depleted and another snowstorm — anywhere near the intensity of the one they had just endured — would certainly doom them all.

In truth, Caleb and Joshua figured they had experienced their full share of bad luck, and things just had to get better. Fortunately, Mother Nature seemed to share this belief. While finding the going extremely arduous through the heavy snow, the boys were blessed with crisp but sunny weather. Though nothing could ever erase the memory of their lost comrades, the courageous group realized they were finally closing in on their destination. This renewed them with youthful enthusiasm.

During daily hunting parties, the boys always returned with saddlebags full of blue grouse, white-tailed ptarmigan, snowshoe hares, and yellow-bellied marmots. The deep snow made the game easy to find and track down, and — with ravenous relish — the young men ripped into the fresh meat that was grilled on spits over the nightly campfires.

After two arduous days of long descents mixed in with minor uphill slogs, the snowpacks on both sides of the trail mercifully began to diminish. Finally — on a brilliantly-bright but bitterly cold morning in early November 1848 — the boys surmounted a small upgrade. The sight on the horizon beyond — at first glance — took their breath away.

Sitting side-by-side at the peak of the small hill, the boys realized that they were finally looking at the end of their seemingly endless journey. Before them lay the broad, flat, and mostly snow-free environs of what is today California's Central Valley.

In the near distance foothills, the boys could make out the silhouettes of a collection of ramshackle buildings. This was the wild and wooly gold-rush boomtown called Hangtown — so-named because of the numerous hangings that had occurred there.

Yelling like a posse of drunken cowpokes, the boys ignored the snaking switchbacks of the partially snow-covered slopes and spurred their steeds straight downhill toward the open plain below. Caleb and Joshua worried about the boys breaking their horses' legs as they whipped them down the slopes. Fortunately, that didn't happen. Their torturous journey had toughened up the horses as well as the boys. As they rode, the flat land before them glistened just like the gold nuggets that they knew would soon make them each rich beyond belief.

The way Caleb and Joshua figured it, their troops surely set an all-time record riding down from the top of the first valley view and into the main street of Hangtown. And the wild celebrating didn't stop even after they got into town. By the time, they had ridden all the way through town and then back again, every single person — except for the stone-cold drunks lying in the street gutters — knew the rambunctious group from 'somewhere back east' had finally arrived.

The story of Hangtown — which within a few years would become known as Placerville — actually began at nearby Sutter's Mill, some nine months earlier. It was there that James W. Marshall built a sawmill on the South Fork of the American River for his employer John Sutter. On January twenty-fourth, 1848, Marshall — an itinerant carpenter — discovered two tiny nuggets of gold in the tailrace of the mill, and nothing was ever the same. The good news spread like wildfire, and the Great California Gold Rush historically had started. After the discovery of gold at Sutter's Mill, more than two hundred and fifty thousand businessmen, farmers, pioneers, and miners traveled in over the California Trail to the goldfields.

By the end of the next day — after they had so boisterously arrived in Hangtown — the boys had thoroughly scouted the local rocky hillsides. Their explorations led them to establish a gold-panning tent camp near a fast-flowing river that looked like it was a great potential source of the sparkling riches.

While the first few days of panning and prospecting didn't produce any results — outside of a few tiny flakes — the boys' enthusiasm wasn't assuaged in the least. They were all still too pumped up and convinced that their dreams of vast wealth lay just beneath their next shovelfuls of dirt or pansful of gravel. Typical of this group's bountiful and unyielding spirits, their days were filled with hard labor while their nights were full of drinking, singing, and dancing around their camp's central bonfire.

Discovering the Mother Lode

On an unusually warm — actually hot — day in early April 1849, the boys' prospecting luck took a dramatic turn for the better. They had been working diligently now for more than four months, and still did not have anything of substance to show for their efforts.

Late in the afternoon, a frustrated Travis Jackson threw down his shovel, tore off his shirt, and proclaimed, "I'm sure getting sick of this gol-durn heavy work in this hot sun. I'm going down to that river and take me a nice, cool swim!"

Quick as a wink, the rest of the boys peeled off their sweat-soaked shirts and — jumping and laughing as they ran — chased after Travis down toward the riverbank. Stumbling along like drunken sailors while they also shimmied out of their trousers, the boys made a comic sight to see. As soon as they reached the riverbank, each boy launched himself forward, coming down feet-first on the river bottom and sending torrents of water, mud, and rocks bursting skyward.

As always seems to happen when young men and water mix, a massive water fight ensued with arms flailing cold liquid in all heights and directions. After a few minutes the combination of the cool water and intense exercise abated the group's testosterone levels and they all settled in peacefully, scrunching down just enough to let the trailing rivulets flow around their shoulders and necks.

Suddenly, Thackery Thomas, shouted out, "Drat it. You boys made me lose my good luck bracelet. So now, how about helping me find the dadgum thing!" With that, all the boys began to stare down at their feet, trying to find Luke's shiny charm along the rocky bottom.

Josh McCown was the first to react. "Hey, Thackery, I think I've found your silly trinket so how about stopping your belly-aching!" No sooner had he finished speaking those words than Josh's chiding tone turned to a celebratory screaming, "Whoo-wee, ya'll forget the stupid bracelet—I've found me a god's honest golden nugget!"

With that, Josh held up a chunk of glistening yellow rock about the size of a large musket-ball. Just as suddenly, several other boys started thrusting their hands above their heads and dancing wildly through the water — holding their own golden nuggets.

Turns out the group's wild, river-rock kicking afternoon swim had accomplished what months of hard labor had not. They had finally discovered their very own pot of gold.

The lads didn't waste any time exploiting their watery discovery. They blasted out of the water and up the riverbank — making a mad dash in just their skivvies back to where they had dropped their pickaxes and sieves. Minutes later, they were all back in the water, moving rocks around and collecting unearthed nuggets as fast as their hands and arms could move.

Reality Sets In and San Francisco Beckons

During the next four years, all the boys continued to live in Hangtown and most made a decent living doing so. But none of them found the wealth of riches they had hoped for during their arduous journey across the country. While they all managed to build themselves ramshackle homesteads — complete with vegetable gardens plus flocks of chickens and sheep for meat and clothing — none of the boys married. Not that they weren't willing, and they were certainly eligible, but Hangtown was not the kind of place that young women were willing to move and set up families. The town's widespread reputation for being 'wild and wooly' was simply too much for most women to consider.

As was commonplace in Hangtown during the boom days, brazen burglaries cost most of the boys a lot of their hard-earned loot. Because of the generally solitary, hardscrabble nature of the gold mining process, there was little the lads could do to defend themselves when roaming bands of hoodlums came calling on their mining claims. Instead of putting up a fight or waiting for local law enforcement — which in the best of times was ineffective and most of the time was nonexistent — they just threw up their hands and gave up their days' diggings whenever bandits dropped by.

Then on a hot July day in 1853, a wind-driven wildfire nearly destroyed Hangtown including the homes of most of the boys. This event — coupled with the fact that the local mining claims were all rapidly playing out — got most of them thinking about pulling up stakes and moving on. The general discontent became so great that a few days after the great fire, Caleb and Joshua called the boys together for a meeting at the local Methodist Church to decide what to do next.

After two hours of heated debate, the group was split. Five of the boys — including Joshua — argued against abandoning the dreams that had sent them on their erstwhile trek across the wilderness frontier. They still believed that their future fortunes and happiness lay buried somewhere beneath the rugged hillsides and rushing rivulets of the Sierra Nevada foothills.

The other five boys — with Caleb as their leader — said the town fire was the last straw. They were sick of working their fingers to the bone, day-after-day. They were tired of having nothing to show for their labors but parched, sunburned skin and calloused hands. They were ready to make their way westward to the burgeoning mecca of San Francisco with its promise of fine creature comforts. They craved the good food, soft beds and — most of all — marriage-eligible women that were practically non-existent in Hangtown.

The way the boys with Caleb figured it, San Francisco would offer plenty of honest work with a variety of ways for young, energetic men — like themselves — to earn honest livings and raise proper families. It was time — they believed — to give up the dream of golden riches and move on with their lives. With that, the group decided to part ways. Joshua's group stayed on to chase their golden dreams while Caleb's group was off in search of new adventures.

It didn't take long for Caleb and his group of boys to move on and settle into a relative life-of-leisure — partaking of the fun, excitement, and good pay offered in downtown San Francisco. At first, they all lived together in a modest boardinghouse with shared bathrooms and a communal dining hall. But within a few months, four of them had found good-paying jobs and started dating engaging young women.

Nathan Cornbluth got a job as a brakeman with the Union Pacific Railroad, and moved into a house a few blocks from the central train yard. Josh McCown hooked on as a butcher's apprentice and found a walk-up flat in Chinatown. Travis Jackson apprenticed as a carpenter and immediately had all the work he could handle in the midst of the city's building boom. Capitalizing on his significant overtime pay, Travis made enough money to afford moving to the scenic village of Rancho del Sausalito on the north shore of San Francisco Bay. Meanwhile Rhett Baumgardner found a job he loved, working as a driver on one of San Francisco's city stagecoaches and living in a small flat on Telegraph Hill.

Caleb was the only one of the group of five, who didn't find the permanent life he was looking for in the city. He tried his hand at a few jobs — but none of them really suited him. Plus, he found himself becoming more and more conflicted over the extreme damage the boomtown development of San Francisco was inflicting on the surrounding natural landscape.

Caleb was especially concerned over the damage that gold mining was having. In truth — after the surface gold ran out — most individual miners who were panning streams with limited to no success, finally just gave up. In their place, heavily capitalized mining companies moved into the now thriving city. The preferred strategy of these invasive corporations was hydraulic mining. To accomplish this, rivers were dammed, creating reservoirs that supplied water cannons that blasted and washed away entire mountains to get at the gold inside.

This roughshod mining process ravaged much of the surrounding Sierra Nevada landscape — filling parts of San Francisco Bay with more than three feet of silt, sand, and gravel. On top of this, entire forests of ancient redwoods — that surrounded the city's core — were being slashed and burned to make room for the thousands of new families being brought in by the mining conglomerates.

Caleb's abiding love for nature — inherited from his dad, Thaddeus — carried over from his months of guiding his intrepid band of young adventurers across the untamed wilderness of the continental U.S. He soon became deeply enamored with the redwood-covered Sierra Nevada foothills that bordered both the chaparral woodlands and the flat fertility of the Central Valley. The intricate ecological mixing of old-growth forests, woodland savannahs — featuring blue oak and gray pine with a scattered understory of toyon and chamise — and native grasslands captured his childhood vision of how the west was going to look. He also delighted in finding, hunting, and often just watching the abundant wildlife — bison, elk, mule deer, coyote, mountain lion, bobcat, ringtail cat, and gray wolf — that filled these wildlands to overflowing.

Most magnificent of all the animals that Caleb saw on his frequent backcountry sojourns, was the California grizzly bear. Little could he have suspected the irony that would befall this fearsome and majestic beast. Just over one hundred years later — in 1953 — the grizzly bear was designated California's official state animal, even though the last one

250

in the state had been killed some thirty years earlier. The California grizzly bear is still honored as an icon on the state flag.

The wanton destruction of irreplaceable wildlife habitats soon became too much for Caleb to stomach. Plus, he had just met a wonderfully compassionate woman named Suzie Buchwalter. Suzie shared Caleb's passion for nature and avowed his horror at the damage man's callous actions were causing. She reveled in sharing Caleb's love for everything, from the daintiest woodland orchid in a forest of towering redwoods to the leviathan humpback whales often seen breaching just offshore in San Francisco Bay.

Caleb Finds His True Calling

Two years after their first meeting, Caleb Adams and Suzie Buchwalter were married. Then — because of their mutual discontent with city life — it came as no surprise to anyone when the happy newlyweds announced at one of the group's weekly dinners that they were moving out of the city to the coastal countryside.

Caleb had taken a job as a Biological Scientist with the General Land Office (GLO) in the U.S. Treasury Department. He was assigned to manage the federal land in the remote outpost of the Marin Headlands — along the Pacific Coast, some fifteen miles north of the city proper. Although it was the precursor to the federal Bureau of Land Management (BLM), the GLO of the 1850s had a very different function from that of today's BLM.

When Caleb took his position with the GLO, he was ostensibly tasked with dispersing thousands of acres of federal land to the masses of settlers that were flooding into the San Francisco Bay area. He soon realized, however, that there wasn't a lot of demand for the rugged, roadless Marin Headlands area that was his primary jurisdiction. So, Caleb and Suzie spent most of their time living in their cozy, government-built cabin, and enjoying their spectacular natural setting while waiting for intrepid settlers who seldom showed up.

Getting paid to live off the land in a grand natural landscape suited Caleb and Suzie just fine. Every month or so, they would hook up their horse team to their buckboard and bounce and jounce along rutted wagon roads into San Francisco for supplies and a taste of city life. But at the end of each three-day jaunt, they were always anxious and ready to return to the peace and tranquility of their precipice-hugging cabin.

In between their trips into San Francisco, Caleb and Suzie reveled in taking side trips down to the spectacular redwood forests and other ecological gems along their isolated California coastline. At the right time of the year, these temperate rainforests were an explosion of life in every trophic level — from krill and capelin near the base of the food chain, to river channels chockfull of salmon making their way back up to historic spawning grounds.

At times, Caleb and Suzie loved to just sit and watch sea otters as they floated on their backs and used small rocks to crack open sea urchins and clams. On each trip, they also saw sea lions and elephant seals lounging on rocky headlands, plus comical humpback whales bubble-cloud feeding in near-shore coves and bays. Soaring above, around, and through this wealth of oceanic riches were millions of seabirds infused with land-based raptors like bald eagles, osprey, and peregrine falcons.

Perhaps most astonishing — among this glorious display of wildlife — were the marbled murrelets. Shaped like diminutive footballs and flying with the alacrity of wildly blurring wings, these puffin-like birds streamed down by the thousands from their lofty nests high atop the redwoods. During the spring, they were all headed out to sea to capture and return with small schooling fish to feed their nestlings.

Caleb and Suzie spent the next few years living a peaceful and serene subsistence, mostly hunter-gatherer lifestyle amid the natural splendor of their rugged coastline. During this time, they also had a beautiful baby boy named Harrison. Caleb had Harrison out camping and watching wildlife before the boy could even walk.

BOOK ELEVEN
Everything Changes

Disillusionment Enters the Picture

Unfortunately, as time went by, Caleb and Suzie Adams grew increasingly sickened by the rampant deforestation that was taking place — not just in San Francisco proper, but also for new ranches and farmsteads in neighboring hills and valleys. Entire forests were being leveled willy-nilly. Little thought was given to long-term planning, such as replanting cut over areas for land stabilization and future forest management. This massive clear cutting led directly to major environmental impacts. Many wildlife populations were rapidly declining because of the annihilation of their habitats. The widespread loss of topsoil was causing serious sedimentation increases in creeks, rivers, and estuaries. Fishery spawning habitat — especially for salmon species — was being heavily impacted by siltation.

It was as if the general populace believed that California was such a bounteous land that the natural resources had no end. The consensus seemed to be that a land this rich and teeming with natural resources could absorb and endure whatever man wanted to do to it.

Despite this, life in the Marin Headlands remained mostly good for Caleb, Suzie, and Harrison. But — during the autumn of 1859 — something happened that would soon demand a complete change in the family's lifestyle.

Finding Endless Slaughter

The life-altering event began early one October afternoon while Caleb was out on a hunting trip. His goal was restocking his family's meat supply for the coming winter.

Riding along a rough-hewn trail just below the crest of a ridge, Caleb suddenly noticed the carcasses of scores of dead birds and animals littering the slope below. Looking back upslope, he saw several makeshift hunting blinds, positioned to provide a perfect vantage point for shooting anything that moved on the slopes below. Aghast at this scene of carnage, Caleb urged his new mount — Sequoia — gradually down the slope toward the cove at the bottom.

As he neared the shoreline, he came upon more wanton slaughter that turned his stomach so much he had to dismount and vomit. Everywhere he looked were putrid, rotting carcasses of sea lions, seals, sea otters, bald eagles, gulls — plus anything else that could be readily shot. Dead birds and other animals also littered the shoreline rocks and floated out into the adjacent seawater.

Caleb even found a family of magnificent California golden bears — a boar, a sow, and three cubs — massacred, just inside the canopy of redwood trees that sheltered portions of the shoreline. The bodies of the boar and sow had been decapitated and skinned, no doubt to make plush rugs for laying in front of the killers' hearths. The feet and claws of the cubs had also been hacked off — for what ghastly purpose, Caleb could not even imagine. The stench of death that filled the air was both disgusting and overwhelming.

At that moment, Caleb decided that — as the responsible party for land management in the area — he had to put a stop to this random killing. He formulated a plan to pitch a discrete camp where he could watch the blinds until the offending parties came back for another round of shooting. As he had it figured, he would then sneak up behind the culprits and arrest them for brazen destruction of natural resources.

Caleb knew — of course — that this would be risky, since he had no idea how many men were involved or what their attitude might be when he confronted them. But he was so angered by the malevolent carnage he had just witnessed that he didn't care.

When Caleb went back to his homestead and told Suzie about his plan, she pleaded with him to just let it go. She felt the risk was too great, and she didn't know how she could continue to raise Harrison here alone if something happened to him. But Caleb convinced her that everything would be all right, and — just after sunrise the next morning — he outfitted his packhorse with a week's worth of camping supplies, and headed back on Sequoia to the site of the butchery.

Determined to Enforce Justice

Reaching the scene of the slaughter around noon, Caleb tethered his horses to a sapling and began the task of pitching camp uphill from the blinds. He made sure that there was plenty of underbrush between his camp and the blinds so that the murderous heathens would have no idea he was around until he was ready to mount his surprise attack. He also decided to wait until they resumed shooting again, so that he could catch the villainous culprits in the act.

While he waited, Caleb spent the better part of two days building a massive pile of rocks, three hundred feet directly upslope of the men's blinds. As he worked, he used a thick rope to tether together a barricade of stout logs that held the rocks in place. While he was no engineer, he was savvy enough to know how to use the natural force of gravity to create a landslide on a steep hill.

Sure enough, just after dawn on the third morning of his stakeout, Caleb heard guffawing laughter and wild rifle shots coming from the direction of the blinds. Looking down the hill he saw three men — one occupying each blind — firing blindly away at anything that moved and snorting with laughter every time one of their rifle blasts found its mark. The men sounded like they were all drunk. For all Caleb knew, they were probably still all liquored up from the night before.

The good news was that this was exactly what Caleb was hoping for — catching the culprits in the midst of their dastardly deeds. The bad news was that he was outnumbered three-to-one by brazen, cowardly bullies, who were drunk and blazing away indiscriminately with no obvious concern for man nor beast. What's more, they clearly had no respect for laws or authority.

Caleb realized they certainly would have no qualms about mowing him down — just like another defenseless animal — if he tried to confront them in a formal, legal manner. There was no doubt in his mind that — capturing this bunch of disgusting misfits — would require some tricky maneuvering coupled with lots of luck.

To begin his plan, Caleb started pumping rifle shots into the backsides of the blinds, being careful not to shoot in the middle and risk hitting the men inside. His idea was to spook the men into running out of the blinds and into the open where he could draw a bead directly on them.

After the first two rounds of Caleb's bullets, it was clear that his plan was going to work.

The evil trio began wildly cursing in anger and confusion — wondering out loud about who in the world could be taking potshots at them. Two more rounds did the trick. The men bounded out of their blinds — almost as one — and turned to stare back up the hillside to determine the source of the bullets.

Next, using his most authoritative possible voice, Caleb yelled to the men, "By the power vested in me by the government of the United States of America, I order you to drop your weapons and surrender immediately." The three men continued squinting up the hillside — directly into the morning sun — trying to see who on earth could be making such a ridiculous request.

After a few minutes of stunned silence, one of the men yelled back at Caleb, "You gotta be kidding us, Mister. This here's free range wild country and you got no business trying to tell us what we can and can't do! How 'bout if you quit hiding like a coward, and show us yer face so's we can shoot it off and save us all a heapa trouble!"

Caleb pretty well figured this was what would happen. Here he was, alone on a mountainside, confronting three wild-men with no other human beings within twenty miles. Since the three villains obviously had no intention of surrendering, he initiated the third part of his plan. He used his trusty Bowie knife to cut through the rope trip wire which then unleashed his carefully constructed hillside avalanche.

Sure enough — within seconds after Caleb freed the logs holding the rocky debris in place — a hundred-foot-wide swath of the mountainside started rolling and tumbling directly downhill toward the men and their blinds. "It's a gol-dern landslide shouted one of the men, we got to get outta here before we get kilt!" With that, all three men flung their rifles out of the way and started running as the first rocks began pelting them. To avoid the bulk of the rocky cascade, they all dove headlong off to the side and away from the mass of mountainside that was now bearing down on them.

Quick as a wink, Caleb mounted Sequoia and followed the slamming wall of debris down toward where the men had taken their dives. He soon stood directly above the now rifle-less men and shouted, "OK, now — you no account scoundrels — stand up and put your hands in the air. If you don't, believe you me, I'll blow your fool heads clean off your bodies!"

Whimpering in pain, the men began pleading, "Please, Mister — whoever you are — please don't shoot us!" Continuing to whine like the cowards they were, the evil men slowly groveled through the dirt and stood up with their arms raised to the sky.

Caleb could see that his landslide had wiped out the men's hunting blinds as well as their mounts — which had been tethered behind the blinds. He wasn't too happy about killing the men's horses, but he realized it was just as well. Having to make their way on foot — with no firearms — back to the smarmy holes where they lived — would serve these heartless men right. In fact — if there really was any sense of justice in the universe — they would be killed and eaten by grizzly bears or a wolfpack before they made it back home.

Still looking down the barrel of his rifle, Caleb yelled down to the men, "OK, now I want you slimy varmints to skedaddle outta here, and don't ever come back. In fact — if I ever catch you shooting wildlife again — your bloody bodies will be the next ones piled on top of the dead animals!"

Caleb then fired two warning shots at the men's feet, and chuckled contentedly as they leapt up and stumbled down the mountainside as fast as their shaking legs would carry them. As soon as they were out of sight, he dismounted from Sequoia and walked gingerly down the still dusty face of the landslide. He wanted to make sure the men's rifles were completely buried so that there was no way they could come back and find them after he left.

Finding no visible firearms, Caleb made his way back up the rubble pile, remounted Sequoia, rode back up to his campsite, and packed up his provisions for the journey back home. As he rode back toward what he knew would be a sweet and welcome reunion with Suzie and Harrison, he mused about what — if anything — he had accomplished.

Caleb realized that there was a very good chance he had won a battle but very well may have lost the war. He knew that this raw and still mostly unsettled wilderness was full of many more 'ne'er-do-wells' who refused to accept any authority or regulation of their unruly and disgusting lifestyles.

Sadly — as he was soon to find out — Caleb had no idea just how right he was.

The Backlash Arrives

The next few months passed uneventfully — through the rest of autumn and into the early winter of 1860. Caleb patrolled his assigned territory on a weekly basis, each time leading Sequoia and his packhorse in a different direction.

Except for the occasional Native American hunting parties, he seldom encountered other humans. The few white men he ran into were harmless, hardscrabble prospectors out, just poking around, hoping to somehow, somewhere stumble onto a claim.

Then, on a bitterly cold late January afternoon — with snow flurries spitting about — it happened. As he sat shivering and trying to keep warm beside his cook fire, Caleb smelled smoke, wafting up from the hillside below his campsite. Knowing that — in these conditions — it had to be a man-made fire, he crept downhill in the direction of the smoke.

After moving quietly through calf-deep snow for several hundred yards, Caleb could hear human voices — shouting, yelling, and cursing — as if in the middle of some drunken celebration. Creeping even closer, he knelt down behind some fallen brush. He was now only about fifty feet from the roaring fire-pit around which at least fifteen men stood in animated conversation:

"Yessiree, we's going to kill us that high-falootin' lawman that destroyed our hunting camp," ranted one of the men. "Hell, we'll take him and his whole dern family out — now that we know where his homestead is. We'll teach him to come rip-roaring up here and telling us what we can and can't do. Tomorrow, we'll put an end to his kind and send a sure-fire message to them gov'ment boys to never try nothin' like that again. Jest let us live the way we want — we ain't hurting nobody. We's just killing us some worthless animals and making a little money in the process off the skins and body parts. What's the harm in that?"

Caleb immediately recognized the man doing the talking. It was definitely one of the three crazy yahoos he kiboshed with his landslide trickery. He was certain the other two deadbeats were also among the men planning to attack his home and family.

In the back of his mind, Caleb always knew his initial encounter with these violent misfits might come down to this. As he rode steadily through the night back to his homestead to rescue Suzie and Harrison, Caleb thought about the options that lay ahead. He certainly could no longer stay in this backcountry job — risking putting his family at the mercy of ruthless, drunken vigilantes. But he also didn't like the idea of moving his family back to the increasingly over-crowded confines of San Francisco.

In Caleb's mind, the only solution was moving on to some new, unspoiled territory and starting a new life. Now he just had to figure out exactly where to go, how to get there, and — most difficult of all — how to convince Suzie that this was what they had to do.

As he rode back toward home, Caleb remembered the many stories he had recently heard about efforts to settle a new frontier — a peninsula of land in the far southeast corner of the United States. To hear it told, this unsettled country was the land of legends — hot and sodden barrens where Spanish Conquistadors searched for Fountains of Youth. But — instead of eternal life, they found vast bubbling springs of ice-cold, blue water gurgling up to the surface from great depths. All across the lower part of this remote peninsula, sheets of water rushed through boundless grasslands and then into jungle-thick mangrove swamps. These dense, low-growing coastal forests supported a variety of beasts with gaping jaws and gnashing fangs. So, the stories went, most of these strange animals had seldom been encountered — in either the thirteen original colonies or by the intrepid wagon trains of westward trekkers.

Caleb also heard tales of giant wild birds with white, pink, blue, and gray feathers in flocks so dense and thick that they blotted out the sky. The Spanish immigrants called this wild new land 'Florida', and he decided that this was where he needed to go to find a fresh start for himself and his family.

As soon as he got back to his homestead just past midnight, Caleb awakened Suzie and Harrison and told them to pack up everything they really needed and to just leave the rest. He said he would explain on the way, but for now they just had to get out. And they needed do it fast!

Caleb then bounded out the cabin's back door to the barn where he hooked a team up to the family wagon. He also collected several bedrolls and a large tarp that could be used to create a cover if the snow flurries morphed into a full-blown blizzard. But there was really no time to think about other detailed arrangements right now. He knew had to get Suzie and Harrison out of the house and on the road to safety before the drunken posse of vigilantes arrived to kill them all and burn down their house.

Long Passage to Florida

The next day, Caleb reined the team carrying his precious family up to the front of a hotel near San Francisco's waterfront. After he got Suzie and Harrison settled into a room, he hoofed it over to the North American Steamship Company's office and inquired about tickets to the Florida peninsula.

When Caleb explained that he needed tickets not only for him but for his wife and young son, the agent looked up and gently shook his head. "I have to warn you, sir, that this trip is not even for faint-of-heart men, much less women and children. This can be an arduous three-week journey fraught with danger — from exploding boilers to perilous seas and deadly on-board diseases. We have lost — by far — more ships, passengers, and even entire crews on this route than any other place we travel."

Caleb explained to the agent that he understood the dangers of the voyage, but the risks of staying in California were far greater for both him and his family. Hearing this and sensing Caleb's sincerity and urgency, the ticket agent handed Caleb three tickets to the still mostly undiscovered 'paradise' of Florida. The steamship tickets cost Caleb nearly every penny he had saved, but he remained convinced that he was making the right — and only — decision for his family's long-term safety. With the steamboat tickets now in hand, Caleb spent the rest of the afternoon sadly selling his horses, wagon, and most of the family's possessions.

At precisely eight a.m. the next morning, Caleb, Suzie, and Harrison made their way up the gangplank and onto the southbound steamship, S.S. Nebraska. Their journey would take them down the west coast of California and Mexico's Baja Peninsula to Panama City, Panama where they would take a train that connected the Pacific Ocean to the Atlantic Ocean. At the railroad's eastern terminus in Aspinwall, Panama they would then board another steamship for the journey through the Caribbean Islands to Havana, Cuba.

Fortunately for Caleb and his family, the seas held strong and the weather good throughout their Pacific steamship travels and the train ride across the Isthmus of Panama. By the end of the 1850s, many of the unpleasantries of steamship travel — overcrowding, shortages of food and water, passenger abuses (especially toward women), and the like — had been alleviated by a combination of better business practices and government regulations. With the exception of occasional calamitous shipwrecks associated with engine failure and severe weather, steamboat travel was now mostly safe and comfortable — despite the officious warnings of the North Shore Steamship Company agent. Also, before the completion of the transcontinental railroad in 1869 — it was by far the best and easiest way to travel from San Francisco to America's East Coast.

In fact, the only unpleasant events for Caleb and his family during this trip involved what they saw on other ships plying the Pacific coastline. Since their travel along the Baja Peninsula dovetailed with the start of the northward migration of gray and humpback whales, they witnessed — not once, but several times — the violent harpooning and butchering of these magnificent cetaceans.

The flotilla of whaling ships belonging not only to the United States — but to Russia and Japan as well — carried out this bloody carnage. Whenever Caleb spotted one of these vessels on the horizon, he told Suzie to take Harrison below deck so that they didn't have to watch.

In early February 1860 — after arriving in the bustling port of Havana, Cuba — Caleb immediately sheltered Suzie and Harrison in a local lodge and set about the task of finding a boat captain who would transport them across to the fishing village of Key West. From his reading back in California, Caleb knew that most of the Florida peninsula was still untrammeled wilderness and he thought that the best thing they could do was to settle into a pleasantly quiet lifestyle in Key West.

THE IGNOBLE HISTORY OF THE WHALING INDUSTRY

Today, many Americans in the United States believe that our country has always been the 'good guys' in the international whaling controversy. But such has not always been the case. In fact, during the 1850s, there were more whaling vessels registered under the American flag than any other country on earth.

This slaughter of some of the world's most intelligent creatures was being conducted to acquire two substances that were in great demand — whale oil for lamps plus baleen for buggy whips, fishing poles, corset stays, and dress hoops. While Native American tribes always hunted the whales respectfully, most commercial whalers left the massive carcasses of the dead whales to rot in the open ocean — rendering their killing largely senseless and devastating to the whale populations.

In what was dubiously dubbed a 'Nantucket Sleigh Ride', it was not unusual to see a whaling boat riding along after its quarry as if being pulled like a sled by horses through snowdrifts. The idea was that the harpooned and enraged whales would soon succumb to the maximum energy they had to expend hauling the heavy boats through the water. While on these wild rides, the schooners often passed by the rotting carcasses of previously killed adult whales and the forlorn — but still alive — calves of harpooned mothers.

The way Caleb figured it, his wealth of skills as a government backcountry ranger should serve him well in leading exploration parties through the wilderness of this untamed land. He certainly had plenty of experience dealing with unsavory characters, plus he had no fear of any animal that wasn't human.

As it turned out, Caleb's timing was impeccable. In fact, he and his family landed in Havana at exactly the right time. Droves of Cuban immigrants were crossing the Florida Straits seeking political freedom and economic opportunity in the still wide open — but suddenly burgeoning — oceanic outpost of Key West.

So it was no surprise that Caleb quickly found a transport for his family across the scant one hundred and ten miles of ocean that separated Havana from the southern tip of Florida. In fact, the first person he talked with — a bilingual mail boat captain on Havana's bustling docks — told Caleb that he and his family could be on a boat to Key West within an hour.

After paying the captain for passage, Caleb dashed back to the inn and rousted Suzie and Harrison to get ready for one final boat trip. The next day — all giddy with excitement — they debarked on the passenger dock in Key West. They were now more than two thousand five hundred miles away from their rustic but beloved California homestead. In fact, they were more than four hundred miles south of Tallahassee — Florida's provisional capital and closest 'civilized' settlement — but at least they were now safely back on U.S. soil.

Key West Becomes Home

As things turned out, Key West was the perfect location for Caleb, Suzie, and Harrison to continue the lifestyle they had come to cherish while living in California's remote coastal headlands. Of course, just about everything was as different as possible from what they were used to in California. The land was cookie sheet-flat — not even a slight hill in sight. The daytime temperature was usually broiling hot and the humidity hung in the air like a limp dishrag. Day after day morphed into month after month with only the slightest variation in weather. Lightning-and-thunder filled torrents of rain rolled in at practically the same time every afternoon.

The fauna of the Adams family's new home was also a total transformation from the fearsome but impressive array of megafauna — grizzly bears, wolves, and mountain lions — featured around their California cabin. Even the deer here — the so-called 'key deer' — were tiny, not much bigger than a German shepherd dog. Much of the terrestrial wildlife in Key West revolved around birds — everything from the elegant great egrets to the comical brown pelicans and the tide-skittering sandpipers. There were also plenty of curious cold-blooded critters like treefrogs, anoles, skinks, salamanders, turtles, plus a healthy — yet mostly despised — population of snakes.

To be sure, there were also some alpha predators — such as alligators and crocodiles — both of which could grow to be fifteen-foot long behemoths. But just as Caleb expected, the greatest emphasis on wildlife in Key West involved the ocean and its vast array of both commercial and game species — including tarpon, tuna, shrimp, crabs, spiny lobsters, grouper, and redfish.

Relying on Caleb's penchant for getting things done and Suzie's resourcefulness in running a household, the Adams family soon found themselves settled into a rustic cottage — living on the edge of sometimes erratic, but usually quite laidback Key West lifestyle. Located just beyond the outskirts of town, their two-acre plot of land afforded them the same wilderness comforts they had in California while also allowing them to be a part of the human population. It was — in particular — a perfect set up for Suzie, who craved the support and camaraderie of a community.

Despite their proximity to neighbors, Caleb and Suzie still maintained a mostly subsistence lifestyle. Caleb relied on his exquisite outdoor instincts to reap a bounty of fresh seafood from the neighboring ocean, while Suzie applied her green thumb to cultivate crops from their backlot garden. They occasionally supplemented their home-grown food stocks with general store luxuries like hand-made dairy products, fresh-baked goods, and local wines.

Their in-town splurges were made possible by the extra income that Caleb earned by serving as a fishing and hunting guide. He made it known around town that he was available to lead the adventoruous tenderfeet that somehow — usually by steamship — made it all the way down the East Coast. He emphasized that he was the perfect person to lead these rich but inexperienced fun-seekers on fishing trips into the myriad bays and backwaters that surrounded Key West.

Caleb also spent many hours working with local 'shipwrecking crews' — an occasionally lucrative pastime for many Key Westers. In truth, shipwrecking was right up Caleb's alley — coupling his penchant for adventure with his lust for hidden treasures that was left over from his California Gold Rush Days.

For the next seventeen years, Caleb and Suzie reveled in the rustic, but comfortable lifestyle they had found for themselves in Key West. Their son Harrison was now the spitting image of his father. With sharply-chiseled facial features and long lean muscles, Harrison loved the outdoors now even more than his Dad did. In fact — as soon as Harrison became a teenager — Caleb and Suzie barely saw him during daylight hours.

This unquenchable thirst for spending every waking moment outdoors made Harrison the perfect partner for assisting Caleb with his work as a fishing and hunting guide. In fact, Harrison's reputation as a guide grew to such an extent that many of the wealthy adventure seekers — who descended like flies on Key West — often asked for him instead of Caleb.

After this had gone on for a few months, Caleb decided to take full advantage of Harrison's skills. He bought a second guide boat and started advertising that he and Harrison were now both leading out-of-town clients through the wilderness maze that surroundeded Key West. This worked so well that in less than a year, Harrison had made enough money to clear a piece of land and build his own cottage just two hundred feet away from Suzie and Caleb's modest abode.

A Boston Brahmin Arrives

Raised in a family of wealthy 'Boston Brahmins', Marybeth Magruder was always the best student in her school. She graduated first in her class from Radcliffe College at age 18 with a triple major in biology, physics, and general education.

Owing to her exceptional pedigree — both in terms of family blood lines and educational achievements — Marybeth was whisked right to the top of Boston's educational system. But — while always reveling in teaching the cream of the crop of Boston's school children — she always felt that something was missing in her life. Then one morning in early November of 1877 — just after she turned twenty-one — she glanced over at the copy of the Boston Globe her father was reading while he drank his morning coffee.

Marybeth's eye was attracted by these words:

HELP WANTED
FULL-TIME TEACHER IN KEY WEST, FLORIDA
Excellent Pay and Benefits—Relocation Assistance Provided

Marybeth had no idea where Key West was. But she did know something about Florida. First and foremost, she knew the state was far enough south that they did not have any winter. As a dedicated warm weather person who celebrated Massachusetts' short summers, but languished during the state's long winters, she was immediately intrigued by this job possibility. As soon as her father finished reading the paper, she grabbed it and clipped out the help wanted ad.

After a few hours in the Boston Public Library, reading everything she could find about Key West, Marybeth knew exactly what she wanted to do. She made her way to Boston's Causeway Street Station — appropriately enough, through a driving snowstorm — and bought a sequence of railway tickets that would take her to Jacksonville on

Florida's east coast. Then — from Jacksonville — she knew she could hop on a variety of steamships, outriggers, and sailing sloops that would eventually take her all the way down the state's peninsula. If everything went as she had planned, she would be in Key West by the first of December.

The only thing Marybeth now had left to do was talk to her parents. But because she knew they would never agree to let her make this move, she didn't even ask. She left a note telling her parents that she loved them very much and then slipped away to the 'T' station bright and early one morning. Feeling very self-satisfied at her own bravado, she was having dinner in New York City's Grand Central station before dark that same day.

Although she had not talked to anyone in Key West, Marybeth figured that — once she made it there, all the way from Boston — they would have to give her the job. And she was right. By the second week in December of 1877, she was seated behind her desk — looking adoringly out at the twenty-one bright faces that were hanging on her every word.

While vanity wasn't an adjective that applied to Marybeth, she realized the children were all taken in by her freckily, dimpled face, willowy figure, and spitfire personality. In other words, Marybeth knew that she immediately had the entire class in the palm of her hand. Without a doubt, teaching this group was going to be 'easy as pie'.

Since she now had been gone for almost a month, Marybeth realized that her parents were probably beside themselves with worry and concern. But Marybeth didn't care — she was where she wanted to be. She was soaking in Florida's gloriously warm weather while her family were likely all out shoveling sidewalks and scraping ice. Plus, she had escaped from the big city 'rat race', and was living comfortably and quietly amid Mother Nature's glorious bounty.

When Marybeth finally reached her parents by telegraph, their return messages were not pleasant. In fact, they were quite apoplectic in tone — all full of 'how could you's' and 'how dare you's'. But in truth, what could they really do. She was now more than one thousand-five hundred miles away and making a good salary. She was, in fact, as happy as a clam living in a Key West tidal flat.

In all honesty, Marybeth didn't really know how long she would be staying in Key West — so far away from the rest of her family that she dearly loved. She originally thought that it would be at most a two-year fling and then she would make her way back to Boston.

For the first several months that she lived in Key West, Marybeth yearned to get out and really explore the marine ecosystems that surrounded her. She did — after all — have a biology degree and was sure she would immediately be enamored at seeing all the exotic flora and fauna she always heard everyone in town talking about.

Unfortunately, two things were keeping Marybeth from accomplishing her goal. First, she didn't own a boat. This was quite a deterrent — since at least ninety percent of Monroe County, Florida was water. Secondly — since she was a brand new and diligently dedicated teacher — her hours outside of teaching were fully consumed with lesson planning and curriculum building.

Finally in late May of 1878 — as the school year was drawing to a close and her workload was easing somewhat — Marybeth decided the time had come. She started asking around town about the best guides for showing her Key West's natural resources. And ninety percent of the time, she heard the same name — Harrison Adams is the man you want.

Less than a week later, Marybeth was at the town dock joining five other people on Harrison's boat — the Playful Pelican. Just as soon as Harrison turned around to introduce himself and talk about where they were going, Marybeth was smitten. While she really didn't believe in love at first sight, she conceded that there was an exception to everything. Then at the end of the trip — after four hours of listening to his eloquently mellifuous description of Florida Bay's unique amalgam of marine plants and animals — she knew for certain that Harrison was the exception.

As things turned out, Harrison felt exactly the same way about Marybeth. Before she started teaching again in September, she and Harrison were married and living blissfully in Harrison's cabin with Caleb and Suzie — the best in-laws she could ever imagine — living right next door. Marybeth now fully realized that Key West was much more than a fling — it was her true destiny calling.

Within five years, Harrison and Marybeth had extended Caleb and Suzie's family even more — in two very delightful ways. On March twenty-eighth, 1880 Aurora Marin Adams was born followed by Wilson Audubon Adams on June eleventh, 1881.

Growing Up in the Florida Wilderness

Aurora and Wilson Adams grew up in a wonderfully supportive home in Florida's subtropical paradise. The natural world was always literally at their doorstep and immersed throughout their lives. Their property was surrounded by estuarine tidal marsh to the south and east, plus dense mangrove thickets on the west and north. While they were still just toddlers, they were out camping and communing with their parents and the local wildlife community during just about every weekend.

As pre-schoolers, Aurora and Wilson had their days filled with games and learning exercises at their 'Mimi Suzie's' house. Each morning, they couldn't wait to go next door and see what fun activities and tasty snacks their grandmother had ready for them. Then each night, either Marybeth or Harrison read books to them until they drifted off to sleep.

Aurora and Wilson both loved books so much that — before they even started school — they could each read books written for young adults. Then, once they started school, they had the extra advantage of being taught by their own mother — who just also happened to be the best teacher in Key West.

As Aurora and Wilson regularly experienced, the pristine natural beauty of Key West was — in a word — overwhelming. Seemingly endless rookeries teemed with birds displaying almost every feather color imaginable — pink flamingoes and roseate spoonbills; white snowy and great egrets, reddish egrets; and multi-colored herons — including great blues, little blues, and tri-coloreds. Surrounding thickets of red and black mangrove forests — coupled with dense beds of eelgrass, interspersed with tidal marsh — collectively served to create some of Earth's most productive nurseries for oceanic fishes, mollusks, and crustaceans.

Once Aurora and Wilson started school, their 'Pop-Pop Caleb' took advantage of every opportunity he could find to take both grandkids along on his wilderness forays. On weekends when he didn't have paying passengers, Caleb would load the kids into his jury-rigged flat bottom swamp boat. While quite seaworthy, this unusual-looking vessel — which the kids named the Sea Cow — could comfortably carry up to ten passengers and was complete with a sleeping shelter, portable toilet, cook stove, and ice box. After Caleb was confident that Aurora and Wilson knew exactly what they were doing on the water, he often took them out on trips with his clients — at least, when doing so didn't interfere with their schooling.

Throughout his years in Key West, Caleb never failed to provide his mostly city-slicker clients with adventures of a lifetime. He took them places — forerunners to today's famous Florida bone-fishing flats — where they caught hundreds of pounds of fish, with some tarpon weighing in at more than fifty pounds apiece. The fish were so abundant that it didn't make any difference what you threw in the water — as long as it had a hook — it was going to catch a fish. The only problem was trying to decide what to keep and what to throw back.

Of course there were no fishing regulations at the time. But Caleb still had the mindset of a true conservationist — realizing that all immature fish and gravid females should be immediately released after being caught. He instinctively knew that such a practice was critical to maintaining the good health of the local fishery stocks.

Under Caleb's expert tutelage, Aurora and Wilson both became expert fishermen as pre-teens, although they always begged for Caleb to release every fish they caught. It hurt them to see the fish suffering and they cheered each time the hook was removed and the fish slipped away — back down into the tannin-colored depths. Typically, both children most preferred to just sit back and revel in the glory of Mother Nature's always spectacular shows.

While Aurora never held her tongue when she felt something had to be said, Wilson was by far the more talkative of the two. His thick shock of blond hair always seemed to be bouncing on his head as his deep set green eyes darted around — drinking in everything he saw.

With his agilely muscular frame, Wilson moved around the boat with a dancer's aplomb — constantly pointing out and describing new things to everyone within earshot. This seemingly natural-born propensity to be a wilderness guide pleased Caleb to no end. He realized he would soon have another enthusiastic partner for his business.

On the other hand, Aurora's interest in Florida's majestic outdoors was much more difficult to read. While there was no doubt in Caleb's mind that she loved going with him on the boat, he wasn't quite sure that she was really passionate about engaging his clients. In fact, she often parked her long and willowly frame in the bow of the boat — keeping her auburn-colored flowing locks and piercing blue eyes focused on the water ahead. It was as if she was always expecting some remarkable new creature to arise each time the Sea Cow sliced its way through another light chop.

Some days the sightings from the Sea Cow were both unfathomable and unforgettable. One such trip started out as just a typical bright, breezy but unusally warm south Florida day. Small, mixed flocks of gulls, pelicans, terns, and egrets were feeding languidly here and there, as Caleb scanned the near-shore shallows and flats for signs of the bonefish and tarpon he knew his clients coveted.

Then — quick as a wink — everything turned into biological chaos. The surface of the water boiled with fins and tails of schools of hundreds — more likely thousands — of yellow jacks. Caleb instantly realized that this signaled the start of a feeding frenzy. No doubt the jacks were reacting violently to being pursused by a school of tarpon with their mouthfuls of snapping, razor-sharp teeth.

Caleb yelled a warning to Aurora and Wilson — who were perched in their customary 'look-out' seats in the bow — to watch the skies for dive-bombing birds. Sure enough — within seconds — hundreds of brown pelicans, herring gulls, and royal terns began plying the skies above the thrashing jacks. Folding their wings in, the birds hurtled head-first into the broiling milieu below. More often than not, the bombarding birds popped back up with finny quarries flopping in their beaks.

As each group of birds melded back to gulp down their piscatory prey, more birds took their place in the diving hierarchy. This dual layered smorgasbord — predatory fish from below and avian gluttony from above — went on for a good thirty minutes, until the jacks had finally spread themselves out enough to stop the carnage.

The Millinery Trade Rears Its Ugly Head

All through the 1880s and into the 1890s, the two generations of Adamses lived a very comfortable and satisfying life in the southern hinterlands of the 27th state. They continued to supplement their self-sufficient lifestyles — mostly growing their own crops and raising their own meat (chickens and goats) — with incomes from both guiding and teaching.

As attested to by the several national wildlife refuges that now surround Key West, the areas where Caleb and Harrison regularly took their clients were beaming beacons to unfathomable birdlife — especially multitudes of elegantly-feathered wading birds. But herein laid a big problem. The feathered finery of these birds — especially the herons, egrets, and spoonbills — was also attracting the attention of a devious group of money-grubbing villains, known as the millinery industry. Because of this headgear 'fashionista' scourge, the placid backwater lifestyles of peace and tranquility all came crashing down one fine spring day in 1895.

It happened when Aurora and Wilson were heading out with Caleb who was guiding some clients from New York City for a day of trophy fishing. It was a perfect mid-April morning — buttressed by a cooling spring breeze — and the Sea Cow was plying her way through dead-water flats. They were cruising just east of a huge wading bird rookery that Caleb's two now-young adult grandchildren especially reveled in watching.

Being the peak of the nesting season, hundreds of wading birds — great and snowy egrets, tri-colored herons, roseate spoonbills, and wood storks — were flitting all around. They were swooping in and out and up and down — bringing freshly caught food to their never-satiated nestlings.

The cacophony of avian noise — from the squawks, snorts, gurgles, and gargles of the adults to the continual screeching of their chicks —

was unlike anything else in the natural world. Melding in the visual delights of flying feathers of every color imaginable, produced an overall sensory experience that could never be replicated by humans.

Suddenly, all hell broke loose. As Aurora and Wilson watched in horror, at least two dozen men — decked out in camouflage from head to toe — rose up from their mangrove hiding spots and began blasting away at the birds perched helplessly right above their heads. The defenseless birds started falling from all directions — like huge bloodied raindrops. The killing was totally indiscriminate — both adult and young birds succumbed to death by the hunter's blasts.

Caleb started screaming at the top of his lungs that he was going to see that the hunters rotted in prison for their unrelenting bombardment. But it did no good. In less than thirty minutes, it was all over. Save for some newly-hatched chicks — too young to hold their heads up — not a single bird remained alive in the rookery.

It was simply too much to fathom — even for Caleb's clients. They were so shaken that they asked Caleb to discontinue the trip, so they could go back to their rooms and recover. Of course, the biggest impacts were to Aurora and Wilson who sat in the bow helplessly shaking — totally aghast at what they had just witnessed.

Sadly enough, these rookery massacres were being precipitated by an industry located more than a thousand miles to the north of Key West. A high fashion hat craze was rapidly overtaking northeastern cities like New York, Philadelphia, and Boston.

This gluttonously-vain period began when the millinery industry started emphasizing the need for ladies of 'high society' to adorn their headgear with long, colorful, and flowing wild bird feathers. In fashion circles, this suddenly made the tail feathers of many wild birds — at $32 per ounce — more valuable than gold. The spectacularly coiffed feathers of great egrets were considered the *piece de resistance* of the chapeau fashion industry.

To supply this fiendishly-despiccable market, milliners hired teams of 'avian hit men' who descended *en masse* on rookeries throughout South Florida. As Aurora and Wilson had just witnessed, an entire rookery could be wiped out in less than an hour. When they were finished, the millinery murderers plucked the carcasses clean and then left hundreds — and in some cases, thousands — of helpless starving chicks and rotting eggs in their nests.

HEADGEAR HORROR

In a tale seemingly plucked from an Edgar Allan Poe short story, Frank Chapman — founder of *Audubon Magazine* — decided to take a stroll one day from his uptown Manhattan office to the heart of the fashion district on 14th Street. Along the way, Chapman — a talented birder — counted a total of one hundred and seventy-four birds comprising forty species — including woodpeckers, orioles, bluebirds, blue jays, terns, and owls. At first blush, this seemed to be a pretty impressive array of birds for the middle of New York City. The problem was — all the birds Chapman counted that day adorned the hats that sat on the top of women's heads. Throughout the 1890s, millions of birds — representing more than fifty different species — were killed for fashion. Entire populations of shorebirds and wading birds — including herons, egrets, spoonbills, gulls, and terns — along the Atlantic Coast were wiped out.

Aurora and Wilson saw this slaughter of hapless nesting birds happen not just once, but several more times during the next few years. While this ongoing butchery was devestating to the bird populations, there was a silver lining. The whole disgustingly-outlandish scenario so infuriated Aurora that — as she sat helplessly watching these avian bloodbaths — she vowed to do something, anything she could, to stop it.

A Boston Hero Steps Up

From a historical perspective, most successful environmental organizations owe their starts to individuals with a deep and abiding respect for and dedication to the natural world. This was certainly the case with Harriett Lawrence Hemenway and the soon-to-be newly minted Massachusetts Audubon Society.

For much of her life — through early adulthood — Harriet Hemenway lived a life of luxury and privilege at the pinnacle of Boston society. Although she escaped to watch birds along the Charles River whenever she could, Hemenway spent most of her time as a prominent socialite — moving gracefully through all the right places while always decked out to the nines in the latest trendy fashions. That was — at least — until she sat down on a cold winter morning and read a newspaper story that made her blood boil and caused all hell to break loose within the confines of polite Boston society.

When Harriett first read about thousands upon thousands of magnificent wading birds being slaughtered just for feathers to decorate women's hats, she was overwhelmingly infuriated. From that day forward, she became a true 'Champion of Conservation', and girded herself for the battles she knew would soon follow in the male-dominated world of northeastern capitalism.

Harriett's portrait by the famous artist John Singer Sargent shows an arrestingly handsome woman, with a deep-set gaze that practically shouts out, "Don't trifle with me . . . no matter who you are!" Soon after she read the bloodcurdling account of entire rookeries being wiped out in Florida, many of the cocky men who thought they ruled the roost in Boston were being called on the carpet to atone for the sins of the millinery trade.

As a freshly minted activist, the first thing Harriett did was contact her cousin Minna B. Hall. Together, Harriett and Minna organized a series of ladies' teas — with the intent of discussing much more than the latest social goings-on. During these 'high tea' get-togethers, they first told the women about what was happening to wild birds just to assuage society's *haute couture* needs. Next, they beseeched their guests to start refusing to buy hats with bird feathers, and to rally everyone else they knew to do the same.

Of course — while neither woman knew it at the time — Harriett's heroic actions were dovetailing perfectly with the life's goals of Aurora Adams. Aurora was now a handsomely rugged young woman, who was defined by an increasingly burning desire to do what was right for the other creatures with whom she shared the planet.

One cold — for south Florida at least — winter day in 1896, Aurora hitched up the team and drove the family wagon into town to pick up the usual month's worth of groceries, and other supplies. While waiting at the counter, Aurora overheard a group of local women talking about the changes that would potentially make it illegal for rifle-toting zealots to wipe out bird rookeries.

As soon as the conversation ended, Aurora — in her typically polite but affirmative manner — tapped the woman closest to her on the shoulder. "Excuse me, ma'am, I don't mean to be eaves-dropping, but can you give me some more detail about what you all were just discussing?"

Obviously overjoyed at finding another person interested in the cause, the woman immediately replied, "Why of course, my dear, just let me get a scrap of paper and pencil." The accommodating woman then quickly scribbled something down and handed it to Aurora.

The note read simply: 'Protector of wild birds—Harriet Lawrence Hemenway, Boston, Massachusetts.' From that propitious moment, Aurora knew she had found her true calling in life. She didn't know exactly how she was going do it — since Key West was so far south of Boston — but she knew she had to meet with Ms. Hemenway as soon as possible.

Meanwhile back in Boston, Harriett Hemenway's strategy was working like a charm. Using her social networks as a springboard, she reached out to hundreds of scientists and businesspeople and soon had gathered enough support to begin establishing the Massachusetts Audubon Society — the first official conservation organization in the

United States.

A few months after she successfully advanced her Audubon initiative, Harriett received a letter from a place she only knew about as a hotbed of the heinous plume-hunting industry. In carefully and elegantly inscribed handwriting, the letter was from an 'Aurora Adams'— bearing the simple return address of 'Key West, Florida'.

Harriett was both enthralled and surprised by Aurora's thoughtfully written prose. The letter began by providing — in great detail — how much she knew about, and was appalled by the rookery slaughters that she had personally watched taking place all around her.

In poignantly beseeching language, Aurora made the case that her main goal in life now was stopping this glaring assault on the natural world, and she knew that Ms. Hemenway was just the person to give her this opportunity. Aurora's letter was so moving and convincing that Harriett immediately assigned one of her personal assistants to arrange for Aurora to come to Boston for an in-person discussion.

When the word arrived, that Harriett had arranged for her passage to Boston, Aurora was beside herself with joy. Of course, her mother, Marybeth, was also especially delighted. In fact, she told a breathless Aurora that her Brahmin family back in Boston actually knew the Hemenways quite well. Marybeth even remembered playing and exploring along the Charles River and Back Bay with some of the Hemenway children.

The next day, Marybeth telegraphed her family to tell them that Aurora was on her way to Boston and would be staying with them. This message delighted the Magruders to no end — because their family was about to come full circle. As far as they were concerned — although Key West had taken away their daughter — the Florida swampland was now giving them back a granddaughter.

Fighting the Good Fight

Within the week, Aurora was on board a steamboat sailing from Key West north to Jacksonville, Florida. From there, she rode a series of passenger trains, arriving three days later at Boston's North Union Station.

When Aurora stepped off the train and onto the platform, the first thing she saw was a very-refined looking woman holding a sign that read simply 'Aurora'. Turns out, Harriett Hemenway herself had decided to be Aurora's official 'greeting party'.

A warm embrace quickly ensued making Aurora feel immediately welcome and comfortable. "I simply can't tell you how delighted I am to have you he-ah in Boston, my de-ah," said Harriett.

Aurora felt an immediate bond with this elegant, stately woman with a steely gaze that belied her sophisticated upbringing. She instantly knew she had made the right decision — this was definitely a woman who was out to change the world of avian protection and wildlife management.

And change the world of natural resource conservation they did. Harriett — working with Aurora as her right-hand assistant — kept hammering away at the male-dominated landscape of Boston's Copley Square and the city's Financial District. In short order, Harriett's newly-formed Audubon Society applied sufficient pressure to convince the Massachusetts legislature to outlaw the wild bird feather trade altogether within the Commonwealth.

Bird lovers in New York, Connecticut, Pennsylvania, Tennessee, Maine, Iowa, Texas, Colorado, and the District of Columbia followed Harriett and Aurora's lead. Women in all these states started societies dedicated to ending the feather trade and then convinced — actually coerced — male civic leaders and local scientists to join their cause.

Next, the U.S. Congress passed the Lacey Act — which provided the necessary legal teeth for prohibiting the interstate shipment of wild species killed in violation of state laws. By 1905 — operating off this federal legal benchmark — a total of thirty-three states had moved to pass their own versions of the Lacey Act. The millinery trade of wild bird feathers — while still breathing slightly — was now on life support.

The death knell finally started ringing in 1911. First, New York State passed the Audubon Plumage Bill — a legal triumph that banned the sale of plumes of all native birds, and shut down the domestic feather trade in the state.

Then in 1913, the Weeks-McLean Law prohibited the spring hunting and marketing of migratory birds while the Underwood Tariff Act banned all importation of feathers except for purposes of scientific research or education. These two laws placed all migratory birds under federal jurisdiction — ending the wild bird plume trade in the United States for good.

Finally in 1920, the US Supreme Court upheld the most powerful piece of legislation ever passed to protect wild birds. Still in effect today, the Migratory Bird Treaty Act of 1918 gave all migratory birds full federal protection.

Amid her litany of successes working with Harriett Hemenway in Boston, Aurora also found the time to earn a degree in marine biology from Radcliffe College. Given her rigorous work schedule — often involving twelve-hours days and seventy-hour weeks — this was a monumental accomplishment. But holding true to her humble nature, Aurora always told people that it wasn't really that difficult.

After all, she was the daughter of a triple major *magna cum laude* Radcliffe graduate. Plus, her tuition and fees were all taken care of by her Boston 'blue blood' relatives. Of course, what Aurora neglected to add was that — with the generous salary Harriett was paying her — she could have covered all her own college expenses, with plenty left over.

As things turned out, Aurora was able to stash away most of her earnings — since she didn't have to pay for school, lodging or food. In fact, in addition to learning all about conservation policies and issues, she was also able to build up a sizeable bank account during her stay in Boston.

BOOK TWELVE
An Activist for the Ages

Moving to Tallahassee

In 1912 — after sixteen years of working and studying in Boston with Harriet Hemenway — Aurora Adams returned to her Florida roots. She smartly transitioned her now well-honed skill set as a conservation activist into a permanent job working with the freshly-created Florida Audubon Society in the State Capitol of Tallahassee.

Over the next two years, Aurora worked to pave the way for Florida Audubon to become a force in protecting not just wild birds, but all the natural resources of America's duly-named 'Sunshine State'. She spent the majority of her daylight hours rummaging around the halls of the statehouse — often sitting in the balcony to monitor the legislative prodeedings as they were happening.

During one such day, Aurora witnessed a hearing that sent her down a path of decency and integrity that would define the rest of her life. It all started when Morris Delgado — a colonel with the U.S. Army Corp of Engineers — 'Corps', for short — based in Jacksonville, Florida started speaking. While motioning toward a map of south Florida with his pointer, Delgado declared, "Our plan for ditching and draining 2,000,000 acres south of the vast inland sea — that the natives call Lake Okeechobee — will be one of the most momentous events in the history of our great state. We will turn this mosquito-infested land of muck and ooze into bounteous farmland and supporting development. This will not only make those who farm it and build on it rich, but will also open the door for attracting thousands upon thousands of new residents to our great state."

While listening to Delgado's slick, polished — but highly inaccurate — salespitch, Aurora could only hold her head in her hands and sigh deeply. In fact, it was all she could do to keep trom crying out loud. She knew that the work being proposed by this money-grubbing combination of federal and private mercenaries would forever change the south Florida landscape — destroying much of the state's vast treasure trove of natural resources that she had learned to love so much during her youth.

A SEQUENCE OF DEVELOPMENTAL TRAVESTIES

During the early part of the twentieth century, the State of Florida became an embarassing example of poor land development practices. Especially egregious was the natural resource travesty commited against the vast amalgam of freshwater wetlands that once dominated the landscape south of present-day Orlando. This monumental 'comedy of errors' included straightening hundreds of miles of cool, widely meandering streams and diking the sheet flow going south out of massive Lake Okeechobee.

Much of this work was done by the Corps under the guise of 'improvement projects' to help facilitate stormwater runoff, and lessen flooding problems during the rainy season. Of course — by eliminating natural floodplains and their associated groundwater recharge areas — these projects actually accomplished exactly the opposite. These massive federal boondoggles just served to coalesce and transport the flood flows — in much higher volumes — to unprotected downstream locations where they did significantly more damage than normal.

Impacts from 'channelization' — which, at the time, was being practiced by the Corps throughout the country — on aquatic and floodplain habitats were both abominable and unfathomable. The channelized streams essentially functioned as concrete sluiceways with no substrate for fishery reproduction and no vegetation for wildlife food production. The complete loss of connections to the historic floodways of these streams also eliminated most of the hydrologic and nutrient support systems for the adajacent freshwater marshes and floodplain swamps — causing the degradation and eventual loss of much of these critical wildlife habitats and the species dwelling in them.

Arguably, the most collosal ecological disasters foisted by the Corps — and their complicit cadre of developers and politicians — involved twice damming the south side of the broadly shallow Lake Okeechobee. This huge natural lake provided the cookie sheet-flat freshwater flow that supported south Florida's now well-known and invaluable 'river of grass'.

Both of these construction blunders resulted in massive deaths of mostly poor minority farmers. These farmers were led to believe that the Corps dams provided the protection they needed to till the soil and begin farming the fertile lands immediately south of Lake Okeechobee's shallow basin. What they did not count on — as inexplicably neither did the Corps — were the massively destructive forces that would be exerted by a strong hurricane against a hastily constructed and ill-conceived dam.

The first such disaster happened during a 1926 hurricane. When a massive wall of wind-whipped water in Lake Okeechobee smashed up against the shoddy dam, it failed and wiped out an estimated three hundred farmers and their families living downstream.

The Corps' contrarious response to this horrible disaster was to immediately rebuild the dam, under the belief that such a thing could never happen again. But of course, it did happen again — almost immediately and much more catastrophically — when another hurricane clobbered Lake Okeechobee in 1928, killing at least two thousand five hundred people.

The federal government's defense of these twin human and ecological disasters was to shift the blame away from the Corps — stating that something had to be done to counteract Mother Nature's creation of these 'killer Lake Okeechobee hurricanes'. No one will ever know what the feds had in mind with these remarks. Perhaps they were considering somehow filling the entire Okeechobee Basin with dredged material. Fortunately, this was one environmental atrocity that they were convinced not to commit.

As Aurora sat listening to a parade of salesmen prattling on about the untold benefits of their development proposals, she was also taking copious notes. She was building an artillery of knowledge to protect her beloved home. As Florida Audubon's leading lobbyist, Aurora knew she would have her chance to fight back against this environmental tyranny the very next morning.

Activism Becomes A Reality

Bright and early the next day, Aurora again took her seat in the senate gallery — eagerly anticipating being called upon to speak in opposition during the public testimony portion of the hearing. After the bailiff called her name to speak, Aurora strode forcefully up to the podium. Her diminutive frame, loose fitting outdoor clothes, and folksy manner belied the rage that was hiding in her heart.

"Mr Speaker," Aurora began, adressing House Speaker, Joseph Bliss, who was standing behind the dias at the front of the assembled legislature. "I respectfully want to point out that these men — both the developers and their cronies from the Corps — know absolutely nothing of what they speak. It is clear to me — as it should be to all parties here present — that they have not done any homework whatsoever on the topography, hydrology, geology, or soils of south Florida. If they had, they would know that much of Florida's unusual gelology consists of 'karst topography' — limestone bedrock that is honeycombed like a beehive."

"As such, it functions like a piece of cork that can't hold water," Aurora continued. "This means that if the peatland soil that underlies the drained wetlands is stripped off — no matter how much irrigation water is pumped onto these lands — they won't hold water long enough to support crops. Alternatively, if the peat is left in place, the land will again flood during south Florida's typical torrential rainstorms and the crops will be inundated and destroyed. Remember, just because the wetlands have been drained, it doesn't mean that the underlying peat deposits won't still hold water — that's just what they do!

"Furthermore," Aurora continued as she flailed her arms for emphasis, and spun round-and-round, maintaining eye contact with the legislators on the Senate floor, "draining and developing a vast area of wetlands like this will cause the loss of the vital functions that wetlands provide. For starters, you have the flood storage capacity. If the wetlands are no longer there, where do you think all the flood water runoff is going to go?"

Briefly pausing for effect, Aurora continued, "Well, I'll tell you exactly where the flood water will go... right into all the croplands and developed areas where the wetlands used to be! Can you imagine the nightmare of having to deal with severe and extensive flood damages every time it rains in South Florida?"

Now warming to her task, Aurora followed with this, "Next, there is the issue of groundwater recharge that natural wetlands provide. If we crop and pave over all our wetlands, what will we do for drinking water? Will we just be content to go thirsty while we watch everything wash away? Also — once the wetlands are gone — what will happen to all the pollutants that we continuously dump onto our landscape? In their natural state, wetlands serve as giant filters — sucking up and retaining much of the effluent we humans generate. If we eliminate wetlands, where are all these nasty contaminants going to go? Into our waterways and drinking water aquifers — that's where!"

"Finally consider this fact," concluded Aurora, "in Florida, wetlands provide the primary habitat needs for most of our wildlife — especially birds. Now I know — or at least I hope — that most of us living here enjoy the abundance of birds in our fine state. But if we eliminate all their habitats, where are the birds going to go? What will they do? I'll tell you what will happen — the birds will be long gone — either dead or migrating. So, ask yourself — is this the Florida we really want?"

And there it was. Florida Audubon's human hurricane had roared through the State House and made an absolute mockery of all the pro-development testimony that had been presented during the past two days. The rationale for widespread wetland ditching, draining, and filling had been totally blown out of the water by Aurora Adams.

Of course, the army of lawyers and engineers representing the other side wasn't about to give up the fight so easily. They knew they just needed to feign some expertise to win the audience back over to their side. In their minds, the war of words was just getting started.

Immediately after Aurora stacked her notes and walked away from the podium, Colonel Delgado took her place and he was not happy. "This woman's testimony is pure drivel and blasphemy," he bellowed, "she is attempting to steal our God-given right to improve all of south Florida for the interests and needs of the people of this state."

"And why is she doing this?" Delgado continued. "Well — as she just described herself — she wants to protect the plants and animals that are living here in a wild manner. Sacrificing the rights of humans to

295

future wealth, health, and happiness in the name of untamed nature is just not right, it's not the American way, and it's not how we have built our great country. We must not allow such blatant heresy to have standing — much less rule how we manage and use our vaulable land."

This response to her testimony only served to fuel the raging fire in Aurora's heart and head. She had yet to reach her seat, when Colonel Delgado started speaking. His first sentence — accusing her of blasphemy against the people — stopped her in her tracks. She waited in the aisle while he finished talking, and then she wheeled abruptly around and headed back toward the podium.

Grabbing the microphone from Delgado, she started ripping into him. "How dare you question my integrity and motives by saying that I don't value the people of Florida. I'm simply saying that what you and your wicked friends are proposing to do will be bad for all living things — both human and non-human. There are right ways to go about making Florida available for human settlement, but I assure you that it has nothing whatsoever to do what you are proposing."

Before Aurora could finish her rejoinder, Chairman Bliss gaveled her down. "Young lady, you have aready had your chance to speak. Now, I strongly advise you to go back to your seat and be quiet. Otherwise, I will be forced to hold you in contempt of these hearings."

Realizing that Speaker Bliss meant what he said, Aurora walked stiffly away from the podium and — with clinched fists and gritted teeth — made her way back to her seat. As soon as she sat down, she heard Speaker Bliss say, "I now declare this hearing closed and I am next going to ask for a show of hands — first from those in support and then those against the proposed project."

With that, Speaker Bliss asked for those legislators in support of the project to raise their hands. Aurora watched as at least 90% of the assembled hands went up in the air. The next vote then confirmed her worst fears as less than 10% of the representatives voted to turn the project down. Aurora wasn't surprised at the overwhelmingly positive approval — especially after the previous two days of lies, half-truths, and innuendo that the project's supporters presented. But she was still both astonished and dismayed at what had happened.

Starting A Family and Continuing the Fight

In January 1915, Aurora met Jacob Ellsworth, a muscular and handsome local hunting and fishing guide. They first met on what was known as the 'lighthouse dike trail', located in what would become St. Marks National Wildlife Refuge in Florida's panhandle. In Aurora's mind, Jacob was a junior image of her father, Harrison. He had the personality of a rugged outdoorsman which was tempered by a deep, abiding love and respect for all the creatures of the natural world.

Given the fact that their lifestyles and beliefs — especially those related to natural resources and conservation — were so well blended, it's little wonder that Aurora and Jacob fell hard for each other. Just four months after they first met, they were married in an intimate, but movingly beautiful ceremony in the St. Marks' Lighthouse, the second oldest lighthouse in the State of Florida.

During the next five years — while living in Tallahassee — Aurora and Jacob had three children. In order of their birth, the youngsters were named Jason Thoreau, Fathom Walden, and Camilla Hemenway. Camilla's middle name, of course, honored the name of Aurora's beloved mentor — Harriett Hemenway.

While lovingly raising her beautiful children, Aurora continued to fight the good fight in preserving Florida's treasure trove of wetlands, wild birds, and other natural resources. Unfortunately — for the most part — the absence of both state and federal regulatory protection, generally left Aurora feeling like she was trying to stave off a tidal wave with a teaspoon.

With her rabble-rousing personality and unassuaged opposition to ill-conceived development, Aurora soon began being compared to Marjory Stoneman Douglas — the young South Florida activist, and future 'Grand Dame of the Everglades'. These comparisons so intrigued

Aurora that she sought out Ms. Douglas when she came to Tallahassee for a public hearing. Thus began a wonderful friendship and working relationship that lasted throughout Aurora's remaining career as an ardent conservationist.

A New Mentor Takes Over

Ironically, Marjory Stoneman Douglas was born in 1890 in Minneapolis, Minnesota, and grew up in Taunton, Massachusetts — two places and environments that were about as far removed as possible from the South Florida landscape she came to love and cherish. During her undergraduate years at Massachusetts's Wellesley College, Marjory earned straight A's and was voted 'Class Orator' — a prophetic title, as wealthy landowners and their corrupt politicians throughout South Florida were soon to learn.

After college, Marjory moved to South Florida and began working as a columnist for her father's newspaper — the precursor to the *Miami Herald*. Combining skillful writing with a firebrand personality, she quickly gained local notoriety by getting embroiled in battles over racial inequality, feminism, and resource conservation — long before these issues became the focus of the national spotlight.

The state of Florida's outlandishly uncontrolled land development practices provided the perfect fodder for Marjory during her early years as a columnist and poet for the *Miami Herald*. She regularly wrote editorials urging protection of Florida's unique regional character and arguing against the rampant development that was threatening to destroy these irreplaceable natural resources.

In her characteristic Panama hat and horn-rimmed glasses, Marjory typically looked more like a wealthy socialite than the ardent outdoor lover that she was. But as the old adage goes, 'looks can be deceiving'. Marjory worked diligently to turn a lifelong passion for doing the right thing into her own personal environmental crusade. Her diminutive size also belied her zeal for speaking truth to the power interests in South Florida.

Well aware of Marjory's outsized power and well-earned respect, Aurora was nervous about their first meeting. But within five minutes of conversation with the legend, Aurora began to relax. The two women's shared passion for blocking land development in the Everglades to maintain its vital sheet flow provided much fodder for connection. Their union against the many enemies they were sure to encounter — land developers, political hacks, and power brokers — gave them a common bond. From Marjory, Aurora learned how to effectively take on the developers while also earning a great deal of respect from all sides.

After their initial meeting, Aurora often joined Marjory in rallies and public hearings for proposed projects. They repeatedly blended their fierce personalities with their evocative vocabularies to make mockeries of the hogwash that was being spewed in every direction by the vain, greedy land developers.

Each proposed development project was typically represented by an all-male team of lawyers, surveyors, engineers, and bankers — known as the 'money men'. Of course, each project group also included a smattering of local, state and federal officials who were being paid under the table to approve and support each smarmy proposed action.

Aurora and Marjory were almost always in the minority of public opinion, but that didn't stop this diminutive duo of strong-willed women from constantly clamoring for things to be done the right way. Unfortunately, their persistent preaching about protecting the natural environment mostly fell on deaf ears. The dastardly triumvirates of developers, politicians, and federal engineers kept right on conspiring and colluding ways to ditch, drain, and develop South Florida's fast-disappearing natural paradise.

A Land Development Travesty

Aurora and Marjory continued to work tirelessly — trying their best to stem the tide of land development tyranny that was engulfing the State of Florida. Throughout the first half of the twentieth century, the appallingly incessant roar of heavy machinery continued to mow down and fill up thousands upon thousands of acres of South Florida wetlands.

In less than fifty years, this massive illusion of land development grandeur transformed much of south Florida from the peaceful swampland it once was, to the chaos of golf course communties, shopping plazas, blinking traffic lights, and honking cars that it is today.

As Aurora agonizingly experienced far too often during her career, many of the concepts of natural resource degradation and wildlife annihilation hit their zeniths in the state of Florida. Though she was often fighting a battle that seemed insurmountable, Aurora never lost sight of her goals or gave up hope.

THE RAMPANT RAVAGES OF TEAM RODENT

No one was guiltier of the sleazy development of Florida than the 'Mouse King' himself. In their infinite wisdom, the State of Florida welcomed Walt Disney in the 1960s with open arms and widespread checkbooks. Using such clever psuedonyms as 'M. T. Lott' to mask his high-powered name, Disney purchased and filled hundreds of acres of pristine wetlands. Power players in both the private and public sectors told him he could do whatever he wanted as long as he put his massive new 'theme parks' in the middle of the state. Many people will tell you that Disney World — because of the rampaging development it still fosters — is the worst thing that ever happened to Florida.

Carl Hiaasen is a bestselling novelist and columnist for the *Miami Herald*. In his 1998 book, *Team Rodent: How Disney Devours the World*, Hiaasen suggests that Disney World changed the face of an entire state. He writes, "Three decades after it began bulldozing the cow pastures and draining the marshes of rural Orlando, Disney stands as — by far — the most powerful entity in Florida; it goes where it wants, does what it wants, gets what it wants… the worst thing Disney did was to change how people in Florida thought about money… suddenly there were no limits. Merely by showing up, Disney dignified blind greed in a state pioneered by undignified greedheads."

At Last Success

In 1947 — after more than thirty years of fighting with politicians, bureaucrats, and local land developers — Aurora helped Marjory publish her landmark book, *The Everglades: River of Grass*. In this masterpiece — which has been favorably compared to Rachel Carson's *Silent Spring* and Aldo Leopold's *A Sand County Almanac* — Marjory lovingly described the unfathomable beauty and untold treasures encompassed by Florida's Everglades.

The *River of Grass* sparked a movement to protect the Everglades from uncontrolled filling, land development, and wanton destruction. It also opened the eyes of the rest of the country to see and appreciate the many critical functions — including flood control, water quality protection, aquifer recharge, and wildlife habitat — provided by wetlands.

Her tireless efforts as a conservationist, earned Marjory many awards. In 1986, the National Parks and Conservation Association established the Marjory Stoneman Douglas Award 'to honor individuals who often must go to great lengths to advocate and fight for the protection of the National Park System.' Then, in 1993, she was awarded the Presidential Medal of Freedom — America's highest civilian honor.

Aurora served as Marjory's trusted proof-reader and second set of eyes for the *River of Grass*. Through her intense involvement with the inimitable Ms. Douglas, Aurora knew that she would fight until the end of her days to protect the remaining treasures of the Everglades and the State of Florida.

And she did just that.

BOOK THIRTEEN
Passing the Torch

Twin Conservationists Are Born

While Aurora Ellsworth was constantly tangling with evil developers throughout the Florida peninsula, her youngest daughter — Camilla Hemenway Ellsworth — was watching and listening with rapt attention. Clearly inheriting her mother's love for all living things, Camilla graduated at the top of her class from Tallahassee's Leon High School. She then continued her studies and — in the spring of 1947 — achieved dual degrees in wildlife biology and journalism while graduating *summa cum laude* from the University of North Carolina in Chapel Hill.

Throughout her scholastic years, Camilla Ellsworth had no doubt about what she wanted to do with her life. Watching her mom struggle — day after day, hearing after hearing — with no regulatory tools to support her cause — left an indelible impression. She vowed that she was going to dedicate her life to correcting this unfair situation.

Capitalizing on her mom's long and dedicated career with Florida Audubon, Camilla contacted National Audubon Society's Office in Washington, DC. Fortunately, they offered her just the deal she was looking for. They needed a cracking good lobbyist in their DC Office who could really shake up the local establishment with a deft combination of actions and words.

With her disarmingly persuasive personality, well-honed writing skills, and strong knowledge of Audubon's national agenda and goals, Camilla was the ideal choice for this job. She didn't have to be asked twice. In fact, she was not the least bit apprehensive about leaving Florida behind.

Camilla knew that working in the Nation's Capital would provide her with the perfect location and access to get her goals accomplished. In just two days time, she was aboard a passenger train whisking her up the East Coast to what she felt sure would be her long-term career.

Within days of her arrival in Washington, DC during the first week of July 1947, Camilla met a man who was about to change her life in many ways. It happened as she was moving into a tiny — what would today be called 'a studio' — but furnished apartment near Capitol Hill.

Camilla was struggling to lug her rather bulky belongings up the steep stairs of her brownstone building. Suddenly, a dapper young man with a sleek handlebar moustache and golden blonde hair — parted neatly in the middle — appeared behind her and asked, "Hey my good lady, it looks to me like you could use some male muscle!"

Never wanting to admit weakness, especially not to some macho stranger, Camilla replied, "Oh well thank you, kind sir, but I'm managing just fine on my own!"

At this point, in a perfect case of impeccably humorous — if somewhat painful — timing, Camilla slipped and tumbled backward down the staircase. She fortunately caught herself enough to mostly break her fall, but she looked totally forlorn and embarassed, with one of her suitcases planted indiscretely in the middle of her chest.

Noting that Camilla was not seriously injured, the winsome passerby immediately jumped to her assistance while remarking obsequiously, "Ah yes, I can see you have everything well under control!"

As the man lifted the suitcase off of her, Camilla jumped quickly to her feet, dusted herself off, and harumphed, "I am perfectly fine, good sir, and certainly would have been so — even without your assistance!"

Laughing lightly under his breath — the man knew he had a challenge on his hands if he expected to get to know this petite, but fiercely determined young woman. He graciously extended his hand, saying, "Pleased to make your acquaintance, I'm Horace P. Greenleaf. May I ask your name?"

Camilla turned and faced the man squarely, peering deeply into his eyes. He certainly seemed to be a gentleman, and was handsome enough. "Yes, sir, my name is Camilla Hemenway Ellsworth and I've just moved to Washington, DC from Tallahassee, Florida."

"Well then, Miss Camilla from Florida," asked Horace, "what is it that has brought you up here on such a long journey?"

"I'm a lobbyist for the National Audubon Society," replied Camilla, "I'm here to find better ways to protect our Nation's wildlife — especially birds — and the natural habitats that support them."

"Very interesting," replied Horace, "I'm a wildlife biologist with the

National Park Service and my primary charge is setting aside more federal land — as national parks and monuments — with the specific goal of protecting more habitat for our Nation's wildlife. It sounds like once you get settled, we should have lunch and discuss our common goals. DC is a wonderful restaurant city — very diverse, as you might expect — and I would be honored to introduce you to some of its best spots."

Camilla and Horace's first lunch — just a couple of days later at an authentic Morrocan café on North Capitol Street — turned into many follow-up convivial colloquies. Many of their discussions focused on the mixed public opinion about natural resource issues, infused with myriad social and political concerns. They talked about how World War II ended and how the Nazi scourge had blessedly been eliminated. They debated the merits of the Manhattan Project. They both agreed that — while it may have finally won the war — the inglorious death and destruction, wreaked by dropping atomic bombs on the Japanese cities of Hiroshima and Nagasaki, had changed the world forever.

As ardent wildlife lovers, however, they talked the most about the fates that had befallen so many of America's once bountiful species. In particular, they lamented the eradication of wild flocks of Carolina parakeets and passenger pigeons — both of which used to fly in such enormous flocks that it was impossible to imagine their extinction.

They also reveled in glimmers of hope for wildlife — such as the Smithsonian Institution's William Temple Hornaday single-handedly saving the American bison from extinction. While millions upon millions of these free ranging symbols of the American West had been senelessly slaughtered by marauding bands of trophy hunters, at least several hundred — enough to save the species from disappearing forever — were now permanently protected.

As things turned out, Horace Greenleaf and Camilla Ellsworth really did have a great deal in common. Their 'soul mate' dream continued three months later, when they married in a simple ceremony at a small Episcopal Church in the Georgetown Section of DC. Their wedding reception was held at one of Georgetown's justifiably famous telescoping pubs and attended only by family and close friends.

Then in October 1948, Camilla and Horace Greenleaf welcomed

fraternal twins into their lives. They named the girl Abbey Brower and the boy Aldo Marshall. Little could they imagine — at the time — that the names they had chosen for their baby daughter would go down as indelible heroes in the annals of the U.S. environmental movement. In defining her illustrious career, Abbey Brower Greenleaf would perfectly blend the high adventure, full-spirited advocacy of David Brower — '*The Archdruid*' himself — with the unfiltered, just don't give a hoot journalistic aplomb of Edward Abbey — '*Mr Monkey Wrench Gang*'.

Of course, Camilla and Horace knew that the names they had selected for their son were already a revered part of our country's environmental heritage. In naming him, Aldo Marshall Greenleaf, they paid homage to two of the people — Aldo Leopold and Robert 'Bob' Marshall — they most respected for dedicating their lives to our Nation's natural resources.

In fact, if they had known in advance what the future held for both their daughter and their son, Camilla and Horace would most certainly have been delighted beyond belief.

Dominance by the Bureau of Reclamation

The U.S. Bureau of Reclamation was created as a separate bureau in 1907, for the expressed purposes of 'watering the west' and 'making the desert bloom'. Under congressional directives, the BuRec's administrators attacked their task with great vigor — knowing that the only thing that could hold back westward expansion was a lack of water in the parched western landscapes. Accomplishing this required that the agency's phalanx of planners, engineers, and hydrologists first find and commandeer sites that lent themselves well to construction of mighty dams backing up immense volumes of irrigation water. Hoover Dam and Lake Meade in Arizona and Nevada, Grand Coulee Dam and Roosevelt Lake in Washington State, and Fort Peck Dam and Lake in Montana were all prototype BuRec projects.

These marvels of human engineering did — in fact — allow crops to be produced and people to survive in places where only greasewood, tumbleweed, sidewinder rattlesnakes, and roadrunners were supposed to live naturally. But from a natural resource and aesthetic standpoint, these towering concrete edifices — and the inland seas they backed up — were catastophes of the highest order. Once each dam was completed and the reservoir was filled, everything for miles and miles upstream of the dam was drowned and lost forever.

These inundated resources included thousands upon thousands of acres of often very rare wildlife habitat — such as 'cottonwood-willow riverbottoms' — the long, meandering inland oases of life that characterize the floodplains of many western rivers. But also lost were scads of irreplaceable human resources — petroglyphs, artifacts, and constructed civilizations of the Native American tribes that occupied these areas millennia before the European colonists arrived.

Camilla Greenleaf's first real test as a National Audubon lobbyist was a daunting one. She was assigned to testify on Capitol Hill against the mighty federal Bureau of Reclamation's (BuRec) overly ambitious dam building program. Derogatorially known in some circles as the 'Bureau of Wreck the Nation', BuRec was charged with taking desolate areas of landscape — located throughout the western United States — and turning them into lush valleys full of irrigation canals and verdant farmland.

In assuming her role as protector of the natural landscape, Camilla dutifully and brazenly stepped to the microphone and went after a project that reached deep into her psyche. The BuRec had a proposal for 'programmatic approval' — meaning no natural resource impact assessments were required — of the Colorado River Storage Project, which encompassed construction of multiple new dams and reservoirs across several western states.

"How can you — the representatives of the people — turn a blind eye toward the obliteration of hundreds of natural habitats that support thousands upon thousands of wild animals," Camilla asked. "Why are these animals and the places they live being sacrificed? I'll tell you why — for pure speculation that if you build something, people will come and use it.

"But there's no guarantee that anyone will actually use this water for growing crops. Most of these projects are located in the middle of nowhere," continued Camilla, "there's a good reason no one lives there now — these lands are not fit for permanent human habitation. It's like a young child trying to drive square pegs into round holes. They just won't work. The difference is the young child eventually realizes the futility and gives up. But not so with BuRec planners and engineers. You just keep on slamming away until something breaks — how utterly foolish!"

For the most part, the federal legislators just listened quietly while Camilla spoke. Some acted like they were taking notes, while others simply dozed off. In the minds of most D.C. politicians of the day, any projects that created real estate for sale were a good thing and should — therefore — be allowed to go forward. As a consequence, every BuRec project that came along was expeditiously approved. In fact, the legislators wished they had even more 'water reclamation projects' to vote on, since they were always favorably received by the majority of their constituents.

This 'approval by rote' procedure made Camilla's job both frustrating and boring. After two years of being mostly ignored, she was ready to find something that would give her a better shot at making a difference.

Career Frustrations Build

Things really weren't much better for Horace over at the National Park Service (NPS). He was dedicating his life to researching and finding new landscapes — especially in the American West — that merited full and permanent preservation under the auspices of the NPS. Many times, his studies involved traveling with a team of scientists to some remote western landscape for first-hand review and documentation. He was not totally rebuffed in his efforts — as Camilla was in presenting her anti-dam testimonies — but the 'no' answers to his protection proposals happened far too often.

In many ways, Horace's troubles with the NPS' mission left him dumbfounded. After all — from a natural resources protection standpoint — the agency was our federal government's most important resource protection model. It was — and still is — being emulated throughout the world.

As an ardent student of the conservation movement in the United States, Horace knew full well that the NPS was the torch bearer for the successes that could be achieved. That's the main reason he decided to work for them. The agency's record for acquiring permanent protection for our vital natural resources — even before 'land conservation' was a real thing — was remarkable.

Gleaned from his detailed research, Horace considered John Muir to be his ultimate life hero and role model. Often called the 'Father of Our National Park System', Muir lived his life to the fullest. Through his writing and speaking, he made others aware of the joy he found in his famous western cathedrals: "Climb the mountains and get their good tidings. Nature's peace will flow into you as sunshine flows into the trees."

But Muir also realized the importance of fighting for the protection of these iconic landscapes as a way to honor the entire natural world; "When we try to pick out anything by itself, we find it hitched to everything else in the universe." In the final analysis, he gave his life — battling corporations, city officials, and federal bureaucrats while trying unsuccessfully to save a sacred piece of his hallowed cathedral — the Hetch Hetchy Valley — in the High Sierras.

Emphasizing his devotion to Muir's thoughts and practices, Horace sincerely believed that every piece of land he 'discovered' was worthy of federal protection. But the rejections he received were far too often based purely on economic factors — in lieu of carefully studied natural resource values.

In fact, several times his scientific teams were attacked by gangs of shotgun-toting men, who told them flat out to 'get the hell off our land'. This happened despite the fact that Horace knew full well that the land he selected for review was all open space and unowned.

The Park Service's reponse to each of these events was to immediately give up, instead of pursuing legal action against these wild west bullies. Such repetitive experiences led Horace to finally and fully agree with Camilla — enough was enough. It was time to get out of the madding city and into living on open land where their actions would make a difference — at least at the local level.

Finding a Virginia Home

One oppressively hot and humid July day in 1951, Camilla picked up her phone and heard Horace's almost delirious voice proclaiming, "I've just found the job we've both been looking for! It's with the U.S. Fish and Wildlife Service (USFWS). We would be co-managers of a wildlife refuge located in southeastern Virginia. It's absolutely perfect for us and I'm sure — with our resumes — we would be shoo-ins to get it!"

After Camilla hung up, she was just as excited as Horace. She couldn't wait to get home and hear about the details.

There was a huge reason both Horace and Camilla were so thrilled with their new job. The USFWS — and their country-wide network of national wildlife refuges — was focused solely on protecting existing habitat and creating new habitat for wild birds.

So — on paper, at least — this was a federal agency that combined Camilla's unabiding love for wild birds, with Horace's quest to continually identify and protect the habitat of wildlife species that were rapidly declining in number. In fact — while many of the USFWS's refuges were managed for waterfowl hunting — they were also bastions of protection for wildlife species that were in limited abundance.

THE MAN WHO SAVED DUCKS

Created in 1940, the U.S. Fish and Wildlife Service supports the following mission statement: *'working with others to conserve, protect, and enhance fish, wildlife, plants, and their habitats for the continuing benefit of the American people.'* By 1945, the national wildlife refuge system, under the direction of the USFWS, was the fastest-growing federal land agency in the country — protecting thousands of acres of natural wildlife habitats.

The USFWS owes its start to the man with the best name in the history of the U.S. environmental movement. Jay Norwood 'Ding' Darling — the 'Man Who Saved Ducks' — combined an artist's eye with a humorist's ear and — over fifty years — produced Pulitzer Prize-winning political cartoons that amused the American public while galvanizing their support for landmark conservation initiatives.

Darling was in large part responsible for establishing the network of national wildlife refuges that now spread across the country. The Federal Aid in Wildlife Restoration Act of 1937 (also known as the Pittman-Robertson Act) — which provides money to states for the purchase of game habitat and helps fund wildlife research through a tax on sporting firearms and ammunition — also owes its existence to Darling's work.

In the fall of 1951, Horace and Camilla — along with their children Abbey and Aldo — moved into the manager's house in Back Bay National Wildlife Refuge (NWR). Established in 1938, Back Bay NWR now occupies nine thousand acres in the southeasternmost part of Virginia. At the time that the Greenleafs moved there, the staff's housing on the refuge could only be accessed by boat. Although the living conditions were both rustic and remote, Camilla and Horace loved the immersive experience of hands-on living with wildlife.

Living in Back Bay gave Camilla and Horace a prime opportunity to home school Abbey and Aldo. Far removed from the rigors and constant diversions of their previous DC homes and office jobs, they were free to concentrate on inculcating both children with the same conservation ethic that so strongly influenced their own lives and careers.

Since they were refuge co-managers, Camilla and Horace shared both administrative and field responsibilities. To accomplish this, they rotated their work on a daily basis. Camilla would take the refuge's Boston Whaler patrol boat out on rounds one day while Horace stayed in their home office, doing paperwork and answering the phone. Then — the next day — they switched tasks with Horace going out on patrol and Camilla handling the desk duties.

This worked especially well for Abbey and Aldo, since they also alternated between home and the field with their parents. When either child went out riding patrol, they always learned new things about the refuge's ecology.

Since both Camilla and Horace were exceptional birders, Abbey and Aldo soon could identify every bird in the refuge — both visually and 'by ear'. They even knew how to differentiate each bird species' songs and calls as well, parsing out the regional 'dialects' of birds within the same species.

When they were out on the boat with Abbey and Aldo, Camilla and Horace also concentrated on explaining the inner workings of the refuge's complex ecology. For example, they described how each species of wading bird uses a different feeding style that best fits its physiology. Snowy egrets poke around with their 'golden slippered' feet to scare small fish and amphibians out of their hiding places in the marsh grass. Meanwhile, great blue herons and great white egrets both slowly stalk and then stand stockstill until their prey forgets that they are there. Then it's one quick stab, and dinner is served. Meanwhile, the reddish egret's 'drunken sailor routine' confuses the bait fish so much that they don't know which way to flee.

While the wading birds are feeding, double-crested cormorants — slickly and quickly dive under the water and then pop back up with fish wriggling in their mouths. Each cormorant displays its dexterity in always flipping a flopping fish around in its beak so that it can be swallowed head-first. Then, suddenly — from high above — an osprey dives feet first to secure its prey in sharp talons before flying off to a nearby nest to feed its young.

On days when Abbey and Aldo alternated staying at home — Camilla and Horace instructed them in the educational basics — including English, math, physics, chemistry, and biology. They even included time for music lessons, with Camilla teaching Abbey how to play the console piano in the refuge's house and Horace teaching Aldo how to play his six string guitar.

Many of the refuge's visitors were families with children. Whenever they stopped by, Camilla and Horace let Abbey and Aldo lead the visitors on interpretive hikes or boat rides. This had the dual benefit of educating the public about the refuge's wildlife and ecology while honing Abbey and Aldo's social and scientific communication skills.

317

A Poaching Event

During the fall and winter hunting seasons, the sounds of duck and goose calls reverberated throughout the marshland habitat. Shotgun blasts periodically interrupted the cacophonic blend of birdsongs as hidden hunters rose and took aim at their quarries. For the most part, the refuge's hunters all had the appropriate licenses and followed the established bag limits set for each species of waterfowl that the refuge supported. Only occasionally did Horace or Camilla have to write tickets for either lack of a hunting license or exceedance of a species 'bag limit'. There were, however, a few exceptions involving disingenious poachers with a plan.

After receiving a tip from one of the refuge's most frequent and trusted hunters, Horace boated out well before sunrise and sequestered himself in a dense patch of reeds. He chose his hiding spot to be near the blinds that the poachers were said to be using. Sure enough — still under the cover of darkness — Horace heard the putt-putt-putt of a boat motor and the muffled chatter of a crew of four men coming directly toward him.

Once the boat was within one hundred yards of Horace's hiding place, it veered off toward the suspect blinds. The next thing Horace saw and heard let him know that these fellows were indeed up to no good. He could see their arms flailing about and the hear the sound of the feed corn they were flinging hitting both the water and the adjacent marsh vegetation.

Once they started hunting, Horace now had them 'dead to rights' since hunting over bait — the feed corn they were dispersing — was illegal. He could have arrested them on the spot, but Horace waited, because he knew a much greater and judicially more intense infraction — waterfowl poaching — was likely to occur.

While Horace waited and watched, the malicious gun-toters manoeuvred their boat into a blind right next to the illicitly baited area. Soon after sunrise, skeins of ducks — mostly mallards and wood ducks

— began arriving and cantilivering down into the baited area like heavy raindrops at the beginning of a thunderstorm. As soon as the ducks started descending, an unrelenting bombardment of number five shot began.

The carnage was sickening. It was akin to shooting fish in a barrel — birds were dropping from the sky so fast that Horace couldn't even begin to estimate how many had been killed. But he did know one thing; these yahoos were certainly exceeding their legal limits, and by a very high number, indeed!

After the blasting subsided, Horace watched disconsolately while the men waded out and collected their feathered corpses, guffawing all the while about how many birds they had shot. Within an hour, the deviants had finished collecting most of the dead birds.

This was by far the worst case of poaching that Horace had ever witnessed on the refuge. Plus the complete lack of remorse — and, in fact, downright glee — these low lifes demonstrated for both the law and the birds completely infuriated Horace. He knew what he was about to do was risky — since he didn't have any backup — but he just couldn't let these scofflaws get away with it.

He drew his pistol and demanded, "Drop your weapons and raise your hands, I'm a federal wildlife officer and you're all under arrest for illegal baiting and taking of waterfowl." The surprised men reluctantly did as they were told while grumbling such banalities as 'they didn't realize they were violating the law' and 'they didn't intentionally kill more ducks than they should have.'

Horace just rolled his eyes as he listened to their inane whining. Using one hand on an oar, while still training his pistol on the men with his other hand, Horace pushed his way over to the offenders' boat. Once alongside, he started writing arrest warrants for all four of them telling them that — once they got back to the mainland — they would follow him to the Princess Anne County Courthouse where they would be booked for waterfowl poaching.

Since he had to use both hands to write the warrants, Horace assumed his suspects would be civil enough to abide by the presence of federal authority. So he dropped his guard and put his pistol on his boat seat while he wrote.

Of course, trusting these miscreants was a big mistake. Scant seconds after Horace laid down his weapon, one of the poachers picked up an oar and smashed Horace in the head, knocking him unconscious into the back of his boat. Howling with laughter, the jack-booters yelled in unison, "OK, we done took care of this loony lawman. There ain't nothin he can do to us now. Let's get the hell out of here and no one will be any the wiser."

Then something happened that they least expected. From all four corners of the surrounding marsh, other boats appeared — each carrying more duck hunters with raised shotguns. The only difference was that these were legitimate law-abiding hunters, who had heard about Horace's daring mission and decided to be 'in the area' just in case he needed help.

"OK, you liver-lillied scumbags, raise your hands and shut your mouths. It's idiots like you that give us honest hunters a bad name and decimate the waterfowl populations we rely on. We're not going to put up with it. So you can either go quietly with us back to the mainland, or we'll just blast you right here on the spot since you just attacked a federal law enforcement officer. It's your choice!"

By the time they all got back to the mainland, Horace was fine. He dutifully thanked his rescuers, four of whom insisted on helping him cart the law breakers over to the courthouse for booking.

On final count, the poachers had taken a total of more than eighty ducks — three times the legal limit. During their hearing a few weeks later, the court told the men that they had to make restitution for the birds they killed. Plus the shotguns they had used were confiscated. Since the shotguns were all top-of-the-line, the overall judgment was going to end up costing the men about a thousand dollars each. More than enough — hoped Horace — to keep them from thinking about pulling such a stunt again.

The Director's Visit Brings a Change

An especially memorable event occurred on a sunny, but blustery and cool morning in the middle of October, 1954. Camilla was out making her morning rounds, while Horace whipped up breakfast for himself, Abbey, and Aldo. The wood fire snapped and popped as the smell of bacon frying filled the room. Suddenly, the two-way radio crackled to life: "Good morning, this is the Princess Anne Base Station. Please come in. Over."

Thinking this was just a routine morning check to make sure everything was all right; Horace picked up the receiver. "Good morning to you. This is Back Bay Station. All systems are in fine shape and running smoothly here."

"Well, maybe not," replied the voice on the other end, "depending on what I'm about to tell you."

"Oh — what could possibly go wrong on a fine day like today?" Horace queried in his always upbeat voice. "Hit me with the bad news."

"OK, here goes: The director himself, Mr. John Farley, and his entourage will be stopping by your place in less than an hour — as soon as their patrol boat can make it through the choppy bay to your dock. Are you ready for them?"

Horace summoned his best example of a confident, casual response, "Okey dokey, no problem on this end. We'll be out there waiting for the director as soon as he arrives."

After he switched off the radio, Horace let his anxiety show. He was simultaneously both exhilirated and exhausted. A first hand meeting with the Director of the USFWS was both a superb delight and a supreme honor. But there was so much to do and so little time to do it.

He grabbed the radio again — with a trembling hand — and called Camilla. "Guess who's coming to breakfast?" he asked, trying to sound as matter-of-fact as he could.

"I have no idea — who could be visting us this early in the

morning?" Camilla responded. It wasn't like they had any next door neighbors who would be dropping by to share some coffee.

"I'll give you a hint," replied Horace. "He's from Washington, DC and he has a big traveling party with him."

"Oh my gosh," exclaimed Camilla, "not President Eisenhower!"

"No, not quite — but close. It's Director Farley — he wants to see first hand what we're doing out here. And — here's the real news — he'll be here in less than an hour."

"OK, I'm on my way back right now," Camilla said, as she simultaneously turned the Whaler back toward their dock. She sensed the urgency in Horace's voice and realized he needed help getting ready.

Right on schedule, an officious-looking Cabin Cruiser — named the 'Refuge Rider' pulled up to the refuge dock, and disgorged six people with Director Farley bringing up the rear. They were all dressed in their best LL Bean outerwear, and looked as if they were headed out for a month long African safari.

"Well hello there, you must be the Greenleafs — safe keepers of this magnificent wildlife paradise," said Director Farley with a broad, mischevious grin adorning his round face. "And I see you've brought your future replacements," he continued while motioning toward Abbey and Aldo, "who I assume are already receiving *beaucoup* training in what it takes to run this place."

"A hearty welcome, sir, to you and your party!" beamed Horace. "Please come inside our humble abode. We've got fresh pots of coffee and tea and from-scratch biscuits with homemade strawberry jam just waiting for your arrival."

Horace led the field party into the refuge house. By assembling chairs from all the rooms around the kitchen table, they had — just barely — enough room for everyone to sit.

While Abbey and Aldo dutifully served coffee and biscuits, Director Farley opened his briefcase, rummaged through it, and finally withdrew two manila envelopes. He opened the first and sorted the contents — copies of the beloved 'Ding' Darling's political cartoons along with boxes of fresh Crayola crayons — to both Abbey and Aldo.

"Let's see what you youngsters can do to spice up some of my hero's curmudgeonly work," said Director Farley as he winked at the kids' excited faces.

With that, Director Farley took another bite of his jam-drizzled biscuit, opened the second envelope and withdrew the contents — some scribbled talking points — and began speaking in his affably articulate manner.

"I want to start off by congratulating both of you — plus your little ones — for the wonderful job you have been doing. I've done a little research, and I know you two epitomize what we are trying to accomplish. Keep in mind, that the U.S. Fish and Wildlife Service has only been around for fifteen years. But in that time, we have made great strides in ferreting out and protecting — through the establishment of new refuges — invaluable natural wildlife habitats and the species living therein that are in peril of declining populations."

"As you know, our focus is — and must be — on protecting and expanding habitat for waterfowl and the folks that hunt them. This is because our primary funding for managing our refuges comes from the federal 'duck stamp program' which is money accrued from hunters when they purchase their licenses.

"But I want our refuge system to be much more than just preserves for duck hunters," Director Farley continued. "And that's why you two fit in so perfectly. I know that you really pay attention to everything that's going on here in Back Bay — looking at much more than just your populations of ducks and geese. I know you are paying special attention to the populations of shorebirds, wading birds, and raptors that use this refuge — and how they fit into this overall ecosystem.

"I know you are tracking population numbers — annual increases and decreases — for more than fifty 'non-game species'. You are building databases that will allow the determination of trends in food supplies and migratory patterns for each of these species. This is exactly the type of information that will allow us to implement efficient and effective management programs for all the wildlife — both game and non-game — that live throughout our refuges."

Then, Director Farley delivered his main talking point. "Your dedication to holistic ecosystem management is something I want to feature as a management prototype for all of our current and future refuge managers. To acomplish this, I am herewith designating both of you —

323

Camilla Greenleaf and Horace Greenleaf — as roving wildlife management ambassadors with responsibility for traveling to refuges all over the country, and teaching our field employees how to set up management programs exactly like the one you have established here. The good news is that this will be a significant step-up for you both — in terms of both prestige, as Assistant Directors, and financial compensation. But — since I know how much you both like living and working in the field — the bad news is, this job will require you to move back to Washington, DC."

Camilla and Horace were both completely surprised and flummoxed by Director Farley's offer. They both sat in stunned silence — glancing first at the director, then at each other and their kids, and back again at the director.

Realizing he had suddenly planted a very large seed of disarray, Director Farley quickly tried to ameliorate the shock effect of his offer. "Oh wow, folks, my apologies — I now realize I should have soft-pedaled this whole situation a bit. I should have given you some advance warning, instead of gliding out here and dropping a bombshell like this on you.

"Let me be perfectly clear — this is strictly an offer — actually quite a selfish one on my part," Director Farley continued. "After studying what you have been doing here, I realized what a potential administrative windfall you represent for both the agency and my mission as director. Let me assure you that — if you decline — it will have no effect on your record or status whatsoever. I will still consider you to be a tremendous asset and will be grateful for the wonderful work I'm sure you will continue to do here at Back Bay Refuge. Why don't you take a few days to think things through, talk it over, and then get back to me with your decision. I will certainly remain in awe of your service no matter what decision you make."

With that, Director Farley stood and shook hands with both Camilla and Horace, patted Abbey and Aldo on their heads while admiring the way they had colored Ding Darling's cartoons, and headed for the door and the dock.

As the motor launch backed away from the dock, Director Farley waved vigorously and shouted, "Thanks very much for a wonderful visit.

I assure you that your delicious biscuits, strawberry jam, and hospitable conversation will continue to warm my heart for the rest of the day."

For several minutes after the director's boat had disappeared into the marshy horizon, Horace and Camilla gazed lovingly at each other without speaking. Finally, Horace remarked, "Well… while we'll certainly miss the quiet but meaningful lifestyle we have established here, this seems like a once-in-a-lifetime opportunity. The director has just laid out the next big step — call it a giant leap — in our careers. But we have a really good thing going here, and we love our life in the bay. On balance, what do you think, my love?"

Camilla thought for a moment. While they did have a good, simple life, this was the chance she had been hoping for since she started her career as an Audubon lobbyist. The two of them could now shape the nation's overall wildlife refuge system, which would have far-reaching effects — way beyond their management of a single refuge. She thought of how many birds they could save working together, plus all the ways they could strengthen the habitats that the birds relied on. She raised her cup of coffee toward the end of the dock and said, "To Back Bay — thank you for the good life we've had here. But the time has now come for us to make a much bigger splash."

With that, Camilla and Horace gently embraced each other and their kids, then turned and walked quietly — but confidently — back into their refuge home for their last few months of bliss on the bay.

BOOK FOURTEEN
Being Wildlife Ambassadors

Following Leopold

Because of a comprehensive relocation package, Camilla, Horace, Abbey, and Aldo Greenleaf were comfortably ensconced in their new DC digs — by January 1955 — less than three months after Director Farley's visit to their Back Bay home. They realized that having the federal government taking care of everything — their housing needs on both ends, plus packing up and moving all their household goods — sure made things a lot easier. While moving can be a very traumatic experience — especially for the children — their move to a comfortable three bedroom brownstone in DC's Georgetown Section went off without a hitch.

Another aspect of this move that was both totally new and completely transformative for both Camilla and Horace was their office space. They now enjoyed the prestige and spaciousness of side-by-side executive offices in the Department of the Interior's main office building on K Street — just a five minute stroll down from Capitol Hill. With Director Farley's assurance that all the resources of the USFWS were now at their disposal, they dove right into their major task at hand.

Working in close concert with the USFWS's Senior Management staff, Camilla and Horace wanted to create a plan that would increase the number of national wildlife refuges across the country. Along with this expansion, they also wanted to dramatically increase the public's awareness of and appreciation for these bastions of habitat protection and biodiversity preservation. Their ultimate goal was to elevate national wildlife refuges to the same plane of respect and reverence currently reserved only for our nation's national parks.

In formulating their overall plan, both Camilla and Horace understood that — before they could achieve their life's goals — they had to gain a much better understanding of the new science of 'wildlife ecology'. In 1955, the majority of the U.S. population inexplicably still held fast to the religious belief that the early colonists first brought with them to the 'new world'. The dominant thinking was still that humans had a God-given right to exert dominion over all of nature's creatures. This general idea was that the beasts of the forests, fields, rivers, and streams were put there to serve human needs. Almost one hundred and eighty years after our nation was founded, not taking full advantage of this natural bounty was still widely considered a sacrilege and an affront to a person's divine duty.

During their first week on the job, Horace and Camilla sat down together in Horace's spacious office to discuss what should be the centerpiece of their new refuge management strategy. Not surprisingly, the first name they both thought of was Aldo Leopold — 'the Father of Wildlife Conservation in the United States'.

Camilla began by emphasizing why Leopold was the perfect choice for their collation-building idea. "You know — when he was a young man with boundless energy —his life totally revolved around killing as many wild animals as he could. But then, do you remember his transformation expressed in that incredibly moving passage from his book, 'A Sand County Almanac', that was published in 1949 — just a year after he died fighting a forest fire near his Wisconsin home?"

"Oh yes, how could I ever forget that — it's the best conservation quote I've ever read," exclaimed Horace. "I've got his words earmarked right here."

With that, Horace grabbed *A Sand County Almanac* off his bookshelf. "Remember Mr. Leopold had just shot a female wolf with his high-powered rifle and — after he reached the animal's dying body — he wrote these words:

"We reached the old wolf in time to watch a fierce green fire dying in her eyes. I realized then, and have known ever since, that there was something new to me in those eyes — something known only to her and to the mountain. I was young then, and full of trigger-itch; I thought that because fewer wolves meant more deer, that no wolves would mean hunters' paradise. But after seeing the green fire die, I sensed that neither the wolf nor the mountain agreed with such a view."

After he had finished reading, Horace pulled his handkerchief out of his back pocket and started dabbing at his eyes. "Sorry, I can never read these words without tearing up. It always makes me realize how much there is left to accomplish."

"Don't worry, I fully understand," replied Camilla, wiping away her own tears. "That's exactly why Mr. Leopold's words must be the guiding light for where we want to go."

"Remember how his experience with the dying wolf changed his life forever — from a man who took great pleasure in killing animals to one who often relished just watching and documenting what they did," continued Camilla.

"Right," added Horace, perfectly picking up Camilla's theme. "In his younger years — before his 'fierce green fire' experience — he was seldom seen without a hunting jacket on, and a rifle slung over his shoulder. Then — afterwards — he was more likely to have a long-stem pipe poking out of the corner of his mouth, and a pair of binoculars hanging around his neck. It's amazing how this dramatic event changed Mr. Leopold's personal thinking and led to the publication of '*A Sand County Almanac*'. His book has now altered the thinking of much of the U.S. environmental movement and ushered in a totally new field — the science of wildlife management."

"Yes," continued Camilla, "in his stirring essay entitled '*The Land Ethic*' that concludes '*A Sand County Almanac*', Mr. Leopold emphasizes his amazing and heartfelt beliefs that everything on Earth is interrelated, and that humans and nature actually co-exist in a harmonious relationship."

"What incredible concepts for our purposes," exuded Horace, "Mr. Leopold's beliefs that we humans are just a part of the overall global ecosystem and — as the most intelligent component of this worldwide ecosystem — we have the moral obligation of being the caretakers of all living things."

"Wow, my dear, I think we have just discovered where we need to be right now," replied Camilla. "Mr. Leopold also stressed that all living things are owed the right to a healthy existence. As you know, some people working in our field right now, unfortunately still think that Mr. Leopold's concepts — while incredibly innovative — are also far ahead of their time. But I think we both agree that — for what we want to accomplish — this Leopoldian philosophy is right on the money!"

In concluding their most satisfying first strategy session, Camilla and Horace selected the following quotes from '*A Sand County Almanac*' to guide their work as national wildlife refuge ambassadors:

"Like winds and sunsets, wild things were taken for granted until progress began to do away with them. Now, we face the question whether a still higher 'standard of living' is worth its cost in things natural, wild, and free.

"The last word in ignorance is the man who says of an animal or plant: 'What good is it?' To keep every cog and wheel is the first precaution of intelligent tinkering."

From that day forward, Camilla and Horace used these quotes as an *ipso facto* mission statement when they were making decisions. In all their work, they continually emphasized the importance of human's connectedness to the planetary ecosystem. As such, they viewed themselves — and the entire human race — as part of Earth's circle of life. In concert, they worked hard to replace the wrong-headed notion that humans should dominate and control nature. Instead, they emphasized the idea of a symbiotic relationship where humans are just a highly functioning part of the whole.

A Presentation by Roger Tory Peterson

Before venturing forth, on what they knew would be extensive travels to educate the public and gain political 'buy-in' for their refuge expansion plan, Camilla and Horace completed a detailed study of two of their other natural resource heroes. They knew that effective communication would be critical to engaging the public with their initiatives. They hoped that by turning to some of their favorite experts, they would better hone their message and find the mutual inspiration they needed.

Camilla and Horace's next conservation hero was Roger Tory Peterson who gained their attention because of the impeccable accuracy and value of his field guides. The *Peterson Field Guide Series* had proven to be invaluable resources for them in identifying and documenting the abundance and diversity of birds living in the Back Bay NWR. Peterson's ubiquitous popular articles also boosted the public's interest in birds — and, accordingly, their interest in the national wildlife refuges. Before long, he became known to some twenty million birdwatchers around the nation as simply 'Peterson' — as in 'quick, look it up in your Peterson.' As refuge managers, Horace and Camilla both agreed that they owed much of their success to Mr. Peterson.

That's why when Peterson scheduled a July seventeenth, 1955, presentation for DC's Andrew W. Mellon Auditorium. Camilla and Horace were among the first in line to buy tickets. From what they had heard about Peterson's unusual combination of a cantankerous personality often mixed with a playful wit, they fully expected his talk to be highly entertaining. While the marketing posters promised detailed dialogues on the life histories of wild birds, both Horace and Camilla suspected they would also get a healthy dose of how Peterson became the person he was. And that was exactly what they both wanted to hear.

On the evening of July seventeenth, Horace and Camilla excitedly joined approximately seven hundred ardent *Peterson Field Guide* fans — almost a sellout — in welcoming Peterson to the stage. And he did not disappoint. Openly displaying his handsomely craggy features and somewhat obstinate personality, he started off telling tales about his younger self. As he put it, he was known to his teachers and other townsfolk in Jamestown, New York — where he was born and raised — as a constant troublemaker. He was always pulling pranks and raising hijinks. His schoolmates called him 'Professor Nuts Peterson', since he was atypically — for a kid his age — totally absorbed by insects, bugs, and biota.

He next moved into telling how his true bird-loving epiphany occurred. At the ripe old age of eleven, he joined the local Junior Audubon Bird Club Chapter. After he latched onto his first birding field guide and pair of binoculars, his wayward days ended, and his life-long passion began. Then in his early twenties, while he was struggling to make a living as an artist, his two life passions began to slowly come together. He started to notice that each bird species had distinctive field marks that clearly set it apart from other — even closely related — species. From these initial observations, Peterson realized that he had discovered a way for birds to be quickly identified — even at a distance.

Barely able to contain his excitement, Peterson set to work drawing and writing his first book, 'A Field Guide to the Birds', which was published in 1934. Near the end of his entertaining presentation, Peterson told his legion of hero worshippers that, after numerous reprintings, more than five million copies of his primary field guide had been sold. With that, the entire audience rose as one in hearty applause, in response to which Mr. Peterson — again, belying his irascible reputation — graciously bowed several times in deep appreciation.

After the applause finally died down, Mr. Peterson demonstrated his commercial side by plugging his 1948 book — 'Birds Over America'. In doing so, he emphasized that this book clearly showed his depth and breadth as a dedicated conservationist. In fact, most conservationists agreed that 'Birds Over America' bridged the gap between professional ornithologists and amateur backyard birdwatchers. As both Horace and Camilla fully realized — while primarily describing birds and birdwatching across North America — 'Birds Over America' was also notable for its explanations of both ecological principles and environmental ethics. In particular, this book also features the interconnected web of all living things, especially emphasizing how hunters and farmers affect conservation, the ominous threats posed by invasive species, and the importance of protecting endangered species and their critical habitats.

GUIDES TO THE NATURAL WORLD

Roger Tory Peterson's entire series of field guides — which included identification books on everything from amphibians to butterflies, fish, reptiles, wildflowers, and even seashells — fostered an appreciation for the natural world and helped set the stage for ramping up the U.S. environmental movement during the sixties and seventies. It became impossible to find someone who was interested in the natural world who didn't have at least one '*Peterson Field Guide*' on their home or office bookshelves. In 1984, Peterson founded the Roger Tory Peterson Institute of Natural History in his hometown of Jamestown, New York, to further educate people about nature and conservation.

While Leopold's writing provided the backbone for Camilla and Horace's environmental ethos, Roger Tory Peterson helped shape their philosophy of focusing attention on invasive species while providing special protection for endangered species habitats. Camilla and Horace always took several copies of Peterson's birding guides with them on their travels to visit other wildlife refuges. They were convinced that the breathtaking and comprehensive illustrations of the avian species in Peterson's books would turn any would-be nature lover into a serious birder.

Becoming Best Friends with Rachel Carson

The next one of Camilla and Horace's environmental heroes was the renowned scientist Rachel Carson who — as it so happened — worked in the same building where they were stationed. Two weeks after settling into her new office, Camilla mustered the courage to venture down the hall in hopes of striking up a conversation with Ms. Carson. As she walked up to the closed office door with a glass upper half, Camilla noticed Ms. Carson hunched in deep observation over one of the microscopes that lined the office's back wall.

In response to Camilla's gentle tap-tap on the door, the famously reticent biologist looked up and said, "Yes, how can I help you?" but then proffered a warm smile upon recognizing one of the USFWS's dynamic duo she had recently heard about. "Ah, you must be one of our new wildlife refuge ambassadors. Please come in," motioned Rachel. Camilla immediately felt overwhelmed by the graciousness of her personal heroine.

Even though Rachel had not yet written her most famous book, 'Silent Spring', she was widely known and venerated in conservation circles for her prescient writing on marine biology, and keen insights on environmental conservation. Rachel motioned Camilla over to a chair, which she enthusiastically accepted. Camilla then sat engrossed in ecological royalty — as she listened to Rachel describe how her work with the USFWS evolved.

"Well, my dear," she began, "to make a long story short, I was born on a farm near Springdale, Pennsylvania — just up the Allegheny River from Pittsburgh. My love for nature came at an early age as I spent most of my daylight hours outdoors — happily romping around, over, and through my family's sixty acres."

"That must have been such fun for you, Ms. Carson," replied

Camilla, "but please tell me how you first got into writing about nature."

"Oh yes, I was very fortunate with that as well," responded Rachel. "I read a lot as a child and started writing stories about animals on our farm when I was eight. Then when I was only ten, I had my first story published, although — I hate to admit this — I can't really remember what it was about. That's awful, isn't it?"

"Well, I certainly wouldn't say that," commiserated Camilla, "just having something published at such a tender young age must have really made you feel great!"

"Yes — thinking back now, it really did," continued Rachel. "In fact, that early success with publishing really lit a fire under me. I began reading voraciously — more often than not about our planet's oceans and the creatures that dwelled therein. This interest in marine biology stayed with me through my graduate studies at Johns Hopkins University in Baltimore."

"So how did you end up here with the US Fish and Wildlife Service?" asked Camilla, now totally enraptured by Rachel's life story.

"OK, I'll just cut to the chase on this one," replied Rachel, her handsome face framing her steely blue eyes as she looked directly at Camilla. "In 1937, I first started working in what was then called the U.S. Bureau of Fisheries, which later became the Fish and Wildlife Service. Then — as Chief of Publications with the USFWS — I began writing my book, 'The Sea Around Us'."

"Oh, my goodness, yes," exuded Camilla, "I've delighted in reading your exquisitely written book. In fact, I keep it right on the top of my bookshelf — as a primary reference guide. Wasn't that a New York Times #1 Bestseller for quite a while?"

"Yes, and you are so kind for remembering that," replied Rachel, now smiling broadly at Camilla. "In fact, 'The Sea Around Us' opened the door, for me to write two other closely associated bestsellers, 'Under the Sea Wind' and 'The Edge of the Sea'."

Now completely blown away at talking face-to-face with such a humble conservation legend, Camilla asked one final question, "Ms. Carson you're absolutely incredible — you've already accomplished so much. But what are the major projects that you are concentrating on right now?"

"Ah hah, now you've opened Pandora's Box," replied Rachel, "but since you asked, I'll tell you about my latest — and probably the most important — project I've ever undertaken. I can't really tell you many details because it involves something that really rankles a lot of high-powered people. In essence, I'm researching the long-term effects of the vilest poison ever spread across the American landscape. The stuff is a chemical compound known as 'dichloro-diphenyl-trichloroethane' or DDT, for short. Right now, it is threatening to wipe out hundreds of wildlife species, most notably our regal raptors — eagles, falcons, hawks, owls, and osprey. Like I said, I have to keep my work against the horrors of DDT very low key — at least for now. But let me assure you, my dear — if it's the last thing I ever do — I will eventually rid the Earth of this noxious scourge."

After Rachel had finished talking about DDT, it took Camilla a couple of minutes to fully absorb what she had just learned. She was amazed to hear that such a serious environmental problem existed, but she had no doubt that — if it could be solved — Ms. Carson would be exactly the person to do it. Little could Camilla have known at the time, how prophetic her thoughts would be within the next two decades.

Glancing over her shoulder at the clock on Rachel's office wall, Camilla could not believe that she had been sitting there for more than an hour, talking with the woman who was her ultimate role model for what she hoped to accomplish as a career biologist. Taking advantage of the break in the conversation, Camilla stood up, extended her hand to Rachel, and thanked her profusely for her time and profoundly interesting information.

The rest of the day was a mental blur for Camilla. She simply could not get her mind off her meeting with this legendary biologist long enough to accomplish any other work.

Through her years of employment with the USFWS, Camilla regularly talked with Ms. Carson during coffee-breaks and lunches in the building's cafeteria. Because of her close association with her new best friend, Camilla also never missed an opportunity to rail against the wanton and widespread use of DDT.

Watching a Snow Goose Spectacle

In late February 1955, serving in their capacities as ambassadors of our nation's wildlife refuge system — Horace and Camilla took their first overnight field trip to the Pocosin Lakes National Wildlife Refuge (NWR) located on the coastal plain of eastern North Carolina. They felt like this would be a good place to start, since this refuge had a great deal in common with their previous assignments in Back Bay NWR. Also — since they were traveling there during the winter — it would give them a wonderful opportunity to see first-hand the awe-inspiring migration of snow geese and tundra swans they had heard so much about.

Covering one hundred and ten thousand acres, Pocosin Lakes NWR comprises a vast phalanx of farm fields and dirt roads. On the weekend that Camilla and Horace visited, the bone-crackingly cold weather was driven by a biting northwest wind. As they were driving to their prime viewing locations, the refuge manager — Donovan O'Brien — briefly explained the life history of the snow geese.

The bird's name comes from its coverage of brilliant white plumage — which is everywhere except on its black wingtips. The North American populations nest in huge colonies in remote areas above the Arctic Circle — in Canada and northern Alaska — and over winter along the Pacific, Atlantic, and Gulf coastal areas of the United States. Each year, vast overwintering flocks of both snow geese and tundra swans stop at Pocosin Lakes NWR, to gorge on leftover grain, before continuing on to their far-north nesting grounds.

Fortunately, Manager O'Brien had been closely monitoring the vast flocks of snow geese and knew exactly where the largest assemblages would be congregated. For forty-five minutes, the trio bounced and jounced along the refuge's dirt roads traveling through cornfield after cornfield in the tabletop-flat coastal plain of eastern North Carolina.

Suddenly — as they rounded a sharp bend — Camilla and Horace looked straight ahead and saw a field completely buried in snow. At least

— at first glance — that's how it looked. Then, drawing closer, they noticed that the 'snow' was moving around and was — in actuality — thousands of snow geese blanketing every square foot of the landscape.

The next thing Horace and Camilla witnessed, was a mind-boggling cacophony of sight and sound. Resembling some sort of ethereal cornfield levitation, the entire flock of snow geese lifted off as one. The resultant display — of white flapping wings and gabbling honks — was both breathtaking and earsplitting.

As Camilla and Horace sat watching in rapt attention, the huge flock of geese circled around the perimeter of the cornfield and then flew right back to where they had been — descending down in a continuous funnel cloud of white. Once they were back on the ground, the geese resumed feeding as if they had never taken off in the first place. For the next hour, the geese repeated their routine of taking off *en masse* every ten minutes or so, circling around, and then dropping back down into the field.

Throughout the remainder of the day, Manager O'Brien treated Horace and Camilla to similarly amazing avian spectacles all over the refuge. While O'Brien didn't know exact numbers, he estimated the wintering population of snow geese at more than 1.5 million birds — buttressed by an additional fifty thousand tundra swans. As they prepared to return to DC, Horace and Camilla profusely thanked Manager O'Brien for providing them with one of the greatest wildlife viewing thrills of their lifetimes. In addition to being astonishingly memorable, this field trip reinforced their perspective on the irreplaceable wildlife resources that are permanently protected by our national refuge system. The sights and sounds they experienced on the North Carolina coastal plain remained with Camilla and Horace during the rest of their USFWS careers.

Challenging the Bureau

Camilla and Horace used their lofty positions with the USFWS as bully pulpits to address many of the crises they saw creeping into the complex milieu of wildlife management throughout the United States. In so doing, they enjoyed reasonable success as USFWS ambassadors. During their first few years, the national wildlife refuge system added millions of acres of newly protected habitat. Camilla and Horace took special satisfaction when invaluable western wildlife habitat was yanked away from under the bulldozers of strip mall and big box store developers.

One of Camilla's first assignments in the summer of 1955 — as an environmental investigator — took her to northwestern Colorado and the dusty cow Town of Craig. Her job was to oversee the potential impacts to wildlife habitat associated with the proposed — and soon-to-become notorious — Echo Park Dam project, located in Colorado's Dinosaur National Park. The project was being proposed by none other than the U.S. Bureau of Reclamation ('the BuRec') — Camilla's arch-nemesis from earlier days of her career.

During the early 1950s, Colorado's Dinosaur National Monument confined the confluence of two of the Colorado River's major and most magnificent tributaries — the Yampa and the Green Rivers. At the time, the fantastic palette of scenic, archaeological, and paleontological beauty in this remote corner of Colorado was known only by Native Americans and white colonists living in the sparsely settled local communities. In the minds of the BuRec's chief administrators, however, these characteristics offered them exactly what they were looking for — another success story like Nevada's Hoover Dam. Decades after it was 'opened for business', Hoover Dam was still being touted as a boon for farmers and settlers in both Nevada and Arizona.

The BuRec's engineers began their work in Dinosaur National Park by focusing their attention on Echo Park — a remote canyon that snaked its way around an eight-hundred-foot-high sandstone monolith called Steamboat Rock. Steamboat Rock stood in the riverbed just below the confluence of the Yampa and Green Rivers and, topographically, provided the ideal location for constructing a massive dam.

The channel's narrow trough at this location would require a relatively minimum concrete span which would back up the water in both channels of the two major rivers. The resulting long expanse of open water would provide plentiful hydroelectric power and 'boundless recreational opportunities' — serving as the perfect complement to other downstream dams and reservoirs that were also represented by future plans on the engineers' drafting tables.

Camilla's initial findings on the wildlife impacts of this proposed hydrologic monstrosity were — in a word — devastating. In addition to wiping out thousands of acres of virgin riparian (riverside) habitat, the project would destroy five populations of rare, native fish species; the Colorado pikeminnow, the humpback chub, the bonytail chub, the razorback sucker, and the Colorado River cutthroat trout.

During the series of evening public hearings held for this project at the courthouse in Craig, Camilla let the panel of BuRec engineers and hydrologists have it with both barrels. "Mr. Chairman, as I think you know, I am here representing the interests of the US Fish and Wildlife Service — one of your fellow agencies in the Department of the Interior. But regretfully, I have to say that I don't believe any time or concern whatsoever has been given to the immense impacts this project would have on wildlife habitats and rare fish species."

"Quite frankly," Camilla continued, "this whole situation is totally appalling and places shame on our entire department. The area that would be permanently flooded by this reprehensible action is extremely valuable for both natural resources and human archaeology. Instead of being forever inundated and lost, this river reach should receive additional special designation, as land that is critical for protection of both rare fisheries habitat and irreplaceable prehistoric human artifacts."

"Thank you for your opinion, Miss," replied Joe Waldrop — BuRec's Chief Engineer and Hearing Chairman, "but you are totally off base by placing your concerns for wild creatures and their primitive living spaces above the desperate needs for the advancement of human civilization." Waldrop then took the inflammatory step of waggling his index finger in Camilla's face while repeating, "Shame on you, shame on you, shame on you!"

This total condescension of her professional opinion caused Camilla to experience *déjà vu*. In a mirror image display of her previous BuRec testimony as a member of the National Audubon Society, Camilla grabbed the microphone, yanked it out of its holder, and stomped out from behind the speaker's podium. "How dare you, sir, treat me like a child! You certainly know that I have every right — indeed it is my sworn duty — to state my opinion in this matter as a professional wildlife biologist and senior federal environmental scientist."

"As to your assertion that this project is somehow essential for the existing human condition," Camilla proclaimed, "that is narrow-minded and self-serving. The Native American tribes — that once dwelled here — were long ago driven from their ancestral homes and onto reservations. Aside from the occasional itinerant prospector, there aren't even any humans now living in the vicinity of this proposed project.

"Your assertion of human value is strictly predicated on the belief that 'if you build it, they will come'," elaborated Camilla. "In other words, you want to provide water in a place that none has ever existed, so that you can convert pristine western prairie habitat into an artificial 'Garden of Eden'. Your whole premise is couched on speculation — once you have created this false green façade — that people will just suddenly show up and settle in. Your supposed foresight is nothing but blind ambition!"

"OK, now you've gone too far," stammered Chairman Waldrop, his round face now beet red and his voice filled with anger. "I suggest you step away from the podium and take your seat before I find you in contempt of this hearing!"

At this point, Camilla realized that a continuing verbal battle would serve no purpose and might end with her losing her job, so she acquiesced and returned to her seat. The rest of the hearing went as she expected. The vast majority of the testimony was presented in favor of the project and since there were — at the time — no legal or regulatory tools for mandating consideration of impacts to wildlife habitats and rare species, the approval process was a foregone conclusion. But what Camilla didn't realize was that the power of a newfound personality type — the 'citizen environmental activist' — was suddenly about to burst forth on the scene.

Back in Washington, DC, all systems were indeed 'go' for this Echo Park Project — or so the Washington politicians and BuRec engineers figured. But until now they had not met up with the dissenting minds of the Sierra Club, led by Executive Director David Brower. To Camilla's everlasting joy — far from becoming another showcase for the western water controllers — the proposed Echo Park Dam was on its way to becoming one of the most momentous victories ever recorded in the nascent history of the U.S. environmental movement.

The forceful opposition to Echo Park first started when a group of downstream river guides in Utah got wind of what was being bandied about upstream. The guides moved quickly to rally support for their cause and invited Brower and other conservation leaders to join them for a trip to see exactly what would be lost if the canyons were flooded. They also asked Camilla to go along as a federal agency representative. And she certainly didn't need to be asked twice.

After spending a few days with the guides, Brower and his fellow conservationists oversaw the formation of an alliance that challenged the BuRec's claims about the project's major benefits and limited impacts. The opposition group that Brower formed had a catchphrase:

'We're not opposed to development. We're not opposed to dams. We're just opposed to dams in national parks.'

Faced with such difficult to refute logic about the absurdity of a dam in a national park — alongside withering opposition led by a master organizer like Brower and compelling evidence for the destruction of resources from scientists such as Camilla — the U.S. Congress eventually removed Dinosaur National Monument and Echo Park Dam from the act that created the Colorado River Storage Project.

THE ARCHDRUID IN HIS GLORY

David Brower enjoyed a litany of ecological successes throughout his career. He became the first Executive Director (ED) of the Sierra Club in 1952. In this position, Brower first achieved national fame — leading the opposition to several other Bureau of Reclamation (BuRec) dam proposals in addition to Echo Park. His advocacy as Sierra Club ED also helped establish nine national parks and seashores — including three in his native California — Redwoods National Park, Kings Canyon National Park, and Point Reyes National Seashore. Under his direction, the Sierra Club also began publishing their now-famous large-format, coffee table books — combining mind-blowing outdoor photography, with poignant and powerful conservation messages.

Nominated for the Nobel Peace Prize three times — in 1978 and 1979, and then jointly with Professor Paul Ehrlich in 1998 — Brower earned international respect because of his passion for Earth and its inhabitants. In 1998, he also received the Blue Planet Prize for his lifetime achievements. His successful advocacy for many environmental causes led acclaimed author John McPhee to publish a series of articles on Brower, and then a 1971 bestselling book called '*Encounters with the Archdruid*'.

In the final analysis, David Brower was one of the foremost environmental activists and natural resource preservationists in U.S. history. He singlehandedly founded more national environmental conservation groups than any other person. Included among Brower's organizations were the Friends of the Earth, the League of Conservation Voters, and the Earth Island Institute.

Echo Park Dam — The Rest of the Story

Unfortunately for David Brower, Camilla and the cadre of opposition environmentalists, the story of Echo Park didn't end with the project's defeat. In their crusade to preserve Echo Park and Steamboat Rock, Brower and his band of activists accepted a tradeoff — a loss downstream that would anguish them and others for years to come. The deal involved an agreement not to oppose a dam on the Colorado River — constructed between 1956 and 1966 — in a little-known place called Glen Canyon.

Still smarting from the damming of Hetch Hetchy Valley in Yosemite National Park, the Sierra Club's focus in the 1950s was squarely on national parks and monuments — but Glen Canyon had no such protected status. The rationale was that since Glen Canyon wasn't in a national park, it probably wasn't all that valuable. But this time, the Sierra Club was wrong — very wrong — and Brower deeply regretted his compromise decision. Camilla had hoped to get to Glen Canyon to provide the same type of assessment she pulled together for Echo Park Dam, but competing priorities kept her away. By the time she finally got there and realized the importance of the area, it was too late — construction had already started.

The Glen Canyon Dam drowned more than one hundred miles of spectacular canyon, a rippling desert wilderness that few had ever seen. When Camilla first saw the canyon, it took her breath away. The area was filled with ancient, still-colorful pictographs and pit houses that were an important slice of history. The area held a beauty and wildness that was captured by the stunning nature photographs in Eliot Porter's 1963 book, 'The Place No One Knew'. Camilla owned the book, but sadly — for the rest of her career — it remained on her coffee table in memoriam to a canyon long-gone.

Despite the less-than-perfect victory, Echo Park became a symbol of wilderness, and the battle to save it was documented in a 1994 book. The project's showdown between Congress, the BuRec, and the Sierra Club — led by Brower — and other opposing conservation organizations and environmental scientists like Camilla, was widely acknowledged to be a major steppingstone that led to passage of the Wilderness Act of 1964. After her Echo Park Dam experience, Camilla's steadfast belief about always stating the truth as a professional wildlife biologist and senior environmental analyst never wavered. She believed strongly that including an assessment of follow-on environmental impacts from any construction project was critical to ensuring the sustainability of the overall ecosystem — for both humans and wildlife.

Little could Camilla have known — at the time — how important her stance against the Echo Park Dam would become. Fifteen years later in 1970, the newly promulgated National Environmental Policy Act (NEPA) mandated that every 'major federal action' — which Echo Park certainly was — must be subjected to detailed scrutiny and preparation of a comprehensive Environmental Impact Statement (EIS).

America's Last Best Place

One especially memorable — for all the wrong reasons — event occurred in the late summer of 1956, when Camilla and Horace travelled to the wondrous backcountry of Alaska — 'America's Last, Best Place'. They were tasked with finding territory for new wilderness areas that would forever preserve the untold bounty of natural resources in what was soon to become our Nation's 49th state.

Just getting to central Alaska amounted to one of the greatest adventures of Camilla and Horace's lives. Their grandparents, Aurora and Jacob, delightedly agreed to keep the twins while their parents pursued their adventure-filled trip. Abbey and Aldo, now eight years old, begged to go with their parents, but Camilla felt that the travel would be too arduous for the youngsters. First, there was the more than twelve-hour flight — counting layovers — from Washington's National Airport to Elmendorf Airfield in the City of Anchorage. Next came the awesome, but tediously long, passenger train ride from Anchorage to the City of Fairbanks — one hundred and forty miles south of the Arctic Circle.

After arriving in Fairbanks, Camilla and Horace boarded a sturdy, but rattletrap military bus, that carried them across several mountain passes to the Kantishna Roadhouse on the doorstep of Mount McKinley National Park — now Denali National Park and Preserve. Finally, they hopped on a bush plane that ferried them to a large island in the middle of the broad floodplain of the Savage River — along the park's eastern boundary. There, the pilot summarily dumped them off along with all their gear, which included a week's worth of supplies.

"Now don't forget," yelled the pilot as he bumped along taxiing for take-off, "if you have any troubles or forget something, just call me on your radio. If I'm not too busy, I'll come right away to help you out. That is, unless the weather's too bad to fly, which, unfortunately, it is about eighty-five percent of the time up here. But don't worry, somebody will probably come — eventually. Oh, and make sure you watch out for the

348

grizzlies — the females can get pretty aggressive when they're with cubs, and the males are always a pretty cantankerous lot!"

With that, the pilot gunned the engine, threw back the stick, and the plane powered off — disappearing quickly into the low-hanging clouds.

"Well, here we are," said Horace, sheepishly grinning at Camilla's chagrined expression. "Alone in the Alaska wilderness — just as we have always dreamed about."

"Yes, but I didn't expect us to be quite this alone," winced Camilla. "What if the bears decide we look good enough to eat?"

"No problem," promised Horace as he unpacked an M-16 rifle from its case. "Just as with most wild creatures, if we don't mess with them, they probably won't bother us. But just in case they do, we do have this deterrent. Now let's get busy pitching camp. We've got a long hike tomorrow to meet up with the miners who seem to believe this land all belongs to them. To tell you the truth, I'm a lot more worried about them than I am about the local grizzly population!"

By following all the rules for camping in grizzly country — primarily hanging all edibles in a tree away from their camp site — Camilla and Horace enjoyed an extremely pleasant sleep under the clear, starry skies of a magnificent Alaskan night. While they could occasionally hear grizzlies snuffling and snorting along the riverbanks, the imposing creatures didn't come close to their tent site.

Rising well before the sun the next morning, Camilla and Horace busily built a campfire and cooked a hearty breakfast that they would need to sustain them on the day's journey. According to Horace's detailed topographic map, they had more than ten miles of rough-hewn logging roads to travel before they reached their destination — one of the many miners' cabins scattered throughout the surrounding foothills.

After packing up their camp and beginning their long hike, Camilla and Horace were astonished at the stunning beauty revealed to them by the rising sun. Since it was early September — actually peak foliage season in central Alaska — the landscape was bathed in vividly-glorious colors. From her meticulous research on Alaskan ecology, Camilla remembered that 'taiga' was the name given to stunted trees growing on top of permafrost. This made for a very atypical forest with only scattered black spruce trees — most less than fifteen feet tall — overtopping a thick layer of shrubs dominated by golden-hued willows, and bunchberry bushes with their bright red berries and leaves.

Since they were hiking directly up a broad mountain valley along the side of a tributary river, glaciated foothills surrounded them on three sides. This gave them exquisite views of a natural cornucopia that actually surpassed the splendor of the autumnal landscape. Not only was this the best time to see Alaska's fall colors, but it was also the best time to see the native wildlife. Everything was now on the move, getting ready for the long winter season that was starting to descend.

Everywhere Camilla and Horace looked, they could see small groups of caribou grazing gracefully among the berry bushes in preparation for the great mass migration that would dovetail with the season's first fresh snowfalls. For now, these massive beasts — with their curvaceously-cupped 'reindeer antlers' — didn't exhibit any of the signs of anxiety that would soon cause them all to come together and move *en masse* to their lowland wintering grounds. Their family groups — gently ambling through the colorful landscape — were visual delights that would be forever etched in Camilla and Horace's memories.

Closer inspection of the terrain immediately surrounding their trek yielded views of smaller creatures — such as the mottled-brown Arctic ground squirrel and the willow ptarmigan. Still primarily speckled gray, brown, and rust, the ptarmigan's feathers were beginning to moult into pure white for winter camouflage. Surprisingly, these smaller animals paid little attention to the presence of Camilla and Horace — somehow sensing that these strange human creatures were not predators.

Near the tops of the adjacent foothills, Camilla and Horace glimpsed the white dots of Dall sheep — Alaska's high mountain denizens — gingerly making their way through the still snow-pocked boulder fields in search of green foliage to nibble on. These sheep stayed white year-round, since the high country they live on seldom — if ever — completely loses its snow cover. From a wildlife perspective, however, the biggest thrills by far for Camilla and Horace were associated with the Alaska's largest land animals — one a six hundred-pound, meat-eating bear and the other a strict vegetarian, with a reputation for being the most fearsome beast in the backcountry.

For a time — as Camilla and Horace walked along the side of a braided tributary stream — they were paralleled by a family of grizzlies. A sow and her three cubs were sauntering lazily along looking for anything edible on the stream's opposite side. Normally, such a situation would be one to avoid at all costs. By all accounts, a female grizzly with cubs is the most dangerous animal to be encountered in the Alaskan bush. Of all the fatal bear attacks on people ever recorded, the majority involved adult females defending their young from offending humans.

In most cases, these bear attacks were predicated on the bear's natural instincts and humans making poor choices. The humans had either approached too closely or were doing the unthinkable and harassing the young bears. Far too often, the deadly interaction involved both taboo activities. But — of course — whenever a bear killed a human, an immediate hue and cry went out calling for the 'offending' bear to be killed.

In this case, however, the bears were more than one hundred yards away across the widely braided stream and they weren't paying any attention whatsoever to Camilla and Horace. The ursines were preoccupied with rooting around in the loose dirt for grubs and gleaning bunches of fresh berries off the shrubs that were growing along the floodplain. In fact, Camilla and Horace took great pleasure in watching the bears as the cubs stopped every now and then to bump and bat against each other, while tumbling about in the freshets of standing water.

The biggest fright for Camilla and Horace occurred as they were making their way through a dense, high thicket of willows along the floodplain's edge. Since the fast-growing willows had formed a canopy over the logging road, they were having to push their way forward while barely able to see five feet ahead. They knew full well that this situation could lead to another prime reason for a bear attack on humans — the element of surprising an unsuspecting grizzly. So, they were already very tense while moving ever so slowly, and keeping up a running back-and-forth discourse of 'hey bear-bear-bear' to make sure that any grizzly hidden in the brush would know they were coming.

Then it happened. A massive brown head poked out a scant ten feet away from where they stood. But it wasn't the bear they had been anticipating. Instead, a mouth full of gnashing teeth topped by a huge rack of bleached white antlers was coming straight at them. They did the only thing they could think of doing under the circumstances. Camilla flung her body straight off the road to the left while Horace dove headlong off the right. As they both lay covered in the sodden mud of the roadside ditches where they landed, they looked up just in time to see a full-grown bull moose pounding down the road at full gallop.

After the eight-foot-tall body had lumbered past them, Camilla and Horace stared at each other — sighing in total relief. They both realized how close they had come to being trampled by Alaska's most fearless animal. As any backcountry aficionado can attest, a bull moose does not yield ground to anything, including grizzly bears, tourist buses, and — most certainly — not to a pair of dazed and confused human hikers.

Another four hours passed, and Camilla and Horace sensed they were nearing the end of their laborious hike. The width of the valley had narrowed considerably, and the logging road was now pocked with clusters of granite. The mountains of the Alaska Range were looming ever higher and higher above the adjacent foothills. Their wildlife viewing had continued unabated but had settled into a more genteel — less threatening — experience.

In particular, they were treated to a variety of raptors soaring high overhead — including bald eagles, peregrine falcons, and red-tailed hawks. They had also seen several more denizens of the tundra high country — snowshoe hares, ermines, and Arctic foxes — scampering furtively through the low-growing brush. All three of these species adapt to the onset of snowy weather by turning white during the winter.

A mile further up, they rounded a bend, looked straight ahead, and immediately felt as if the wind had been knocked out of their chests. There, immediately before them in all its grandiose glory, stood North America's highest peak, locally called Denali, 'The Great One'. They stood in sheer awe for several minutes, knowing that the visual delight that now rose before them was something few visitors were privileged to see.

Since Denali stands 'head and shoulders' above all the surrounding peaks, its summit generates its own weather. This means that storms typically occlude the top of the mountain from low level views almost year-round. But due to the elevation Horace and Camilla gained during their hike, they were experiencing the majestically imposing peak silhouetted against the bright blue sky.

A Most Unpleasant Experience

Although Camilla and Horace were still almost fifty miles away from Denali, its massif completely dominated the horizon in front of them. In fact, the mountain was so engrossing that they at first didn't even notice the miner's cabin — their destination — sitting beside the road only about a quarter mile ahead. Upon closer inspection, they noted that the small structure was neatly crafted of rough-hewn logs that must have been doggedly dragged upslope from the nearest forests several miles below.

The outside of the cabin was festooned with bleached white antlers of both moose and caribou. This made it easy to understand how the inhabitants obtained their primary supplies of protein each year. The source of water for the cabin was a spring that had been piped and valved near the right side of the front porch. No doubt, this convenient water source was the reason why the cabin had been built at this location.

A classic outhouse with a quarter moon carved in the door stood about fifty feet away from the cabin's left side. Finally, a small stock pen — containing a cluster of clucking chickens with at least one rooster, a gaggle of goats, and two sturdy-looking mules — stood behind the back of the house.

Camilla and Horace surmised that the chickens and goats provided other primary sources of food — eggs, meat, and milk — while the mules were used as work animals. But they weren't quite clear as to how the residents obtained their other basic needs — corn meal and flour, for example.

Camilla and Horace's quiet musings about the cabin's inhabitants suddenly took a turn into harsh reality. The door to the cabin flung open and smashed ignobly into the side of the porch. Immediately, two grizzled men with floppy hats, long-greying beards, and rawhide clothing burst forth. Each pointed a double-barreled shotgun directly at Camilla and Horace.

"This here's private propitty — what in damn tarnation do you think you're doing here?" shouted one of the men. He was working over a big wad of tobacco and, as he talked, he hocked a glop of spit at Horace.

Camilla reached in a pocket of her vest and took out a badge that identified her as a federal enforcement officer with the US Fish and Wildlife Service. "We're here, sir, to talk about your mining activities. You see, this is actually not your own personal land. It belongs to the federal government and — as such — is owned by all citizens of the U.S."

"You got it all wrong, lady," shouted the man, still spitting tobacco to emphasize his words. "We're the Hartfield twins, and we've lived on and worked this land for the past forty years. It's our'n by squatter's rights and taint nobody gon' take it away from us — especially not some no-good-for-nothin's from the federal gov'ment — like you two. Now git off our land, or my brother and I might just decide to blow your blame heads off! We'd jest bury your bodies up here on this mountainside and nobody would ever know what happened to you!"

"Please, sir, understand that we mean you no harm," responded Camilla. "You and your brother will be able to keep living and doing exactly what you've been doing. We just need to document that we've talked to you about a potential change in land use. The government is considering designating a wilderness area here and we want you — as well as the other miners living around you — to be aware that this is taking place."

"Look, lady," responded the still fuming man, "we moved up here to git away from the infernal gov'ment intrusion and regulation down thar in the lower 48. We sure as hell ain't goin' put up with no feds comin' up here and tryin' to take over. That just ain't gonna happen. And I can flat dab guarantee you that ever'one else living up here feels exactly the same way we do about you gol'darn gov'ment intruders. So, like I told you, git out of here now while your head is still attached to your shoulders."

With that, both brothers raised their shotguns and fired double blasts right above the heads of Camilla and Horace. The blasts were so close, Camilla could feel the wind from the shot blowing through her hair. That was all the motivation they needed to realize that they were never going to get anywhere trying to talk to these two mountain men, and it was time to leave. They hightailed it back down the logging road as more shotgun blasts and the sounds of the brothers' guffawing laughter chased after them.

After arriving back at their designated pickup spot on the river floodplain, Camilla and Horace used radio links to connect with their USFWS headquarters back in Washington. When they explained what had happened, Camilla and Horace were appalled to hear the tone of plausibility in the voice of Director John Farley. It was almost as if he expected this to happen.

"Well, I'll tell you what," explained Director Farley, "those people that live up there — out in the Alaskan boonies — just don't have tolerance or respect for any government people. We've tried to reach out to them several times and some version of what happened to you always seems to be the result. I suggest you just give up and come on back home. It's no use trying to deal with anyone else up there. We'll just have to work around them and manage the land how we see fit with them right in the middle of everything. Maybe they'll eventually tire of the rustic lifestyle and move on or maybe they'll just die in place. In either case, the best we can do is to make sure no one else moves in after they finally leave."

The Director's response was not exactly reassuring or comforting to Camilla and Horace — considering that they had just risked their lives, taking an action that was apparently doomed to fail. But all was not completely lost. They did manage to wrangle a few more days of camping and exploring the awesome resources of Alaska's backcountry.

Plus, a seed was planted in both of their minds about the reality of land management; the need for balancing the connection that humans develop to a land they call home with the need to maintain that land for all future generations. While there was nothing further that Camilla and Horace could do in this situation — neither was interested in another interaction with the shotguns of the miners — they filed the experience in the back of their minds and made note to pull from it for future career land management decisions.

A week after they first landed, the bush plane swooped back down to their river channel's 'landing strip', loaded Camilla and Horace up, and ferried them back to Kantishna to start their long journey home.

Protecting America's Vanishing Wilderness

Experiencing the jaw-dropping beauty and magnificent wildlife in Alaska increased Horace and Camilla's concern for the preservation of wild areas throughout the nation. To re-center their thought processes, they decided to revisit the work of a man they knew as the chief proponent of wilderness designation and preservation in the United States.

Robert 'Bob' Marshall waged a lifelong battle to protect wilderness areas — especially those found in Alaska. His poignant 1930 essay — 'The Problem of the Wilderness' — became one of the most influential works in conservation history. Camilla and Horace had both studied Marshall's venerated essay early on in their careers and they connected most profoundly with his assertion that there are many reasons for preserving wilderness — beyond its intrinsic value as 'landscape untrammeled by human activities'.

As Camilla and Horace reflected on their Alaska trip, they tried to piece together why they believed wilderness is so important that it is worth disrupting the only life the miners they met had ever known. Searching for an answer, Camilla came across this quote in Marshall's essay and read it aloud to Horace, "Fundamentally, the question is one of balancing the total happiness which will be obtainable if the few undesecrated areas are perpetuated against that which will prevail if they are destroyed. What do you think Marshall means by that?" she asked.

Horace sat pensively for a few moments. "I think," he ventured, "that our revered Mr. Marshall is giving us a seminal call to action. He views wild areas as fundamental to human happiness. Personally, you and I both know the peace and soul-filling joy that being out in nature provides. But Marshall is saying that truly wild lands have irreplaceable values for all humankind. Because of this, we must keep them wild to provide places where people can retreat to find themselves and rekindle their souls."

"Horace, you know that I fully embrace that philosophy," mused Camilla, "but I can't help but think about those miners and what might happen to them if their land becomes a wilderness area. Did I like them as people? Well, not really — not with their shotgun blasts whizzing past my ears. But — at the same time — I don't want them to be homeless."

"Remember that Bob Marshall was also a staunch advocate for Native Peoples," continued Camilla, "he spent years living with and studying the native Koyukuk in the remote Alaskan village of Wiseman. Because of this, it seems to me that he would have some sensitivity to the importance of home for everyone and the injustice of a federal entity managing land for the government without regard to its current inhabitants and their dependency on the land. Is taking the land away from the miners we met that much different from taking it away from Indigenous Peoples?"

This was a tough question, for which Horace didn't have an immediate answer. For much of their careers, he and Camilla had fought for the preservation of wilderness areas. As a result, they both knew how critical they were for future generations and for supporting humanity's place within the overall ecosystem. But Camilla's point prompted him to think more critically about the land in Alaska and the wilderness that might be established there.

"I dunno, Cam," said Horace. "I think that communication is critical in both situations. The main reason we went to Alaska was to talk with the miners and help them determine how they could live with the proposed change in land management. But — legally — the land they are on is *not* their land. It belongs to the federal government and the decisions we make are decisions that must be for the greater good of all Americans."

"When the European colonists came along and took land from Native Americans," continued Horace, "we were taking *their* land. The white settlers had no claim to the land; but they had guns and they had power and they used both to undermine the sovereignty of the Native Peoples. Plus, we exploited both the people and the land. The Native Americans were so careful with natural resources and thoughtful about wise management of the ecosystem and its abundance. In the final analysis, the way land was taken from the Native American tribes is a dual tragedy — comprising both human and ecological injustices."

"Agreed," replied Camilla, resting her head in her hand as she thought deeply, "but I know that the plans we have for the wilderness area in Alaska are not self-serving for us or for the government. We are just trying to return the land to management practices that echo the careful way Native Americans originally stewarded the land."

"And I also know," Camilla continued with emphasis, "that if we don't preserve that land from future desecration, we will very well see the delicate ecosystem — that we so vividly witnessed during our visit to Alaska — collapse. The moose, the grizzly bear, the caribou, the Dall sheep, the willow ptarmigan, the Arctic fox, the timber wolf, the snowshoe hare, the ermine — these species are all part of a food web that keeps all populations in check. But if the land is developed and used by humans — without more stringent regulatory controls — the entire system could fail in ways we might not expect."

"You know what, love," smiled Horace, "this whole discussion reminds me of our favorite Bob Marshall quote, 'How many wilderness areas do we need? How many Brahms symphonies do we need?'"

Their discussion, while far from settled, left both Horace and Camilla feeling better about their encounter with the miners in Alaska. Over the course of their careers, Bob Marshall's sage philosophies and prescient words often provided the guidance they needed to fight their battles for protecting wild lands from development.

A National Environmental Malaise Settles In

Along with their triumphs, Horace and Camilla also faced many frustrations and defeats. The basic problem was with the 'Life of Riley' suburbanite lifestyle that permeated middle-class America after World War II. For the most part, the 1950s skittered along with most Americans striving for prosperity epitomized by sparkling new homes, festooned with immaculate green lawns, two-car garages, and all the latest appliances from General Electric and Bendix. The song about the rows of little houses all made out of 'ticky-tack' certainly seemed apropos for defining the new 'American dream'.

Since they often contradicted the prevailing emphasis on finding and living 'the good life', environmental considerations soon disappeared from the American psyche. The majority of U.S. citizens just assumed — off-handedly — that natural resources were there to serve their recreational needs and provide family enjoyment. Indifference and callous misuse of the environment was rampant. Litterbugs were everywhere. Piles of rubbish accumulated along the nation's roadsides and in recreational areas. People blindly tossed their garbage out of their car windows as they drove along.

Most national parks, monuments, and forests suffered severe overuse as more and more vacationers fled to these scenic outposts to escape the drudgery of their urban jobs. People just wanted to be entertained — without any thought of being sensitive to the native flora and fauna in these areas. Unfortunately, most federal recreational areas were not sufficiently staffed to deal with the increased hordes of seasonal visitors. Because of this, the quality of the natural resources on federal lands all across the nation was being severely impacted — often, irreversibly so. Something desperately needed to be done. But no one in a position of leadership volunteered to step forward — or even seemed to know exactly what actions needed to be taken.

Even the federal government seemed to be making all the wrong decisions and taking all the wrong actions. President Dwight D. Eisenhower — retired general and World War II hero — appointed a Secretary of the Interior who became known as 'Giveaway McKay'. During his tenure as Interior Secretary, Douglas McKay repeatedly tried to turn federal energy projects over to the private sector, abolish national wildlife refuges, and transfer federal game reserves to state agencies.

Despite difficulties associated with this environmental negativity, Camilla and Horace kept their noses to the grindstone working to protect wild areas. Throughout the remainders of their careers, their battles to set aside more and more land as wildlife refuges continued unabated, but too often ended in failure. Whenever their arguments came down to a choice between protecting valuable wildlife habitat or choosing economic gain from land development, they usually ended up with the short straw. They simply didn't have the legal basis or regulatory authority to support their impassioned appeals for natural resource protection.

There were times during this period that a type of environmental depression settled over the couple. It was devastating to care so passionately about wilderness, only to have so many obstacles in their way. To provide some solace during this tough period, they often talked about Howard Clinton Zahniser, known as the Father of the Wilderness Act. They did not know 'Zahnie' — as he was called by those who knew, loved, and respected him — but they followed his work and were advocates for him whenever the opportunity arose.

After working for twelve years as a writer and editor with the Department of Agriculture's Bureau of Biological Survey — the successor agency to the USFWS — Howard Zahniser took a pay cut to serve as executive secretary of the Wilderness Society and editor of the *Living Wilderness* magazine. During almost twenty years — from 1945 to 1964 — in this position, he worked with other conservationists across the nation to lobby for a piece of federal legislation called the Wilderness Act.

Zahniser was a gifted writer and an eloquent speaker, and he passionately shared his love for wild places and made arguments for their preservation. He used a variety of media — magazine articles, radio addresses, professional speeches, and congressional testimony — to get his message about the value of wilderness across to the general public and the legislators on Capitol Hill.

Often going more than twenty-four hours without sleep, Zahniser pushed himself to the breaking point to finally get the Wilderness Act passed. In the final tally, this legislation sailed through the U.S. House of Representatives by the remarkable vote count of 373–1. Sadly, the incredibly dedicated individual who made this possible — writing sixty-six drafts of the legislation over an eight-year period and leading eighteen congressional hearings — was not around to see the landmark act put into force. Zahniser died from a heart attack just four months before President Lyndon Baines Johnson signed the act. But anyone who knew this friendly man could sense him there, looking down and smiling at them when the president handed the now-famous signing pen over to his widow, Alice.

Zahniser's story always made Horace and Camilla tear up. They often saw themselves in his position — working tirelessly for a cause that may not be addressed to their satisfaction during their lifetimes. But they also took inspiration from his indefatigable commitment to wilderness preservation and its ultimate success in the 1964 Act. During some of their darkest moments, after a particularly contentious hearing, or after they lost yet another proposed wildlife refuge to a strip mall development, they would look at each other and say, "Remember, Zahnie." And that was all it took to keep them moving forward.

DEDICATING A LIFE TO WILDERNESS PROTECTION

When it first took effect, the Wilderness Act of 1964 protected 9.1 million total acres in fifty-four locations in thirteen states. Over the nest fifty years, the number of areas in the Wilderness Preservation System grew to more than eight hundred — protecting more than one hundred and ten million acres in forty-four states and Puerto Rico. Regrettably — in all of these wilderness areas — there is not a single feature named in honor of Howard Zahniser.

Never in the limelight like some of his more widely acclaimed contemporaries — including David Brower, Rachel Carson, and Aldo Leopold —Zahniser was always content with staying in the background and subtly pushing his basic message. As journalist Don Hopey describes it: "Zahniser was an early proponent of the ethic that without untrammeled wilderness, mankind would be materially and spiritually impoverished."

Zahniser firmly believed that Congress needed to pass wilderness protection legislation to keep these wild lands from being used as pawns among greedy politicians who were playing one-upmanship with our nation's public land legacy. His son Ed is quoted as saying, "It was not just an environmental ethic my father had. He viewed conservation as part of a broad humanism. Thoreau said that in wildness is the preservation of the world, and my father believed that."

BOOK FIFTEEN
Welcome to the Environmental Movement

Environmental Activism Becomes a Catch Phrase

The 1960s ushered in a new era for environmentalists. While they didn't quite fit the mold of the flower-power generation, Camilla and Horace Greenleaf were uplifted — along with the vast majority of our Nation's young people — by the transformation they saw taking place daily on the streets and in meeting places throughout the country. They were especially encouraged by what dissenters often derisively referred to as the 'tree-hugging' mentality that was rapidly overtaking America.

From the Beat Generation to hippie communes; civil rights marches; anti-Vietnam War demonstrations; and sex, drugs, and rock and roll; the 1960s were known as the decade of social upheaval, civil unrest, and cultural shifts. In particular, many Americans finally became fully aware of environmental concerns. The severe impacts that human activities were having on land, water, and air could no longer be ignored or tolerated.

Spurred on by the replacement of consumerism and materialism with free-spirit simplicity and lifestyle mellowing, Americans began demanding better care of Earth's natural resources — advocating for clean air, clean water, and enhanced biodiversity, plus more open land, green spaces, and recreational amenities. 'Progress at all costs' was renounced in favor of finding a balance between comfortable living and preserving — instead of constantly altering — the natural environment. In summary, the wild social and political radicalism of the Sixties was the best thing that ever happened to the U.S. environmental movement.

Throughout the environmental heydays of the late 1960s, media — both print and television — began to be used as a primary tool to promote environmental activism. One of the most famous examples is the public service television spot, 'Keep America Beautiful', showing a 'Native American brave' — who was, in fact, an Italian-American actor —

canoeing down a river until he arrives at a trash-laden, pollution-spouting urban waterfront. There — after he drags his canoe out of the water — a tossed bag of garbage explodes at his feet. A close-up zoom shows a single tear drop rolling down the man's cheek and instantly captures the nation's attention.

While Camilla was thrilled to see the rising interest in environmental concerns, alarm bells went off in her head about ads that pointed to the behavior of individuals as the root of the problem. Everything in her career had taught her that the greatest environmental problems emanated from developers and corporations who were constantly putting their profits above all else. In fact, the 'Keep America Beautiful' ad was a prime example of this. While it was not widely known at the time, this ad was produced by a group of beverage corporations who were fighting against environmental initiatives — such as 'bottle bills' — that could significantly impact their bottom lines.

Camilla was not alone in her convictions about the hazards of corporate greed. She was especially pleased to see that her old pal David Brower — now Executive Director of the Sierra Club — was still around harassing the U.S. Bureau of Reclamation. In 1966, Brower developed an ad campaign attacking a federal program designed to build dams and flood unprotected portions of the Grand Canyon. His showcase ad read, 'Should we also flood the Sistine Chapel so tourists can get nearer the ceiling?' Public reaction to these pro-environmental protection ads was enormous and instantaneous. They generated almost unanimous support against building dams anywhere in the Grand Canyon.

The Washington politicians who had been feverishly pushing the dam-building initiative were so incensed that they dispatched an Internal Revenue Service (IRS) agent to the local Sierra Club office in DC. The agent carried a letter stating that the group's nonprofit status was being revoked. But Brower and the Sierra Club had no intention of giving in to such brazen threats.

Camilla knew that while many people may not be familiar with the Sierra Club, the IRS was a common household name — and usually not a popular one. While she was not thrilled to see Brower's efforts being officiously punished, she was giddy over the backlash they were causing. Membership in the Sierra Club skyrocketed as people railed against the

366

unjust actions of the IRS.

In fact, the resulting public reaction was so intense that the federal government was forced to change its plans. Instead of supporting the proposed dams, Congress expanded Grand Canyon National Park and prohibited dams from being built anywhere within its boundaries. In the final analysis, the Sierra Club had used a series of simple print ads to change the course of history and become the fresh face of the now burgeoning U.S. environmental movement.

As one of the narrators in the film '*A Fierce Green Fire*', environmental activist Doug Scott states, "Every now and then some issue arises that is elevated into the stratospheric focus of public attention, then becomes the symbolic rallying cry for a whole generation of activists." In the 1960s — much to Camilla's elation — that issue was the proposed damming of the Grand Canyon.

Fortunately for Camilla and Horace, their twins — Aldo and Abbey — entered college in 1965; just at the right time to mesh their chosen careers with this onrushing tidal wave of national environmental concern. Aldo was studying marine biology at Florida State University (FSU) in Tallahassee while Abbey was majoring in the newly established field of wildlife ecology at Virginia Tech in Blacksburg. While their parents continued to fight their battles for clean air and water, Aldo and Abbey took a deep dive into the future of environmental activism.

One summer afternoon in June 1969 — fresh after graduating from FSU — Abbey came rushing into the house waving an issue of *Time Magazine*. "Dad! Mom! Did you see this? An entire river caught fire in Ohio!"

Abbey spread the magazine out on the dining room table and stared wide-eyed at the photos of the flaming Cuyahoga River — an absurdity that even Hollywood producers could hardly imagine. Abbey later discovered that the photos she had shown her parents were from a much larger fire in 1952 — the 1969 fire was too small and too quickly extinguished to capture on film. Nonetheless, the article ignited more than just the Cuyahoga River. Abbey — along with much of the nation — rose up in force against the rampant pollution of our Nation's waterways.

In the meantime, Aldo was consumed with other Nationwide

environmental woes. Like his mother, he was an ardent fan of Rachel Carson and her work. As an avid birdwatcher, and a particularly keen observer of raptors — including the iconic bald eagle and the spectacular peregrine falcon — Aldo had latched onto Carson's crusade against DDT.

In fact, on that same June 1969 afternoon, Aldo reminded his mother about a conversation they had right after 'Silent Spring' was first published. In response, Camilla just shook her head and said, "Oh yes, it is truly awful stuff, Aldo. Do you remember the times in the summer when we watched clouds of what was then called 'mosquito spray' spewing out of tank trucks rolling along our residential street in DC?".

Aldo thought for a moment and then replied, "Yes, you and Dad always complained about how awful the smog was and how it made your eyes hurt."

Camilla nodded, "Well, we didn't know it at the time, but that was DDT. They have since found this poison in mother's breast milk. Plus, chicken farmers have commented that their eggshells break much more easily than they used to, and bluebirds have steadily disappeared from their open landscape habitats. Anyone with any sense can plainly see that this chemical is causing deleterious effects and should be banned."

"So then why hasn't it been banned?" Aldo asked, impatiently. "If DDT is clearly causing all these problems, why is it so difficult to stop using it?" Camilla sighed and shook her head again. Indeed — at the time — that was certainly one of the environmental questions of the day.

Now, after hearing both of her college-educated children expressing their strong environmental concerns, Camilla decided it was time to talk to them about the destructive power of corporate misinformation. She started by explaining that most of these outrageous ad campaigns filled viewers with ideas that were false — such as that banning DDT would create a world full of pests. Worst of all, these ad campaigns were massively effective and hard to undo once they were locked into the public's psyche.

To provide a specific example of this, Camilla talked about what happened right after 'Silent Spring, was published. "I know you both have heard a lot about Ms. Carson's book, but I don't think I've ever told you the gory details about what she went through after it first came out. Before she passed away in 1964, I talked with her a lot about DDT."

"Yes, I know she had a really rough time of it, but I'm not sure exactly why," replied Aldo. "Please fill us in."

"Well, for starters," began Camilla, "the things corporate America did to besmirch the credibility of both Ms. Carson and her book were unfathomable."

"I know I'm about to become enraged by what you are going to tell me next, but please go on. I really think I need to know all about this," said Aldo, wiping his brow in mock preparation.

"All right, you asked for it, my dear," replied Camilla, "but if my discourse gets too intense for either of you, just raise your hand and I'll stop."

"OK, let's go for it, Mom," gulped Abbey, "we'll summon our strongest environmental fortitude!"

"I apologize that this may sound a little biblical," continued Camilla, "but in the beginning — after 'Silent Spring' was first published — it was met with a bitterly negative reaction from the corporate world. The resistance started with small-time farmers and moved all the way up to the mega-giants — the Monsantos — of the agricultural world. This antagonistic pushback also went sideways to the corporate chemical conglomerates — the DuPonts and the Union Carbides — who were used to getting whatever they wanted, wherever and whenever they wanted it."

"Ouch," winced Abbey, "sounds just like the 'through-the-ringer' process so many environmental initiatives receive nowadays."

"Yes, you're exactly right," agreed Camilla, "but this knee-jerk negative reaction toward Ms. Carson went quite a bit further than normal."

"Double ouch," grimaced Abbey, grasping her head in her hands.

"Yes, it is certainly very painful for me to recall," lamented Camilla. "The chemical giants threatened to sue Ms. Carson over her 'inflammatory statements' in 'Silent Spring'. They argued that her 'outlandish opinions' were crippling American agriculture while also threatening human health. The horrific rhetoric was so bad that I can still remember a statement from a chemical-industry spokesman. He said that following the teachings of Ms. Carson would lead our return to the Dark Ages, allowing the insects and diseases and vermin to once again inherit and rule the Earth."

"Yikes, now that's not just biblical, it's scurrilous," exclaimed Aldo, squirming in his seat.

"Yes, well unfortunately, that's not the worst of it," continued Camilla. "Ms. Carson's most vehement critics tried to push her to the far left of the political spectrum. They argued that she was consorting with unsavory parties who were trying to undermine American agriculture and free enterprise. While the word 'Communist' — the most potent of insults in the decade following the 1950s scourge of McCarthyism — wasn't used directly, it was certainly implied."

"You have just got to be kidding me. How could anyone say such things about a dedicated conservationist and high-quality person like Ms. Carson?" railed Abbey.

"How, indeed," commiserated Camilla, "but — as we're learning all too well, lately — any time big business is threatened, they will go to any extreme to make sure they continue to get their way. Monsanto even published and distributed five thousand copies of a brochure which parodied 'Silent Spring' by describing a bleak world — wracked by famine, disease, and uncontrolled hordes of insects — which existed because chemical pesticides had been banned. Can you believe that?"

"No, I absolutely can't, Mom," Aldo replied, "but you know what I've really learned from our discussion today? I now realize just what a remarkable conservation champion Ms. Carson really was. Standing firm in the midst of such slanderous and withering corporate criticism is really phenomenal!"

"Right you are, my dear son," concluded Camilla. "That's why we all need to work extra hard to defend and continue her conservation legacy."

SILENT SPRING BECOMES A HEROIC LANDMARK

It would be difficult not to vote for the publication of Rachel Carson's book, *'Silent Spring',* as the most pivotal environmental accomplishment of the twentieth century. This landmark publication led to the eventual eradication of DDT — a pesticide that had monumental environmental and toxicological effects. The toxic effects of DDT were most exemplified by the deaths of massive numbers of birds of prey — also known as raptors — and their offspring. Thanks to the publication of *'Silent Spring',* bald and golden eagles, peregrine falcons, brown pelicans, and ospreys still fill our skies with their dramatic flights.

In *'Silent Spring',* Carson's revelations about the myriad horrors of synthetic pesticides such as DDT scared money out of people's pocketbooks and forced letters to Congress out of their pens. Carson wrote that, "We have allowed these chemicals to be used with little or no advance investigation of their effect on soil, water, wildlife, and man himself. Future generations are unlikely to condone our lack of prudent concern for the integrity of the natural world that supports all life."

In the final analysis, not even the debilitating effects of the cancer that was ravaging her body deterred Carson from defending the content of her now-famous book. She endured all of the witheringly negative personal attacks with dignity and professionalism, assuring the American public that what she was saying deserved to be heard and heeded. In 1972 — eight years after Carson's death in 1964 — the U.S. Environmental Protection Agency (EPA) finally banned DDT nationwide, though U.S. corporations continue to be among the largest producers of the chemical for use in other nations. Today, *'Silent Spring'* is credited with generating a groundswell of grassroots activism that eventually opened the door for the massive environmental movement of the late 1960s and early 1970s.

Camilla and Horace were both heartbroken and proud of the passion and concern building up in their precocious twins. They could see the anguish these environmental calamities were causing, but — in equal measure — they could see the determination in her children's eyes to do something about it. Immediately after her misinformation talk with Abbey and Aldo, Camilla turned to Horace and said, "Well, my dear, I think we may have just passed the torch." Indeed, the twins were now fully activated and driven to make a difference in what was now their world.

Having finished their undergrad studies with a thirst for more expertise, Aldo and Abbey immediately enrolled in graduate school. They were soon both immersed in obtaining advanced degrees in the relatively new field of environmental management and communication; with Aldo studying at Johns Hopkins University in Baltimore, Maryland while Abbey matriculated at Carnegie-Mellon University in Pittsburgh, Pennsylvania.

Just after ringing in the new decade of the 1970s, Abbey and Aldo agreed to meet in Washington, DC, for a special land conservation event that they had been hearing a lot about. Little could they have guessed — at the time — that what was envisioned as a rather modest get-together among like-minded concerned citizens would become one of the most momentous happenings in the history of the U.S. environmental movement.

A Series of Environmental Firsts

On April twenty-second, 1970, Abbey and Aldo met in Washington, DC to attend an environmental rally being touted as the First Annual Earth Day. The night before the event, the twins shared drinks in their hotel bar and talked excitedly about how this happening could be a much-needed harbinger of the serious interest in environmental protection that was beginning to take hold across the U.S.

After the first Earth Day was over, Abbey and Aldo again met in the hotel bar to discuss what they had just experienced. "Wow — what an amazing day, Sis," began Aldo. "That was so much more than I ever expected. What were they saying about the crowd size on the National Mall? I think it was more than one hundred thousand people. But then everyone kept talking about how millions of people were actually involved nationwide, plus more than one billion across the globe. I mean who could have possibly predicted that kind of turn out?"

"Yes, it was overwhelming all right," replied Abbey. "I don't think that Wisconsin Senator Gaylord Nelson — who organized the whole deal — ever imagined he would get such a massive response. I'm really pumped that this will be the beginning of lots of good things to come for our environmental movement."

"Plus, the speakers were all phenomenal," added Aldo. "They hit all the hot buttons — water pollution, dying lakes, atmospheric heating, strip mining, oil spills, dwindling natural resources, endangered species, overrun parks. It was all right there, presented in a nutshell to show exactly how bad things have become."

"You're so right, little brother," replied Abbey — again demonstrating the propensity of twins to channel each other's thoughts. "At first, everyone was talking about how our nationwide obsession with industrial growth and consumerism is straining our environment to the breaking point. But then the discussion turned to how we can best solve these problems by accepting and practicing the idea of living lightly on the Earth. That's exactly what we all have to start doing. We need to figure out how to live sustainably by protecting our natural resources instead of using them up."

"There you go again," admired Aldo, "you always come up with another perfect term; 'living sustainably'. Somehow, I suspect that just might become the catchphrase for how we humans need to structure our lifestyles."

"Thanks for the compliment," demurred Abbey, "but you know you don't do too badly yourself. Someday, we might just make a really great team!"

"So, just wrapping everything up," concluded Aldo. "I think the media coverage was also just what we needed. It seemed like every time I turned a corner, I saw another mobile media unit from either NBC, CBS, or ABC. That's really the best way to get our message out across the country!"

As things turned out, Abbey and Aldo were right on with their assessment of the first Earth Day. The event was the greatest demonstration of public support for a cause in U.S. history. To pull it off, Senator Nelson had organized twenty million people, ten thousand grade schools and high schools, two thousand five hundred colleges and one thousand communities in three and a half months. And he did it all on a total budget of just $190,000. The key to all of this success was the grassroots response — getting the word out and then having it spread like wildfire from the heartland to the suburbs.

The unexpected magnitude of the response to the first Earth Day clearly proved what can be done when the political and social moods of the country collide, coming together with a message that says, 'Let's get something done, instead of continuing to drag our feet'. As a testament, the resulting outpouring of federal environmental legislation proved that Congress was listening to what the people wanted. Such a groundswell of public opinion — all speaking with the same voice — certainly went a long way toward building the first bastion of environmental laws and regulations.

The public outcry for fixing the environment became so pervasive that when President Richard Millhouse Nixon — one of the most unpopular leaders in U.S. history — took office in January of 1970 he was forced to acknowledge that something had to be done about the environment. Nixon made his feelings quite evident during his first State of the Union Address, saying, "The 1970s absolutely must be the decade when America pays its debt to the past by reclaiming the purity of its air and its waters. It is literally now or never."

The flurry of environmental legislation coming from Capitol Hill in the early seventies offered solid proof that Nixon and Congress were committed to putting federal funds where their mouths were. The demand for more national environmental protection was so great that no administration could ignore it, including one staffed primarily by conservative and often — as proven by the sordid and shameful Watergate Affair in 1972 — criminally unscrupulous politicians.

Fittingly, the first piece of federal legislation to pass during the 1970s was the National Environmental Policy Act (NEPA) and — along with it — the president's Council on Environmental Quality (CEQ). While officially intended to be representative of a national policy promoting enhancement of the environment, NEPA, in actuality, turned out to be something quite different. In fact, it quickly became a controversial vehicle for debating the pros and cons of what was enigmatically referred to as… "proposed federal actions that may or may not have significant negative or positive impacts on the quality of the natural or human environments". Say what? Yes, NEPA was certainly not an easy thing to understand.

Unfortunately, federal environmental scientists — like Camilla and Horace — who were assigned to conduct 'NEPA analyses' and then write corresponding 'Environmental Impact Statements (EISs)' really had no clear idea about what they were supposed to do. In fact, Camilla spent the better part of a year, writing inquiries to Congress and asking members of CEQ to clarify the 'NEPA Regs'.

Camilla's continuous clarification efforts did earn her an invitation to make a keynote presentation to the North American Wildlife and Natural Resources Conference (NAWNRC) at DC's Shoreham Hotel. She and Horace put together a multi-media presentation entitled, 'The Troubles with NEPA', that they presented to a standing room only crowd of more than one thousand people. While the idea of deriding both the understandability and the usefulness of the nation's new environmental legislative showcase rankled Horace and Camilla's supervisors at the USFWS, the positive response they received was overwhelming.

As a result of Horace and Camilla's presentation, NEPA's purpose and applicability became much better defined during the next few Congressional legislative sessions. In the final analysis — even though the first version of NEPA might have been difficult to interpret — everyone at the NAWNRC agreed that it represented a legitimate effort on the part of Congress to embed an environmental ethic and consciousness into the U.S. land-development community. And this was — in fact — a big improvement over what previously had been required from an environmental analysis and evaluation standpoint, which was pretty much nothing at all.

Next, in 1973, the US Congress passed the federal Endangered Species Act (ESA) and placed it under the jurisdiction of the USFWS. Under the ESA — if a species was deemed to be in jeopardy — the agency made a determination, declaring the species to be either 'threatened' or 'endangered' by extinction. Since monitoring and protecting individual members of a listed species proved, in most cases, to be extremely difficult — if not impossible — the ESA sought to protect the 'critical habitats' of each species.

Despite some regulatory rough patches, both Camilla and Horace realized that the ESA was certainly a big improvement over having no jurisdictional protections for wildlife species faced with extinction. In fact — throughout its history — the ESA has had many notable successes, including such 'showcase' (high visibility) species as the bald eagle, the American alligator, the peregrine falcon, the osprey, and the brown pelican — all of which are now common or even abundant in their natural habitats.

BOOK SIXTEEN
Abbey's Federal Career

Moving to Colorado

Upon completion of their graduate coursework in 1974, Abbey and Aldo Greenleaf chose career paths that followed those of their parents — albeit with quite different directions. Abbey used her master's degree to attain an excellent entry-level position with the federal government at Colorado's Denver Federal Center (DFC). Specifically, (dovetailing her parents' careers) she started as a GS-9 Environmental Scientist with the Rocky Mountain Regional Office of the USFWS. It was — as they say — an offer that Abbey couldn't refuse.

The first weekend Abbey spent in Colorado, she drove Trail Ridge Road — up, over, and through Rocky Mountain National Park — three times. During each trip between Estes Park east of the continental divide and Grand Lake to the west, she ignored her own rule about no playing music in national parks and sang along with John Denver's then number one hit song, 'Rocky Mountain High'. She just wanted to celebrate the fact that she had found her true calling in life, settling in a place where she had dreamed about living for a long time.

Abbey's pay and benefits were terrific — most federal entry-level jobs were either GS-5 or GS-7. Plus, she was hired as a Professional Environmental Scientist (PES), which meant she would be in charge of reviewing the impacts of proposed projects under the brand-new suite of federal environmental regulations — including both NEPA and the ESA. Bolstered by these new regulations, Abbey believed that she now had the regulatory clout she needed to balance the scales between human development and natural resource protection. Or at least, that's what she hoped.

Meanwhile, Aldo took his master's degree in environmental management, and moved to the Boston area to start his own environmental consulting firm. Teamed with the twins' friend Holton O'Leary and two other partners who were versed in a variety of natural resource disciplines, Aldo bought a three-bedroom ranch house with an oversized two-car garage in Marshfield — a coastal town on Boston's South Shore. Then, he hung out his first business shingle reading 'Allied Environmental Scientists' or just 'AES' for short.

Now comfortably ensconced in Colorado, Abbey wanted to totally dedicate her life to her new-found clout as a first-order reviewer of the wildlife impacts of development projects. This meant that she — at first — eschewed any ideas about starting a family. While she always had plenty of opportunities, she only dated occasionally. She was content, career-focused, and living solo in her rented one-bedroom apartment just outside of the western gate of the Denver Federal Center.

When she wasn't on the road, Abbey exercised daily at a health club called The Point while working twelve to fourteen hours a day. During her first three years as a PES, she also spent time — following in her parents' footsteps — working with Congress and the CEQ to improve exactly how a NEPA EIS was structured and how the findings could best be determined and presented.

In the process, Abbey received a lot of detailed feedback from both members of Congress and federal administrators. But — as she was about to discover from writing her first EIS — the fledgling federal environmental regulatory process still had a long way to go in changing the way 'things had always been done' within the hallowed halls of Capitol Hill.

Sage Grouse Shenanigans

Abbey's assignments while working with the USFWS were rich and varied. Just a few weeks after starting, she was tasked with determining how federal grazing allotments on Bureau of Land Management (BLM) land in northwestern Colorado were impacting native populations of greater sage grouse.

To begin her research, Abbey traveled to North Park, Colorado — a tiny town located on a mountain plateau which had the reputation as being the one of the coldest human inhabited places in the Lower forty-eight. Rising at five a.m., she joined a small caravan of four-wheel-drive vehicles motoring out across the sagebrush flats to a location where she soon learned that sometimes Mother Nature provides a perfect imitation of human life.

In the gloaming moments before sunrise, Abbey watched an annual ritual that had all the elements of a human happy hour at a favorite neighborhood bar. In reality, she was staring at a circular, sagebrush-free area — known as a *lek* — and watching some very strange behaviors indeed. The 'bar patrons' she was observing were chicken-sized wild birds known as greater sage grouse. And the *lek* where they were performing was — appropriately enough — the Swedish word for 'playground'.

As Abbey sat shivering in the pre-dawn dark, she was enthralled by the activity occurring right in front of her. Totally full of themselves, male sage grouse were strutting around in tight circles with their hairless chests puffed out. As they walked, they repeatedly made burping and belching sounds while aggressively posturing toward any other males that came too close to their domains.

Populations of greater sage grouse have been performing their mating rituals on leks for eons. Every February through April, they puff their chests out and proudly display their sharply-pointed tail feathers while aggressively defending their territories. They repeatedly leap high in the air with their feet and spurs fully extended, striking out at their nearest competitors to garner feminine attention.

The largest grouse in North America, greater sage grouse live on the high plains of the American West — at elevations of four thousand to nine thousand feet — including populations in Washington, Oregon, Idaho, Montana, South Dakota, North Dakota, Nevada, Utah, eastern California, and western Colorado. Like many wildlife mating rituals, the 'dancing' of the male sage grouse around a *lek* is all about influencing female choice.

Abbey watched intently as the female sage grouse skittered demurely in, out, around, and through the displaying males — acting as if they didn't actually exist. In reality, she knew that only the males with the showiest exhibitions — typically less than five percent of those trying — would be able to mate with all the females. Meanwhile, the losing males would skulk off to recoup their grouse-hood in hopes of faring better when the next morning's activities began anew.

Rusty Longtree, a colleague of Abbey's noted for his unruly mop of curly red hair, nudged Abbey as they watched the last few birds leave the *lek.* "My uncle nearly got killed by one of these show-off grouses! He swears that these birds sit hidden in their sagebrush hollows, secretly plotting the precise moment to burst up with wings beating wildly askew in front of horses galloping across the open range. He claims that one of them did that to him, causing his horse to rear up and fling him — derriere first — into a clump of sagebrush.

Abbey smiled knowingly at Rusty, "Yes, I have heard a tale like that before. But wow, isn't it special to be able to sit here and watch their strutting in person? It's actually quite beautiful!"

Unfortunately, after months of studying these fanciful birds, Abbey's findings were not good news for the local ranchers that were benefitting from the BLM's generous — almost altruistic — structure of grazing fees. The rates the BLM were charging, were more than ten times less than the rates charged by private landowners for similar grazing rights.

But this wasn't the most disturbing part of Abbey's findings. She determined that the sage grouse populations were being severely impacted, first by 'chaining' of their habitats, and then by the helter-skelter construction of barbed wire fences that partition off ranchers' grazing allotments.

Sagebrush 'chaining' involves attaching a heavy steel chain between two bulldozers, and then literally knocking down all the woody vegetation — including all the sagebrush shrubs — in one hundred-foot swaths. This activity promotes the growth of more grazing grasses, which means that the ranchers can add weight and — in effect — marketing dollars to their cattle at a much faster rate.

Meanwhile, barbed wire fences are literally torture and death traps for sage grouse. These birds prefer to scurry on the ground like chickens rather than fly. When they do decide to fly, they do so at low elevations over mostly short distances. This means that they regularly get caught up in barbed wire fencing where they hang until they die.

As Abbey quickly discovered, both chaining and barbed wire fence construction were illegal on federal land. The BLM grazing leases clearly stated that the lessees — both ranchers and farmers — could not modify or impact any of the land they were using to feed their domestic cattle and sheep.

But when Abbey submitted her draft EIS describing these impacts, complete with heart-breaking pictures of grouse — plus antelope, hawks, and other animals — ensnared on the barbed wire, she learned another shocking lesson about the 'good ole boy' western lifestyle. The 'powers-that-be' summarily instructed Abbey to remove the negative language and photos showing how cattle grazing was impacting sage grouse and their habitats. When she asked her supervisor why, he said, "This is the way things have been done for decades, and all the new regulations — including NEPA and the ESA — therefore do not apply."

In other words, the chaining of sagebrush habitat and construction of barbed wire fences were both 'grandfathered into' — excluded from — the new environmental laws. With a devastated heart, Abbey accepted this decision; she didn't have a choice if she wanted to keep her job. But it really bothered her. Her review of the new environmental statutes and regulations made it clear that 'grandfathering' did not apply in this situation.

To assuage her hurt feelings, Abbey made it a point to hike regularly through the high plateaus of the Rocky Mountains, freeing any sage grouse she found. She also tied long flags of fluorescent wetland tracking tape — paid for on the government's dime — to the barbed wire to help scare the birds and other vulnerable wild animals away from the dastardly fences.

Abbey couldn't know this at the time, but this experience with her first EIS would be a problem with environmental regulation — in particular, those involving impacts to wildlife habitat — that would continue long after her time in government was over. Call it what you will, favoritism or cronyism, but environmental decision-making often came down to 'who' (what person and/or entity) was proposing the development.

As Abbey continued to find out — unfair and unfortunate as it may seem — the whole EIS process often revolved around how money was being distributed in political campaigns. In the case of the sage grouse, the ranchers who were benefitting from the grazing leases were holding all the cards.

In sparsely populated western counties, ranchers were the power brokers who decided who will be and who will not be elected. So, if the ranchers are suddenly told they can no longer go about 'business as usual', it is all but certain that the Congressional representation in their districts will dramatically change during the next election cycle, as will the BLM District Supervisors in those same areas.

In Abbey's defense, she was right on the money with her EIS findings. When she did her study in the mid-1970s, the greater sage grouse was a relatively abundant species. Today — primarily because of the loss of their high plains' sagebrush habitat — greater sage grouse are being considered by the USFWS for listing as an 'endangered species'. This is, indeed, a sad commentary for federal protection of wildlife species and their 'critical habitats'.

Rocky Mountain Reflections

Working for the USFWS in Denver also gave Abbey ample opportunities to explore what quickly became her favorite location in the Rocky Mountain West — Rocky Mountain National Park. She was assigned to work closely with the National Park Service staff in 'Rocky' — as the park was affectionately known. She concentrated on mitigating — or lessening — the potential impacts that visitor facility development might have on the park's resources. In the long run, this environmental oversight assigment provided her with significant insights into one of the most pressing conundrums associated with managing natural resources.

During her first week of exploring and evaluating the park's cornucopia of resources, Abbey had plenty of time for introspection. She also had a willing and quite capable associate — Rusty Longtree. Abbey was not positive, but she had a suspicion that Rusty wanted to be more than just friends. But she enjoyed his company and his willingness to sit with her and philosophize about land management.

Just before dawn one morning, she and Rusty sat on the edge of a rock beside Trail Ridge Road — the park's only through highway — drinking their morning coffee and soaking in the magnificent panorama that was just lighting up before them. The centerpoint of their magical vista was the massif of Longs Peak, which, at more than fourteen thousand feet, is the park's highest mountain.

As the rising sun sent its golden shafts spinning down into the deepest recesses of the valley below, Abbey asked Rusty, "Do we really appreciate what we have in a place like this? I mean, just look at that mountain! I can sure understand why the song '*America the Beautiful*' calls Colorado Mountains 'purple mountain majesty.' But what is the true value of our national parks and monuments?"

"Oh c'mon Abbey, can't you just sit and enjoy the view for once?" Rusty teased, but then — seeing her blush with embarrassment — responded, "In part, national parks are like an insurance policy, right?

They are reservoirs of genetic diversity for preserving as many different species of wild animals and plants as possible. I like to think of them as living museums — preserving intact examples of every kind of ecosystem in the United States.

"If they are museums, then should we be here, crushing plants and scaring away animals with our presence? The roads that we cut to get here and trails that we keep clear for hiking impact wildlife habitat. Wouldn't it be a better insurance policy if it was untrammeled and left completely to nature?" Abbey mused.

Rusty sat, contemplative. "If a tree falls in the forest and no one is around to hear it, does it really make a sound?"

"What?" Abbey looked at Rusty, bemusedly. She then caught sight of the smirk on his face and sucker-punched him. "Knock it off, Rusty, I'm serious!"

Rusty laughed, "So am I! Really, if we just leave nature to itself and never interact with it, how can we ever connect to it? How can we get people to bind with something that they aren't allowed to touch or don't know about the beauty that exists within? We need these access roads and hiking trails so that people can come here and see what we are seeing — to get away from the day-to-day grind and let off steam. To climb, hike, explore, and be happy!"

As they mulled over these questions, Abbey thought about one of her favorite quotes from Henry David Thoreau: "In wildness is the preservation of the world." To her, Thoreau's statement summarizes the thoughts that anyone who values nature must have from time to time: There's just something in the natural world that we know we can't live without. It's an intangible feeling — very difficult to describe — and yet its always there, in the back of our minds. It's an irrepressible urge that makes us all — hikers, campers, sightseers, hunters, fisherman, birdwatchers, photographers — yearn to get into the outdoors and return to nature's wonders.

Because of this, Abbey thought, we place an intrinsic value on our national parks and wildlife refuges. Somehow — even if we never get to visit these special places — just knowing that they're there is quite comforting and satisfying.

Later that evening, when she was reflecting on the morning's discussion in her journal, Abbey wondered what we would lose if we lost our national parks and wildlife refuges. As she often did, Abbey explored this question by writing about one of her favorite showcase wildlife species — the grizzly bear.

This 'Great Bear' once roamed throughout our United States from the rolling plains to the mountain tundra. Now — in the Lower forty-eight — it is mostly confined to remnant populations in and around Glacier and Yellowstone National Parks.

Abbey knew that Enos Mills — the famous naturalist and founder of Rocky Mountain National Park — spent a great deal of his lifetime tracking and studying the grizzly. Mills poignantly summarized his findings by stating that, "Without the grizzly, there can be no true wilderness." Abbey knew that many members of the ecological community agreed with Mills' statement.

So does the disappearance of the grizzly, Abbey wondered, mean that there is no longer any true wilderness in most of the continental United States? Is it possible to have a true national park without wilderness? How many wilderness values — such as the grizzly bear — can we afford to lose before we have lost a park?

A better question to ask, Abbey wrote, is how can we best protect the wilderness values we have left? She suddenly remembered a book, 'The Yearling' by Majorie Kinnan Rawlings, that she read as a youth. This book contained another one of her favorite quotes; "We were bred of the earth before we were born of our mothers. Born, we can live without our mothers or our fathers but we cannot live without the earth… or apart from it. And something is shriveled in man's heart when he turns away from the earth and concerns himself only with the affairs of men."

At that moment, Abbey realized that Ms. Rawlings' message was actually quite clear: We should strive to live in harmony with the earth instead of constantly struggling for dominance over it. Every potential impact should be looked at like a piece in a gigantic jigsaw puzzle.

If the rest of the puzzle has been well thought out, then the new piece will slip easily into place. But if the puzzle has been hastily and sloppily constructed, the new piece won't fit. And forcing the new piece into place will cause the entire puzzle to buckle and break apart.

Abbey realized that this same thing happens to our natural

environment. Ill-advised, poorly planned development does not fit. It destroys critical, natural resources and creates a ripple effect — like a stone tossed into a pond — that sends shock waves throughout the entire ecosystem of interrelated organisms.

Abbey next thought about how this all related to the task before her. In her mind, she began examining the ultimate questions of park management. Should we manage our parks strictly as wilderness enclaves, while minimizing the construction of visitor facilities and transportation routes? So doing would provide maximum protection for the park's natural resources. But what about the park's human visitors who don't have the ability or time to hike or backpack? How could they see and enjoy our national parks?

Should the NPS provide facilities and access points to accommodate every type of visitor? This would ensure that each of our citizens would have an equal opportunity to see and enjoy our national parks. But this could jeopardize the quality of the natural resources that our parks are supposed to protect. Is it possible to successfully accommodate both human visitation and natural resource protection?

As Abbey mulled over this dilemma, it occurred to her that the answer had to be a balanced approach. The emphasis had to be on park facilities that minimized resource impacts while still allowing visitor access.

Park buildings and roads had to be made of all natural and long-lasting — sustainable — materials that blended in with the natural environment while requiring only minimal maintenance. Energy sources must all be renewable — wind, water, and solar power — that would be inexhaustible, and the use of which would minimize impacts to air and water quality and other natural resources.

When Abbey presented her ideas for facility development that would be most harmonious with the natural environment, she realized that she was — unfortunately — a few decades ahead of her time. The park supervisors reminded her that renewable energy sources were not dependable enough — especially not in a relatively remote setting like Rocky Mountain National Park.

But Abbey's ideas did make her assembled management team sit up and take notice. They realized that continuous communication and cooperation among all parties — ecologists, engineers, park managers, concessionaires, visitors — was the key to optimal development of resource management plans.

In the final analysis, Abbey realized that everyone must be willing to sit together and hammer out compromise concepts that will allow needed facility development to take place in harmony with natural resource protection. This will allow the public to rest assured that our national parks and wildlife refuges will forever remain as lasting tributes to the preservation of our natural heritage.

Ramblings in the High Rockies

In addition to her professional work in Rocky Mountain National Park, Abbey spent many hours of her free time as a park volunteer, working out of the visitor center. She knew that Rocky's proximity to Colorado's Front Range and accessibility from several major highways made the park a must-see for most people vacationing in Colorado. Yet, she also knew that the majority of the park's visitors seldom experience what the park is really all about.

The average length of stay is only seven hours — just long enough to stop at a couple of scenic turnouts, view the magnificent mountain panoramas, and maybe take a short stroll along one of the park's interpretive trails. In Abbey's mind, this was very unfortunate, because Rocky offered so much more than a couple of snapshots for the family photo book taken during a quick drive across Trail Ridge Road. Impressing this fact on each and every visitor she met was her primary goal as a Park Ambassador.

She wanted people to know that the true allure of Rocky is the subtle splendor that can best be seen by those who venture off the asphalt and away from the crowds. It's the pastel fragance of a bouquet of streamside blue columbines — Colorado's state flower. It's the chattering of a chickaree from high up a lodgepole pine. It's the slap of a beaver's tail on a sunset-emblazoned subapline pond. It's all the magical qualities of nature that come together in the backcountry to make Rocky Mountain National Park what it truly is — an ecological showcase for the entire western U.S.

Abbey knew that no other national park offers a better opportunity to see and experience the different wild plants and animals that make up the various 'life zones' found throughout the Rockies. Driving up Trail Ridge Road, in a distance of less than ten miles, a park visitor travels — ecologically speaking — from the open ponderosa pine forests so typical of the Colorado foothills to the treeless tundra that characterizes northern

Alaska.

Whenever she led families through Rocky, Abbey never failed to emphasize her favorite fun facts about the park's wildlife. It always pleased her to see the bright-eyed responses of her charges — especially the children — to her 'behind the scenes' revelations of what really happens 'out there' in nature's world.

Abbey Starts a Family

In 1975 — in the midst of her busy and often-hectic government workload — Abbey also found time to get married. To Rusty Longteee's great disappointment, however, it was not to him. They remained friends for decades — Abbey was even a bridesmaid in Rusty's wedding years later — but Abbey never had romantic feelings for him. As fate would have it, the lucky man she married was, like her, a staunch conservationist and environmental activist. They spent hours discussing the philosophy of land management and shared an affinity for many of the same conservation authors.

Plus it didn't hurt that Randall ('Randy') Childers graduated *summa cum laude* with dual advanced degrees in civil engineering and landscape architecture from the Massachusetts Institute of Technology (MIT) in Boston. He also had an excellent job, working as a Senior Project Engineer with the National Park Service in their Denver Service Center — less than a mile from Abbey's USFWS office. After they married, Abbey and Randy bought a comfortable 'bonus ranch' home in the new Sixth Avenue West Subdivision — less than a half-mile from the Denver Federal Center's western gate.

Whenever she could, Abbey drew on Randy's vast expertise in evaluating the planning and design qualities of the project impacts she was assigned to assesss. Randy — in turn — pulled from Abbey's knowledge of wildlife ecology and systems thinking to help him view his engineering projects with a holistic approach.

After a year of marriage, Abbey and Randy gave birth to beautiful and healthy identical twin girls named Shiloh and Sunny. The happy couple could not have been more excited. For the first few hectic years of raising twins, they were lost in the land of diapers, feedings, and ten-cups-of-coffee-to-get-through-the-day-after-another-sleepless-night, new baby bliss. And bliss it was, despite the insanity. Their girls were both happy babies and brought immense joy to their days, acting as a salve for the tough problems that began to befall the U.S. environmental movement in the mid to late 1970s.

Unfortunately, the environmental movement was perceived — and for the most part, justifiably so — as catering to wealthy white Americans. The idea of environmental justice, or lack thereof, was clearly at play. Clean water and air, abundant wildlife, and plenty of open spaces and wilderness areas began to be viewed as amenities only for the establishment rich. The members of environmental and conservation organizations primarily belonged to upper socioeconomic classes — people who could afford to travel and experience the values of our nation's natural resources that were now protected by the environmental regulations passed during the first half of the decade.

Abbey and Randy, in the rare moments they had for conversation without twins in hand, often fretted about the exclusivity of the environmental movement. Abbey, in particular, worried that the movement was isolating itself from a critical network of vital support. Without diverse voices and perspectives, how could they ensure that they were managing land in ways that were fair and just for all people? Additionally, by excluding a large swath of the population from engagement or participation, they were losing valuable voices, both in numbers and perspectives. She remembered the countless conversations her parents, Camilla and Horace, had at family dinners about the way white-dominated governments forced laws onto the land without thought to the people living on that land.

At the same time, Randy wrestled with the conflict of his discipline's solution to every problem — engineer a way out of it. All around him, engineers, chemists, physicists, mathematicians, and other people working in the 'hard-science' fields — where single, definitive answers could usually be found — started questioning the biologists, ecologists, and the other 'soft-science' folks. In these softer sciences, there was usually not just one right answer, but many possible outcomes. Many hard scientists began to go back to the old ideas of thinking that humans could figure out how to deal with anything Mother Nature might throw their way. They believed that — no matter how disastrous a situation seemed to be — engineers and mathematicians would always find a way to solve things and prevail.

Randy and Abbey — literally — were a marriage of hard science and soft science. They provided essential perspective to, and abiding respect for, each other's discipline. Though, admittedly, Abbey often commented to Randy about how preposterous it was for the hard scientists to think that nature functions only in specific spheres. "It is like you hard science folk think that the natural world only operates in terms of either physics, chemistry, or math. Well, it doesn't — it is all interconnected. You *know* my favorite John Muir quote —" began Abbey.

Randy laughed, and cut her off, "Yeah, yeah I know — when you try to pick out any one thing by itself, you find it hitched to everything else." He poked her cajolingly. "It's true, Abs, nature doesn't fit into a single discipline. But we — engineers — want it to. It is a challenge, and that is why we rely on brilliant minds like yours to keep us straight!"

Abbey smiled at Randy, and gave him an affectionate hug. "I knew I married you for a reason!"

A Peanut Farmer Finds the White House

Because of the general loss of motivation in the environmental community when Jimmy Carter beat incumbent Gerald Ford in the 1976 presidential election, Carter inherited a difficult situation. A Georgia peanut farmer, Carter emphasized that he was a Washington 'outsider' — working against the dismal financial baggage and Watergate legacy that was attached to Ford. In the long run, this scenario did not serve Carter well. His clear lack of Washington insider knowledge and strength weakened his decision-making powers and — in 1980 — led to his defeat as a one-term president.

Abbey and Randy lamented the loss of a president that did more for the protection of public land than any other president since Teddy Roosevelt. Whenever they could, Abbey and Randy worked side gigs as freelance writers and photographers for both *Empire Magazine of the Sunday Denver Post* and the newly minted *Colorado Homes & Lifestyles Magazine*. They did this for two primary reasons. First, it gave them a creative divergence from the bureaucratic humdrum of their government jobs and — secondly — it provided an outlet for expressing their personal views about President Carter's accomplishments in the natural world.

For example — in one of their major cover pieces for *Empire Magazine* — Abbey lauded Carter's historic efforts in achieving passage of the Alaska National Interest Lands Conservation Act of 1980. This legislation protected one hundred and four million acres of America's last frontier, and represented the single largest conservation initiative in U.S. history. Abbey's piece elaborated on how Carter's bold action created a splendid tapestry of national parks and monuments, wild and scenic rivers, wildlife refuges, national forests, and wilderness areas.

In preparing her expansive photo-essay, Abbey pulled liberally from the stories and photos her parents — Camilla and Horace — accumulated during their Alaska trip in 1956. As a child, she had heard these stories so many times they were literally etched into her brain.

Whenever Horace started out saying, "Did I tell you about the time in Alaska when…" Abbey would always finish his sentence with a laugh.

"…you watched an eagle swoop down on an osprey and steal its fish? Or when you rounded the corner of a trail and nearly lost your footing at the sight of the full massif of Denali bathed in early morning light?"

Abbey always poked her dad teasingly when he started on his stories, but now she was thrilled to have this first-hand knowledge to illuminate her writing for *Empire*. As a final tribute in her piece, she stated that the American public owes President Carter a vote of deep and abiding gratitude for ensuring the preservation of a legacy of unrivaled scenic beauty and untold natural resources of the 'last great place', for all future generations of Americans to visit and enjoy.

In coffee-room conversations with their colleagues, Abbey and Randy also never missed a chance to applaud Carter for his foresight in establishing a new cabinet department — the Department of Energy (DOE) — that was tasked with researching and implementing alternative renewable energy sources. Their colleagues started to call them the 'Carter-Crazy Couple' or C-cubed for short. It is no surprise that when solar power became a big deal, their colleagues were the first to drop the newspaper articles on C-cubed's desks — which, of course, Abbey and Randy already knew all about! Carter set up the DOE to be the world's authority on research into fossil fuels, biofuels, nuclear fuels — plus solar and wind power.

In fact, Abbey and Randy were living in Golden, Colorado when solar power in the United States first hit a home run at the federal level. To their great delight, the Carter Administration's new DOE established funding for the Solar Energy Research Institute (SERI) — located less than five miles from their house.

Of course, Abbey and Randy fully supported SERI's mission. Many of their neighbors also jumped at the chance to get a free color television set in return for putting solar panels on their roofs. At the time, most everyone Abbey knew basked in the glow of having an international solar research center right in their own backyards.

Years later, Abbey and Randy often thought about how different the

U.S. energy future might have been if not for changes initiated by the next political administration. They also often wondered aloud about what happened to SERI. Then, one day in 1981, Randy somberly walked into the kitchen, carrying the morning newspaper. Shaking his head dejectedly, he looked at Abbey and said, "Not only did Reagan take Jimmy Carter's solar panels off the roof of the White House — 'a joke', he called them — he has essentially wiped-out SERI's budget. How are we going to keep solar energy moving forward with no budget for research and development? Don't people like free hot water heated by the omnipresent electrons of that great ball of white-hot gas in the sky? I just don't understand this at all."

The Great Communicator Creates A Backlash

Owing in large part to new President Ronald Reagan's policies, the 1980s were a time of transition, with environmentalists struggling to maintain their gains while conservatives — proponents of smaller governments, lower taxes, less regulation, and no support for renewable energy — took a more active role. As Benjamin Kline wrote in his book '*First Along the River*': "Although many people still sympathized with the need to protect the environment, there was a backlash against the perceived liberal agenda of the 1970s. Government and public support for the environmental issues waned in the glare of the emerging conservative beliefs."

After taking office, Reagan decimated the research and development budgets and eliminated tax breaks for anything related to renewable energy at Carter's Department of Energy (DOE). "The Department of Energy has a multibillion-dollar budget, in excess of $10 billion," Reagan boldly proclaimed during an election year debate, justifying his opposition to Carter's renewable energy policies. "It hasn't produced a quart of oil or a lump of coal or anything else in the line of energy."

Ironically, in April 1981 — less than three months after Reagan took office — the USFWS assigned Abbey the task of evaluating the potential environmental impacts of two renewable energy projects. Both projects — which were proposed by Abbey's old friends at the U.S. Bureau of Reclamation (BuRec) — were located in south-central Wyoming, near the tiny prairie outpost of Medicine Bow. The first project called for construction of a 'wind farm', one of the first in the western U.S., consisting of one hundred state-of-the-art large turbines located in a topographic vortex — only twelve miles from the town.

The second project — creating a pumped-storage hydroelectric generating system — was much more complicated from an engineering and design standpoint. It called for linking two existing reservoirs along the Medicine Bow River. The two reservoirs were separated by 1.8 linear miles and two thousand feet of vertical elevation. The linkage would be created by constructing twin penstock tunnels between the powerhouses of the two existing dams.

Once these tunnels were completed, water from the lower reservoir would be pumped up to the higher reservoir during periods of low energy demand. The flow would then be reversed during periods of high energy demand with water flowing downhill from the higher reservoir into the lower reservoir. In so doing, this design concept — known as hydroelectric pumped storage — would produce extra energy when it was most needed. The proposed design also called for constructing five total miles of new electric transmission lines to efficiently tie into the local power grid.

Since the proposed pumped storage project was also located less than ten miles from Medicine Bow, the BuRec determined it could most efficiently conduct the required environmental analyses for both projects by leasing the town's Virginian Hotel and setting it up as the project team's headquarters. This historic edifice was the only reasonable accommodation option for more than twenty-five miles in any direction from Medicine Bow. It was also the most famous building in south central Wyoming, being made so by Owen Wister — the famous author of 'The Virginian' and many other western novels. Because of the BuRec's lodging decision, Abbey joined twenty other EIS Team Members living in Medicine Bow during four-day work weeks while traveling back to her Golden home for Thursday, Friday, and Saturday nights.

For Abbey, this living situation was unlike anything she had ever experienced. Each team member was assigned an individual hotel room that served as both a living space and a field office. Then — since there was really nothing to do in 'downtown' Medicine Bow — the hotel's vintage 'Old West Dining Room & Saloon' was where all meals and off-duty hours had to be spent. As the project team settled into their daily routines, the discourse in the Virginian Hotel's cozy confines — among a group of highly-educated, but strongly-opinionated team members — often became quite lively and challenging.

One night, a group of engineers from the BuRec invited Abbey to join them in the saloon to discuss where she stood with her environmental assessments of the two projects. After ordering two pitchers of the local lager — High Plains Drifter — Raul Pagano, the BuRec's Chief Engineer, led off with the question that was on everyone's mind, "As the lead environmental scientist, how can you say anything negative about either of these projects, since they both represent clean energy development?"

Abbey took a sip of her still-frothing beer, stared thoughtfully at Raul, then replied, "I definitely understand your point. Since President Reagan has wiped out all the efforts President Carter made to advance our Nation's clean energy agenda, we should be taking advantage of every opportunity we have to approve all renewable energy projects — including solar, wind, and hydroelectric. But — since Reagan has not yet gutted our federal protections for wildlife — it is still my duty to review each project in terms of how they might negatively affect the endangered black-footed ferret, the threatened bonytail chub and razorback sucker, and a host of migrating hawks, eagles, and other raptors."

"Ah, yes," replied Raul. "From a professional standpoint, you're obligated to determine the regulatory impacts of a project — no matter how you feel personally about the project's value. But here's the thing. Don't you have to admit that President Reagan is not really the bad guy here? He's just trying to help us all out financially by cutting our taxes, reducing the size of the out-of-control federal bureaucracy, and cutting back the interminable delays caused by the federal regulatory process. Our President just believes that environmental protection and conservation issues should be subordinate to the needs of the people."

The quick shift in Raul's response — from project specific to overall policy analysis — caught Abbey totally off-guard. Taking a deep breath followed by two big gulps of her draught, Abbey shook her head at Raul and then calmly told him, "Based on what I know about the President's policies, he would be fine with doing away with all protections for natural resources — especially wildlife. If it were totally up to him, our government would abolish all the federal environmental statutes put into place in the late 60s and early 70s and go back to the days when all proposed federal projects would be approved straight away — no matter how much they contaminated our air, fouled our water, or caused species extinctions. Is that really what you want?"

Now things were really getting heated. Raul's face was almost as red as the close-cropped beard that framed his round face. Jerking his head toward Abbey, Raul drained the rest of his draught and seethed, "You are completely misunderstanding and disrespecting our duly elected leader. He understands and respects the need for, and value of, protecting our nation's resources. He just thinks that protecting the quality of life for humans is more important than protecting the life cycles of bugs, bunnies, and birds."

Picking up the verbal lance, Abbey charged forward, "So, you're saying that President Reagan fully understands what environmental protection is all about. If that's true, then how do you justify his Secretary of the Interior working to eliminate our landmark Land and Water Conservation Fund, drafting rules that would de-authorize new national parks, and recommending new oil and gas leases in federal wilderness areas? Also, how you defend his Director of the Environmental Protection Agency who is cutting hundreds of millions of dollars and a third of the staff from her own agency? Do you really believe that's the best way to protect our environment?"

The discussion continued back and forth like this for the better part of two hours. Finally — after many rounds of lubricating lager — the evening evolved into a friendly team competition of 'pong', one of the world's first video games that had somehow found its way into this remote western watering hole. As they departed for their rooms, Abbey winked at Raul. They both knew that — out of mutual respect and professional courtesy — they would agree to disagree about Reagan's policies and conduct their workloads as the consummate professionals they both were.

Abbey's field assessments for both BuRec renewable energy projects were something special. For the team's biologists, the wind farm project centered on assessing potential impacts on the black-footed ferret — one of our Nation's showcase endangered species. As members of the weasel family, these diminutive but vicious predators are primarily nocturnal. After the sunset light has faded, they slink into the burrows of the unsuspecting prairie dogs, and carry off their squealing catches to dine in the comfort of their own purloined burrows.

Because of this, much of Abbey's work on the proposed wind farm had to be conducted as surreptitiously as possible — always under the cover of darkness. This meant that the three other USFWS wildlife biologists — under the direction of Abbey — had to rotate night shifts. They also had to work with infrared headlights and several clothing layers to ward off the always frosty nights and typically strong winds at an elevation of more than six thousand feet.

Documenting the ferrets' activities and routines also meant that the biological team had to become very adept at setting up remote 'camera traps' that were triggered by trip wires. Under this system, animals moving through pre-determined locations — usually along obvious game trails — essentially took their own portraits.

On the other hand, the field work required to evaluate the potential impacts associated with the proposed pumped-storage project presented a completely different challenge. Efficiently accomplishing a detailed survey of the wildlife species and habitats in and around the project reservoirs, required the use of two six-person Bell helicopters buzzing around at 'pipeline pilot' elevations of less than one thousand feet and speeds of around fifty miles-per-hour. The pilots of these choppers were masters at making steep, pinpoint turns whenever a project team member asked to take a closer look at something on the ground.

As Abbey quickly discovered, this was not field work for the weak of stomach or faint of heart. But the rewards of hours of aerial surveillance of central Wyoming's remarkable assemblage of hoofed ungulates — including herds of Rocky Mountain elk, pronghorn antelope, and bighorn sheep — were well worth any minor moments of physical distress that might also occur.

On a typical field day, the copters would load up the teams and then take off from the hotel parking lot. Next, they would conduct an overview — flying at about five hundred feet above the previously delineated 'project area'. Consisting of four sections — 2,560 acres — of land, the project area was designed to encompass both reservoirs as well as the surrounding lands that appeared to have the highest wildlife habitat value. Each project team member understood that — as the field work moved along — the project area would be modified to best fit the findings of Abbey and her team of biologists.

After completion of the aerial overview — guided by voice requests from team members — the pilots would zoom down to elevations of less than one hundred feet for close-up views of ground details. This was when Abbey truly felt in her element. As her chopper crisscrossed the Wyoming prairie, she imagined that she was floating along in a dreamworld. Below her, herds of elk — often numbering in the hundreds — roamed the rolling hills, grazing placidly on billowing tufts of switchgrass. Meanwhile scattered small herds of pronghorns nibbled away in the sagebrush and greasewood flats and — in the higher elevations — groups of bighorn sheep mastered their steep terrain with all the skills of ballet dancers moving on point.

The most appalling thing Abbey noticed during her weekly overflights were the impacts that free range cattle ranching was having on the local wildlife populations. The entire project area — beyond the two BuRec reservoirs — was owned by the U.S. Bureau of Land Management (BLM). In line with the BLM's stated mission, this land was all being leased at ridiculously cheap rates by local ranchers.

This meant two things; neither of which were good for the local wildlife populations. First, cattle herds — sometimes numbering in the thousands — were free to roam the project area's habitat. Of course, these hordes of domestic livestock reduced the amount of grazing land available to the native elk and pronghorn herds. Second — in order to control their individual herds — the ranchers constructed mosaics of barbed-wire fencing that honeycombed the four sections of land. As Abbey had previously learned during her first field assignment, constructing barbed-wire fencing on federal land is illegal. But just as they did with their grazing fee gifts, the BLM conveniently looked the other way when it came to any fencing restrictions.

When Abbey and the other biologists conducted follow-up field inspections, their worst fears were often confirmed. At least once a week, they found a dead pronghorn, sage grouse, or raptor, impaled and left grotesquely hanging in the spikes of the unforgiving wires. Many times — as she lay in bed, trying to ignore the nearby rumblings of the coal trains that rattled the seams of the ancient hotel — Abbey thought that the wildlife in the project area would be better served if she was working to do away with inequitable federal grazing allotments, instead of assessing impacts of projects that — in all likelihood — would never be built.

In the final analysis, Abbey's midnight misgivings about the future of her projects proved to be correct for two primary reasons. First, the fossil fuel companies still not only owned, but actually dictated the world's economy. Second, the anti-government attitudes of the Reagan Administration were now all the rage.

As a result — in the second year of their existence — both of the Medicine Bow renewable energy projects were officially 'back-burnered' for future consideration'. In bureaucratic parlance, this meant that the BuRec had canceled both projects for lack of internal support. So, after eighteen months of field assessments and working in their sequestered hotel rooms, the project team packed up their files and headed for home.

As far as Abbey knew, her team's intense scrutiny and detailed assessments of impacts to endangered species, critical habitats, and overall wildlife populations in two separate locations never even saw the light of day. Extremely frustrated by what amounted to an immense waste of money and brainpower, as soon as she was settled back in her Denver office, Abbey politely asked her supervisor to never again assign her to another environmental assessment of an energy project.

In retrospect, Abbey almost had to admit that maybe President Reagan had a point about the slovenly size, redundancy, and unwieldy functioning of the federal government. She just wanted to go back to finding, researching, and evaluating new federal wildlife refuges. At least — she figured — these conservation projects had a realistic chance for approval and if so, they would provide her with an honest feeling of professional accomplishment.

Throughout the rest of her time working in the Reagan Administration, Abbey became more and more disenchanted with her USFWS job. She began to feel that anything she tried to do — even in the realm of expanding protection for wildlife and other natural resources — was destined to be buzz-sawed and obliterated by the existing anti-environmental backlash. Sadly — in typical bureaucratic fashion — most of her reports promoting new national wildlife refuges just seemed to vanish during the review process.

BOOK SEVENTEEN
A Dramatic Career Change

Considering Extreme Activism

While her conservation efforts at the USFWS continued to be ignored, Abbey wrestled with the question of whether she should or could be doing more to further the cause of environmental activism. After all, her first name reflected the exploits of one of the most famous — or infamous, depending on who you're talking to — environmental activists of all time. In fact, Abbey decided she at least needed to get to know more about Edward Abbey and his 'side of the coin'.

One night after dinner, she opened another beer for Randy and herself and then asked him, "How much do you know about my namesake, Edward Abbey?"

Randy paused for a moment, took a couple of swigs of his beer, and said, "Well I know he is quite a controversial and cantankerous old coot. But he is also an incredible writer and staunch conservationist. Why do you ask?"

"Because I'm trying to determine if becoming an activist will help me feel better about making a difference in the world right now. I have to admit that this government bureaucracy is finally getting to me. I feel like I'm just spinning my wheels; like I don't really even have a career."

In his normal calm and soothing manner, Randy said, "Well, let's talk about it then. Tell me more about Mr. Abbey, my love."

"Well, let me think," began Abbey, "he's actually best known for his outlandish 1975 novel '*The Monkey Wrench Gang*'. This book really set the tone for the rebellious environmental movement, you know, using whatever tactics it takes to get the job done. It even emphasizes protesting environmentally damaging activities through the use of violent force. Right now, the term 'monkey wrenching' is used to define any sabotage or law-breaking practices needed to preserve natural resources — including rare wildlife."

"Wow, that sounds pretty radical," responded Randy, "way beyond the pale, if you ask me. Tell me more."

"OK", continued Abbey reflectively, "Edward Abbey also has a softer side that — unfortunately — is not nearly as well-known as his hard edge. For example, his nonfiction book '*Desert Solitaire*' is a series of sublime yet powerful stories about his year as a ranger in the backcountry of Arches National Park. Of course, in many of the book's chapters, he also expresses his deep-seated beliefs about the faults of modern Western civilization. This includes his aversion to the lack of ethics in U.S. politics and the closely associated disintegration of America's environment. In sum total, '*Desert Solitaire*' is now considered a classic piece of natural-history narrative — on par with Thoreau's '*Walden*' and Leopold's '*A Sand County Almanac*'."

Randy took another swig of beer and looked pensively at Abbey, "Now that really tells me something important about this man, Abs. He certainly isn't preoccupied by fame and fortune — even though he has clearly achieved both. Sounds to me like he just wants to change the world for the better!"

Hearing Randy's words, Abbey reached out to him with her beer bottle, and they clinked the glass tops together. "Oh, you're just too perceptive, my love," she gushed. "In fact, I've read that he has already told his family that after he dies, he wants to be buried at night in the Arizona desert — wrapped only in a blue sleeping bag near a granite rock that is inscribed with the words: 'No Comment'."

After reading most of her namesake's books, Abbey realized that — for the most part — environmental radicalism has never quite achieved the level of mayhem and destruction espoused in the '*Monkey Wrench Gang*'. In fact, most of the new environmental non-profits (NGOs) relied on getting the public's attention through carefully planned protest rallies and peaceful activism — such as conservation voting record-tracking.

In Abbey's mind, the main exception to low-key environmental activism was the organization known as Greenpeace. More than any other NGO, Greenpeace was now emphasizing the media to gain attention to their causes. But in the past, Greenpeace — often described as the most visible environmental organization that ever existed — has always been controversial.

Throughout the 70s and early 80s, during thousands of dramatic protests, Greenpeace activists infiltrated nuclear test sites, shielded whales from harpoons, and blocked oceangoing barges from dumping radioactive waste. Then, in 1985, '*The Rainbow Warrior*'— flagship of the Greenpeace fleet — was mined and sunk by the French foreign intelligence service in the port of Auckland, New Zealand. The ship had been in route to protest a planned nuclear test in Moruroa in French Polynesia when it was sunk. This dramatic event also claimed the life of Fernando Pereira — a freelance Dutch photographer.

After spending time studying both the writings of Edward Abbey and the activities of Greenpeace, Abbey realized that radical environmental activism has two primary downsides. First, there is the very real possibility that extremism may prove to be a turnoff to the masses and, as such, would result in a loss of credibility for the overall environmental movement. The other problem is that civil disobedience often involves breaking the law — either as a result of simple sit-in protests, or something more volatile, such as blockading fossil-fuel extraction activities. As a result, civil disobedience often means arrests, trials, prison sentences, negative press, and possible loss of voting rights, which stirs up resentment and opposition, instead of support for the cause.

Abbey also fully understood that there is a place for well-organized activism. Indeed, both woman's suffrage and the civil rights movement leaned heavily on peaceful protests. Without people putting their bodies on the line and risking arrest, those important causes would not have moved forward. But though she wanted to live up to her namesake's legacy, Abbey knew that getting arrested was not in the cards for her. So, she turned her attention to the legal pathways she had available to channel her activism and make a difference in the world.

In the long run, this approach worked beyond Abbey's wildest imagination.

Becoming a Professional Wetlands Scientist

While her efforts at expanding the national wildlife refuge system continued to meet dead ends, Abbey started searching for ways to expand her career choices. At the time, the Clean Water Act (CWA) had become the most powerful federal tool for protecting wildlife habitats. Primarily aimed at preserving the quality of our nation's waters — including everything from major rivers to rivulet streams — the CWA also protected quite a bit of upland habitat in the form of 'land adjacent to wetlands', often referred to as 'upland buffer zones'. In July of 1985, Abbey talked her Bureau Chief — Rachel McQuade — into letting her attend a week-long training course at the U.S Army Corps of Engineers' (the Corps) Wetlands Research Technology Center (WRTC) in Vicksburg, Mississippi.

While she hated to drop the ball on Rachel — with whom she had become fast friends over the years — Abbey knew that being trained as a wetlands scientist would open up the way for her to move from the public sector to the private sector. And, at the time, she knew that was exactly what she wanted to do.

On the first day, the training coordinator, Colonel Reginald — just call me 'Reggie' — Phrateri, walked into the conference room, turned to the blackboard, and wrote, 'So why is the Corps the lead agency for protecting America's wetlands? Aren't you the guys that usually dredge and fill wetlands?'

After writing these two questions, Colonel Phrateri turned back to the class and, with a wry smile, said, "Ha — got ya, didn't I!" He waited for a minute for the looks of total surprise to disappear from his twenty-five trainees, then continued, "You see, when you do something long enough, you learn a few things. And I quickly learned that these are always the first two questions on the minds of the people taking my training. Even though, at first, no one is bold enough to ask them."

With that, Phrateri pushed his granny glasses back up to his fully bearded face, and stalked his heavy-set but obviously agile body over to his lectern. "Well, fellow scientists, before the rumor mill gets to swirling, here are the answers. Straight from the water buffalo's mouth, so to speak. You see, the Corps has been around for quite a while — longer by far than most other federal agencies. We were actually established by President Thomas Jefferson in 1802. In 1899 — under Section 10; the federal Rivers and Harbors Act — we were tasked with maintaining all 'navigable waters' of the U.S. The reason for this was, of course, to make sure our waterways remained usable for interstate transport, foreign commerce, and, as necessary, protection from our enemies. So, in 1972, when the federal Clean Water Act came along protecting all other 'waters of the U.S.' under the CWA's Section 404, it just made sense to roll that into our regulatory framework. Now for those of you tree-hugging wimps that may not agree with this logic, I say deal with it, because that's the way it is!"

Phrateri paused again to let the uneasy cringing die down, put his elbows on his lectern and smiling broadly said, "Ha — got y'all again. You guys are just too easy. Seriously now, I welcome all of you to this class and look forward to hearing your diversity of opinions. So, don't be timid about challenging me with your questions. OK now... who's first up?"

Never one to hesitate, Abbey immediately raised her hand and said, "I'm Abbey Childers, Senior Wildlife Biologist with the US Fish and Wildlife Service in Denver, Colorado. Look... I realize that one of the Corps' primary tasks is continually dredging rivers and harbors to keep them open for shipping. And I also know that all rivers and harbors are now protected 'waters of the U.S'. So, how does the Corps deal with having to regulate itself?"

Abbey immediately knew she had struck a nerve. Phrateri whipped around like a bowlegged man jumping off his horse and glared straight into Abbey's steely blue eyes. "Whoa, Nellie", he exclaimed, "now that's quite a question to start things off!"

"OK, we might as well dive right into it — so here goes," continued Phrateri. "First off, you are correct. The Corps dredges literally millions

411

of acres of regulated waterways a year. But here's the thing. Since Section 10 of the Rivers and Harbors Act says we must maintain the 'navigability' of waterways, we are exempt from regulating dredging or removal of material from waterways and wetlands. Now under Section 404 of the CWA, we are only charged with regulating the filling — or deposition of material or pollutants — into wetlands. The pollution component of our jurisdiction also deals with both 'point source discharges' — such as the outflows from factory and sewage pipes — and 'non-point source discharges' — meaning the contaminants contained in stormwater runoff."

"OK, young lady, have I answered your question satisfactorily?" asked Colonel Phrateri, again staring at Abbey. Seeing Abbey's affirmative smile and nod, he turned back to the group and said, "OK, who's next — please step right up!"

Several hands again shot up. Peering over his glasses, Phrateri pointed to a tall fellow in the back of the room, "All right, let's hear it. Name, position, and location first — if you will."

"Hi Colonel, I'm Jackson Landis from Knoxville, Tennessee and I work as Fishery Biologist with the Tennessee Valley Authority. My question is pretty simple: How do you folks decide who needs a permit and who doesn't?"

"Ah yes — an excellent question indeed, my good man," replied Phrateri. "Well, first off, let's take a look at what you're proposing to do. If you're looking to do something that will involve permanently altering a wetland, then we will take jurisdiction. Then — if your proposed action is permittable under the CWA, we have three types of permits we can issue."

Phrateri paused to gaze around his audience and make sure no one was dozing off. Satisfied that he mostly had everyone's attention, he continued. "Eighty percent of the permits we issue are Nationwide Permits, which means that your proposed action is a type of general activity that occurs all over the country — for example, building a boat ramp or a family fishing dock. Your project design just has to conform to pre-specified minimal wetland impacts for us to permit it."

"Regional Permits are the next type of permit we issue," continued Phrateri. "These are specific to each Corps district office and also require

412

a finding of minimal impacts to wetland resources and their associated functions. A permit for constructing a lobster-handling facility in our New England District is an example of a Regional Permit. Finally, we require what we call an Individual Permit for a proposed project that would involve greater than 0.5 acres of impacts to the 'aquatic environment'. As you might expect, these are the projects that involve — by far — the greatest loss of wetlands and waterways. Before, we can issue an Individual Permit, we have to be convinced that the proposed action satisfies our Section 404(B)-1 Guidelines. This compliance will prove that your overall project is designed to minimize wetland impacts."

Phrateri had barely gotten these words out of his mouth before another wildly waving hand shot up from the middle of the room. "Oh sir, you just said the magic words for me. My name is Marjorie Tannenhurst and I live in Southborough, Massachusetts. I work for the U.S. Environmental Protection Agency (EPA). I just started six months ago, and it seems like everywhere I turn at work, I hear someone talking about the Section 404(B)-1 Guidelines. If you can explain these to me, I will be forever grateful!"

"Wow, I guess I'm really in the hot seat now," responded Phrateri with a distinct twinkle in his eye. "I know that at first, these Guidelines sound like gibberish to most people. But they're actually quite simple — they just involve a sequential series of three tests."

Sauntering over to the blackboard, Colonel Phrateri was now really in his element. He started writing as he was talking. "You see, these 'B-1 Guidelines' are the basic method we use to determine the impact significance of your proposed project and — accordingly — whether we have to approve or deny your Individual Permit. In other words, this is where the rubber meets the road in wetland permitting.

"So", continued Phrateri, "before we start the B-1 review process — we must determine that your project is justifiable for either infrastructure enhancement, economic growth, or reasonable use of private property. Now the first B-1 test assesses whether your project is suitably designed to avoid impacts to aquatic resources. For example, can the size of the marina you're proposing be reduced by one hundred slips and still be economically viable? Next, the second B-1 test — after you pass the avoidance test — is have your unavoidable impacts been sufficiently minimized? Sticking with our marina example, can the re-sized facility be shifted two hundred feet southward to avoid impacting two seagrass beds and an oyster reef? Finally, the third — and typically the most difficult B-1 test — is mitigating for or replacing the aquatic resource impacts that cannot be avoided or further minimized. Again, with our marina example, mitigation might involve creating new seagrass beds and an oyster reef adjacent to the new facility."

"So that's basically how it works," concluded Colonel Phrateri, "now please tell me what you think."

In truth, Abbey didn't like much of anything she heard about the 'Section 404(B)-1 review process'. She saw it for what it was: a regulatory tactic for justifying projects that either had sufficient financial clout, or the political backing to make it through the permitting gamut. Still, she was excited enough about becoming a wetlands scientist that she kept her mouth shut.

Most of the remainder of Abbey's week in Vicksburg included intensive field training. The emphasis was first on how to delineate — or define the limits of — a wetland. This involved using a tool called a Dutch auger to dig test holes for analysis of the hydric characteristics of soil profiles. While Abbey found this work to be somewhat tedious, she — not surprisingly — picked up the process quite quickly. By the end of the week, she was an expert at determining whether a soil profile had the necessary factors — low chroma color, mottling, fine grain size, etc. — to be officially designated a wetland soil type.

Actually, the most exciting thing that happened during the three days of wetland delineation field work was something that wasn't actually on the program. As Colonel Phrateri was bending down to show Marjorie Tannenhurst how to extract a soil column from her auger, he slipped. As he was falling, he grabbed Marjorie's arm and they both tumbled straight back into the oozing salt marsh behind them. The resulting splatter of organic muck covered them both, as well as Abbey and many other class members who were standing nearby.

Slowly rising to his feet as he wiped the gooey mess off his clothes, Colonel Phrateri looked wryly at the group and said, "So, how do you like me now? I just went out of my way to give you all a first-hand demonstration of how you know when you're really in a wetland. When you smell those good ol' rotten eggs and feel that slimy soil texture, you know for sure you're in my jurisdiction!"

The rest of the time in the field, the group watched as Phrateri and his assistants explained and demonstrated the basic functions and values of wetlands. They used columns of soil types with different grains sizes to demonstrate how wetlands suck up stormwater runoff. They did this by showing how water — with red dye added — flows right though sandy, large-grained upland soils, but is trapped by silty, fine-grained wetland soils.

They then explained that this provides two vital functions. First, wetlands are like giant sponges that reduce the intensity and extent of flood flows. In fact, an acre of wetland can store up to 1.5 million gallons of floodwater. Second, wetlands trap and absorb many of the pollutants contained in stormwater runoff before they can contaminate our surface water resources and our groundwater supplies. Plant roots and microorganisms in the wetland soil commonly absorb foul liquids, while other pollutants stick to the soil particles themselves.

Every morning, Colonel Phrateri and his field crew also led the class on wildlife walks. They used these jaunts to prove that wetlands enhance both the size and biodiversity of local wildlife populations. As the Corps instructors walked and identified species that they saw and heard, they also threw out a lot of factoids for the group. For example, up to 50% of North American bird species nest or feed in wetlands. And — although they make up less than 5% of land surface in the U.S. — wetlands are home to more than one-third of our plant species.

Abbey already knew most of this information, since — every time she conducted an environmental assessment — she had to analyze potential impacts to wetlands and waterways. But overall, she still considered her week in Vicksburg valuable for two important reasons. First, it was an excellent refresher course on all things, wetlands. Next, it provided great networking with other wildlife biologists and wetland scientists from all over the country. She suspected that many of the folks she got to know during her Corps training week would play a role in her future career — and she wasn't wrong!

When she got back home, Abbey immediately set to work on submitting her Professional Wetland Scientist (PWS) application to the

Society of Wetlands Scientists. She featured the Corps training course she had just completed as a cherry on the top of the more than ten years' experience she had studying wetlands and assessing their impacts from proposed federal development projects. Less than a month later, she was pleased to find out that her application must have sailed right through the review process. By the end of August 1985, Abbey was proudly displaying her PWS Certificate on her office wall.

Teaming Up With Aldo

Obtaining her PWS certification was especially important to Abbey because of where she decided to take the next step in her career. For the past year, Aldo had been bugging her — sometimes it seemed almost daily — to come and work with him.

Aldo's consulting business — AES — was being overwhelmed by trying to serve both new and returning clients. He and his partners had moved from their garage 'start-up' to a permanent six thousand square foot office space right on the waterfront in downtown Gloucester, Massachusetts — north of Boston. AES now had more than fifty employees, but they needed many more — especially-certified professional scientists and project managers like Abbey.

In June of 1986, Aldo made Abbey an offer she couldn't refuse. He increased her government salary by more than 50%, said he would pay her moving expenses, and set her up with a staff of ten — including eight professional scientists and two administrators. Somewhat reluctantly, because she had loved the myriad of challenges and travel involved with a federal land management agency — Abbey accepted Aldo's generous offer as a 'Senior Wetland Scientist'.

At first, after accepting Aldo's offer, Abbey was concerned about the fact that most of Aldo's clientele were land developers, and, given the out-of-control pace of development in New England in the mid-1980s, they were all chomping at the bit to get as much steel in the ground as fast as they could. Many of Aldo's clients were constantly pestering him to 'just get our permits ASAP'. They didn't even care what it was going to cost them to do it. They knew they could make tens times what they spent as soon as a project was finished.

But because he was her brother, Abbey knew beyond the shadow of a doubt that Aldo would play strictly by the rules. This meant that, even though his clients might push him to do so, he would never even think about cutting corners or playing games with the regulatory process. In fact, Abbey knew Aldo would do just the opposite, even if it meant costing him a hefty payday. If it came down to a question of not following the mandatory procedures for environmental protection, Aldo would — even in the middle of a project — not hesitate to tell his clients to find another consultant.

Beyond sharing all of Abbey's ideas about how things should be done, Aldo also knew that any consultant who didn't adhere to the regulatory 'book' was playing with fire. You might get away with fooling the permitting folks once or even twice, but as soon as you get caught, you will be out of business. As is the case with just about any business, once you lose your professional credibility you can never regain it. You might as well shutter your business and just walk away.

During their many late-night discussions before she took the job, Aldo also guaranteed two things to Abbey. First, he told her that she would function as his personal gyroscope — making sure that everything he did remained constant and above board — while never deviating from his personal mission to balance top-quality human development with necessary resource protection. The second thing Aldo promised Abbey was that as soon as she had her feet on the ground, he would let her choose the types of clients and projects she wanted to work on.

As Abbey was soon going to find out, Aldo's second promise was the most important assurance her career would ever receive.

A Trip Down Memory Lane Backfires

As part of moving to her new job, Abbey decided to detour by the national wildlife refuge where she had so many wonderful memories and experiences as a young child. On her series of flights from Denver to Norfolk, Virginia, Abbey rested peacefully and daydreamed about her childhood exploits in and around Back Bay National Wildlife Refuge (NWR).

She fondly recalled days filled with dangling rotten chicken necks in front of blue crabs, braving head-high waves to sling blood worms into the surf — and when the moon was right — catching buckets of croakers and spot. Generally considered trash fish by local sportsmen, these small, surf-schooling fish were all trophies to her.

Unable to sit still on a beach for more than about a minute, Abbey always hated the lounge chair, beach umbrella, and sandcastle-building beach routines. Instead, she opted for long walks along the wrack line at the top of the intertidal zone — always dashing and splashing her way through each breaking wave. She loved the squish of wet sand squirting up through her toes while she stopped to examine every oceanic treasure that caught her eye.

It was during just such a beachcombing venture that she had her first up-close-and-personal encounter with mollusks — although she didn't know them by that name at the time. She noticed that each breaking wave unearthed a palette of shiny organisms — all furiously digging in unison back down into the wet sand.

A call to her dad brought a typically stellar, "Let me show you something really fun to do!" With that, Horace Greenleaf marched down into the breakers, turned his backside to the ocean, and screwed his feet down into the sand. As soon as the next wave passed by and began to recede, he dug his hands deep into the sand and pulled up hundreds of miniature, multi-colored shells.

Now Abbey was really hooked! She rushed back to the refuge house, grabbed her plastic bucket and shovel, and sped back to the beach to collect some new 'pets'. She just couldn't believe that this soggy, seemingly sterile, sand was hiding hundreds of tiny jewels — each one with its own distinctly different colors and patterns. With each double handful of sand, she was unearthing a new gallery of nature's art.

The creatures Abbey was finding that day of her youth were tiny bivalve mollusks known as Atlantic coquinas. They were filter feeding in the surf — continuously being uncovered by outgoing waves — and then using their tiny 'feet' to dig back down before the next set of waves exploded across the intertidal zone.

After driving through the urban confines of Norfolk, Abbey couldn't wait to get back to her Back Bay beach and share the joys of these tiny jewels with Randy and their twin girls, Shiloh and Sunny. But as soon as she turned her rental car south onto Sandpiper Road toward the refuge headquarters, Abbey was worried that she might be making a big mistake.

All of Sandbridge Beach — a residential development north of Back Bay NWR — was now packed with row upon row of tightly spaced houses. And the worst part was that the lovely foredunes that used to shelter and buffer the inland areas from the ocean's waves were all now gone — completely replaced by the lawns and decks of the beachfront mansions.

After finally coming to the refuge gate, now reachable by an access road, Abbey was relieved to find that at least the refuge property looked mostly the same. But when she grabbed her plastic bucket from the back of her car and scampered over to the beach with Shiloh and Sunny in tow, her worst fears were realized.

Right on cue as a wave rolled in and out, Abbey pulled up soupy handfuls of wet sand and, to her complete chagrin, not much else. Another wave rolled in and again she dug down deep and pulled up nothing. She changed positions several times, moving first several hundred feet up the beach and then several hundred feet down the beach. Every scoop brought the same results — mostly sterile sand with absolutely no 'tiny jewels' to be found.

In fact, there was not a coquina anywhere on the refuge's beach that day — or during the rest of the Childers family's brief visit. Apparently, something had caused the local population of coquinas to go from millions to seemingly nonexistent in just over three decades.

Also, the beach's former resident crustacean community — notably sand fleas and ghost crabs — were mostly missing in action. Abbey asked everyone she could find about these missing beach denizens and was told that this tragic loss of natural resources was not due to just one 'something' but actually a long, interrelated string of poor land management decisions.

Oceanfront Development Fiascos

Finally, after they had beachcombed their way north for about a half mile, Abbey, Randy, Sunny, and Shiloh came across an elderly gentleman who was sitting comfortably in a beach chair, and minding two surf rods that were stuck down in the sand in their plastic holders. Realizing that this fellow probably lived in Sandbridge Beach and had obviously been around for quite a while, she decided to give it one last shot. "Excuse me, kind sir, can you tell me why this beach has changed so much in the past thirty years?"

"Why, just what on earth do you mean, young lady?" replied the man as he rubbed the sweat off his mostly bald head, and then wiped his hand across his evenly-tanned chest.

"Well, sir, my parents were the refuge managers here when I was a child," replied Abbey, "and I fondly remember how much fun I had whenever we went to the beach, and my dad would show me all the coquinas, sand fleas, and ghost crabs that lived here. There were literally millions of critters living all over this beach. Now I'm back with my husband and young daughters, and we can't find anything like what I remember. It's so sad."

With that, the man stood up and walked over to Abbey and her family. "Hoo boy, do I ever have a story to tell you. How much time do you have?"

"All the time in the world right now," responded Abbey, "we're here for a couple of days."

Stroking his chin stubble, the man said, "OK then — let's do this. My name is Frank Thurlow, and I've lived in Sandbridge for the past fifty years — so I can tell you anything you want to know about what's happened here. Let me give you my address and phone number. Do you happen to have a pen and paper?"

Abbey pulled a pen and piece of scrap paper out of her beach bag and handed them to Frank. He scribbled something on the paper and handed it back to her.

Looking at what he had written, Abbey read '304 Sandfiddler Way' and asked, "Is this near here?"

"Yes, of course, it is, my dear," replied Frank. "It's just a few miles up the road, very easy to find. Just stop by any time. My wife, Liz, and I will be there and we'd be more than delighted to talk to you over some nice lemonade and snacks."

"Oh — that's wonderful," replied Abbey, "how about five o'clock tomorrow afternoon?"

"Perfect," replied Frank. "At that time of day, we can switch our repast to brews and boiled crabs. Now, you folks enjoy the rest of your walk and be thinking of all the questions you want to ask. But fair warning, you may not be too happy with my answers."

The next day at five o'clock sharp, Abbey, Randy, Shiloh, and Sunny picked their way along the plank walkway that led up to Frank's front door. The house itself was rather small, but the expansive screened porch on the right side revealed where Frank and Liz spent most of their time. As soon as they stepped through the front door, they were taken aback by the fact that the house appeared to still be under construction. The 'walls' consisted of tar paper nailed to studs, and sheets of unfinished plywood made up the floor.

"Now don't be too fast to judge us on the quality of the house," sniffed Frank as he welcomed them in. "When I was building this place, I thought, shoot, this is just a beach house — so let's live in it like we're at the beach. We decided we really didn't want a place that required a lot of fuss to keep straight. So, I stopped working and we started living. Best decision I ever made. Now, all we do is sweep the sand out every day and prop our feet up out on the porch.

"Speaking of which, let's head out there now," continued Frank, gesturing toward the porch door. The shrimp and crabs are boiling, the beer is nice and cold, and the picnic table is all set. Plus, I've got some of Liz's tasty lemonade and cookies for your girls."

After everyone had comfortably settled into the porch's eclectic array of chairs, Frank started the conversation. "OK, let's get started. First, let me give you a thumbnail history of Back Bay and Sandbridge Beach before we hit the grub."

Gently rocking in his favorite chair, Frank took a swig of his Princess Anne Nut Brown Ale and started, "As you might guess from it's name, Sandbridge is essentially a barrier island — in fact, many folks call it 'Virginia's Outer Banks' — with the Atlantic Ocean to the east and Back Bay to the west. As a natural feature, it provided protection to the mainland by buffering — or lessening — the impacts of winter's nor'easters and summer's hurricanes. Because of this essential function, it should never have been developed in the first place."

Always curious, Shiloh immediately raised her hand and asked, "Do you mean that barrier islands can't have houses? Why is that, Mr. Frank?"

"Ah, now that is a most perceptive question, young lady," replied Frank, taking another long quaff of his beer. "You see, since barrier islands absorb the energy of storms, they are always moving and shifting. They perform like opposing battering rams — slamming against a storm's fury and diminishing its destructive energy."

"Depending on the strength of a storm, a barrier island may look completely different in size and shape after the storm has passed," continued Frank. "Now this is all fine — if only crabs, mollusks, and barnacles live on the island. But if there are human structures present, what do you think is going to happen to them when the sand starts moving around?"

Once again raising her hand, Shiloh exclaimed, "Well that can't possibly be very good for the homes or the people living in them. They're going to get wrecked!"

"Right you are, sweetie," Frank nodded, "many of the houses will have their foundations washed away and they will collapse. Of course, most of the people — at least the smart ones — will have evacuated, so they will be all right. But the buildings are a different story. I'm sure you all know what the devastation left by a major hurricane looks like."

"Yes, it's not really very pretty," interjected Shiloh.

"But", contined Frank stroking his chin, "as my old radio buddy Paul Harvey always says, 'now for the rest of the story'. When Sandbridge was being built, the nimcompoop land developers let the wealthiest folks build their mansions next to the open Atlantic — right on top of the foredunes. So now not only did Sandbridge no longer have any flexibility to move in response to storms, it also no longer had any protection from the force of the massive waves and the surges generated by the storms. So, winter after winter, many of the largest, oceanfront houses on Sandbridge were damaged and some were even destroyed. And then, when this happened, what do you think those wealthy homeowners did?"

Now it was Sunny's turn to get into the act. "Well, I can imagine they weren't very happy. Did they try to get their money back for their houses?"

"No, they couldn't do that, because no one was stupid enough to give them flood insurance," replied Frank. "But — as you suggest — they did raise quite a ruckus. And you won't believe what happened next. But before we get into that, let's all take a seat at the table and enjoy these heaping platters of Chesapeake Bay blue crabs, boiled shrimp, fresh corn-on-the-cob, and home-made hush puppies — Liz's specialty."

After downing their sumptuous Frank-and-Liz buffet, everyone cleared and washed their own dishes, and then scurried back to their seats to hear the rest of Frank's Sandbridge Beach story. Abbey and Randy were especially thrilled to see how much Shiloh and Sunny were really into the narrative — but they realized that it may be because Frank was such a master storyteller.

Clearing his throat and then taking a gentle sip of his piping hot after-dinner tea, Frank started again, "Let's see now, where were we? Oh yes — almost every winter, many of the beachfront homeowners were reguarly losing parts — and sometimes all — of their homes. So they all started calling their local Congress folks and demanding that something be done."

"Gee, Mr. Frank, why did they do that?" asked Sunny. "Wasn't the real problem that they had built their homes where they shouldn't have? So how could they expect someone to bail them out?"

Frank took another sip of his tea, gave Sunny a thumbs up, and said, "Right you are on all counts. But unfortunately, in the world of politics, as the old cliche goes, 'money talks'. And because most of the beachfront homeowners were major contributors to their fiancial campaigns, the politicans gave them what they wanted — and almost right away. Before anyone could say 'grease the skids', our friendly Corps was on site pounding a wall of forty-foot-long steel girders down into the tidal zone and then guy-wiring them back into the property owners' lots. The federal government was, in effect, trying to a recreate a massive, five-mile stretch of protective bulkheads that the foredunes provided before they were wiped out by construction of the beachfront homes."

Since Frank was now talking about a major federal action, it was Abbey's time to ask a question. "Mr. Frank, how were they able to do this so fast. Didn't they have to prepare an Environmental Impact Statement (EIS) under the National Environmental Policy Act (NEPA)? Seems to me that these artificial walls would have totally messed up the beach and coastal dynamics for miles in both directions!"

"Uh huh — you've hit the nail squarely on the head, my dear. Now, I understand what you must be doing in your government job. But before I answer your questions, let me tell you about the comedy of errors that happened next."

"In many cases," lamented Frank, "the steel girders didn't even make it through the next season of winter storms. The storm surges simply overtopped the bulkheads and then mashed them flat from the inside out. After just two years, except for the unsightly mess of twisted and broken girders lying around, the artificial wall was essentially completely gone."

"Wow, that's incredible, Mr. Frank," remarked Randy. "I can't imagine what happened next."

"Not only did Sandbridge homeowners lose the money they invested in the girders," continued Frank, "but they also lost their once wide and beautiful beaches. While temporarily stabilizing Sandbridge, the bulkheads caused a significant and permanent change to the local coastal flow dynamics. Storms began eroding sand from the Sandbridge area then depositing it further south. Soon, Sandbridge's beaches were completely gone at high tide, the breakers just slammed against the remaining bulkheads and reduced the beaches to just barely walkable slivers at low tide."

"But then after the bulkhead debacle…" Frank took a thirty-second pause for dramatic effect, "the Corps initiated what they called an annual 'beach nourishment program'. Now I'm not even sure who asked them to do this. But many of my neighbors and friends are convinced they just decided to do it on their own. They wanted to atone for their bulkhead boondoggle. Anyhoo, this nourishment program consisted of dredging millions of cubic yards of sand from offshore banks and then pressure pumping it onto all five miles of the Sandbridge oceanfront. And they've been doing it every year now for the past fifteen years. In fact, they just finished this year's sand dump last week!"

"Uh oh, that can't possibly be good for all the creatures that were living in the tidal zone," remarked Sunny, holding her head in her hands in exasperation.

"You're so right, sweetheart," concluded Frank. "While this sand dumping succeeded in temporarily restoring the depleted beaches for each coming recreation season, the tons of imported sediment buried billions of mollusks, crustaceans, and other sand dwelling critters. And — since this beach renourishment process had to continue each spring — to make up for the sand lost during each winter's nor'easters — the populations of the coquinas, ghost crabs, and sand fleas may now be lost forever."

"But since this was a 'federal action', I still don't understand how the Corps was able to do this work without NEPA compliance," persisted an obviously frustrated Abbey.

"All this work was done under something I believe they called… uh, let me think here… 'categorical exclusions', yes — that's it. And because of this, no environmental assessments at all were done. The Corps just came out here and started pouring sand onto our beaches. Now the actual extent of how much the bulkhead building and sand pumping projects have screwed up Sandbridge's beaches is still being debated. Most of the scientists at the Virginia Institute of Marine Sciences (VIMS) think that both the negative hydrogeological and the ecological impacts are permanent and that Sandbridge Beach will never return to the beautiful, wide open expanse of beach life that it once was. So sad but true, folks — I'm sorry to say."

As soon as the last words were out of Frank's mouth, everyone sat in stunned silence for several minutes — mulling over his words they had just heard. Finally, Frank broke the silence, "But hey, this is the beach and what are you supposed to do at the beach? Have fun — that's what. Now, I understand that Ms. Liz has some big bags of marshmallows that aren't going to roast themselves. So, what say we all head over to the beach, build a big bonfire, and get to it!"

"Yay!" shouted Shiloh, tugging at Sunny's shirt. "Come on, slowpoke, I'll race you. Last one there has to collect driftwood for the fire!"

Understanding what had happened to her beloved Back Bay beaches spurred Abbey to study more about the history of oceanfront development. As she soon learned, coastal land development practices in the United States have been abysmal throughout the 1900s. And — as she had just experienced — the most egregious mistakes involved the development of barrier islands like Sandbridge Beach.

Abbey's research revealed that land developers have always taken advantage of the public's lustful desire for oceanfront properties. Seaside mansions, roads, and supporting retail establishments now cover many barrier islands. In effect, this amounts to real estate suicide, since all barrier island developments are doomed to fail sooner or later. No matter how much money is spent trying to stabilize oceanfront developments with seawalls and bulkheads, the ocean's power will eventually win out and cause the catastrophic loss of property and lives. It's not a question of if, but when a barrier island development will be obliterated by a hurricane or powerful winter nor'easter.

In studying this shameful land development practice, Abbey read about hundreds of examples of catastrophically poor judgment from Bar Harbor, Maine to Brownsville, Texas. They all had had massive impacts on the local coastal flow dynamics, causing changes in erosion-deposition patterns and cycles that bury marine resources — especially oyster beds, clam flats, and — as Shiloh and Sunny had sadly just experienced — billions of tiny coquina shells.

BOOK EIGHTEEN
Establishing a Career Legacy

Making Gloucester Home

By the first of September 1986, Abbey, Randy, Sunny, and Shiloh Childers were settled into a comfortably-cozy townhome in Rocky Neck section of Gloucester, Massachusetts. They were all beside themselves with excitement and anticipation. The family was now surrounded by an *avant garde* enclave of artists and writers intermixed with a dazzling view of the bustling harbor with a cadre of gourmet 'seafood shacks' just down the street. Abbey was now ready to begin her new journey as a private environmental consultant.

Gloucester, Massachusetts, was still exactly what it has always had been — a no-holds-barred, heavy-duty fishing port. The city is rightly famous for many things, including its unparalleled history. Located on the waterfont, the 'Man at the Wheel' statue honors the hundreds of brave boat captains and crews who never returned from their intrepidly-daring voyages. The city is also the home of Gorton's of Gloucester and Birdseye — arguably the two most famous names in the seafood industry. And Rocky Neck is the oldest continuously working art colony in the nation. Through the years, the area has featured the lives and works of such notable painters as Winslow Homer, Edward Hopper, and Fitz Henry Lane.

The irony was not lost on Abbey that she had started working in the private sector near the end of Ronald Reagan's presidency. From an genvironmental perspective, Reagan's policies had a ground-breaking effect. She knew his 'Reagonomics' spurred land development and private economic gain like nothing else had done since before the Great Depression of the 1930s. But his simultaneous de-emphasis on environmental regulation and natural resource protection also had a galvanizing effect on the conservation community.

Enjoining the public's typical response to a widespread tragedy, supporters of environmental quality grabbed their pens and opened their wallets as never before. Much to Abbey and Randy's delight, the popularity of some of their favorite conservation groups skyrocketed. Organizations like the Sierra Club, National Audubon Society, National Wildlife Federation, and The Nature Conservancy had to hire extra people just to keep up with the massive influx of new members. It seemed to Abbey that — from the standpoint of protectionist power — America's myriad of natural wonders never had it so good. In many respects, Reagan's anti-resource rhetoric achieved the opposite of what was intended.

Because of the Reagan Administration's pro-development policies, the Boston metro area — along with most of New England — was booming in the mid to late 1980s. As a result, Randy was eagerly anticipating hanging out his own shingle as a professional land surveyor and civil engineer.

Based on his recent conversations with Abbey, Randy knew that her brother Aldo and his company — AES — was completely overwhelmed by droves of new projects coming in the door each day. Accordingly, Randy also happily agreed to be an 'on-call' subcontractor for Aldo to help ease the workload whenever and wherever his services were needed.

With the crazy speed at which land development was happening, turning down new work wasn't even an option. Developers were so anxious to get their projects in the ground and on the market that they didn't even haggle about price. The over-riding mantra was 'just get it done, send us the bills, and we'll pay you whatever it costs'. As Abbey and Randy were about to experience, these were — indeed — good times to be engineering and environmental consultants.

Abbey and Randy were also ecstatic about the school situation for Shiloh and Sunny. Located just south of Gloucester in Beverly, MA, they found The Waring School — a co-educational private school for students in grades six to twelve. Offering the usual array of basic courses, the school also featured extensive studies in humanities, music, art, and theatre, capped off by a curriculum of French language and cultural exchange. Since Abbey and Randy were both avowed Francophiles, this last educational option was the just the ticket that sold them on the school.

Traveling to Martha's Vineyard

Beginning on the first day Abbey walked into the AES office in Gloucester — only three blocks from her family's new townhome — her workload jumped from the frying pan into the fire. Her typical work week went from a previous forty hours to more than sixty hours. In fact, there just didn't seem to be enough hours in the day for her to keep up with all her project work. Yet strangely enough, the increased workload made Abbey feel much healthier and more satisfied with what she was doing.

Plus, Abbey now believed that every task she undertook was of great importance — probably because each permit application she filed meant either success or failure for the clients who were paying her bills. While her work with the USFWS was usually both engaging and enlightening, it didn't carry the same onus as her work for Aldo. In fact, although she never approached her job this way, her government work often amounted to little more than 'window dressing'. In other words, she was just there so that the USFWS could show a presence — not to actually have a say in the decision-making process. Working as both a professional wildlife biologist and a certified professional wetland scientist (PWS) with Aldo made her feel for the first time in her life like she finally had a real career and was making a difference.

Within minutes of Abbey setting up her desktop on that first day, Aldo whisked in and plopped a project file down in front of her. Before Abbey could even say 'good morning', Aldo excitedly started talking about tomorrow's travel plans. Abbey quickly realized how Aldo had earned his office nickname of 'Captain Chaos' — because when he was around, complete turmoil was typically busting loose. While Aldo had always featured a relatively high-strung, passionate personality, this whole new whirlwind scenario was, Abbey had to admit, a step above anything she had been used to when they were growing up together.

As Aldo talked, Abbey soon understood why he was so excited. Jacoby Jefferson was a former world class downhill skier who owned several resorts in both the Rocky Mountain West and the Swiss Alps. Just last month, Mr. Jefferson had strolled into AES and presented Aldo with a set of concept plans for a high-end residential subdivision named Chadwick Estates on the *hoity-toity* Island of Martha's Vineyard.

Abbey quickly learned that Jefferson traveled everywhere on his personal fleet of Learjets, one of which was now poised to take her and the entire project team to Martha's Vineyard for three full days of commission meetings and public hearings. In fact, they were leaving tomorrow from the Beverly Airport at seven a.m. sharp so they could be on 'the island' for a breakfast *tete-a-tete* with Susan Brockenborough — Director of the Martha's Vineyard Development Board (MVDB) — and several of her senior staff.

The next morning as the team bordered the ten-passenger jet, the golden orb of the rising sun was just beginning to glint in sparks and spackles off the airport runway. Aldo reached over and gently clasped Abbey's shoulder, "I don't want to scare you, but this flight will be like nothing you've ever experienced before. It's like riding a rocket — we'll be on final approach to the Martha's Vineyard Airport in less than twenty minutes after we take off!"

As soon as the pilot punched the throttle forward for takeoff, Abbey understood exactly what Aldo meant. During her career with the USFWS, she had flown on just about every type of aircraft imaginable — helicopters, bush planes, pontoon planes, cargo planes, even skydiving planes — but never a high performance private jet like this. The plane felt like it was thrusting straight up, sending her body deep into the cozy recesses of the plush leather seats. After they leveled off, she looked over at Aldo who, sensing her exhiliration, winked and gave her the double thumbs up sign.

At that very moment, Abbey knew she had made the right decision in changing jobs. It was as if this rocket she was riding on was transporting her from the obscure, mundane, and often tedious work of a federal bureaucrat to the constant excitement of high profile private land development. If she could have reached Aldo across the aisle, she would have given him a huge 'thank you' hug!

In another significant difference from commercial aviation, five minutes after they landed, the project team was standing by the curb outside the terminal, waiting for the entourage of three rental cars to pick them up. No security gates, no baggage claim, none of the ground *accoutrements* that slow down the typical commercial flight process. Easy as pie, they zipped right from the airport to their breakfast restaurant — The Egg and I in West Tisbury — in less than fifteen minutes after they landed.

While they feasted on gourmet breakfast fare — featuring a variety of seafood benedicts, Danish *ebelskivers*, and French pastries — MVDB Director Brockenborough laid out the schedule for the day. The first order of business was a preliminary meet-and-greet with the full MVDB staff at the town hall.

Next up was lunch at the Lobster Shack in Menemsha — the shooting locale for the classic horror movie, *'Jaws'* — followed by a question-and-answer session with the general public at the local high school auditorium. Then, since Jefferson didn't particularly care for dinner served at any of the Martha's Vineyard restaurants, it was back to the airport for a ten-minute Learjet hop over to Nantucket Island.

After landing in Nantucket, the team was whisked in taxis to Jefferson's favorite restaurant — *Chateau Chanticleer* — for a sumptious *pre fixe* meal. While everyone indulged themselves, the taxis waited with their motors running to make sure they all got back to the Martha's Vineyard Airport before 7.30 p.m. The formal project hearing with the MVDB started at eight p.m. sharp and they could not afford to be even a minute late.

This whirlwind of activity made Abbey's head spin. She knew the federal government was often, and rightfully so, accused of wasting money and excessive budgeting, but this was way beyond anything she had ever experienced. She couldn't even imagine what the total cost — including jet fuel, pilots' fees, rental cars, taxi time, and gourmet meals — was going to be. And this was for only the first work day!

What Abbey did not know — in fact, could not possibly have known at the time — was that this project would eventually forever change the way humans view and deal with the natural world. In the end result, humanity's whole attitude about other creatures — with whom we share our planet — was going to be summarily flipped upside down.

And it all started with a ghostly-gray and-tan, four-inch long creature found only in the highlands of the Town of Chilmark on the Island of Martha's Vineyard, Massachusetts.

A Rare Salamander Changes Everything

The project team made it back to the Chilmark Town Hall without a minute to spare. They quietly found their table in the front of the venerably-appointed but musty-smelling courtroom. As they took their seats, they could sense the looks of disquieted disdain pouring forth from both the packed audience and the row of board members lined up in front of the array of flags — American, Commonwealth of Massachusetts, and Town of Chilmark. From her prior public hearing experiences, Abbey knew that it was all just part of a well-honed procedure to let project presenters know that they were in for some serious scrutiny.

Casually clearing his throat, the rotundly-figured, balding Chilmark Town Councilman, Alistair Chapman, began in a thick Boston accent, "Well, it's nice to see that the project team has decided to actually join us tonight. We were just beginning to wondah if you had gotten cold feet and left town. But now that you're finally heah, let's get on with these proceedings forthwith. Mr. Greenleaf, the floor is all you-ahs. We are all quite anxious to heah what you have to say and please don't scrimp on the details!"

With that, Councilman Chapman settled back into his chair with a distinctive plop and began reflectively stroking his black-and-gray peppered beard.

In a model of efficiency, Aldo thanked the councilman, acknowledged the commission, and then unfurled his bundle of two-foot by three-foot site plans — supported by an easel — one by one. In the process, he deftly explained all the key aspects of the Chadwick Estates Project — from initial grading and topographic configuration to housing plots, access roads, landscaping, and site drainage.

Aldo's project plans also showed the restricted areas — including delineated wetlands, streams, and associated buffer zones plus designated upland open (green) spaces — on the one hundred and twenty-acre property. In sum, the project called for constructing forty homes — averaging 3,500 square feet (SF) each. This amounted to three acre minimum lot sizes which was well within the Town of Chilmark's zoning requirements that specified two-acre minimum lot sizes.

Before Aldo could introduce presentations by the members of his project team — including Abbey's description of the site's natural resources — Councilman Chapman interrupted the proceedings for what he called 'a piece of breaking news that is of paramount importance'.

Responding to those words, a massive man clad in flannel and denim and wearing LL Bean swamp boots forcefully strode onto the stage behind the commission table. "Folks, for those of you who may not know him, this is Dr. Trevor Wallace — our town Natural Resources Agent. He has a critical finding to announce," continued Chapman. "OK, Dr. Wallace, take it away!"

Adjusting his granny glasses and tightening the red bandana that held back his brownish-gray pony-tail, Dr. Wallace stepped up to the podium and began speaking, "As anyone here who knows me can attest, I am a widely-recognized expert in the field of herpetology. Just today, I have found a creature on this project site that may render these hearings moot. I have discovered a salamander that I firmly believe has never before been found anywhere else in the world. I am so confident in this discovery that I have given it a preliminary scientific name of *Chilmarkii wallacius*."

"I am also a great believer in the teachings of biodiversity", continued Dr Wallace, "especially those espoused by the esteemed Harvard Professor E.O. Wilson. Professor Wilson makes no small thing of our moral obligation to protect every species on Earth. He touts the value of every species for their potential contribution to medical or sociological benefits. He also notes that energy depletion, economic collapse, conventional war, and the expansion of totalitarian governments can be connected to species loss. But while those problems may be repaired in a few generations, the biggest problem he emphasizes with species extinction is best exemplified directly from his writing."

Holding up his notes, Wallace then quotes Professor Wilson: "The one process now going on that will take millions of years to correct is the loss of genetic and species diversity by the destruction of natural habitats. This is the folly our descendants are least likely to forgive us. The earth is our home. Unless we preserve the rest of life, as a sacred duty, we will be endangering ourselves by destroying the home in which we evolved, and on which we completely depend. We should preserve every scrap of biodiversity as priceless while we learn to use it and come to understand what it means to humanity."

"Based on Professor Wilson's rationale which I just quoted," concluded Wallace, "I am against taking any action on this site that could jeopardize the continued existence of *Chilmarkii wallacius*. Especially before we have a chance to learn what secrets this creature may hold for the advancement and preservation of humankind."

With that, Councilman Chapman stood up, pounded his gavel on the table, and said, "I hereby declare this hearing of the Martha's Vineyard Development Board adjourned until we have time to investigate this new information."

Almost immediately, the courtroom was abuzz with animated conversation and people milling about. Ever since it was officially announced, the Chadwick Estates Project had been one of the island's main topics of conversation. But Aldo, Abbey and the rest of their team just sat there in stunned silence, wondering what in the world had just happened. Collectively, Aldo's team had just finished putting weeks of overtime into preparing for this night, this public hearing, and now they were faced with the realization that all of their work may have been for naught.

Abbey was both dismayed and distraught. She was worried that Aldo and the team of investors led by Jefferson were considering blaming her for this situation. She was, of course, now the lead biologist responsible for representing the natural resource inventory of the site — including wetland delineations and identification of potentially endangered wildlife. She had stayed up almost all night reviewing the project files — including all the on-site natural information the AES scientists had collected. She knew that she had not missed anything that had been previously documented. But how could she have been expected to know about a species that — until today — no one even knew existed?

On the quick flight back to Beverly from Martha's Vineyard, Jefferson made his displeasure with the project team quite evident by his silence. In fact, no one said a word during the return flight, preferring instead to stare disconsolately out of their windows at the clear starry night and the mosaic of scattered lights down below.

After the plane landed, Abbey pulled Aldo aside for a quick word. Then, they both approached Jefferson with Abbey taking the lead. "First of all, sir, I would like to apologize for the unsuccessful results of our hearing tonight. I am disappointed that we did not know about this salamander ahead of time, but I'm also quite angry about the whole chain of events. I strongly believe that tonight's hearing was a grandstand play on the part of the town to make us look as bad as possible in front of the public."

"Now don't get me wrong," Abbey continued, "the rare salamander is a genuine issue and obstacle to our permitting process. But if we had known about its presence ahead of time, we would have definitely taken provisions that would have allowed our project to go forward as planned — instead of being continued for another month. In fact, I already know what we have to do to make things work out to the satisfaction and approval of all parties involved. I can almost promise you that by this time next month, we will all be celebrating the success of Chadwick Estates."

"Well, I certainly hope your confidence is borne out by our results during next month's continuance. Believe me, I don't like spending all the money it costs to attend these hearings and then come away with nothing. I'll see everyone back here on the morning of October 20th at seven a.m. sharp and we'll give it another shot." With that, Jefferson spun around in his $500, hand-stitched Italian loafers and sidled off to his chauffeured Maserati that would transport him back to his oceanfront home in Hingham.

As the uber luxury car squealed away from the curb in a cloud of dust, Aldo glanced at Abbey and gave her a sigh of relief. She smiled back at him and said softly, "Don't worry, I am confident my plan will work." And Aldo — knowing full well about his sister's unyielding ferocity when faced with a problem — had no doubt that she was right.

Abbey's Sustainable Design Solution

The next morning well before dawn, Abbey was leaning over her light table — armed with a full set of site plans and a fresh packet of multi-colored *Sharpies*. The first thing she did was to demarcate all the potential salamander habitat that was present on the one hundred and twenty-acre Chadwick Estates site. Assuming that *Chilmarkii wallacius* had the same basic habitat requirements as other terrestrial salamanders, this meant shading in all the *vernal pool* wetlands that could serve as breeding areas. She then used another color to mark the forested uplands located within one hundred feet of these breeding pools. These were the dryland areas that provide potential winter hibernacula; sites where the adult salamanders spend ninety percent of their non-breeding time.

Once Abbey had finished marking these 'critical habitats', she linked them all together with migratory corridors. This process connected the salamander's upland hibernacula with their spring breeding pools. When Abbey was finished, she took a deep breath and sighed at what she saw. The combination of the habitat footprints and their connecting pathways eliminated all but six of the forty house lots on the original design plans.

Deeply chagrined, Abbey pushed back from the light table, took off her reading glasses, and rubbed the sleepiness out of her eyes. "This will never do," she thought to herself, "everyone on the project team — including even Aldo — will flip out if I show them this." As Jacoby Jefferson was always fond of saying when he was being slammed by natural resource permitting constraints, "I'm not in this business to build homes for birds and bunnies. I do this to make real money — and lots of it!"

Since Abbey hadn't bothered to eat breakfast and it was now after eight, she left her office and walked the few blocks down to her favorite pastry shop — 'The Delectable Danish' — where she bought a French roast coffee and an everything bagel with chive cream cheese. As she sat

— melancholily sipping her coffee and nibbling her bagel — she mulled over everything she knew about sustainable design and associated low impact development. She thought back to the conversations she and Aldo had before he hired her. Well, she thought, he promised me I would be able to do things my own way. But I'll just bet he wasn't expecting to have to prove it quite so quickly.

Suddenly the solution came to Abbey. It was actually as clear as her hand in front of her face. She trashed the rest of her breakfast, raced back to her office, and grabbed a book off her bookshelf that she had known for (literally) her whole life. From her earliest remembrances, Aldo Leopold's '*A Sand County Almanac*' was always close at hand to where her parents were working. They both revered this book, so much so — in fact — that they considered it their career bible for guiding them in successfully managing wildlife refuges.

But what Abbey didn't remember — until this morning — is the essential message of Leopold's landmark treatise: 'Humans and wild animals can co-exist in harmonic peace'. She riffled through the book's well-worn pages until she came to the text she was looking for, '*The Land Ethic*'.

Revisiting Leopold's words made Abbey realize that — with her plan revision — she was only applying one part of the basis of sustainable design. Consistent with her profession as a biologist, she was considering just the ecological integrity of the Chadwick Estates property. She was forgetting all about the other two primary legs of sustainable design's 'three-legged stool'; economic opportunity and environmental equity.

Abbey hastily grabbed a fresh site overview plan and began marking it up with an entirely different vision. This time as she worked, she concentrated on 'The Three Big E's' — ecological, economic, and environmental (human) factors — that must be harmoniously blended to bring truly sustainable, low-impact development to long-term fruition. She remembered that — in practice — sustainable design includes both indoor and outdoor components. Plus, this process always begins with a due diligence evaluation of natural resource constraints on a proposed development site.

As a first step, Abbey had to identify all of the zones to set aside for protection of the property's most significant wildlife habitats and other natural resources. She called these 'no impact zones'. Next, she looked at all the places that water would travel — the natural drainage patterns — based on the existing topography of the project site. Her emphasis was on making the best use of the site's existing natural features and original drainage patterns.

Abbey knew that doing this work up front would reduce the number of trees that needed to be cleared, the amount of land area that needed to be bulldozed, and the re-contouring needed to make the overall site 'developable'. For Abbey, this was a critical step to get Jefferson on board with her new design, since it would result in big-time savings in initial construction costs that are typically associated with extensive site earthwork.

She also realized that designing to preserve a property's natural features can produce a significantly higher economic yield than the standard clear-strip-and-grade development practices. Such designing with the natural landscape typically produces fewer total lots, but the extra amenities associated with the site's preserved open space and natural features boosts the market value — and sales prices — of the lots that remain.

Abbey knew that the commissioners and the townspeople — most notably Dr. Trevor Wallace — would be blown away by her new site design. To ensure the approval of her plans, Abbey first linked all the most important natural features — the regulated wetlands and stream belt, an old-growth stand of hemlocks, a meadow-full of native grasses and colorful wildflowers — as open space design nodes. Next, she connected these open space areas by walking paths that looped through and around the perimeter of the development. Then she further enhanced the walking paths by placing interpretive bump-outs/rest-stops for birding, fishing, picnicking, and exercising at key locations.

A final provision of Abbey's plan was to have these natural resource features — plus their connecting pathways — designated as 'open lands/green spaces' owned and maintained by the Town of Chilmark. This would serve to permanently preserve the property's key natural features while also designating them as recreational amenities for both the resident homeowners as well as the townspeople — another huge plus in favor of garnering project approval.

Abbey was sure that this sustainable design plan would be a win for everyone. The townspeople would be happy because the site is 'greener' and now provides permanent protection for the wildlife — especially Chilmark's newest salamander — inhabiting the site. Next, the town's decision-makers would like the fact that they have a project they can take pride in saying that they permitted. Then the people who buy the homes on the property would be thrilled that they have their own personal plots of park-like open space. And, finally, Jacoby Jefferson and his associates would be ecstatic, because they would make more money while adding a cutting-edge, sustainable design project to their portfolio that they can market as demonstrating their 'green pride'.

Aldo Buys In

As soon as she had finished sketching her revised plan, Abbey blasted across the hall and into Aldo's office.

Jerking his head up from spreading cream cheese on his morning bagel, Aldo looked at Abbey and knew right away that something big was up. "Well excuse me there, Sis", he chided her kiddingly, "don't I even get to eat some breakfast before you assault me with work?"

Settling into the chair in front of Aldo's desk, Abbey blurted, "Whoa now, I'm just so excited Aldo — I don't even know where to start!"

Now laughing out loud, Aldo said, "OK, now I'm worried. You're sounding just like me. You're always supposed to be the calm one — remember? Just slow down, take a deep breath, sip your coffee, and then tell me what you're thinking. I'm prepared to be blown away!"

"OK, here goes," started Abbey, exhaling deeply. "You're not going to believe this. What is the book you remember always seeing on both Mom and Dad's desks when we were kids?"

"Are you kidding — 'A Sand County Almanac '," exclaimed Aldo. "How could I ever forget that — my namesake, you know!"

Clearly enjoying Aldo's excited response, Abbey continued, "Where do you think the inspiration for my new design concept came from — three guesses, the first two don't count!"

"No way," interjected Waldo, "how can we go wrong now? Let's hear the details."

"OK, here's where traditional land development goes wrong," explained Abbey. "In most cases, the natural environment is totally ignored. The first thing a land developer does is come in and strip the site in a process referred to as 'site preparation'. Typically, minimal consideration is given to working with the site's natural topography or drainage patterns. In Leopold's essay, 'the *land ethic* ', he emphasizes that human interests should be balanced with a diverse, healthy natural environment."

"All right, I'm with you so far," replied Aldo, "so how does that translate to your new concept for land development?"

Abbey smiled at Aldo — she knew he was getting the picture. She plopped her new concept sketch down in front him and continued, "Well, re-reading Leopold's *'land ethic'* made me realize how to best revise Chadwick Estates to protect the new salamander. Our site design now works for both its future human residents and its current wild occupants — thereby achieving the balance Mr. Leopold calls for in his now famous essay."

Fortunately, the hydrologists and site engineers working for Aldo were very open-minded. Abbey wouldn't have expected anything less. They quickly latched onto Abbey's innovative design concepts — in fact, most of them liked her ideas very much. In three days — after two more iterations of design plans and reviews — Abbey had exactly what she wanted to present.

Now Abbey couldn't wait for October twenty to come. She anticipated that this was going to be the ultimate first test of the site design philosophy, that would become the business model for the rest of her environmental consulting career.

Achieving Unanimous Acclaim

The morning of October twentieth, 1986 finally came and Abbey stood on the Beverly Airport tarmac waiting for the rest of the project team to arrive. It was a clear, but chilly morning — the overnight air temperatures lingered in the low twenties, and a brisk wind made it feel even colder.

Abbey stood and shivered, wearing her dress clothes and heels under a utilitarian trench coat. She would have been much warmer wearing her down mountain parka and mukluks, but she didn't want to do anything that might appear unprofessional. She also knew that she would be much better off inside the terminal, but she was too nervous to sit down. Plus, she wanted to make sure the rest of team saw that she was the first one on the scene.

From the time the team boarded Jacoby Jefferson's Learjet to when they were all seated at their table in the Chilmark Town Hall, the day progressed exactly as it was scripted. In fact, almost nothing changed from their previous trip — a quick gourmet breakfast at West Tisbury's Egg and I Café followed by one-on-one meetings with various town officials, including everyone from the fire chief to the head selectman. It was Jefferson's practice to make sure he didn't miss a skid when he was liberally applying the grease to project decision-makers.

Next, it was off to Menemsha Harbor for another lobster picnic on the seawall followed by more meetings with town VIPs — as determined from thorough research conducted by Jefferson's staff. Then back to the Vineyard Airport for the ten-minute flight to Nantucket and another grand dinner at *Chateau Chanticleer*.

The only difference was that this time, they all — well at least most of the team, including Abbey — refrained from imbibing any potent potables. Plus, Jefferson stayed on top of the wait staff, practically demanding that they do away with some of the typical dining formalities — especially the time spent between courses. As a result, the project team arrived at the Chilmark Town Hall at 7.30 p.m. — well before any of the board members or townspeople arrived.

At five minutes after eight, Councilman Alistair Chapman gaveled the meeting to order, welcomed the overflow crowd, and asked Dr. Trevor Wallace to come forward and elaborate on the findings he had announced at the conclusion of last month's hearing.

After thanking the board and acknowledging the project team, Dr. Wallace started his presentation by showing the locations on the project site where he had found specimens of his new salamander species, *Chilmarkii wallacius*. "I have now filed the proper paperwork with the U.S. Fish and Wildlife Service to have this species formally listed for review as 'endangered' under the federal Endangered Species Act of 1973. Since the Fish and Wildlife Service's review process for proposed listed species — threatened or endangered — generally takes several months, at a minium, I don't see how this project can proceed at the present time. I therefore recommend that the board deny this project without prejudice, at least until the federal government has made a ruling in this matter."

Dr. Wallace's presentation set the courtroom buzzing in anticipation of another very short night. But before Councilman Chapman could respond, Aldo jumped to his feet — practically flying up out of his chair. "Mr. Councilman, before you make a decision in this matter, we would like to respond to Dr. Wallace's findings. We believe that we have come up with a significantly revised site plan that will not only protect the rare salamander — as well as much of the other significant wildlife habitat on the site — but also make the salamanders a featured natural resource amenity for the long-term benefit and enjoyment of the entire town. Will you please let us be heard?"

"Well, OK, I guess," replied Councilman Chapman, "but please make it brief — I really don't see how we can continue here tonight while facing such a serious outstanding conservation obstacle as this."

With that, Aldo motioned to Abbey to take the podium which she did — displaying her usual jaunty verve which was now brimming with confidence. "OK, folks, tonight I'm going to show you all something that I think you're really going to like!", beamed Abbey. "It's a brand new site concept that we call 'Harmonic Equilibrium Design' — or HED for short. HED balances the three Big Es — *Ecology, Economics, and*

Environment that should be the focus of any good site development plan."

Abbey was experienced enough to know that if a multi-faceted development concept scheme could succeed on Martha's Vineyard, it could play well just about anywhere else in the country. What she was presenting tonight was analagous to a playwright's production that had made it all the way to Broadway. Once a play has been a proven commodity on the Great White Way, it can go anywhere else in the world and be a success.

"Now let me explain the details," continued Abbey, "let's start with the most sensitive *'E'* — the *ecologic resources* — first. In fact, I'd like to thank Dr. Wallace and his *Chilmarkii wallacius* for helping me craft this completely new approach to land development on pristine properties."

"So, as you can see from this plan overview," continued Abbey, "the first thing I have done is preserve the areas on the project site that provide either breeding or overwintering habitat for salamanders. Next, I've also set aside the other most valuable natural systems — wetlands, streams, old-growth forests, and native meadows — on the property. Then I've connected these natural features with untouched fifty-foot-wide corridors. Please note that, as designed, these natural corridors provide a duality of benefits. They serve as important migratory pathways for the site's wildlife, while also including low-impact walking paths for both site residents and townspeople.

"Now — of course — we have to be realistic about this new site design," Abbey continued, trying hard to lighten her tone so as not to sound like she was lecturing. That means that — since this is a residential development — we have to accommodate the second *'Big E'* — the *Environment* for humans on the site. So what I've done to further minimize impacts to *Ecology*, is to cluster the house footprints in three separate areas consisting of ten homes each. Please note that this housing layout still conforms with the board's two-acre minimum house lot regulation since there are now only thirty houses on the one hundred and twenty-acre site."

"For those who are counting," continued Abbey, "that's an average of four acres per housing unit over the entire property. Next, clustering the houses reduces the total amount of impervious surface — important for decreasing stormwater runoff — on the site by fifty acres, from the previous eighty-six total acres now down to thirty-six total acres. As you can see from my site overview, this is accomplished mainly by reducing the amount of asphalt needed for access roads and individual driveways as well as concrete for sidewalks throughout the property."

Abbey could feel it now — she was really rolling, and she knew she had the audience sailing right along with her. She also sensed that she had the rapt attention of all of the board members.

"Now here comes the tricky part," Abbey said, coyly winking over at Aldo. "We still need to address the third *'Big E'— Ecomonics* — and we all know that if this factor doesn't work, neither does the project. So, let's look at how my re-design is financially viable. The answer is actually quite simple: Although the number of total house lots has been reduced from forty to thirty—a twenty-five percent reduction — the value — that is, the sales price — of each lot has increased by more than forty percent."

Now, Abbey aggressively challenged both the board and the audience. "I can assure you that these will be highly sought after properties, increasing the value of all of the homes in Chilmark. How am I so confident? Well, think about it. If you are looking to buy a house in a beautiful place like Martha's Vineyard, the natural environment undoubtedly means a lot to you. So, would you rather buy a house with a typical pattern of development, featuring large, artificially landscaped properties with lots of asphalt roads and driveways, or would you rather own a home surrounded by open green space and natural wildlife habitat. I'm guessing that most of you would opt for the latter."

"To sum up, if you look at the total economic value of the completed development," declared Abbey — making direct eye contact with all of the board members who were by now totally mesmerized, "you have a net gain in the *Big E Economic* factor. And this overall increase in market value of the full development is directly attributable to honoring the first *Big E Ecologic* component of our 'Harmonic Equilibrium Design' — namely our new best friend Mr. Salamander, aka *Chilmarkii wallacius.* Yes, we're now using the natural resources of the site — specifically Dr. Wallace's rare salamanders — as marketing amenities. The atypical —

some might say unprecedented — amount of permanent green space and protected wildlife habitat serves to entice buyers to pay a significantly higher price than they would pay for a house in a more traditional development setting."

"In the final analysis," concludes Abbey with a knowing flourish, "the Chadwick Estates development project has now been optimized to the extent that everyone should be happy. The primary wildlife species and their key habitats are preserved in perpetuity, the residents have a *beaucoup* of permanent open space amenities to enjoy, the townspeople have direct access to a host of new natural areas, and the development increases property values throughout Chilmark. So everybody wins!"

At first, Abbey's concluding remark was met with stunned silence. Then it started somewhere in the back of the courtroom — a slow staccato of clapping that gradually swelled into a standing ovation that encompassed everyone in the room, including all of the board members. Abbey wasn't sure what to do. She thought about taking a bow, but realized that doing so might not be considered proper decorum for a land development team.

Once the applause had subsided, Abbey sat down and Councilman Chapman took the microphone. "Well, young lady, I have working with this board for more than 25 years and I can honestly say I've nevah seen a reaction quite like this. Yah Harmonic Equilibrium Design concept is definitely a big winnah heah tonight. My heartiest congratulations to you and yah team!"

"Because yah presentation has been so well received," continued Chapman, "I've changed my mind about a continuance. I think it's time to call for a vote tonight. All in favah of approving Chadwick Estates — as currently designed — please raise yah hand." All but one hand went up immediately — so there were eight votes for approval. "All opposed?" No hands went up. Abbey turned to Aldo and whispered, "Looks like one of the board members decided to abstain — I wonder why?" But it didn't matter. Chadwick Estates on the Island of Martha's Vineyard was now a reality — an approved project!

The flight home was a raucous, celebratory affair with champagne toasts all around. The congratulatory back-slapping — including lots of hoorays and huzzahs — spilled out onto the tarmack after Jefferson's

450

Learjet touched back down at Beverly Airport.

Before the project team retreated to their vehicles, Jefferson called everyone together. "I want to acknowledge to everyone that this has been a momentous night. You have all done a spectacular job — especially you, Ms. Childers. I have to admit that I've always considered any sort of natural feature — especially a potential endangered species — to be an enemy of a project, an obstacle to success that must be overcome and defeated."

Now unabashedly gushing, Jefferson continued, "Abbey, you have shown me something here tonight that I've never even considered. Turning protected natural features into site amenities and then using them to enhance the marketability of a project is just crazy clever. I believe your concept of Harmonic Equilibrium Design is a revelation; a development strategy that is here to stay and that will make a real difference in the quality and value of all future high-end land development projects. My hat is off to you and the whole AES team!"

With that, the group broke up. Then — as everyone moved off toward the parking lot — more staccato applause broke out, this time accompanied by enthusiastic chants of "Abbey — Abbey — Abbey!" Before they departed, Aldo hugged Abbey tightly and told her that — to paraphrase President Franklin Delano Roosevelt — they were about to embark on a brilliant new deal that would change both of their lives forever.

Aldo had been totally impressed with Abbey's presentation to the Martha's Vineyard Development Board. She had truly knocked his — as well as the MVDB's — socks off. So much so, that before the vote was even taken, he had decided to make her design philosophy a major component of AES. He now knew for certain that a balanced approach — giving equal weight and consideration to the three *Big E's; Ecology, Environment, and Economics* — was going to be the dominant trend in high-end land development both in the United States and throughout the world.

After more than two hundred years in the U.S., the days of treating natural resources as second-class encumberances to man's dominion over the planet were finally going to disappear forever. With her HED concept, Abbey had brought Professor E.O. Wilson's beliefs in

451

biodiversity — equal status for all species on Earth, including humans — to the forefront.

Now, there was no longer a reason to avoid giving due diligence to non-human species occupying a project site. Abbey's HED designs proved that — in most premium situations — many of the non-human species on a project site could actually be permanently protected by site development. It was just a matter of inculcating multi-tasking thought — in lieu of univision — into the site design process.

HED Becomes the Gold Standard

When Abbey walked into her office the day after the Chadwick Estates approval, she found a message to come to Aldo's office. As soon as she entered his office, Aldo closed the door, put his hands behind his head, propped his feet up on his desk, and said, "Congratulations, Sis, you are now the first CEO of Harmonic Equilibrium Design, Inc. — the brand new high-end land development arm of AES. From now on, all of our premium projects that have any natural resource issues from wetlands to rare wildlife will be under your purview!"

Abbey immediately began shaking her arms above her head and bouncing up and down. Aldo smiled because he had such fond memories of his twin sister's 'happy dance' from their childhood days. She always did the same thing when she was pleasantly surprised.

After she had calmed down, Abbey hopped over to Aldo, threw her arms around him and hugged him tightly. "Oh, thank you so much — this is the ultimate dream for me!" Then she sat down, buried her head in her hands, and began sobbing — big happy tears. Abbey now knew exactly where her career was headed. She was now certain that HED would be a huge success.

In fact, HED's reputation spread so rapidly, and the projects came in so fast and furiously that Abbey had a difficult time keeping up with the flow. This, despite the fact that she only took on projects which had a 'quality-first' emphasis — especially when it came to protecting a site's high-valued natural resources. This meant that HED's projects were typically located on sites with first-class natural resources and spectacular settings.

Abbey's role as a 'land developer with a heart' stemmed from the business model often employed by the conservation organization she most admired; The Nature Conservancy (TNC). A TNC project typically starts off by identifying a site's most important natural features. Then, the project team coordinates development of the portions of the site that are either already impacted or have relatively lower natural resource values.

Next, the money gained from this site development is used to purchase and preserve the portions of the property with the highest-value natural resources. In summary, the TNC model typically uses proceeds from partial site development to acquire and permanently preserve a property's most valuable natural features.

To Abbey, the whole concept behind her HED plans was quite simple and basic — at least to anyone who approaches land development with a flexible, open mind. Her sustainable design concept just meant that any proposed land development must be able to continue in perpetuity without significantly impacting the long-term quality of the natural environment.

Abbey had mounted a quote on a square of foam board in her office. It was the Brundtland Commission's recently released definition of sustainable design: '*An ideal of intergenerational equity that balances considerations for the environment, the economy, and society... while meeting the needs of the present generation without compromising the ability of future generations to meet their own needs'.*" As she gazed at this quote, she knew she had nailed it. The key to creating a sustainable future is recognizing that three key components form the interlocking links in the human chain of long-term well-being. As featured in Abbey's HED philosophy, these three components are economic opportunity, ecological integrity, and environmental equity.

As Abbey's HED professes, the pursuit of one of these components without the others — or in opposition to the others — ultimately jeopardizes future progress. But — when properly understood, designed, and practiced — sustainable development results in simultaneous achievement of overlapping economic, environmental, and ecological goals.

Abbey knew that the basic design concepts — 'Sustainable Design', 'Green Building', and 'Smart Growth' — she was using with HED were really not new ideas at all. Based on her extensive research, she understood that more than two hundred years ago, none other than our first President, George Washington was applying sustainable design concepts to the Virginia properties he owned.

GEORGE WASHINGTON'S LAND ETHIC

As described in a 2005 article written for Land Development Today Magazine by Tony Wernke, *'The Father of Our Country'*, purposely designed a house on his Mount Vernon estate that was both remarkable and original. His innovative ideas featured open quadrant arcades, cupolas, and the great piazza — all of which violated contemporary architectural dictates. In fact, each of Washington's design features emphasized utilitarian functions: helping to cool the building, providing shelter from the elements, and taking advantage of natural breezes to improve living conditions.

Washington's landscape design also featured a 'naturalistic' approach, which was a radical departure from the formalized gardens of his time. The key elements of his design took advantage of the natural beauty of the site. Accordingly, Washington surrounded his property with dense tree plantings. He planted the walkways in grove configurations rather than formal alleys, while underplanting the shade trees with dense copses of small trees and shrubs.

Washington later developed a plan — which was ultimately carried out and documented in 1787 — to have his mansion house surrounded by every possible specimen of tree or shrub native to his Virginia landscape. The plan was ingenious for its time, and included the revolutionary idea of restoring part of the landscape to 'wilderness'. He continued such work long after it could benefit him personally and right up until his death. In a time of land and natural resource abundance that must have seemed completely inexhaustible, Washington's land development and farming experiences led him to become the first American conservationist and environmental restorationist.

As Abbey's litany of successes with her HED projects continued to build, Aldo kept busy accruing the overall massive achievements of AES. New work was pouring in so fast that Aldo could barely hire people quickly enough. In fact, he now had so many engineers and other non-scientists on staff that he added a subtitle — 'Engineering and Design Consultants' to the AES name. Aldo also hired Abbey's husband Randy as a full-time Principal Engineer. Randy was already doing so much subcontracting work for AES, that most of the people in the company just assumed he was part of the permanent staff.

Aldo was also occupied with opening offices in other states. AES Engineering and Design Consultants now had an office in each New England state. Plus, Aldo also found a bargain-priced space for a twelve-person office in the upscale community of La Jolla, California — ten miles north of downtown San Diego.

The California location was especially appealing to Aldo. Land development in the state was booming even more than it was in New England. Plus — while he dearly loved the city and suburbs of Boston — the long winters were becoming too much for him to endure. From June through the end of October, New England was the best place on Earth to live. But after the last leaves fell, it was depressing to think about trudging through seven long months of ice and snow before being able to see green trees again.

Aldo firmly believed that a California branch would have multiple benefits for both his and Abbey's career. The State of California's economy was larger than most of the other countries in the world. Plus, the liberal leaning politics and progressive approach to land development were perfectly suited to the types of projects both Aldo and Abbey were now featuring. Finally, southern California — with its wealth of highly-educated, forward-thinking people — provided the ideal landscape for showcasing their innovative land development concepts to the world.

Based on this reasoning, Aldo's plan was to move to La Jolla as soon as the office was operating and profitable. Plus — while he didn't share this with Abbey right away — he wanted her to join him in California as soon as she could work out the details.

BOOK NINETEEN
Westward Ho, Once Again

Portfolio Building in La Jolla

In April of 1991 — in conjunction with Aldo Greenleaf's successful company expansion plan — Abbey and Randy Childers relocated their family to work in the recently opened AES office in La Jolla, California. Fortunately, the real estate gods were watching over their family. Within a week of arriving in town, they found the perfect property — a recently restored Spanish villa styled home with sweeping ocean views and an olympic-sized swimming pool.

After moving to La Jolla, Abbey's HED approach to land development continued to thrive. Her design portfolio accrued many award-winning, highly-accoladed projects throughout the United States and in seven other countries. At the same time, her innovative ideas were pushing the world of land devlopment into places never before envisioned and accomplishments never before achieved.

Abbey and Randy spent much of their free time introducing their teenaged twins — Shiloh and Sunny — to the natural wonders of their new California home. As dedicated parents, they staunchly believed in teaching children the importance of balancing their academic skills with a comprehensive understanding of and appreciation for the wonders of the natural world. In their minds, it was equally important for a child to know how to tell the difference between a spruce and a fir or how to identify the liltingly-beautiful song of a hermit thrush as it was for them to solve a complicated mathematical problem.

In between the family hikes and scavenger hunts, Abbey and Randy also managed to shoehorn in time for their personal passions — nature photography, traveling the world, classical music, and baseball. Their family travels always had an outdoor-oriented, natural theme — again to emphasize this with their daughters — and included such pristine locations as the Galapagos Islands, South Africa's Kruger National Park, New Zealand's South Island, and French Polynesia. Plus, whenever they could during the summer, they took in the Los Angeles Philharmonic performing at the Hollywood Bowl or the Los Angeles Dodgers playing at Dodger Stadium in Chavez Ravine.

While Abbey and Randy continued achieving their stunning array of business accomplishments, Shiloh and Sunny were also accomplishing outstanding success during their high school years in La Jolla. They were both student council leaders while also participating in a variety of extracurricular activities.

Shiloh was all-state in field hockey. As a two-year captain, she led her teams to state championships during both her junior and senior years. Meanwhile, Sunny excelled as point guard on the basketball team — where she achieved all-county honors three years in a row and played in two state championship games. Both girls were also track stars, with Shiloh taking first place in the 1500-meter and 800-meter races at the California State Track Championships during her freshman and sophomore years, and Sunny holding the title of 400-meter hurdle champion for three straight years.

On the academic side of things, Shiloh and Sunny both achieved 3.92 GPAs making them co-valedictorians when they graduated in 1993. Their myriad accomplishments at La Jolla High made them shoo-ins for attending the colleges of their choice.

Shiloh chose to stay relatively close to home by attending Stanford University in Palo Alto. There, she earned a double major in Environmental Engineering and Public Policy. Then, she continued on to graduate school at University of Michigan's School for Environment and Sustainability, garnering a PhD in Environmental Management and Sustainability.

Meanwhile, Sunny chose to matriculate across the country at Duke University in Durham, North Carolina, where she earned a Bachelor of Arts degree in Environmental Science and Policy from Duke's prestigious Nicholas School of the Environment. She followed this up with a PhD degree in Natural Resource Management with a focus on Environmental Social Sciences.

As Abbey's career matured into the 2000s, HED began attracting the attention of forward-thinking land developers worldwide. These were astute money men and women who realized that the days of 'maxxing out' every site for sheer profits were a thing of the past. They fully understood that balancing human progress with natural resources — in lieu of caving in to sheer financial greed — was the wave of the future. Now — less than fifteen years after the startling and landmark success of her Chadwick Estates Project — Abbey's 'Eco-Village' projects were scattered across the globe.

Not only did Abbey's HED approach produce more visually pleasing — and thus, more marketable — projects, but they also attracted buyers who were in the forefront of sustainable living. Her follow-up research on her 'as-built' projects revealed that many of the owners now occupying her HED development sites drove hybrid cars and had solar panels on their roofs.

Abbey took great pride in knowing that her HED projects were on the cusp of what was to become a burgeoning mandate to shift the world's corporate dynamics — away from the polluting practices of the past and toward the sustainable living lifestyles of the future. Her biggest clients understood that America's current corporate power structure — namely Big Oil, Big Coal, and Big Autos — would eventually be replaced by new companies that featured renewable energy sources, updated transmission grids, and regional power plants. They were among the forerunners of the oncoming battle to curb the climate crisis and give the world a fighting chance to preserve basic 20th Century landscapes and lifestyles.

Abbey's HED residential designs were touted as being model examples for sustainable living communities. All of her developments featured neighborhood organic gardens, restaurants emphasizing local cuisine, shops, accommodations, art galleries, performance centers, and conference facilities. While the individual houses included all the modern conveniences — typically associated with luxury homes — they still emphasized ecofriendly living and sustainable lifestyles. Thoughtfully designed networks of footpaths — including signage that interpreted the local ecosystems, featuring native plants and wildlife — connected each home with nearby town centers. This reduced the need to drive places to access basic amenities and services — further reducing the CO_2 footprints of each community.

Whenever and wherever they were built, her HED communities garnered superb accolades and publicity. Her designs along Florida's

461

Gulf Coast featured eco-villages with tightly-clustered developments and xeriscaped — low-water need — landscapes that were surrounded by broadly-connected open spaces and fully walkable town centers.

Her design emphasis with Sand Dollars on Alabama's Gulf Coast protected an ecologically significant, 1,000-acre system of coastal lakes and dunes. Nature-based lifestyles — including hiking, biking, canoeing, kayaking, windsurfing, birding, and fishing — were the focal points. The homes were throw-backs to the days of genteel, gracious southern living. They each had large wraparound porches, wooden columns, and metal roofs with deep overhangs. Walkable amenities that knitted each community together included a swimming pool, fitness center, tennis courts, parks and gardens, shopping and restaurants, golf courses, and a large beachfront bed and breakfast resort for housing visitors and family members.

Desert Waters — one of Abbey's residential designs on Mississippi's Gulf Coast — mimicked the look and feel of a Mediterranean oasis. Emphasizing a strong sense of town connectedness, amenities were located in and around homes to promote walking, talking, and general socializing. Neighborhood shops, service providers, and recreational amenities were located within walking distance of every front door. In addition to providing a striking contrast with the clear blue Gulf waters, the pure-white surfaces of the concrete masonry houses and shops — plus the adobe-like thickness of roofs and walls — provided excellent insulation. These design features also reflected away heat and sunlight, keeping the homes and neighborhoods cooler while significantly boosting energy savings.

Along the southern tier of states, Abbey also designed a unique cadre of super markets and open-air shopping centers. Her supermarket chain — which was branded as 'Eurythmic Foods & More' (EFM) — featured stores with pods for the in-house production of seafood, poultry, pork, and dairy products.

The emphasis was on maintaining a clean and sustainable commodity flow, while also providing household foodstuffs at bargain prices that reflected the elimination of the middleperson in the production chain. In every community where EFM stores were constructed, they dominated the local grocery store market within a year or less. This phenomenal success rocketed the short-term value of EFM's IPO shares — making savvy investors very wealthy and very happy while demonstrating that large-scale sustainability concepts can be very beneficial for both health and economics.

HED's designs for open air shopping centers capitalized on the demise of the now mostly defunct enclosed malls that were built willy-nilly across the American landscape in the 1970s and 1980s. Even when the enclosed malls were in their heyday, Abbey predicted that they would soon be done in by the monotony that dominated their designs. She knew that the traditional 'mall experience' — which was essentially the same no matter where you lived — would spell the doom of these monolithic tombs of uninspired commercialization. And she was oh so right!

Her design strategies for her erstwhile commodity centers featured the open, 'Main Street USA' theme that began being favored for shopping center design in the late 1990s and early 2000s. But Abbey's HED design concepts took things one step further — or backwards, as the case may be.

In addition to the stores selling goods, she added on-site pods for product production. These amounted to small-scale factories that churned out tailor-made items for many of each center's stores. For example, a cobbler shop produced the shoes while a tailor shop produced the clothes that were sold on-site. The resultant opportunities to purchase truly one-of-a-kind, hand-made attire — for prices far below those of traditional factory-produced replicas — strongly appealed to consumers. With the rapid expansion of the direct production to customer linkage of Abbey's designs, sustainability once again won the day.

Abbey knew that on-site production and purchase of consumer goods benefitted all parties involved. Cheaper production costs — resulting, again, from eliminating the middleperson — meant significant price reductions for the consumers while reductions in the overall number of employees needed also meant less commuting miles traveled, and less CO_2 emissions to the atmosphere.

Worldwide, Abbey's innovative designs often incorporated a country's most famous natural features. Her office park in Sao Paulo, Brazil centered around a biosphere containing a fully-functioning Amazon rainforest. Plus, her 'treehouse office' cubicles allowed workers

463

to commune with the world's greatest biodiversity while eating their lunches on wooden decks some two hundred feet above the ground.

In Abu Dahbi, Abbey's plans created a desert oasis with a water feature that used a 200-foot spout to turn briny desert water into potable water. The desalinized flow then serviced five high-rise office buildings supporting a collective total of more than five thousand residents.

Arguably Abbey's most phenomenal design, invovled creation of a mini Great Barrier Reef next to her waterfront office park in Sydney, Australia. To accomplish this, she dredged out a small cove that was polluted with toxins, but incorporated the local tidal regime. She then introduced living coral imported from a site that had been impacted by prior development.

While this proved to be an incredibly expensive appurtenant appendage to her project design, Abbey was deeply devoted to creating a permanent homage to the world's coral reefs. These phenomenally biodiverse ecosystems were dramatically declining — due to ocean acidification and increasing water temperatures caused by global warming.

To make her created coral reef habitat as authentic as possible, Abbey imported many of the species that populate the real Great Barrier Reef. Her reef species list even included such top predators as moray eels, Pacific octopuses, and great white sharks. In addition to providing a truly one-of-a-kind work environment for office park employees, Abbey opened the reef — free of charge — to the public, providing everyone with an opportunity to see, appreciate, and — she desperately hoped — advocate for protecting the world's remaining natural reefs.

When the Scandanavian countries called, Abbey took advantage of their already strong support for sustainable living standards. Her office parks in Oslo, Norway, Stockhom, Sweden, and Helsinki, Finland included on-site solar, wind, and geothermal generating facilities that not only fully powered the office parks but also many of the surrounding communities.

Abbey's multiple residential communities in the progressive country of Costa Rica also emphasized sustainable living. The ecological designs of the housing in these communities included creating minimum construction waste and pollution, using all local materials, producing food from neighborhood organic gardens, and merging energy, water and waste systems. These designs created homes that optimized living conditions while producing almost no unused materials.

Along the Mediterranean Coast in southern France and Italy, Abbey's HED projects featured a variety of progressive housing styles — including earth homes, geodesic domes, and tree houses. These communities also emphasized lifestyles and gatherings that reflected the local color, history, and folklore of the region.

In the Himalayan Mountains of Tibet and Nepal, her Eco-Villages featured biospheric settings which emphasized harmony, trust, support, and mutual understanding among all residents. The primary emphasis in these communities was creating sustainable lifestyles that balanced human needs with respect and reverence for the natural world.

Wherever she could, Abbey worked to make her projects compliant with local, regional, and national sustainable design standards and certifications. In the U.S. — for example — her project designs adhered to the specifications of the Green Building Council (GBC). In fact, her U.S. projects always qualified for the 'platinum level' of sustainable design, which was the highest level certified by the Leadership in Energy and Environmental Design (LEED) Process.

Perhaps the most important lesson inspired by Abbey's HED designs, was dissuading the widespread notion that sustainable living meant uncomfortable housing with no modern conveniences. In fact, her communities proved that 'green lifestyles' did not mean giving up the creature comforts and stylish appointments of upscale living. To the contrary, residents living in her site developments enjoyed all the comforts they were accustomed to while reveling in the fulfillment that comes from taking action that is helping to protect the overall quality of life around the globe.

The Climate Crisis Emerges

While Abbey's HED Eco-Villages were maintaining unprecedented success, human society was being buried in grief, fear, and — in some cases — outright dismay and utter disgust. Unfortunately — to be bluntly candid — many of the world's problems could be dropped squarely in the lap of an increasingly militaristic U.S. government.

One of the most bizarre events in the history of US presidential elections occurred in the fall of two thousand, when the governor of Texas, George W. Bush — informally known as just 'W' — defeated Al Gore, the sitting Vice President of the United States. It wasn't so much who won this election as how it occurred. On election night — as everyone watched the nail-biting returns with eager anticipation — the television networks twice called the winner, only to renege on their projections both times.

Watching this scenario unfold throughout the seemingly unending election night was unbelievably excruciating for both Abbey and Randy. They knew that the future of their carefully-crafted business models lay in the balance. If Gore won, he would be a staunch advocate for sustainable living and green development. As a congressman and then senator, he was well known for his progressive viewpoints — including being the first person in Congress to advocate for solving Global Warming. On the other hand, Bush was pretty much Gore's polar opposite. He was the privileged son of a former president and a devoted Texas oilman. His policies would take the country in the absolutely wrong direction for combating both the climate crisis and biodiversity loss.

When Abbey and Randy finally gave up and went to bed, they woke up to hear the devastating news. After long months of campaign ads, debates, barbs, and innuendos, the deciding vote for the next president of the United States rested solely with the State of Florida. And the vote was simply too close to call — triggering a mandatory recount.

The next six weeks were a mental whirlwind for Abbey and Randy. They went to work, but spent much of their time meeting with the AES Long-Term Strategy Committee (LTSC) that Aldo assembled to decide what to do if Bush won. Then, it finally happened — the U.S. Supreme Court declared 'W' the winner in Florida by only 537 votes — the closest presidential election in U.S. history. Although Gore had won the overall popular vote, he lost the electoral college vote by the thinnest of margins.

The morning after the landmark Supreme Court decision, Aldo summoned the AES LTSC into the conference room to decide what to do next. Aldo led off the discussion, "Well folks, we all know that if Gore had won, we would be on the road to making great strides on the national conservation front — especially with regard to solving both the global warming and biodiversity loss crises. But that didn't happen, so now we have to plan for dealing with greatly reduced support for both AES and HED projects — at least at the federal level. So where do we go from here, troops? I'm open to any and all suggestions."

Arnie Chatwood, Senior Regulatory Affairs Specialist, raised his hand to speak, "Well with Veep Dick Cheney actually running things, I guess we'll have a lot easier time getting federal permits because he wants to — pretty much — do away with the whole federal regulatory process. And he certainly doesn't give two hoots about protecting any natural resources. Remember, before he got into politics, he was in charge of the world's largest military contracting firm. What was it called?"

"Halliburton," replied Aldo.

"Ah yes — Halliburton, that's it," responded Arnie.

Hearing Arnie's remark was too much for Abbey. She immediately shot back, "But that's not us, that's just not how we do things. I say we stick by our principles and continue designing everything exactly how we've been doing it — keeping natural resources as a centerpiece for each project. Our clients know what to expect from us and I don't think that's going to change no matter who is in the White House!"

"Great point, Abbey," concluded Aldo, "the only choice we have is to keep charging forward. So, let's buckle our seat belts and get back to it, gang!"

After 9/11 — with the attention of the United States and most of the rest of the 'civilized world' so focused on fighting terrorism — there was limited time and incentive left for even thinking about long-term environmental issues. Most Americans were preoccupied with potential and immediate threats to their personal safety and security and totally distracted by our two new wars in the Middle East.

In the meantime, while American thoughts were occupied by the 'War on Terror', the U.S. environment was not really all that healthy. Forty percent of Americans were breathing unhealthy air, twenty-five percent lived within four miles of a toxic waste dump, seventy percent of the nation's commercial fisheries were overexploited, and — worldwide — twenty-three billion tons of CO_2 were being unabatingly spewed into the air every year. Plus, the world's population had tripled to more than six billion people in just the past fifty years.

The Bush Administration also instigated the most insidious regulatory free pass — now infamously known as the 'Halliburton Loophole' — in the history of the U.S. environmental movement. The Halliburton Loophole (which was part of Bush's Federal Energy Policy Act (FEPA) allowed the new fossil fuel technology known as 'fracking' to proceed across the American landscape unencumbered by any federal environmental regulations or reviews.

In tandem with the Bush Administration's anti-environmental rhetoric, the seeds of a new, worldwide environmental threat began to germinate. The global temperature curve was beginning to increase so steeply that the decades-old 'Global Warming Theory' slowly began to gain some national attention. Various conservation NGOs started advocating for reduced fossil fuel consumption and increased renewable energy development to staunch the now-documented steady increase in Earth's Greenhouse Gases (GHG).

Meanwhile the Intergovernmental Panel on Climate Change (IPCC) — formed in 1988 — continued their work. Consisting of more than two thousand scientists and technicians, the IPCC was charged with using existing climate models and research information to predict the future impacts of the 'Greenhouse Effect'. These dedicated experts — working strictly on a voluntary basis, without pay — contributed to writing and reviewing the IPCC's Assessment Reports (AR's).

For expediency, each IPCC AR contained a 'Summary for

Policymakers', which was subjected to line-by-line approval by delegates from all participating governments — representing more than one hundred and twenty countries. The IPCC's First AR — published in 1990 — concluded that the Earth's temperature had risen exponentially during the past century, and that human emissions of fossil fuels were significantly adding to this rise. All of the subsequent IPCC AR's have verified and, in most cases, expanded on these initial findings.

Abbey, Randy, and Aldo took serious note of these continuous and unprecedented worldwide increases in GHG emissions. They knew that all of their recent projects emphasized living lightly on the land which meant minimizing the use of polluting resources — like fossil fuels — while maximizing the use of wind, solar, and other sources of renewable energy.

Although Abbey couldn't yet fully realize the dramatic effects global warming would have on her family's future, she personally thought it was something the world needed to address — and right away. Unfortunately, as she gradually came to understand, the climate crisis and the associated global warming were not being taken very seriously at the time. In the minds of most American citizens, the issue just seemed to be something that could occur at some future time. But right now, with global terror and all the other issues that were swirling around, it was not important enough to justify a lot of concern or attention.

Despite being deeply by bothered by this apparent lack of empathy about the diminished quality of life for future human generations, Abbey still had plenty to keep her busy. Brother Aldo kept piling new projects on her office desk. His gleeful ramblings, whenever he bounded into her office, reminded Abbey he was still quite proud of the business they had built together, and the widespread 'green and sustainable' benefits their projects continued to have on the human environment.

The Twins Come to Fruition

Throughout their child-rearing years — as is the bent of most parents — Abbey and Randy had always hoped for great things from their precocious offspring. But little could they have imagined the phenomenal impacts that Shiloh and Sunny would eventually have on the long-term preservation of the quality of life on Earth.

After they completed their extensive college careers, Shiloh and Sunny — with financial assistance from their now legendarily successful parents — rented office space in downtown La Jolla, pooled their remarkable arrays of education and expertise, and in the spring of 2006, started an environmental consulting organization called '*ECO-Truth: Protecting Our Natural Environment with Facts*'.

Despite all of the environmental and regulatory turmoil emanating from the Bush-Cheney Administration, Shiloh and Sunny kept stiff upper lips and their noses to the grindstone. Through their NGO 'ECO-Truth', the multi-talented twins pursued both individual legal actions and class action lawsuits regarding a variety of conservation issues.

Demonstrating their astute foresightedness, Sunny and Shiloh structured their ECO-Truth staff to be especially effective at providing expert witness testimony for anything involving the dual crises of global warming and biodiversity loss. They realized early on that these would become the showcase environmental issues for preserving the quality of life on Earth. And time would soon prove how right they were.

In less than a year, ECO-Truth had a staff of twenty-five environmental scientists, with expertise ranging from archeology to zoology. Plus, more than half of their staff held PhD degrees and the rest had at least a Master's degree in their fields of expertise. With this broad array of talent, ECO-Truth was soon known throughout the Nation for speaking truth to power, and holding corporate powers accountable for any damage they wreaked on natural resources.

During ECO-Truth's first two years of operation, Shiloh and Sunny led their teams of experts in winning landmark court cases involving fossil fuel disasters, impacts to critical habitats of endangered species, massive western wildfires, illegal oil and gas drilling activities, and non-compliance with federal statutes — including the Endangered Species Act, the Clean Water Act, and the 1918 Migratory Bird Treaty Act.

Then, on a clear and cool mid-summer Wednesday in July 2007, a call came into the ECO-Truth office that would cement the company's legacy in stone.

A Desperate Call for Help

Shiloh picked up her quacking — it was the only wild bird sound available at the time — cell phone and was greeted by a pleasant but pleading voice. "Hello, this is Viola Hamner in Edinburgh, Pennsylvania and I — we — desperately need your help. For the past three years, just about everyone in town seems to always be coming down with something — headaches, stomach aches, kidney stones, itchy skin — you name it. Plus, townspeople have been getting various types of cancer at more than twenty-five times the normal rate. This is called a 'cancer cluster' — I know because I looked it up."

"Then — just yesterday," continued the frantic voice, "one of our teenage sons turned on a spigot in the kitchen and — instead of a stream of water — a flare of flame spewed out. Next, my husband went out to check on our well, and when he pushed down the handle, the durned thing exploded in a fireball. Fortunately, he wasn't hurt — except for some minor burns on his fingers — but the shock near gave him a heart attack!"

Speaking in a calm, measured tone, Shiloh told Viola that she fully understood what was going on and that ECO-Truth could — indeed — help her out. Being extremely well-versed in issues associated with the fossil fuel industry, Shiloh knew that Edinburgh, Pennsylvania was located in the Marcellus Shale formation — prime fracking territory. This fact was all Shiloh really needed to know to understand what was going on with the Hamners.

Obviously relieved by Shiloh's reassuring voice, Viola continued, "The townsfolk have been complaining so much to the local officials that they have finally scheduled a public hearing next week to tell us what's going on. It sure would be great if you could be here to listen in and help us understand what they're talking about."

Bright and early the next day, both Shiloh and Sunny boarded an American Airlines flight to Dallas with a connection to Erie,

Pennsylvania. They were scheduled to meet with Viola Hamner and her husband, Julius, at their home on Friday morning. Since their total flying time was more than ten hours, the twins had ample time to discuss what they knew must be happening with the Hamners and — quite possibly — the entire Town of Edinburgh.

Since it was a crystal-clear day all across the country, Shiloh and Sunny enjoyed one of their favorite travel activities. They always booked at least one window seat wherever they flew. This allowed them to study both the natural landscape as well as land development practices along their travel routes.

Because the emphasis of this trip was fracking, the twins especially looked for signs of oil and gas activity. And — in certain areas of the country like West Texas — they were absolutely appalled and dismayed by what they saw. In many places, fracking pads and their spiderweb of interconnecting access roads stretched out below in seemingly endless mosaics of ugliness.

As Shiloh and Sunny animatedly pointed out, the different fracking sites they saw, they caught the attention of a man sitting across the aisle from them. "Excuse me," he said, revealing a voice of velvet and a charming South African accent, "I don't mean to eavesdrop, but your animated conversation is hard to ignore. Can you explain to me what fracking is?"

Shiloh, who was seated closest to him, completely lost her train of thought in his wide and welcoming smile. She shook herself and responded, "Oh, sure. My sister, Sunny, and I get very worked up about fracking. I hope that our histrionics aren't disturbing you too much!"

"Not at all, not at all," he laughed. "I figured it must be important based on the passion with which you both speak. Please, tell me about it — oh, and my name is Zane. What is yours, sister of Sunny?"

Shiloh blushed a little and said, "Oh, right! Sorry, my name is Shiloh. Nice to meet you, Zane." She composed herself and continued. "Fracking is the more commonly known term for hydraulic fracturing. It is a nasty way that the oil and gas industry pumps natural gas out of shale rock. Basically, to get the gas out of the rock, a drilling rig is used to inject a high-pressure mix of water, sand, and chemicals down into a shale formation. This fracking fluid is awful stuff — most companies

473

won't even tell you what is in it. They say it is a proprietary mix but that it is totally harmless. But we know that isn't true. We have heard horror stories about the radioactivity and noxious materials that is in the fracking fluids." Shiloh was back on her stride. Why had this guy knocked her off her game? She was usually unflappable!

"I see," said Zane, "but why do they need to inject this poisonous water into the ground? How does that get the gas out?"

"Good question. The high-pressure fluid fractures the shale; that's why they call it hydraulic fracturing, you see?" Zane nodded, so Shiloh continued. "The water is withdrawn from the shale, but the sand stays behind, propping the cracks open. These cracks then release the natural gas, which gets collected into a well. Supposedly, the fracking water is either reused or pushed deep into disposal wells that are below groundwater, but it turns out that isn't always the case."

Sunny jumped in, "That's why we are headed to Pennsylvania. There is a high density of fracking in that area, and, as it turns out, a high density of sick people. We are going to check it out and see if the health problems are related to the fracking. We think the fracking chemicals are getting into the drinking water."

Zane whistled, "Sounds like you two are a force to be reckoned with. It makes my business trip sound very mundane."

The twins chatted with Zane on and off for the remainder of the flight. They explained how, for the past few years, the oil and gas industry had been touting fracking as the solution to both the warming climate and the ongoing U.S. energy shortfalls. They debunked the fossil fuel industry's claim that fracking would give the U.S. energy independence while significantly reducing CO_2 and methane emissions to the atmosphere.

"The best way to get energy independence is to collect all our own energy here, in this country, using the abundant natural resources the earth provides; wind, water, and solar!" proclaimed Shiloh.

As the plane landed, the twins parted ways with Zane and wished him well in his business ventures. He, in turn, gave them a small bow and thanked them for their good work to keep people safe in Pennsylvania.

Touring the Fracking Battleground

The next day, after a brief kitchen table meeting and home-made breakfast, Viola and Julius Hamner loaded Sunny and Shiloh Childers into the back seat of their Ford F-150 pick-up and rolled off to survey the town. As they approached the town center, Viola proudly briefed the twins on the borough's highlights.

With a population of around five thousand people, Edinburgh is located in Pennsylvania's so-called 'snowbelt region'. It is both a college town and a resort community, featuring all sorts of winter sports.

As is common with many eastern U.S. settlements, Edinburgh's first known residents were Native American tribes. The Eriez, Iroquois, and Cornplanter tribes first called the region Conneauttee, meaning 'land of the living snowflake'.

Shiloh and Sunny also saw and learned that Edinburgh sits along a south-flowing tributary of French Creek. Plus the borough's overall drainage area lies within the immense Allegheny River, Ohio River, and Mississippi River watershed. Based on this overview, the twins realized that any surface water or groundwater impacts that were being caused by local fracking operations could potentially have large-scale, multi-state effects.

The first stop was the town hall, where Shiloh and Sunny could get details on next week's public hearing. As is the case with just about every small town, everyone in Edinburgh knows everyone else. So as soon as they walked in the front door, the slender, horn-rimmed glasses wearing town clerk, Alice Sherman, walked out from behind the counter and scurried over to greet Viola and Julius. After quick introductions, Clerk Sherman briskly walked Shiloh and Sunny directly back into the document filing room.

The twins quickly ascertained that the fracking business had become a big deal in Edinburgh. The map case was chock-full to overflowing with topographic maps and heavily marked-up drilling plans. Plus, one entire sliding drawer of a three-drawer filing cabinet was labeled and devoted to Hydraulic Drilling, Inc. (HDI).

Shiloh and Sunny were elated to learn that the town-wide public hearing before the Edinburgh Planning and Zoning Commission was scheduled to start at seven p.m. on Monday night. Since Shiloh and Sunny had filled out the paperwork that qualified them as 'expert witnesses', Clerk Sherman agreed to let the twins check out all the information they wanted. This meant they could sequester themselves with their laptops in their motel rooms and use all weekend to prepare for the hearing.

After they had spent thirty minutes reviewing and selecting key materials from the file drawer and map case, Shiloh and Sunny packed up their briefcases and walked back out of the file room. There they found Viola and Julius engaged in animated discussion with Clerk Sherman and a gaggle of other townsfolk.

The twins chuckled to themselves as they envisioned what was being discussed. They were certain that it had to be about what HDI was doing to their town, and that much of what was being said was likely not for polite ears.

As they corralled Viola and Julius, they profusely thanked Clerk Sherman and turned to head out the front door into the parking lot. While they were walking away, Clerk Sherman looked back over her shoulder and said, "Oh, by the way, don't forget that Mike Wallace and his Sixty Minutes crew will be here Monday night. They're featuring us as part of their in-depth analysis of the pros and cons of the nationwide fracking industry."

Hearing this, Shiloh and Sunny shared knowing glances. Their suspicions that this project was a much bigger deal than they had originally thought had just been confirmed.

The Hearing Commences

On Monday evening, Shiloh and Sunny met the Hamners at the community Allegheny Diner where they enjoyed the finest in Pennsylvania Dutch cuisine. Their meals included a smorgasbord of such specialties as *schnitz un knepp*, sauerbraten, red-beet eggs, hog maw, corn fritters, scrapple, and chicken and waffles. Of course, the whole gustatory affair was topped off by the requisite slices of shoofly pie. After dinner, they ambled around town before arriving at the town hall a little before seven.

As soon as they walked into the hearing room, Shiloh and Sunny knew they were about to become an integral part of a small-town media event. The place was packed — all the seats were occupied, and more residents stood all along the back wall.

A section that was roped off for 'the press' was like-wise fully occupied by TV and newspaper reporters plus all of their technicians with gear in tow. In the midst of this media morass stood the unmistakable visage of Mike Wallace, who was conversing with his cameraman and taking notes as they spoke.

At 7.00 p.m. sharp, Planning and Zoning Commission Chairman, Rachel Brennehan, gaveled the hearing to order and introduced the team from HDI to give an introductory description of what they had already done plus their future plans for Edinburgh. With that, Mike Mondragon — CEO of HDI — confidently strode to the podium and spouted the company line about how everything they were doing and would continue to do was, of course, a 'win-win situation' for everyone involved.

Mondragon boasted that on a mega-scale, their work would contribute to America's energy independence. Plus, HDI would bolster the local economy by creating many new jobs and supporting local businesses. Of course — best of all — they would accomplish all this without causing any significant impacts to the local environment or quality of life.

CEO Mondragon then proceeded to introduce a succession of geologists, engineers, hydrologists, and environmental scientists who presented a series of maps and testimony that supported his conclusions. Listening to the HDI team's unfettered testimony, one could only draw the conclusion that fracking was — indeed — a glorious gift to the good citizens of Edinburgh.

According to the HDI team, because fracking reaches greater depths than other extraction methods, it allows tapping deposits of natural gas that were previously inaccessible. This means extending the use of fossil fuels for much longer than anyone expects. Meanwhile, the search for viable renewable energy alternatives like wind energy and solar power, can be continued without fear of rolling blackouts.

Also, since fracking makes access to fossil fuel deposits easier, taxes on gasoline and other energy essentials will be lowered. Finally, the CO_2 emissions generated from natural gas are much lower than emissions from coal-fired power plants. This will result in an overall improvement in the region's air quality.

Mondragon concluded his team's presentation by saying, "In summary, fracking provides a mother lode of less polluting natural gas while doing away with our dependence on foreign oil and putting the United States on a fast track to becoming the world's largest fossil-fuel producer."

After sitting for an hour-and-a-half listening to the HDI team's gibberish, Shiloh and Sunny couldn't wait to get up to the podium. They agreed beforehand that Shiloh would take the stand first and describe how the Bush Administration had totally stacked the regulatory review deck in favor of the fracking industry. Then Sunny would follow up by telling the real story of how fracking was severely impacting both the lives and livelihoods of local citizens.

In short order, Chairman Brennehan smacked her gavel, introduced Shiloh and Sunny as expert witnesses from ECO-Truth, and the show was on.

"Good evening, commissioners and ladies and gentlemen in the audience," began Shiloh, "my name is Shiloh Childers. I'm a Principal Environmental Scientist with ECO-Truth and I greatly appreciate the opportunity to speak with you tonight. I would like to begin by familiarizing you with something called the 'Halliburton Loophole'.

"Now you are all probably familiar with the name Halliburton," continued Shiloh. "It's the oil services conglomerate and military contractor presided over by Dick Cheney before he became the current Vice President of the United States.

"The Halliburton Loophole is insidious because it explicitly exempts hydraulic fracturing — also called fracking — from the key regulatory provisions of both the Clean Water Act of 1972 and the Safe Drinking Water Act of 1974. These exemptions from some of America's most fundamental environmental protection statutes provide the oil and gas industry with the *carte blanche* immunity it needs to implement a highly polluting and dangerous drilling process on a grand national scale."

With this onslaught of opening testimony, the twins knew they had done a terrific job of setting the stage. They could hear — and even feel — the murmurings and general uneasiness of the citizens in the packed gallery. They also heard a few expletive-filled, under-the-breath mutterings coming from the HDI team members' box.

Shiloh continued testifying about how the Halliburton Loophole effectively turned the nightmare of fracking loose on the American landscape — quite possibly, never to be contained. As she had just witnessed on her plane flights to Erie, Shiloh stated, "Anyone looking down from an airliner flying at thirty-two thousand feet can easily see the ravages of this regulatory exclusion.

"In many places," continued Shiloh, "fracking roads and pads stretch as far as the eye can see. Since most of these fracking networks are constructed on undeveloped land, the impacts on the local wildlife populations are extreme. In addition to directly eliminating thousands of acres of pristine habitats, the fracking pad matrices also fragment and destroy critical wildlife migratory corridors. And — due to the Halliburton Loophole — all of this has taken place without any federal environmental impact documents being filed or public hearings being held."

Shiloh knew she now had the entire town hall in the palm of her hands, as she put forth these final salvos. "Because our foreign oil dependency has been a thorn in the side of U.S. diplomats since before the Arab oil embargo in 1973, Congress — on both sides of the aisle —

479

has seized on this newfangled fracking practice as a once in a generation worldwide business opportunity. Almost everyone on Capitol Hill has agreed that any environmental damage resulting from fracking would be immaterial to solving our growing energy crisis for the foreseeable future. As a result, the enabling 2005 Federal Energy Policy Act (FEPA) was written, verified, and approved posthaste."

"But the Halliburton loophole wasn't the only fracking enabler in Bush's FEPA," continued Shiloh who was now on a passionate roll — exceeding any testimony Sunny had ever heard her previously give. "The other glaring regulatory misstep was placing the Federal Energy Regulatory Commission — or FERC — in charge of fracking oversight and compliance under the National Environmental Policy Act — aka NEPA. This is truly akin to putting the fox in charge of the henhouse."

Finally, Shiloh wrapped up her testimony with this *coup de grace.* "The FEPA insidiously grants FERC sweeping authority to supersede both state and local decision-making and regulatory authority when it comes to choosing the locations of infrastructure — including morasses of new access roads and product pipelines — to service the fracking industry."

The gallery was now buzzing as Shiloh thanked Chairman Brennehan and Sunny stepped up to the podium. It was now her turn to put the final nails into the HDI coffin.

Glancing directly into the eyes of the assembled townspeople, Sunny began with this powerful statement, "A study published by the National Academy of Sciences has confirmed that high-volume hydraulic fracturing techniques can contaminate drinking water. There have been numerous reports by citizens across the country of fouled tap water. It is a fact that some of the tap water has even turned bubbly and flammable, as a result of increased methane."

"Well blowouts," Sunny continued, "also happen on a regular basis. In total, the companies conducting the fracking industry cannot be trusted. Roughly one in five chemicals involved in the fracking process are still classified as 'trade secrets'. Many of the drilling companies receive dozens of regulatory notices of violation, but these do no good. The companies know that — if they end up in hot water with local commissions — their cronies in FERC will always bail them out as 'essential energy supply operators' that are excluded from municipal rules and regulations."

"So, let's look at some of the specific impacts caused by fracking," Sunny steadfastly continued. "For starters, the access roads and drilling pads needed for an operation destroy entire swaths of formerly untrammeled landscapes. As we mentioned previously, areas where fracking has already occurred look like hundreds upon hundreds of rows of barren squares, all tethered together with access roads with very little room in between.

"Whatever natural habitat that might have existed before fracking took place is all but obliterated," lamented Sunny. "The fate of the wildlife that used to exist in these areas is anybody's guess. Remember what I said earlier — FEPA removes the need for federal or state environmental analyses. So not only are impacts to wildlife not being avoided, minimized, and mitigated, they are not even being identified or studied in the first place."

Sunny turned her unwavering gaze directly at the HDI team as she concluded with this, "At ECO-Truth, we find it both frustrating and unsettling when we learn that fracking companies consistently coverup the compositions of the toxic chemical solutions they blast into the earth. Fracking-associated contamination of groundwater drinking wells has now been proven to be a serious threat to human health and safety. But astonishingly, even doctors who are treating patients with fracking-related health issues cannot access information on the types of toxins that are causing these problems. That's just deceitful, disingenuous, and — quite frankly — disgusting."

Then markedly shaking her fist for final emphasis as she walked off the stage, Sunny kept staring at the HDI project team as she said, "This is all simply inexcusable — each one of you should be ashamed of yourselves!"

The audience reaction was immediate and total. As Sunny walked back to her seat, the gallery exploded up into a standing ovation. Chants of, "Liars — liars — liars," filled the town hall. It took a full five minutes for the cheering to finally subside. With a wry smile on her face, Sunny leaned toward Shiloh and whispered, "Should we do an encore?"

The encore actually came a few minutes later when Mike Wallace himself walked up to the twins, congratulated them on their rousing testimony, and asked if he could interview each of them separately. The ensuing '*Sixty Minutes*' episode — which incorporated segments of the twins' testimony as well as their follow-up responses to Mike Wallace's questions — became the most watched network show during the month of August 2007.

As the twins boarded the plane for the return trip home, Sunny nudged Shiloh. "Don't look now, but standing a few people behind us is a tall, dark, and handsome man with a smooth South African accent boarding our plane to go back home!"

Shiloh stifled a gasp — it was Zane! He caught sight of them when they turned around and he flashed his disarming smile. As they settled into their seats, he passed by them and stopped to chat for a few minutes before moving to his seat a few rows back.

Shiloh couldn't believe the coincidence that he was on their flight again. She admitted to Sunny, who already knew from reading Shiloh's body language, that she found Zane intriguing and briefly wondered if she should give him her phone number. But the twins had so much to discuss following their momentous weekend in Pennsylvania that Shiloh quickly moved on from the thought.

It caught Shiloh by surprise when Zane came up toward the end of the flight and told the twins how nice it was to see them again. He asked about their trip and then, looking directly at Shiloh, he offered his business card to her, saying, "I am sure you are very busy, but I would be delighted if you would do me the honor of staying in touch." For the second time since meeting him, Shiloh felt herself — much to her chagrin — blushing. She smiled graciously and looked at the card, 'Zane W. Nkosi, Esq., Del Mar, California'. Shiloh tucked it into her business card holder and made a note to call him once things settled down in La Jolla. Two weeks later, Shiloh and Zane enjoyed a remarkable and leisurely repast at the Fairmont Grand Del Mar — the first of many convivial dates to come.

Both twins knew that their Pennsylvania trip had been a big leap forward for their careers. And, indeed, it was. From that time forward, the reputations of Shiloh and Sunny Childers as 'powerhouse environmental consultants' were permanently sealed. Working from their waterfront office overlooking the sea lions, harbor seals, and brown pelicans of majestic La Jolla Cove, the talented twins were now continuously in demand.

Their services were regularly sought for solving environmental crisis throughout the United States and — occasionally — even in other countries. For the time being, life was exceptionally good for Shiloh, Sunny, and ECO-Truth. The Monday after their *Sixty Minutes* piece ran, the twins met with their rapidly growing staff and assured them that the process of protecting the planet was now going to be both easier and much more satisfying.

Visiting the Great Bear

From the standpoint of global biodiversity loss, the year 2008 brought some sad headlines. The polar bear — Earth's greatest living icon of the frozen barrens of the Far North and the largest land carnivore on the planet — was officially being described as a 'vulnerable species' by the U.S. Fish and Wildlife Service. One of our most revered and fearsome predators, the alpha animal of its territory, was suddenly in danger of disappearing from the wild forever.

The cause of the polar bear's decline was simple. Since the great bear lives in a frozen landscape, with no land beneath the ice for thousands of miles, it depends on this ice for support and hunting platforms. With the warming seas in the Arctic regions, the bear's critical habitat — ice floes — were rapidly becoming fewer and fewer, even vanishing altogether in some places during the summer months. And once the sea ice disappeared altogether, so did the polar bear populations in those areas.

News about the polar bear potentially going extinct was the last straw for Shiloh and Sunny. They had to go and see this magnificent animal in the wild, while it was still possible to do so. Turned out, they were in luck. It was near the middle of October 2008 — right in the middle of what their travel literature described as 'prime polar bear viewing season'.

At this point, Zane and Shiloh had been dating for six months. It was going well, so Sunny suggested that Zane come along. Sunny would bring her good friend Maeve, the daughter of her parents' college friend, Savannah Andrelton. Within a week, the enthusiastic group of four had updated their field gear and were on a series of flights taking them to the 'Polar Bear Capital of the World'; Churchill, Manitoba, Canada.

The first thing the group of friends realized was that Churchill, Manitoba was one of the most difficult places in the world to reach. Situated at the mouth of the Churchill River on the Hudson Bay's western shore, the town is located two hundred and fifty miles north of the village of Thompson — the next closest settlement. Winnipeg — Manitoba's provincial capital — lies some six hundred and twenty miles to the south of Churchill.

Accordingly, the twins and their compatriots' travel to Churchill involved more than twenty-four hours of total flight time, taking them from San Diego to Denver to Calgary to Winnipeg before concluding with a private charter flight from Winnipeg to Churchill. As is the case with many of the world's most remote locations, Churchill has an airport only because of the U.S. military presence in the area during World War II.

When Shiloh, Sunny, Zane, and Maeve finally arrived in Churchill, they were actually quite surprised to find a rather sizeable community — supporting around one thousand residents. As the group expected, most of the population consists of Indigenous Peoples, many of whom still practice a subsistence existence, that depends on harvesting the local populations of whales, seals, walruses, caribou, and muskox.

One of the things that drew the twins to this trip was Churchill's amazing ecological pedigree. The town sits on an ecotone — the Hudson Plains — at the juncture of several distinct ecoregions. To the south, lies classic boreal forest, featuring subsurface permafrost that supports a sparse growth of weather-stunted black spruce. Iconic Arctic tundra is located to the northwest with the maritime environment of the Hudson Bay on the north. Finally, the east side of the town borders Wapusk National Park.

The polar bear-driven tourist trade — numbering around twelve thousand people in any given year — started in earnest in the 1980s. Because of this seasonal visitor influx, the village features an assortment of lodging and restaurant options.

Even in the town proper, the polar bear is king. Many locals always leave their cars unlocked just in case a quick escape is needed from a town-wandering ursine. Town officials also maintain a 'polar bear jail' where bears — mostly adolescents — that refuse to accept the sanctity of the town are detained until they can be moved back into their wild habitat.

The tour company the twins selected — Nanook Tours — had

booked them into a plain, but comfortable-looking domicile named Bears or Bust Lodge. Being dead tired after more than a full day of flying, the group grabbed a quick dinner at the Poutine Diner.

After dinner, since the northern lights were putting on a spectacular display, they spent an hour watching green and red curtains splashing across the ink-black sky. Witnessing this iconic display of the *aurora borealis* proved to be the perfect sedative. Shiloh and Sunny were both asleep, almost before their heads hit their pillows.

Quite well rested, the group was up long before the 9:30 a.m. sunrise the next morning. Maeve had risen even earlier to fit in a long run before the tour — she was an avid marathoner and had plans to run the New York City Marathon in November. After chowing down the quick cold breakfast provided by their hotel, all four were the first members of their tour group to arrive at the Nanook Tours Tundra Buggy loading station. Listening to the tour naturalist's canned spiel, they were all relieved to learn that the tour operators minimized impacts to the bear habitats by using a system of previously designated trails laid out by Canadian and U.S. military operations.

Their first day's tour started smoothly enough as the naturalist provided a detailed description of the polar bear and its rugged lifestyle. He described how polar bears are able to endure month after month of extreme cold because of their thick layers of fur which overlay even thicker layers of blubber. They also feature black skin under their outer fur layers, which helps them stay warm by soaking up sunlight.

Polar bears also have a rather unusual feeding behavior that keeps them alive throughout the seemingly endless Arctic winters. While they are excellent swimmers, the bears aren't fast enough to reliably catch their favorite prey — ringed seals under water. Instead, a clever polar bear finds and then stakes out an ice-bound breathing hole used by the seals.

There, lying at the edge of the ice surrounding the hole, the bear waits for the prime moment. When a seal surfaces to breathe, the bear pounces; pinning the unfortunate pinniped to the ice and then chowing down. During the winter, an adult polar bear typically needs to eat one seal every five days to survive.

To protect their young from the harsh Arctic environment, female polar bears give birth to their cubs in snow dens. The cubs typically spend the first two years of their lives learning hunting skills from their mothers. After that, the young adult bears are on their own to negotiate survival in habitats that are among the fiercest on earth.

In around an hour, the tundra buggy arrived at their first grouping of bears — two adult females and an adult male surrounded by five frolicking cubs. As soon as the tundra buggy stopped, allowing everyone to revel in this peaceful and wondrous scene, the unpleasantries started.

Most of the twenty or so other tour 'guests' seemed to be treating the outing with a party atmosphere. In fact, even though it was now barely past eleven in the morning, quite a few buggy passengers had already sidled up to the bar to order beers and bloody marys. As the twins soon learned, this celebratory mentality was probably due to the fact that most of the passengers were all members of a 'Travel the World Party Club'.

While the naturalist was trying his best to continue his discussion of polar bear habitat and ecology, the group started a bantering babble of crude jokes and toilet humor. These were the sorts of comments the twins had heard before from groups with no understanding of or appreciation for the sanctity of the natural world: "Well, would you look at that — that dude is one lucky bear, he's got hisself two females and he don't even have to take care of the kids," or, "How does a bear go in the woods, if there aren't even any trees around?" At one point, Shiloh had to hold Sunny back when one of the tourists said, "Boy — those little ones are sure cute. I bet they'd look even better if they was stuffed and sitting back home on my kids' beds!"

To make matters worse, each crude comment was met with rolling guffaws of laughter and snickers of derision. After thirty minutes of listening to this inane discourse, this time Shiloh had heard enough. One of the primary perpetrators was standing right next to her. Stockily built with a round face and bushy beard, he was wearing a backward baseball cap and decked out from head to toe in camouflage. Shiloh first thought about asking him why he needed the camouflage, since the trip patrons were forbidden to leave the security of their tundra buggy. But she demurred and decided to only ask him about his behavior.

"Excuse me, sir," quizzed Shiloh, "but why is your group trying to turn this experience of nature's majesty into a comedy club routine?"

"Well young lady," responded camo man, "my name's Joey Thomas and I can tell from the tone of your question that you just don't understand who we are. We're all well-educated professionals. I have my own dental practice — specializing in orthodontics. But we're also all Christians. As such, we believe that God's creatures were put on Earth for both the control by and pleasure of humans. So — you see — having a little fun with these bears just fits right into our beliefs. We don't mean them no harm, we're just here to have a good time."

"Okay Joey, I guess I sort of understand," replied Shiloh, "but don't you think — as a Christian — that your experience here should be tempered by reverential respect for these remarkable creatures and the raw, unbridled beauty of this awesome place where they are living?"

"Oh — fer sure," responded Joey, "but just look at these bears. We aren't bothering them in the least. In fact, they look like they're having fun themselves. They're just as curious about us as we are about them. Too bad we can't toss them some meat to watch how they fight over food!"

Shiloh drew her breath to launch a retort, but Zane — who now knew her well enough to realize she was gearing up for one of her famous man-withering lectures — put his hand softly on her shoulder. "Shi, he doesn't deserve your valuable energy or impactful words," Zane murmured. "Save them for the real fight."

Shiloh knew Zane was right; it wasn't worth pushing the conversation with Mr. Thomas any further. For the rest of the day, both Shiloh and Sunny just sat back and soaked up the wonder of seeing family groups of polar bears — along with arctic foxes, snowshoe hares, and small herds of barren land caribou in the wild.

But as they reveled in this arctic glory, they also wondered how — in the year 2008 — so many people in the U.S. still accepted the biblical myth about 'man's obligation to exert dominion over nature'. For the remaining two days of their arctic tour, Shiloh, Sunny, Zane, and Maeve successfully ignored the ongoing and unwelcome shenanigans of their tour group partners. They concentrated — instead — on maximizing their enjoyment of nature's far northern bounty and sharing an amazing adventure with each other.

At night — while dining on such traditional Canadian cuisine as poutine, tourtiere, bannock bread, and butter tarts — the group discussed how this experience was providing them with additional insight into why biodiversity loss is such a critical problem — both nationally and globally. Zane almost always joined in these discussions, and sometimes Maeve did as well, if she wasn't in bed early to accommodate her morning runs.

The twins both loved talking to Zane. He was becoming as passionate about environmental issues as they were, and had even started directing some of his law work toward environmental causes. But his background in environmental science was not as strong as theirs, so he was constantly seeking the twins' knowledge.

One evening, as the four friends sat by the huge bonfire that the hotel built each night, bundled in down parkas and fur-lined hats, they reminisced about the amazing predator-prey interactions they had watched on that day's tour into Wapusk National Park.

The day's action started when an adult polar bear ambushed a ringed seal on the edge of a hole in the arctic sea ice. After swiftly dispatching the hapless seal with a slash of its dagger sharp claws, the bear dragged its lifeless quarry further up onto the ice where the rest of the family — three cubs and another adult — could feed. Obviously quite hungry, the white bears were soon covered from head to chest in splatters of crimson.

Next, the Tundra Buggy tour guide instructed the driver to take the group into the interior of the park. Shiloh, Sunny, Zane, and Maeve weren't sure exactly what the guide had in mind, but they suspected it might be something special. And they were not wrong!

After about thirty minutes of trammeling along the snow-and-ice blotched tundra track, the group arrived at a gentle rise overlooking an expansive river valley. There below them, a herd of close to one thousand barren ground caribou moved slowly along — like an ink blob being absorbed into a paper towel. Emphasizing caution, the tour guide told the driver to ease the Tundra Buggy down the slight gradient and toward the migrating herd. Once they were within one hundred feet of the closest animals, the guide signaled for the driver to stop and wait for the herd to move past.

The scene they were now witnessing made Shiloh, Sunny, Zane, and Maeve especially thankful that the Travel the World Party Group had departed Churchill the day before. In stark contrast, the new tour group was extremely quiet and respectful of the wonder of nature moving ahead right in front of their eyes. Then, what happened next was the crowning touch on an already royal day of sightseeing.

Without warning, a pack of eight timber wolves blasted out of the scattered taiga trees and ran right into the middle of the caribou herd. The target of their attack was quickly apparent. A yearling caribou — appearing to have some sort of leg injury — was doing everything in its power to keep up with the herd. Within what seemed like only seconds, the wolfpack was on top the struggling youngster, ripping it apart as it squealed in agony.

Mercifully, death came quickly. In less than an hour, the ravenous canines had consumed all the flesh off their quarry and were lying around licking the blood off their fur. In their stead, a squawking gaggle of vultures and ravens had moved in to pluck the remaining flesh off the caribou's bones.

As their campfire comfortably snapped and crackled in front of them, the group again talked about the caribou kill they had witnessed earlier. "That wolf attack literally took my breath away today," marveled Sunny.

"Agreed," responded Shiloh. "I really felt bad for the helpless caribou, but I know that the predator-prey relationship is an integral component of *'the circle of life'*."

Maeve wrinkled her nose, "As is, I suppose, the polar bear eating the seal, but I can't believe you were all able to watch the wolf attack on that poor, squealing animal. That was just too much — it really turned my stomach."

Sunny poked her playfully, "Maeve, everything turns your stomach. Maybe it's all that running you do!" Maeve rolled her eyes in response, but cracked a big smile.

Zane looked thoughtful. "Tell me," he said, "in these situations, there is a clear balance. The wolves eat the caribou to help return it to the earth and the polar bears eat the seal to feed themselves and help ensure future generations. Everything is in equilibrium." Zane paused and gathered his words, "I apologize for my ignorance here — that is why I hang out with you two, so I can correct my deficiencies — but how does biodiversity fit in? If *'the circle of life'* is complete, why does it need more pieces?"

The twins smiled at both Zane's curiosity and his humility. Shiloh responded with a question, "Simply put, what would happen if the population of wolves were wiped out — say, by human hunters? Without something to step in as an alpha predator to replace the wolves, the caribou would soon overpopulate and overgraze their food supply. Many of the caribou would then die off since their food source is gone. Next, their bodies would overwhelm the landscape and the Arctic wilderness would become a mass of dead animals that are slow to break down without the primary step the predators provide by separating the body into smaller pieces."

"Oh my gosh, gag!" said Maeve, in horror. "Please, let's keep biodiversity!"

"But," Sunny jumped in, knowing — as usual — exactly where her twin was heading with the conversation, "if there is a high diversity of species — say another alpha predator — that can fill in the gaps left from the die-off of the wolves, *'the circle of life'* will be altered, but not broken. Under such ideal conditions, biodiversity props the circle up so that it is not solely dependent upon one chain of interactions." Pulling from her days as a point guard on the basketball team, Sunny continued, "It's similar to having layers of back up when playing ball. One-on-one games are fun, but as soon as you get by the opponent, the shot is in and the game is over. With several layers of defense, there are fail-safes. If the opponent gets through the first line, other defenders are there to fill in and stop the ball.

Shiloh whistled, "Way to connect your two loves from college, Sis — basketball and biodiversity. Impressive!" The group laughed and the conversation wandered to a different topic.

Thoughts about biodiversity and its importance stayed with Shiloh and Sunny throughout the rest of their trip. On their last night in Churchill, they vowed to make researching and solving the world's biodiversity crisis a number one priority for ECO-Truth.

BOOK TWENTY
Evaluating Two Existential Crises

Enter Barack Obama

The November fourth, 2008, election of Barack Obama brought a revelatory sea change to the swirling maelstrom of American politics. As the first minority President in U.S. history, Obama elicited a long-awaited and much-welcomed sigh of relief throughout the environmental protection and resource conservation communities. Joining in with the nation's liberal leaning masses, Shiloh, Sunny, and Zane toasted Obama's election well into the warm, starlit Southern California night.

President Obama provided the twins — and the nation — with hope for climate crisis action. After his election, he stated that "We are not acting as good stewards of God's earth when our bottom line puts the size of our profits before the future of our planet."

While having federal backing for climate initiatives would make ECO-Truth's job easier, Shiloh and Sunny knew they still had their work cut out for them. Like every president before him, Obama was beholden to all his constituents and the political pressure that came with running a country with a two-party system. While he may have wanted to push through an aggressive climate agenda, he was limited by Congress and often by the will of the people as well.

In addition to President Obama's inauguration, another 'main event' in the twins' lives occurred during January 2009. On the six month's anniversary of their first meeting, Zane invited Shiloh out to dinner at one of San Diego County's best known and supremely memorable restaurants — The Marine Room. As the couple sat in awe, watching the waves crash against the restaurant's picture windows, Zane called over a waiter and whispered something into his ear. Five minutes later, a team of waiters arrived — holding the restaurant's signature baked Alaska which they summarily placed in front of Shiloh and flambeed. Demonstrating his typically perfect aplomb, Zane simultaneously asked for Shiloh's hand and then — without missing a beat — slid a diamond ring onto her finger. Gasping in delight, Shiloh could only say, "Yes-yes-yes", as she leaned across the table and gave Zane a joyous kiss.

Restructuring ECO-Truth

As the New Year of 2009 rolled in, ECO-Truth's exceptional reputation for being premiere environmental 'solutionists' continued to spread far and wide. In fact, Shiloh and Sunny were having to turn down more project requests than they accepted.

The twins just didn't want all the headaches that came with continually growing their business. They now had a total staff of fifty environmental professionals; this kept ECO-Truth functioning as a 'small business' — and that's just where they wanted to stay. Plus, they were finding that, more and more, the projects they did agree to take on often involved the two global environmental issues they were most interested in solving; the climate crisis and the worldwide loss of biodiversity.

On January ninth, 2009, Shiloh walked into Sunny's office with a suggestion that forged a permanent path forward for ECO-Truth. "Hi Sis", began Shiloh jauntily, "I've been thinking a lot lately about where ECO-Truth is headed over the long-term. I know you and I both agree that there are two issues we most believe in and feel most compelled to resolve.

"So, why don't we structure ourselves to primarily deal with these two issues," continued Shiloh. "We could set things up so that ECO-Truth has two main teams — one team headed by me and the other by you. Since you're our Sustainability Expert, you would lead the 'Climate Team' and — with my expertise as a Conservation Ecologist — I would lead the 'Biodiversity Team.' Next, we would assign each of our staff — based on their professional backgrounds and individual skills — to one of the two teams."

As soon as Shiloh stopped speaking, Sunny pushed back from her desk, looked at Shiloh, then rolled her eyes, and exclaimed, "Wow, this just has to be a 'twin thing'. I was just getting ready to walk into your office and suggest exactly the same approach. OK, then, let's do it."

With that, Sunny switched on her intercom and asked all the ECO-Truthers to come into the main conference room for a very important announcement. After the staff arrived, Shiloh laid out her plan for the future of ECO-Truth. Sunny was relieved to see the entire staff nodding along in agreement with Shiloh as she assigned team responsibilities. In fact, the ECO-Truth staff fully realized that — if the dual crises of global warming and biodiversity loss were allowed to continue along unabated — the future of global natural resource protection and land conservation was indeed grim, if not gone completely.

As the staff meeting progressed, Sunny named Dr. Philip Nevin — a professional climatologist from MIT — to lead the Climate Team. She also assigned Dr. Evelyn Durnst — a whip-smart recent graduate from the Columbia Journalism School's doctoral program — to be assistant leader. Dr. Durnst also held had an undergraduate degree in Environmental Management and had focused her time at Columbia studying disinformation campaigns — specifically those that related to global warming.

Next, Shiloh selected Senior Wildlife Biologist, Dr. Aubrey Shuster, to lead the much smaller — staff-wise — Biodiversity Team. Dr. Shuster held a PhD from Cornell University's prestigious College of Ornithology and was quite well-known for her entertaining and informative PowerPoint presentations on wild bird behavior.

Finally, Sunny and Shiloh decided to hire a top-notch environmental legal counsel — and they knew just the man for the job. Shiloh's tall, dark, and handsome fiancée, Zane Nkosi, graciously and enthusiastically accepted the position.

The ECO-Truth staff quickly and comfortably settled into their new, dual issue company structure. In fact, they seemed to be even more fervently pouring their hearts and souls into their work. In so doing, the company's array of top-notch scientists was validating the old adage that, 'if you really love what you are doing, you will always be happy'. This phrase held even more meaning, when considering the fact that the ECO-Truth staff's work now concentrated on tasks that were critically important for maintaining the long-term, multi-generational quality of human life on Earth.

When it came down to the issue of climate change — or more

accurately 'global warming' — the ECO-Truth Climate Team needed no further proof that it was really happening and that human activities were the reason why. Unfortunately, despite all the recent supporting research, many Americans still doubted that *global warming* was really taking place and that humans were causing it.

Even the majority of Americans who did believe that *global warming* was a significant issue weren't sure what could really be done to counteract it. The Climate Team's dedicated scientists knew that a great deal of national convincing was still needed to overcome the fountain of falsehoods that kept flowing forth from the climate deniers and the right-wing media.

Understanding that the lack of public commitment to take action was the primary problem, Sunny sat down with her Climate Team leaders, Phil Nevin and Evelyn Durnst, to plan a course of action. They decided that they first needed to produce a document that would encapsulate the issues and potential solutions associated with the climate crisis. Then, once this was accomplished, they wanted to convey their findings to the general public in a form that was both easily understandable and action-inducing. To this end, their final product would be called '*The ECO-Truth Climate Crisis Guidebook (CCG)*'.

From an administrative standpoint, Sunny and Shiloh realized that producing a truly useful and beneficial *CCG* would require a tremendous amount of staff time and effort. They also knew that much of this work — such as researching the causes and potential solutions to the climate crisis — would not be billable.

To keep the ship afloat while they concentrated on producing the *CCG*, Sunny and Shiloh decided to do two things. First, they would solicit only billable work that was associated with either the climate crisis or biodiversity loss. They knew that their reputation would precede them in successfully pursuing these two types of jobs. Some examples, they immediately came up with were farmers who lost their crops and even their livelihoods because of either prolonged droughts or unprecedented floods. Other candidates were the western residents who were suffering catastrophic losses due to wildfires raging across tinder dry landscapes. Then there were the thousands of folks living in coastal areas whose land and property had been washed away by the 'one hundred-year-storms' that were now happening almost annually.

The second step for keeping ECO-Truth solvent — while they tackled the climate change and biodiversity crises — was a bit more delicate. Sunny and Shiloh decided to gain the financial support of both AES and HED by becoming a subsidiary of Aldo and Abbey's companies. Of course — just as the twins expected — their mom and their uncle were ecstatic about becoming a structural component of ECO-Truth's revised business model. Within a week, the AES-HED legal staff, coordinating with Zane, had drawn up all the required paperwork and the deal was finalized. Going forward, ECO-Truth was now bulwarked against financial difficulties by the might of two of the Nation's best known and most successful consulting firms.

As the final step in their week-long strategy session, Shiloh and Sunny compiled a draft protocol for the ECO-Truth Climate Team to follow in producing the *CCG*. A week later, after all the comments from the team members had been addressed, the protocol was finalized, and the Climate Team started enthusiastically working toward their goals. They were all fully aware that the tasks they were now undertaking could very well change the world forever.

Despite their supreme confidence, the ECO-Truth Climate Team could not have imagined how right the future would prove them to be.

Celebrating A Wedding

In the midst of the flurry of travel and research activity that swirled around the *CCG* preparation, there was a paramount cause for celebration and joy in the twins' life. On June fourteenth, 2009, Shiloh, Zane, Sunny and a small group of family and friends gathered on top of Yosemite National Park's famous Glacier Point for a simple, intimate wedding. Silhouetted in front of the iconic Half Dome, Shiloh and Zane exchanged their vows and committed to a life together. At the end of the ceremony, Shiloh threw the bouquet and her Maid-of-Honor, Sunny, of course, caught it. Sunny laughed and said, "Not any time soon, folks — don't get your hopes up just yet!"

Clarifying the Keeling Curve

As a logical first step to assembling their *Climate Crisis Guidebook (CCG)*, Sunny and Shiloh wanted to see where it all started. Accordingly, they asked three key scientists from ECO-Truth's Climate Team to accompany them on a quick trip to the National Center for Atmospheric Research's (NCAR) Mauna Loa Observatory (MLO) on the Big Island of Hawaii. The travel group included team leader Phil Nevin, co-leader Evelyn Durnst, plus Oceanographer Connie Albritton, and Climatologist Charlie 'Thunder' Embid.

On July fifteenth, 2009, they boarded a Southwest Airline flight to Kona International Airport. As soon as they exited the airport a driver greeted them and then whisked them up to the MLO. The minute they walked through the entrance door, a trimly handsome woman met them and led them right into the facility's small meeting room.

Once they were all seated, their guide began, "So, my friends, aloha and my sincerest welcome to you all. I am Professor Simone Kahale and I'm here to show you what we're all about here at Mauna Loa, the world's largest — and yes, still active — volcano. To begin, I know that — as highly trained scientists — you have received a special invitation to visit us here on site. So, I'll skip my usual introductory remarks and just start by asking if you have any questions."

Connie Albritton was the first to raise her hand. "First, thank you so much for inviting us here Dr. Kahale, we are so excited to hear about everything you are doing. But most importantly as far as our research is concerned, we would like to learn more about your CO_2 measurements — the history of the Keeling Curve, if you will."

Professor Kahale smiled brightly. "First, my dear, please call me Simone. We are quite informal around here and although most of our small staff has an advanced degree or two, everyone just goes by their first names. I kind of expected your initial question might be about what became known as our Keeling Curve. In 1958, Dr. Charles David

Keeling, an Oceanographer with Scripps Institute in La Jolla, California — where you folks are based, I believe — became the first person to make accurate measurements of carbon dioxide (CO_2) in the Earth's atmosphere. He chose our facility because we are located high up on the slopes of this still active volcano, at an elevation of more than eleven thousand feet. His goal was to measure CO_2 in air masses that would most closely represent climatic conditions throughout the world. Since we started our monitoring so long ago, we are now considered the world's benchmark site for measuring the concentration of CO_2 in our atmosphere."

Phil Levin was the next to join in, "Since as you said, Mauna Loa is still active, how concerned are you about having all of your monitoring equipment and data destroyed at — potentially — any time?"

Simone again smiled knowingly, "Yes, that's another question we always get. In a way, we just have to take our chances. But since Mauna Loa actually underlies more than half of the Island of Hawaii, just about everyone that lives here is in the same boat. Fortunately, we also have the U.S. Geological Survey (USGS) scientists at the Hawaiian Volcano Observatory (HVO). They are continuously monitoring for indicators of potentially hazardous volcanic activity so that — if anything were about to happen — we could grab our digital data backups and evacuate off the mountain safely before it blows."

Shiloh was next and her question got right to the nitty-gritty, "So, Simone, will you please explain to us why the CO_2 monitoring you are doing here is so important to the rest of the world?"

Pausing for a moment to collect her thoughts, Simone reflected, "Simply put, our monitoring here over the past fifty years proves that the concentration of CO_2 in Earth's atmosphere has now surpassed the 'danger point' that our fellow climate scientist, Dr James Hansen, warned us about back in 1988. We have now documented that the worldwide average of CO_2 has risen from three hundred and fifteen parts per million (ppm) to more than three hundred and eighty ppm in less than twenty years. Our data also conclusively shows that our planet has been warming in direct correlation with these CO_2 increases."

"OK," countered Sunny, "but that's only about a 20% increase — why is this so critically problematic?"

"Ah — your analytical mind is clearly at play here," rejoined Simone, pointing directly at Sunny. "You are correct; statistically the percentage increase may not really be that significant. But you must weigh in the fact that our current CO_2 readings are the highest that have occurred on Earth in more than at least eight hundred thousand years. We know this from measurements of CO_2 trapped in bubbles contained in carbon-dated ice cores collected in Antarctica."

Sunny still had a quizzical expression as she stared back at Simone. "But doesn't this just prove that the CO_2 increases are part of a natural cyclical process — like so many climate crisis deniers still believe?"

"Oh, I see what you're doing, playing devil's advocate with me — and I like it!" winked Simone. "Actually, these recent CO_2 increases are anything but cyclical — and this is where humans get directly linked into the process. You see, it's not so much the total volume of increase that is the concern. It's the rate of acceleration that's most problematic. Since the start of the Second Industrial Revolution — when the proliferation of fossil fuel-powered steam engines and other machines spread throughout the world — the concentration of Greenhouse Gases (GHG) — including CO_2 — in our atmosphere began to increase exponentially. For example, when the Second Industrial Revolution started — say around 1860, depending on who you ask — our world-wide CO_2 concentration was about two hundred and eighty ppm."

Simone paused briefly to pick up some notes on the table in front of her. "Just checking my notes here to make sure that I have the numbers right. So if you compare the CO_2 increase from 1860 to now, you get a one hundred ppm increase in one hundred and fifty years which is roughly an average of 0.67 ppm per year. Then, if you generously consider that the first two hundred and eighty ppm accrued during the eight hundred thousand years prior to 1860, you get an average increase of only 0.00035 ppm per year. Without getting too far into the detailed mathematical calculations, this means that — since the start of the Second Industrial Revolution — our atmospheric CO_2 concentration has increased by a factor of thousands. Do you see what I mean — this rate of acceleration can't possibly have anything to do with natural cycles."

Smiling knowingly, Sunny nodded at Simone. "Actually, you have just confirmed what our team has believed for quite some time now. Your

Keeling Curve data leaves no room for doubting the truth about our increasing CO_2 levels and global air temperatures.

"Now if I may make one final point," continued Simone, "Our climate scientists have borrowed a technique from law enforcement to confirm that humans are definitely responsible for what is happening to our climate. They have established that the carbon dioxide emitted by burning coal, natural gas, and oil has a unique 'fingerprint' and that most of the additional CO_2 in our atmosphere bears this fingerprint. In other words, human burning of biomasses of fossil fuels — which are derived from fossil plant materials — is primarily what is causing our worldwide *global warming* phenomenon!"

Realizing that they had taken enough of the professor's valuable time, Shiloh concluded the meeting, "Thank you so very much for your time, Simone, I think we all just heard exactly what we hoped to learn from our visit here. We're now really energized to go back home and continue putting the pieces of our climate crisis puzzle together."

On the flight back to San Diego, Shiloh leaned over to Sunny and said quietly, "Well, that was certainly instructional. Now where do we go from here?"

Fighting to keep her eyes open, Sunny smiled sleepily and said, "Oh don't worry, Sis, this trip has given me plenty of new ideas. Buckle up — we're about to embark on some great learning adventures. Now please just be quiet and let me sleep!"

Chasing the Greenland Ice Sheet

Shiloh had all she could do to maintain her balance as she stared down into a marbled blue crevasse that bottomed out — two hundred feet below — in a frothy cascade of icy cold water. She looked over at her fully parka-ed and mukluk-ed guide, Professional Glaciologist Sterling Norduff, about what to do next. They could obviously go no further on their dogsleds — unless they could figure how to entice the convivial canines to vault across a one-hundred-foot-wide chasm in the Greenland Ice Sheet.

It was the middle of July 2010, and ECO-Truth's Climate Team was off on another of what they were now calling their truth-collecting expeditions. This time, Sunny was leading a team consisting of team leader Phil Nevin, Glaciologist Walenda Wilkins, Hydrologist Darrell Simpkins, Hydrogeologist Harry Sistrane, and Marine Biologist Latifah 'Moray' Macouri. Their task was to follow in the footsteps of a team of dare devil scientists who were collecting data for world-class mountaineer and *National Geographic* photographer James Balog's Extreme Ice Survey (EIS).

Lined up along the edge of the massive ice gorge, the ECO-Truth team watched in awe as two other members of Balog's research team worked to retrieve data. While one researcher belayed the rope, the other rappelled her way down to a camera wrapped in a heavy-duty case of clear, insulating plastic. The camera was mounted on a steel rod that had been driven deep into the ice that formed the side slope of the crevasse.

As the ECO-Truthers watched this derring-do, they could only imagine what might happen if something went wrong. Certainly, there would be no way to rescue anyone who fell into the icy torrent below. But the confidence of the data retrieval team showed they had successfully accomplished this same maneuver hundreds of times before. In less than ten minutes, the belayer was back on top with the camera's memory card tucked safely into a pocket of her parka. And the camera

— with a new memory card now in place — was continuing to collect data documenting daily changes in the width of the ice gorge.

For the next three days, the ECO-Truth team followed the EIS researchers — up to fifteen miles a day — as they collected data from other cameras installed at strategic viewpoints across the massive ice sheet. At the end of this field work, the ECO-Truth team and Balog's research crew met at the Katuaq Cultural House near Nuuk Airport to discuss their findings and what they meant to the overall framework of the climate crisis.

Before the meeting started, the mixed teams gathered for a hearty repast of traditional Greenland food. The ECO-Truth Team quickly passed on portions of Narwhal blubber and harp seal ribs. But — since their field sustenance had primarily consisted of freeze-dried rations — they welcomed the opportunity to tuck into other Greenland goodies.

First on the menu was the *suaasat* — a broth made from reindeer meat thickened with potatoes and onions. This appetizer was followed by the main course featuring portions of muskox tartare, eider breasts, and — the local favorite — lumpfish fillets christened with their extra-crunchy roe. The whole affair was topped off by a *kaffemik,* which consisted of Irish coffee kicked up with warming dollops of Kahlua and Grand Marnier and then served with slices of *kalaalit kaagiat,* a special Greenlandic coffee cake.

After dinner, the combined group of scientists gathered in the facility's conference room. After a round of introductions, Sterling Norduff stood up. "Hi there everyone — I think you all know me quite well by now. We've certainly covered a lot of southern Greenland during the past few days. Fortunately, the weather cooperated perfectly. I mean sunny skies and twenty-five degrees is about as good as it ever gets around here. Plus, our heroic sled dogs literally worked their hind ends off for us all week!"

Pausing for a minute to let everyone get settled, Sterling started his spiel. "I know you all are here to find out exactly what we're trying to accomplish. So, here's the short version — then I'll take questions about the details. Quite simply, we're documenting — in real time — how rapidly Earth's ice sheets and glaciers are disappearing. And, as the world will soon see in the documentary we're producing, our findings are quite astounding, but unfortunately not in a good way. Now, who has questions for me?"

Sunny started by asking, "Can you please explain to us how this whole complicated process got started?"

"Certainly," replied Sterling as he put his hands behind his head and took a deep breath. "In 2007, the *National Geographic Society* asked our esteemed leader — Mr. James Balog — to study the effects that *global warming* was having on Earth's freshwater resources. This primarily meant examining the Greenland and Antarctic Ice Sheets, as well some other strategically located glaciated areas scattered throughout the world. Since he is a very accomplished photographer, Jim decided that digital visual documentation was the best way to do this."

"Ah, very interesting," replied Sunny, "but how did he manage to set everything up? It must have been extremely challenging to position fully-functioning cameras in some of the most remote and inhospitable terrain on Earth."

"Yes, you are absolutely right about that," continued Sterling, sipping his coffee as he spoke. "Jim used his skills as a world class mountaineer to put the cameras exactly where he believed they needed to be. And he accomplished this often while he was in great pain, with knees that were about to give out on him."

ECO-Truth's Harry Sistrane quickly raised his hand, "I'm a serious nature photographer myself, so I'm quite interested in how the footage showing the retreating ice masses was captured."

"Oh yes, I anticipated this question," replied Sterling. "For this answer, let me pass you over to Clyde Barksdale — our chief photographic specialist and videographer."

Clyde took the reins, "OK, thanks Sterling — now this gets a little technical, but let me break it down for you as simply as I can. We currently have time-lapse cameras — all housed in protective cases — shooting at locations world-wide. Since the spring of 2007, these cameras have been making images — both stills and videos — once an hour for every hour of daylight. As you've been watching for the past few days, our field teams extract the memory cards from the cameras on a regular basis. After retrieval, our post-production team compiles the individual frames into video animations revealing how the glaciers are changing over time."

Next up on the ECO-Truth Team, Glaciologist Walenda Wilkins asked, "I'm curious about the size of these ice masses you're studying. Just how big are they, anyway?"

Sterling spoke up again, "I'll take this one, Clyde — since we're now back in my bailiwick. The Greenland Ice Sheet covers approximately 850,000 square miles — that's almost 300,000 square miles larger than the State of Alaska. But the Antarctic Ice Sheet covers an incredible 5.4 million square miles — an area that is more than five times larger."

"Taken together," continued Sterling, the Greenland and Antarctic Ice Sheets contain about ninety-nine percent of the world's freshwater. If the Greenland Ice Sheet melted completely, the world's sea levels would rise roughly twenty-three feet. But if the entire Antarctic Ice Sheet were to disappear, sea levels would rise an unfathomable one hundred and eighty-seven feet."

Hearing that, Sunny whistled softly and exclaimed, "My gosh, those numbers are quite frightening. If the possibility of being inundated by a hundred feet of water doesn't get everyone's attention, I don't know what will!"

"Yes, you would think that would be true, wouldn't you? But it hasn't happened yet. Maybe — just maybe — after we produce our documentary that we're going to call 'Chasing Ice', that will change..." Sterling let his voice trail off for effect, then said, "So, to summarize folks, we're losing our global icepacks at a rate that could not have even been imagined just fifty years ago. What do you think will happen to our coastal areas if we continue allowing our sea levels to rise exponentially?"

Several ECO-Truth hands shot up.

Sterling pointed at Moray Macouri and said, "OK — young lady — what do you think?"

Moray quickly replied, "Well... I suppose that if our sea levels rise that much, then all the land near the coasts will flood and much of the land development there will be either submerged or washed away."

"Yes ma'am, you bet your biffy," responded Sterling, showing off his Canadian heritage. "Now — here's the really tough question — when that happens what do you think will be our next steps?"

This time, Moray collected her thoughts before responding. "Logically, I guess we'll have to move our coastal developments further inland and sacrifice what's there right now to the rising waters. But won't that be incredibly — maybe even impossibly — expensive, and won't hundreds of thousands — if not millions — of people who don't have the resources to move be left with nowhere to go?"

"Exactly, and won't that be a sad state of affairs if that is actually allowed to happen," lamented Sterling. "But I think we all need to be confident that the indomitable human spirit will figure things out and — working together — we will be able to rise up and fix these problems before it's too late. Now — in conclusion — thank you all for coming and let's get back to work, doing what we can to find solutions to our burgeoning climate crisis!"

PHENOMENALLY FRIGHTENING & HAUNTINGLY BEAUTIFUL

The 2012 production, *'Chasing Ice'* won the Award for Excellence in Cinematography at the Sundance Film Festival, and was short-listed for an Academy Award. The film has also been featured on the ABC, NBC, CBS, and PBS television networks. If you haven't yet seen this phenomenally frightening — yet hauntingly beautiful — documentary film, find it and watch it. There is no way you can view this meticulously crafted production and not be awestruck. Watching sections of an ice sheet — some as large as the island of Manhattan — give way and calve off into the North Atlantic Ocean will have you squirming in your seat in both amazement and agony.

In the production, James Balog's cameras make the invisible visible, and, if seeing is believing, the images Balog has collected prove that we are losing glaciers permanently and rapidly. The loss of this frozen ice is turning into sea-level rise, directly attributing to changing precipitation and temperature patterns. Balog says there is no significant scientific dispute about this: "It's been observed, it's measured, it's bomb-proof information." He refers to these glacial retreats as 'the canaries in the coalmine', saying their rapid melting should be setting off warning bells for the world.

Our first viewing of *'Chasing Ice'* left us mesmerized, exhausted, and enraged. At the conclusion of Mr. Balog's questions and answers, the entire auditorium audience of five hundred people instinctively rose as one in a show of support for the film's dramatic message and the man who had risked so much to put it together. It is impossible to watch *'Chasing Ice'* and come away still doubting that climate change is happening. In fact, it's difficult to watch this epically beautiful, yet supremely sad documentary and not be moved to tears.

Keeping the Coffers Filled

Beginning in 2011 — while both ECO-Truth's Climate and Biodiversity Teams were diligently seeking out the truth in their respective crises, Shiloh and Sunny discovered the primary way to keep working capital coming into the firm. Unfortunately, fossil fuel industry disasters were now happening with morbid regularity throughout North America. In response to each, the fossil fuel company involved was forced to set up a disaster relief fund to compensate people whose businesses were lost and lives permanently disrupted by these catastrophic events.

Of course, the fossil fuel companies did not make it easy to qualify for reparation payments — even when the plaintiffs were clearly entitled. That's where ECO-truth came into the picture. Assisted on the legal side by Zane Nkosi, their teams of expert witnesses efficiently cleared the bureaucratic hurdles and laid out scientifically unassailable proofs of damages to win generous settlements for their clients.

While Shiloh and Sunny were both disgusted that these cases had to exist in the first place, it was satisfying for them to at least make the fossil fuel giants pay for their sins. Plus — to keep everything in perspective — ECO-Truth always gave each client a 70% share of the money awarded. This was by far the most generous split provided by any of the other consulting firms working these cases.

In the meantime — demonstrating total devotion to her work — Sunny's matrimonial aspirations had been put on hold. But that was about to change, and in a most surprising way.

A Whale of a Wedding

One chilly — for San Diego, at least — mid-winter morning in 2011, Shiloh Childers switched on her intercom in the ECO-Truth office and made the following announcement, "Attention everyone, please reserve February twenty-seventh on your calendars. I can't tell you why right now, but believe me, you will not want to miss this event!"

With that, Shiloh turned to Sunny and said, "OK, Sis, there you go — now let's start planning, time is already getting short." Two days later, each ECO-Truth staffer received an information packet that included directions to the Shelter Bay Marina in Point Loma, California and what items to bring for the upcoming trip.

On the designated afternoon, all the ECO-Truthers showed up on time in the marina parking lot. While most of them had figured out they were going on a boat trip of some sort, no one knew exactly where they were headed or what they would be doing.

Since most of the company staff knew each other's families, everyone was surprised to see that Shiloh and Sunny's parents, Abbey and Randy — plus Abbey's brother, Aldo were also coming along. Even more suspicious was the presence of Phil Nevin's parents, Wanda and Willis, all the way from Philadelphia. Plus, Phil's two brothers, Henry and Gabe, both of whom worked for the federal government and lived in Washington, DC, were also standing with the group.

The intrigue for the ECO-Truth staff grew even stronger when a swarthy older man with a Johnny Depp-style pirate's beard, complete with twisted pretzels of hair hanging down in ringlets, limped out in front of the group. He was decked out in tight breeches topped with a waistcoat, a loose-fitting blousy shirt with full bishop sleeves, and a bandana wrapped around his head. The strange man's fearsome look was further magnified by a lit corncob pipe hanging out of the corner of his mouth, a black patch covering his left eye, a stuffed parrot resting on his shoulder, and a skull-and-crossbones earing dangling from his left ear.

Seemingly just off the set of The Pirates of the Caribbean, the man stood, silently surveying the group. At that moment, nobody would have been the least bit surprised to hear him say, "OK all ye lily-livered landlubbers, you're about to shanghaied. If'n ye don't do exactly what I tell ye, you'll all soon be walking me plank and swimming wid de fishes!"

To the relief of the group, the man instead introduced himself as 'First Mate Jack'. He then instructed everyone to follow him — single file — to the other side of the marina. After crossing the street, the group walked along dock after dock through a milieu of several hundred boats. Finally, they arrived beside the boat they were about to board and everyone gasped in awe. They were staring at a three-masted schooner that was the largest sailing ship most of them had ever seen.

"OK, everyone — before we board," smiled Jack, "I want to tell you a few things about our little vessel here. She's the Yacht America and she's actually quite famous — or, at least, her original was."

"Hmm — what exactly do you mean by that, Jack?" asked Gabe Nevin.

"Well, thar, matey, I was just about to tell you, if you give me a chance," retorted Jack. "You see — this here sailing sloop is the spitting image of the world's most famous racing yacht christened way back in 1851. In fact, her ancestor is why the most famous trophy in yacht racing is now called the 'America's Cup'. Doing her civic duty, she's also served our country as a Confederate blockade runner, Union warship, WWII convoy leader, and U.S. Naval Academy training vessel. The original 'America' was destroyed by a German U-Boat torpedo, and the near-perfect replica that you see before you was built in 1995 at a cost of almost $7 million."

"Wow — that's certainly impressive, Captain," interjected Shiloh, "so exactly how big is this ship?"

"First off, thanks for the promotion, Miss, but I'm still just a First Mate," chided Jack, "but to answer your question, this ship is one hundred and thirty-nine feet long bow to stern, and weighs two hundred and twenty thousand pounds dry-docked. She can carry seventy-five passengers which is, according to my manifest, exactly how many of you folks are here today."

"So, we've got a full boat and it's a beautiful day — that's great!" extolled Aubrey Shuster. "But can you tell us where we're going and what we'll be doing?"

"Well, I guess I can now, ma'am," replied Jack, glancing over and winking at Shiloh, "especially since I have to review our safety regs with you. We are about to embark on a sunset whale watching cruise with — as I understand it — a little something extra thrown in for good measure."

Hearing for the first time that they were headed out to watch whales brought memories flooding back to Abbey and Randy. When they lived and worked in Gloucester, Massachusetts, they had gone on so many whale watching trips with the Seven Seas Whale Watch (SSWW) that — after more than twenty-five trips — they no longer had to pay for.

Using her superlative photographic skills, Abbey just shared her best shots with the crew for their use in the SSWW's promotional materials. This arrangement worked out quite well for everyone. Abbey always came back with 'knock-your-socks-off' shots of humpback whales — 'the clown princes of the ocean' — performing every type of activity from fluke lobbing to bubble cloud feeding and full breaching. But Abbey and Randy had not been on a whale watching trip since they moved to La Jolla. So, they were overjoyed to find out how a west coast whale watching trip compared to their Gloucester adventures.

After First Mate Jack finished his Coast Guard safety lecture, he instructed everyone to walk up the gangplank — again, single file — and onto the ship. Following Jack's advice, everyone immediately donned another layer before sitting down along the vessel's gunwales. As Jack so carefully explained — even in the height of summer — the waters of the open Pacific Ocean seldom exceed seventy degrees Fahrenheit. This means that the air moving across the water's surface — even with no significant wind speed — is always quite cold.

As soon as they left the dock, the crew of the Yacht America began pointing out the plethora of marine life that surrounded them. On the left, a family of sea lions was hauled out on an ocean buoy, barking incessantly at everything that moved. Perched all along the seawall on the right, a bevy of Pacific brown pelicans busily preened amid a covey of double-crested cormorants that were coaxing the water out of their feathers by holding their wings out to dry. Flying above the ship, a mixed flock of gulls and terns turned and twisted awkwardly, cajoling the boat's occupants to toss them something to eat.

While the tall ship unfurled its mainsails with the help of many on board, the crew pointed out the local landmarks. These included the U.S. Navy's dolphin training center, where marine mammals were taught to assist frogmen with delicate underwater maneuvers, the Cabrillo National Monument, and both the old and the new Point Loma Lighthouses.

Once the ship moved out into the open water, the crew told everyone to grab their binoculars and scour the horizon for blows that would reveal the presence of their quarries. Finding the first activity didn't take long.

Less than two miles off-shore, the America was suddenly surrounded by a mega-pod of hundreds of long-beaked common dolphins. Weighing as much as five hundred pounds and averaging seven feet in length, these jocular creatures were an absolute hoot to watch. At least fifty of them jumped into the ship's wake and started joyriding the bow — just like kids careening down a water slide. About every two minutes, the dolphins riding near the keel of the ship would peel off — allowing another group of these frivolous fun-seekers to take their place.

Meanwhile, smaller dolphin pods — most likely family groups — were alternately leaping up out of the water and cavorting along both sides of the boat. It wasn't clear if these side-swiping dolphin groups were pursuing prey or just having fun — most likely, it was a little bit of both.

After about thirty minutes of watching this amazing display of marine mammal joy, the crew announced that they were moving on in search of the trip's primary goal — the many species of whales that were known to frequent these waters. According to First Mate Jack and the rest of the crew, the gray whale was the species they would most likely see but humpback whales, fin whales, minke whales, and even blue whales — the largest creatures to ever live on Earth — might also be encountered.

Suddenly — using his best Pirate's jargon — Jack yelled, "OK, maties, nine o'clock — thar she blows!" Realizing that whale watching crews always reference the hands of a clock, everyone on board pushed over to the boat's left side to have a look.

Using her well-honed blow-spotting skills, Abbey nudged Randy and pointed to two grayish semi-circles moving diagonally toward the ship's bow. "Look — they're heading right for us! Oh, I hope they're humpies," she exclaimed, "they're so much fun to watch."

As the whales came closer and closer, one of the crew, nestled high in the rigging, announced that they were looking at a gray whale and her juvenile calf. Displaying their distinctive medium-gray, barnacle-encrusted skin, both animals were moving quite rapidly when the calf suddenly broke off from the mother and — with an air-borne flip of its fluke — dove down and disappeared.

Less than a minute later, the air in the bow of the ship was rife with shouts and shrieks of joy. "Oh wow — can you believe this!" whooped Camille Shuster, Aubrey's daughter. "He's right here in front of me. I can see his eye and his mouth. I can almost reach out and touch him!"

"Oh, please don't do that," implored Jack, as he watched the 'spy-hopping' gray whale calf, "he's just as curious about you as you are about him, but we don't want to frighten these animals. Just be happy that they have enough trust in us to come this close!"

About this same time, the mother gray whale appeared and started pushing her calf away from the ship's keel. In response, everyone groaned. But the excitement quickly returned, when both the calf and the mother started spy-hopping — only this time a little further away from the boat.

"Now that's something we very seldom get to see," chuckled Jack, "a double spy hop. You folks today are very lucky indeed!"

The group enjoyed the close-up views of the gray whale pair for another fifteen minutes until they both dove and simultaneous disappeared.

"Aha, I suspect their hunger must have overtaken their curiosity," explained Jack, "so they're on their way down to grab some muck off the bottom. That's the way they feed; you know. After they make their bottom scoops, they squish out everything that isn't food through their baleen — that's the stuff in their mouth that is like a strainer. Then they swallow all the protein that's left — including worms, zooplankton, larvae, and mollusks — and that's what they live on. So gray whales know how to turn the muck on the bottom of the ocean into their dinners.

That's pretty cool, right?"

"Yes, that was absolutely amazing, Mr. Jack!" enthused Gabriel Macouri, Moray's daughter. "So, now, what's next."

"Wow, you guys are a difficult bunch to keep satisfied — but I love it!" replied Jack. "Well, next we have something that's going to be very special for all of you. And now that everything is ready, will you all please turn and look at me!" Upon hearing these words, everyone — standing along the ship's sides — spun toward Jack who was perched in front of the ship's cabin.

Next—waving his arm toward the cabin steps — Jack pronounced "As you all now know, I'm Jack, as in jack-of-all-trades which includes Justice-of the-Peace. And now, da-da-ta-dah… here comes the bride!"

Everyone suddenly gasped when they saw Sunny, in a wedding dress, and Phil, in a tuxedo, walk up, hand-in-hand onto the deck. With the exception of Shiloh and hubby Zane — plus both the bride's and the groom's parents — no one on the ship even knew that Sunny and Phil were dating, much less engaged.

Next, Jack stepped forward to Sunny and Phil and led the recitation of their wedding vows. As soon as Jack said, "You may now kiss the bride", the ship erupted in enthusiastic applause and then everyone rushed over to congratulate the happy couple. To a person, they all knew they had just been privy to one of the most unique weddings ever — a bride-and-groom being married by a full-blown pirate under the languidly flapping sails of the world's most famous tall ship. As Abbey whispered to Randy, "You just can't make this stuff up!"

But the trip wasn't over quite yet, there was one more miraculous event to go, and it happened just as the setting sun met the serenely-quiet ocean's horizon. Suddenly — as if on cue — another large pod of common dolphins burst forth, jumping and leaping across and directly into the rays of the sun's brilliant orangish-red orb. While this amazing action was happening, Abbey was blasting away with her super-telephoto lens and camera set to record ten frames per second.

Fifteen minutes after the sun had fully set, Abbey sidled over to Randy and elatedly showed him what she had captured. "Can you believe it, my dear, what a day! Our daughter's unforgettable wedding combined with my all-time dream photo — dolphins jumping over the setting sun.

It's all just too good to be true!"

Based on the jovial and celebratory wedding reception that took place at the Marina Landing Resort later that night, Abbey's happiness was certainly shared by all who sailed on the Yacht America on that glorious and most memorable February afternoon.

More Twins Arrive

On June fourteenth, 2011, Zane and Shiloh celebrated their second wedding anniversary by maintaining the family tradition of 'that twin thing', and giving birth to twin boys — named Zane Jr. and Aldo II — at Green Hospital in La Jolla. The Childers-Nkosi family was now comfortably ensconced in a four-bedroom home nestled near the top of Mount Soledad. Their property provided an unparalleled view of the southern California coastline — sweeping from Point Loma on the south to the Scripps Oceanographic Institute on the north. Owing to the 'infinity edge' effect of their balcony, walking outside their house to admire this view was not for the faint of heart.

Meanwhile, the newlyweds, Sunny and Phil, had just finished renovating their house, one street below Shiloh and Zane. Not to be outdone by her 'big sister', on March first, 2011 — one month after their storybook wedding with the whales — Sunny convinced Phil to buy a total fixer-upper.

Right after the purchase, Sunny took complete control of the 'reno'. As she continuously assured Phil during the demolition and reconstruction, "Don't worry about a thing, honey, everything is going to work out just fine. The one really good thing about renovating — instead of buying — is that you know you're going to get exactly what you want!"

Sunny's reassurances could not have been more on point. While Phil had no clue how Sunny found the time to serve as their home's on-site contractor, she ended up — as she so often put it — 'really killing it' with the final product. Six months later — when the still-madly-in-love couple moved into their new digs — they had everything they ever dreamed about. This included, views of the Ocean Beach Pier, the San Diego River Channel, and the wide-open Pacific Ocean.

Sunny's design flourishes were also manifested in a beautifully-landscaped backyard festooned with only native plants, a forty-foot swimming pool with an attached spa, and a bevy of hummingbird feeders and bird baths. Then — in an interior crowning touch — the home's first floor living space encompassed an *au pair* suite, that was specially designed to make visiting friends and relatives feel as comfortable as possible.

During the first few weeks in their 'new' abode, Sunny and Phil were often visited by friends and co-workers who were just dropping by to see if they could help. While the happy couple knew that their frequent visitors were just making excuses to see the results of Sunny's 'reno', each visiting group also brought food — often a complete dinner. This was always most helpful and much appreciated, especially while the home's kitchen was still being set up.

With each new group of visitors that showed up, Sunny always had fun making her 'special announcement'. "Guess what folks, I'm pregnant and — yes — we are maintaining the family tradition of twins. Plus, we already know that this time it's girls. The due date is right after Christmas, so we'll keep you all posted on our progress."

As Sunny accurately predicted, she gave birth to bouncing blonde twin daughters on December twenty-eighth, 2011. In honor of two of their favorite climate crisis heroes, the proud mother and father named their newborns Naomi and Katherine.

Melting Permafrost

A team of awe-struck climate scientists stood atop a gentle hill — beside their tundra buggy — on Alaska's North Slope, staring at the strangest landscape many of them had ever seen. Spindly black spruces were strewn across miles of terrain — looking like giant matchsticks that had just been blasted apart by a category five hurricane. Strings of utility poles that provide critical power to the indigenous villages north of the Arctic Circle were also all catawampus, leaning in every direction but straight up. Trying to put a positive spin on what was actually an ongoing infrastructure calamity, the local town folk call such areas their 'drunken forests'.

From their ongoing research, ECO-Truth's Climate Team knew that the progressive loss of the Arctic and subarctic ice masses meant that the permafrost — which is ice in the ground that remains permanently frozen year-round — was thawing and turning to water for the first time in many millennia. But until today seeing it for themselves first-hand, they had no idea about the massive extent of both human and natural damage this process was wreaking.

This is why; during this third week of August 2012, Shiloh had arranged this trip for a team of ECO-Truth scientists. Using several connections, they had flown from San Diego to Barrow, Alaska and then on to the remote Village of Nasquit — located north of the Arctic Circle in the watershed of the Colville River. Approximately 75% of the town's residents are ethnic Inupiat people. As is the case with most North Slope villages, Nasquit's economy is based primarily on subsistence hunting, fishing, and whaling.

The day after their field review, the ECO-Truth contingent met with Mayor Mildred Enook and Regional Environmental Scientist Charlie Assaluk. They wanted to unravel the details of permafrost loss and — hopefully — ferret out some solutions for the Inupiats as well as the other indigenous peoples who were populating Arctic regions throughout the world.

After enjoying an Alaskan brunch of smoked salmon frittata, eggs Benedict with reindeer sausage, and cherry pistachio scones, all washed down with hearty Kaladi Brothers coffee, the meeting began in earnest. After welcoming everyone and leading a round of introductions, Mayor Enook asked Shiloh what she and her team were hoping to learn.

"Thanks so much for your hospitality, Madam Mayor," began Shiloh. "We are here to understand how the climate crisis is affecting the people of your village — in particular and in general — all the residents of Alaska's North Slope. We all assumed that the warming climate is having some devastating effects on your way of life and our field trip yesterday certainly confirmed our suspicions. But we're here this week to understand from the horse's mouth, so to speak, exactly what is happening and how you're dealing with it."

As soon as Shiloh had finished speaking, Mayor Enook tossed the ball to Charlie Assaluk. "I think it's best to let our Chief Environmental Scientist address your questions. He has been dealing with the on-the-ground ramifications of our global warming for the better part of twenty years."

"Hi — good morning, everyone and thank you for your question," began Charlie, "let me start by explaining what *permafrost* is. As you all know, it's something we Inupiats have been dealing with our whole lives. As the name indicates, permafrost is ground that remains completely frozen throughout the year — for at least two straight years. It is composed of a mixture of different types of soil and rocks all held together by ice. Permafrost is found under an 'active layer' of soil that is not frozen year-round. Depending on the prevailing climate where the permafrost is located, the active layer above it can be anywhere from a few inches to several feet thick."

"OK — I think I understand the basics of permafrost," said Stephanie Stanhurst, an ECO-Truth Professional Soil Scientist, "but can you tell me where permafrost occurs on Earth?"

"Certainly," said Charlie, nibbling on the last of his scone as he talked, "because of its defining characteristics, permafrost occurs chiefly in Earth's polar regions. In fact, almost one-quarter of Earth's Northern Hemisphere is underlain by permafrost — including Alaska's North

Slope where all of us are now sitting."

"So why does our warming climate pose such a risk to permafrost, if it's not even located on the surface?" asked Theo Burnstein, ECO-Truth's Chief Atmospheric Scientist.

Charlie gulped down the last of his coffee and pointed directly at Theo. "Bingo, my man, you have just asked one of the key questions in this whole conundrum that we are dealing with daily. The first thing you must know is this — in its normal state, permafrost stores the remains of many millennia of plants and animals that froze before they could decompose. Because of this, permafrost is one of Earth's best repositories for carbon-based materials. You can think of it as a kind of a giant frozen food locker underlying huge expanses of our planet. But — continuing with our analogy — what happens when you start adding heat to the insulation that is keeping that locker cold?"

"Oh yeah, I see where you're going with this," chimed in Theo, "when you remove the freezing component, all the stored food in our giant locker will quickly decompose and rot. So, applying this thawing scenario to permafrost means that the carbon-based compounds will start decomposing and then be released into our atmosphere, creating a vicious cycle of even more warming and thawing."

"Yes sir," replied Charlie, "you just explained our dilemma in a nutshell. As the global thermostat rises, our permafrost regions start transforming into significant sources of planet-heating emissions instead of vast sheds for carbon storing. And — unless we can figure out how to restore our historic air temperature regime — it's game over!"

"To be more specific," continued Charlie, "in aggregate, Earth's permafrost regions contain an estimated one thousand seven hundred gigatons of carbon. That's more than twice what is currently in our atmosphere. If a warming planet releases this massive amount of carbon — most of which is currently safely confined in our permafrost layers — it would create a permafrost carbon feedback loop. This feedback loop would consist of the following stages; thawing permafrost releases carbon, which causes the global temperature to rise, which thaws additional permafrost, and so on."

"OK, Charlie, can you summarize how this would impact the long-term livability of our planet?" asked Shiloh.

Charlie grimaced and took a deep breath, "Yes, I'm afraid I can and, unfortunately, it's not a pretty picture. Melting Earth's permafrost layers would cause global warming to occur twenty to thirty percent faster than the burning of fossil fuels alone. In summary — if all the permafrost thaws and releases its embedded carbon, the planet will quickly spiral into serious, inexorable global warming. The permafrost carbon feedback loop would then become one of several irreversible processes, along with dry-season rainfall reductions and sea level rise, to which the brakes can no longer be applied."

"Wow, that's really scary stuff," replied Tabatha Graystone, an ECO-Truth Civil Engineer, as she nervously drummed her fingers on the meeting room table. "Are you able to do anything right now to counteract the changing climate here in Nasquit?"

"Yes, we are doing some things locally, but let me pass you back to Mayor Enook since she's in charge of what is going on here in town," replied Charlie.

"Thanks, Charlie," responded Mayor Enook, "everyone living here understands that we're faced with a choice between being 'resilient' and adapting to our changing climate or just giving up and moving. I can tell you that since 95% of our residents have known no other way of life, they are not about to pack up and leave. That's why most of our new homes and buildings are encased in thick foam insulation and powered by solar panels. These 'eco-homes' use eighty to ninety percent less energy than the typical North Slope dwelling. Also, instead of a sewer hookup, the buildings are connected to an external black tank that uses bacteria to compost human waste."

"Wow, I really love the eco-home concept," responded Tabatha while flashing a thumbs up. "How about adjustments to the melting permafrost — what are people in town doing about this?"

"For the past five years, our Town Engineer, Michele Kligut, has been working with home and building owners to come up with solutions to permafrost loss," beamed Mayor Enook. "Each new house in town features an iron foundation that resembles a giant bed frame, built on screwjack pilings. This way — when the ground below the house shifts or sinks — the screwjacks are used to shorten or lengthen the foundation legs and make the house level again. We have also been retrofitting the foundations of some of our older homes and buildings with screwjack pilings to deal with permafrost settlement."

Realizing the time was now early afternoon, Shiloh closed the meeting. "Thank you so much, Madam Mayor. I'm sure you and Mr. Assaluk have plenty of things you need to get done, so we won't take any more of your time. You have given us all plenty of information to mull over during our flights back to San Diego tomorrow. I promise that we will continue soliciting your input as we work to develop solutions to permafrost loss and other key climate crisis issues."

South Florida Is Disappearing

It was the last day of July, 2013. The sun-drenched south Florida sky belied the three feet of water that had flooded and closed Ocean Drive — Miami Beach's main thoroughfare — to traffic. The ongoing sea-level rise on top of a king tide had created a situation where two-pound Florida mullets were now swimming around in the front yards of wealthy homeowners. Carefully wading around in hip boots, a team of ECO-Truthers were looking for other types of sea-dwelling denizens that were now occupying what should be dry land.

Daniel Ruiz, Environment and Sustainability Director, was leading the field group on a demonstration of how the City of Miami Beach was adapting to climate crisis impacts. "As you folks probably already know, Florida is the most vulnerable state in the country when it comes to climate change. Counting both sides of our peninsula, we now have more than nine million people living in the coastal plain — and all of them face the possibility of being relocated if we don't keep this climate crisis in check. The existing man-made infrastructure that is at risk along Florida's coastlines is valued at more than two trillion dollars — and yes, that's trillion with a 'T'."

"Those numbers are just unbelievable," replied Nancy Hartung, ECO-Truth's Coastal Geomorphologist, as she splashed along the highway's centerline. "How in the world are you coping with these sorts of unfathomable impacts?"

"Well, we're certainly not sitting on our hands waiting for a total calamity," huffed Daniel. "Even though we're getting no support whatsoever from our governor, we're moving full steam ahead with infrastructure adaptations designed to accommodate the massive sea level rise that is projected to occur by 2050. The way the City of Miami Beach sees it, we have no choice in the matter. It's either adapt our existing facilities or abandon everything and convert to a floating lifestyle."

"Yeah, I can understand why the first option is the way you want to go," remarked ECO-Truth Civil Engineer, Thad Plimpter, "it's pay me now — or pay me infinitesimally more in the future. So, what infrastructure adaptations have you already made?"

"Excellent question, my fine fellow," responded Daniel, pausing to knock some leeches off of his hip boots, "right now we're undertaking a step-by-step reengineering of our city through the year 2050. In fact — where we're now standing — we have already raised the highway two feet in elevation. And — based on the three feet of water we're now slogging through — this was not nearly enough."

"Our 2050 land-use plan," continued Daniel, "calls for new massive structural adaptations — fortifying seawalls and installing heavy-duty pumping stations — along the most vulnerable portions of Miami Beach's coastline. The more daunting projects, involving moving utilities away from the coast and protecting high-value assets, including educational institutions, hospitals, transportation centers, and the tourist areas that drive Florida's economy will come next."

"But that all sounds a bit iffy — what if it doesn't work out like you hope?" queried Climate Team Leader, Phil Nevin. "What will you do then?"

"Ah — now you're challenging our collective south Florida heart," replied Daniel doggedly dabbing beads of sweat from his furrowed brow. "You see — successfully living here on what amounts to an aggressively stabilized barrier island in the middle of hurricane alley, demands that you incorporate a lot of resiliency in your future planning."

"While it may seem outlandish in terms of lifestyle changes and cost," continued Daniel, "we are prepared to hard engineer the entire city — if it comes down to that. This may mean floating residential areas, elevated highways built on pilings, or transportation corridors that are water instead of pavement. Or when push comes to shove, maybe even all of the above. When people ask me, 'Wow, can that really be done?' I always tell them, 'Of course, it can be done, but can you afford it?'"

"All right, I get that dealing with the climate crisis here on the ground demands a bulldog mentality," responded Adrian Beckwith, ECO-Truth's Chief Hydrogeologist, "but doesn't Florida's unique geology require a much more delicate approach?"

"Hoo boy," whistled Daniel, "now you're hitting on a subject that has us all frightened. When you're talking about a city's drinking water supply, you're truly into matters of life and death. I tell you what — let's get out of this putrid soup, head over to my favorite deli, and I'll bring in Shana Matifico — our Groundwater Geologist. I'm sure she can answer all your questions."

After the group reassembled over premium coffees and the house special cinnamon-pecan rolls at Donifrio's Delectable Delicatessen, Shana Matifico stood up, introduced herself, and adjusted her horn-rimmed glasses, "So, I understand you folks have some questions about what we call our 'honeycomb of life' around here. Well, for starters, you need to understand what 'karst topography' is all about. Quite simply, this term refers to limestone bedrock that is honeycombed like a beehive.

"When it's mined," continued Shana, "the karst limestone consolidates nicely into fill that is fine for creating 'high ground' used for the construction of roads, shopping malls, and community centers. But it's in its natural state, our limestone bedrock is a whole different ballgame. It functions like a piece of cork that has holes poked all through it. Because of this, limestone bedrock can't hold water. Plus, it can't be sealed up. So, while seawalls in the city of Miami Beach can be raised enough to stop most storm surges, they won't stop the water that bubbles up from beneath the ground through this karst topography."

"Yeah, you just confirmed what I thought the situation was," replied Adrian Beckwith, "thank you for that. But — given this situation — how are you planning on stopping saltwater associated with sea level rise from contaminating your groundwater aquifers; essentially, your city's drinking water supply?"

"Ok, now you've hit on our enigma wrapped in a conundrum," replied Shana, hitching up her cargo pants. "As you're surmising, the increased pressure associated with sea-level rise forces saltwater intrusion into our groundwater drinking supplies, contaminates our irrigation supplies, and overruns our agricultural fields. This is, in fact, what's already happening to our 'Biscayne Aquifer' — the principal freshwater supply for southeastern Florida and the Florida Keys.

"But the damage doesn't stop there," continued Shana, folding her arms for extra emphasis, "saltwater encroachment also contaminates our valuable surface water resources. In many cases, saltwater from sea level rise is dramatically altering the fragile salt-fresh water balance in our brackish estuaries — like those preserved in Everglades National Park. Over the long run, these critical changes in estuarine salinity levels will wipe out entire populations of marine species that were sustaining some of our multi-generational coastal families."

"Boy, that's really a tough row to hoe," shot back Adrian, "so how will you handle these complex saltwater contamination issues in the future?"

Shana drew a deep breath, exhaled, and shook her head slowly. "Once the saltwater contamination becomes severe enough, the Biscayne Aquifer will no longer be of value for human use. Then, highly sophisticated, expensive technology must be used to try and make the aquifer potable again. But at this point, it really becomes a crap shoot. In the final analysis, if we can't protect our drinking water supply, no one will be able to live here — no matter how much we fortify our infrastructure!"

On that sad but all too true note, Daniel Ruiz stood up and asked if anyone else had any more questions. Hearing none, he thanked everyone for their participation.

In response, Sunny reached over and shook Daniel's hand. "Thank you and your staff so much for what has been a most informative and profoundly eye-opening meeting. I think I speak for all our staff when I say that we are demoralized to learn first-hand about the pending calamity faced by coastal communities like yours. But we are also all heartened by the bold actions you and your staff are taking, essentially on your own initiatives, to make the best of a potentially bad situation. Please keep us apprised of your ongoing progress, and we'll stay in touch on any potential solutions our research reveals."

Watching California Dry and Burn

The raging wildfire roared up to the edge of the just cleared firebreak, but the hastily constructed stopgap measure was no match for the fire's fury. Jumping from canopy tree to canopy tree, the flames quickly spewed embers onto the shake shingle roofs of the houses and buildings in the California Village of Utopia. Within minutes, the entire mountain community became an inferno of unstoppable devastation. The few residents who had ignored the emergency evacuation order fled the scene with only the clothes on their backs as flames licked the tailpipes of their vehicles. The only good news was that no one died.

Ensconced in their ten-passenger company field vehicle on a hillside safely above the conflagration, the ECO-Truth field team could scarcely believe their eyes. As scientific observers — invited by the U.S. Forest Service (USFS) — the ECO-Truthers were here to sharpen their research about the devastating effects that the climate crisis was having on California. They had spent the past week in the state's Central Valley — often called 'the Nation's breadbasket' — talking to farmers whose crops were withering on the vine and whose fields were turning to dust. But they never expected to see this — the leveling of an entire town.

In fact, this was never supposed to happen. The USFS prided themselves in the expertise of their 'Hotshots'; their expertly trained firefighting crews. The Hotshots were specifically trained in techniques designed to protect human habitation — including everything from trapper's cabins to a remote mountain community. But this was a fire season unlike any of them had ever known.

The ongoing California drought had transformed the forest floor into a tinder box of prime kindling, ready to turn a single spark — from a lightning strike or a camper's fire — into a raging inferno. And as each Hotshot team knew all too well, once the flames — driven by hot and dry Santa Ana winds — reached up into the canopy, it was too late. In heavily forested areas, no method of ground control would do any good. At that

530

point, it simply became a matter of just containing — not controlling — the roaring flames. And that was the sad fate of the Village of Utopia that the ECO-truthers had just witnessed.

After they returned to La Jolla — to fully understand what was happening in Central California during October of 2014 — the ECO-Truth field team combined the notes from their discussions with Central Valley farmers with their observations of the Utopia wildfire. The drought in California had been going on for more than four years now and showed no signs of ending. The ECO-Truth researchers knew that this was especially important since nearly half of the country's fruits, nuts, and vegetables— along with a majority of the dairy products — come from California.

In the final analysis, all of the farmers the ECO-Truth staff interviewed said they had never experienced such prolonged dry conditions in their lifetimes. Now, near the end of 2014, a whopping ninety-two percent of the state was locked into an official 'severe drought'.

Combining this information with what they had witnessed during the destruction of Utopia, the ECO-Truth team was now certain that both the frequency and intensity of western wildfires were being significantly bolstered by the climate crisis. And all of the research they uncovered fit their supposition to a 'T'. For starters, in an interview they found on the PBS television series — *'The Years of Living Dangerously'* — former California governor Arnold Schwarzenegger stated, "There is no longer a wildfire 'season' in the American West — wildfires now happen all year round. As governor, I saw the tremendous changes over the last few years; the amount of land that we have lost, the trees that we have lost, the homes that we have lost, lives that have been lost, and it is due — to a large extent — to global warming."

Through their studies, the ECO-Truth Climate Team also discovered that global warming caused by climate change was creating life-sapping drought conditions all over the world. This triple whammy of misery — no fertile ground, no water, and, eventually, no food — was posing potentially dire consequences for millions of the world's citizens. Sadly, this hydrologic calamity was most severely impacting Indigenous populations, whose lives depend solely on subsistence agricultural operations.

The irony of this situation was not lost on the ECO-Truth staff. They soon realized that here in the United States most people are — at least for now — able to cover their bases during ongoing climate hardships. But the populations of many 'developing countries' are not so lucky. Dramatic drops in crop production often lead to widespread famine and loss of life — especially for infants and young children. Worst of all, prolonged drought can also breed civil unrest and — in extreme cases — revolution and the spread of terrorism.

Decrying Decreasing Biodiversity

Professional Wetland Scientist Aubrey Shuster thought she was losing her mind. She was quite sure that — in this very spot, just three years ago — she would have been standing in the middle of a pristine saltmarsh, teeming with fiddler crabs, clam spouts, oyster bars, and schools of tiny fish. But instead, she was now almost up to the top of her waders in flat, open water — not a blade of *spartina* cordgrass to be seen. What could possibly have happened? As one of the leaders of ECO-Truth's Biodiversity Team, Aubrey was doggedly determined to find out.

Just two months earlier, George Shay, an ECO-Truth Wildlife Ecologist, had come across some very disturbing facts. Between 1970 and 2010, the World Wildlife Fund (WWF) announced that there had been a 52% reduction in the planet's overall populations of birds, reptiles, amphibians, and fish. In total, 39% of terrestrial wildlife species, 39% of marine wildlife species, and 76% of freshwater wildlife species had disappeared from the face of our planet in a span of only forty years.

Meanwhile, other ECO-Truth research revealed that — in the time that our wildlife populations had been cut in half — the human population had essentially doubled. The number of people in the world grew from 3.7 billion in 1970 to almost 7.0 billion in 2010. The bottom line here was that humans are multiplying more quickly than Earth can handle, and there isn't much room left for the planet's other inhabitants.

At this same time, many members of the ECO-Truth Biodiversity Team were reading and discussing Elizabeth Kolbert's 2014 book, '*The Sixth Extinction*', which issued a clarion call for the worldwide protection of biodiversity. As Kolbert, gifted staff writer for the *New Yorker* and Williams College professor, explains it, the fifth extinction — the one that wiped out the dinosaurs — was believed to have been caused by a six-mile-wide asteroid colliding with Earth. But today, we are living through an epoch that many scientists refer to as the 'Sixth Extinction' and this time, human activity — through our overuse of fossil fuels causing climate change — is the culprit. As several researchers have put it, "We are now the asteroid."

According to author Kolbert, "We are effectively undoing the beauty and the variety and the richness of the world which has taken tens of millions of years to reach. We're doing — it's often said —a massive experiment on the planet, and we really don't know what the end point is going to be."

All these pieces of information about biodiversity loss — colliding simultaneously — finally became too much for the ECO-Truth Biodiversity Team to process. They decided that they had to get out of the office and see what was really going on. This is how a contingent of ECO-Truthers — led by Aubrey Shuster and Shiloh — ended up in the middle of the Mississippi River Delta on a breezy and humid June morning in 2015.

As a recent graduate of Louisiana State University's School of Marine Biology, Aubrey knew that the state's spectacular array of wetland resources was being hammered daily by sea level rise. In fact, the Mississippi River Delta was losing more than a football field of coastal wetland habitat every hour.

To be able to see and assess as much of lowland Louisiana's wetlands as possible, the ECO-Truth field contingent booked two airboats from Boudreaux's Swamp Buggies in Houma. After a hearty breakfast, they met their operator-guides at 7.30 a.m. and then spent the rest of the day zipping through the mix of cypress swamps, mangrove thickets, and *spartina* saltmarshes that formed the southern border of the state. In all, they covered some ten thousand acres and — according to Aubrey — much of the watery landscape had changed dramatically in just the three years since she'd last seen it.

When their day on the water ended, the ECO-Truth field team returned to their Hampton Inn Hotel, freshened up, and then reassembled at Deschamps Crawfish Emporium to imbibe on local delicacies and discuss what they had just seen. After delighting in the locally-famous 'Bayou Buffet' of shrimp and oyster poboys, chicken and sausage gumbo, boudin balls, crawfish etouffee, fried catfish, red beans and rice, and mustard greens, Shiloh ordered another round of Ghost in the Machine IPA and then said, "Now that we're all fully satiated from country Cajun cooking, let's get down to the business at hand." Since Aubrey had been guiding the field tour all day — relying on her memories as an LSU grad student — Shiloh decided to also let her lead the discussion.

"Well, I know you all are sick to death of hearing me say this," began Aubrey, glancing around the table with her piercing brownish-green eyes, "but I am — simply put — totally aghast by what we all saw today. In just three years, a large part of coastal Louisiana has totally morphed from a mosaic of vegetated wetlands to a monotypic open water bay. Our goal with this trip was to learn how sea level rise was impacting the overall biodiversity of both plants and animals. Well now we know for sure what's happening down here, and it's certainly a sickening sight to see."

"Yes," picked up Marine Biologist William Goldman, "if this part of Louisiana is any indication — and, unfortunately, I think we have to believe that it is — climate change-induced sea level rise is drowning the world's vegetated wetland systems right and left."

"You are so right, Bill," responded ECO-Truth's John Germaine, "I can tell you from twenty years' experience as a Professional Wetlands Scientist, changing vegetated wetlands into open water has every bit as much impact as actually filling them with dirt. When this transformation is made, many of the vital functions the vegetated wetlands provide — wildlife habitat, pollutant cleansing, groundwater recharge, flood control, storm surge protection — are lost forever."

With that, Airboat Operator Trevor Beacham chimed in, "Hey, I'm not a biologist, but over the past twenty-five years I've led more than three thousand tours around here. And I can tell you for sure that our coastal wetlands are disappearing as fast as gold doubloons lying on a pirate ship's deck."

Tipping his draft toward Trevor, Airboat Guide Jensen Calderone, extended the point, "Well, I've worked these parts for nigh onto fifteen years myself, and I am a wildlife biologist with a degree from Louisiana Tech. I can verify that all of our native habitats are being impacted like nobody's business. In addition to our sea levels rising faster than anywhere else on Earth, our land is also sinking. We're not talking about geologic time frames here. Just in the past five years, I've seen entire tidal marshes — I'm talking thousands of acres, and even whole islands — swallowed up by the ocean."

"Wow — okay," concluded Shiloh as she sopped up the last of her bread pudding with Bayou Rum sauce. "I think we now know that the climate crisis is having hugely horrible impacts on coastal Louisiana. But can anyone relate this to what's going on in the rest of the country?"

With this prompting, ECO-Truth Oceanographer Chandra Jenkins immediately raised her hand and started talking. "Actually, I did my PhD research at the Virginia Institute of Marine Sciences (VIMS) on the estuarine systems bordering our U.S. coastlines. Let me see — if I remember correctly — our nation has more than eighty thousand miles of tidal shorelines, most of which are embedded with brackish wetlands. Serving as transition zones between freshwater and saltwater — these coastal habitats are among the most productive ecosystems on the face of the Earth."

"So, if we don't stop sea level rise in its tracks — what do you think will happen to these ecological treasure troves?" asked Shiloh.

"OK — since you've asked the question," responded Chandra, "I'm going to apologize in advance for the lecture but here goes: If we don't get a handle on the situation in the next decade or less, rising sea levels will obliterate the majority of our coastal salt marshes and seagrass beds. And this would be a real tragedy since these two habitat types are ecologically known as the primary 'nursery areas' for the majority of our oceanic life — including commercially important fishery and shellfish stocks."

"Since you've obviously studied coastal ecosystems all over the place, can you give us some specific examples of harm that might occur?" inquired Aubrey.

"Oh, certainly — if you really want to hear it, it's such sad news," continued Chandra. "I focused my PhD research on our nation's largest estuary — the Chesapeake Bay — which provides habitat for almost four thousand species of plants and animals. Now remember, this was more than fifteen years ago, but my research at the time showed that if global warming proceeded unabated, the rising sea levels would wipe out hundreds of thousands of acres of bordering wetlands and their critical nursery and rearing areas for oceanic fish, crustaceans, and mollusks."

"Ouch — that's so sad," lamented Shiloh, "but based on what we saw today — I think we have to assume this is actually happening right now. Does anyone have anything else to add?"

With that, Hugo Hussene, ECO-Truth's Coastal Ecologist, raised his hand. "Yeah — I've got something else. I know we visited the City of Miami Beach a couple of years ago, but we never really got into talking about the Everglades and the impacts that sea level rise is having there."

"Yes, you're absolutely right, Hugo," replied Shiloh, "so can you tell us about what's going on there?"

"Absolutely," responded Hugo — obviously happy to contribute. "I spent a couple of years studying oceanography at the University of Miami before completing my master's degree at Florida State. While I was at the 'U', I learned all sorts of things about the unique ecology of the 'Glades. First off — in the park — the wetlands dip below sea level at the coast and gradually rise to the north at a slope of about two inches for every mile. This means that every two-inch increase in sea level will cause the loss through saltwater encroachment of a mile-wide swath of freshwater wetlands."

"Oh my — that's amazing," exclaimed Aubrey. "What does that mean for the overall ecology of south Florida?"

"This initial saltwater intrusion starts a domino effect," explained Hugo, "which essentially shifts Florida's remarkable coastal ecology northward. Freshwater areas further upstream become more vulnerable to saltwater intrusion from storm surges. In turn, these storm surges transport mangrove seeds that then become established and begin the process of permanent habitat alteration. Then, if sea-level rise is allowed to continue over the years, the salt-intolerant sawgrass marshes — the 'rivers of grass' for which the Everglades are so famous — gradually die off and give way to more saline and mangrove-dominated habitats. Over the long-term, the entire Everglades could just disappear!"

"Oh dear, losing a world-class ecosystem like that would certainly not bode well for our planet," sighed Shiloh. "Let's all take what we've learned here today, go back to work, and make sure we don't allow that to happen!" With those words, the meeting ended and the ECO-Truthers headed back to their hotel for a well-earned night's rest before their return flights to San Diego.

Australia's Great Barrier Reef

Sunny felt like she was floating in a dream, surrounded by a dazzling crazy quilt of flashing colors and darting shapes. Looking up, she could see a blinding brightness of light split everywhere by an ever-changing array of silhouettes — some tiny and quick, others large, slow, and ponderous. Looking down, she saw an underwater forest of white spicules adorned like miniature Christmas trees with purple, orange, red, and yellow organisms.

Looking over at her fellow divers, Sunny formed a heart with her fingers which she then moved toward her chest. The other divers immediately responded with exclamatory thumbs up — also acknowledging their love for the coral reef they were all now swimming through.

It was the height of Australian spring, 2015, and a joint ECO-Truth Climate-Biodiversity Team was exploring the exquisitely-unmatched beauty of the Great Barrier Reef — the world's largest natural structure. While they were now completely engrossed by the beauty all around them, they knew in the back of their minds that tomorrow's field work would have a completely different look and vibe.

Before their trip, the ECO-Truth field team reviewed everything they could find about Australia's Great Barrier Reef. They knew that many people — especially natural resource aficionados — consider it to be one of the 'seven wonders of the natural world'. Appropriately located in the Coral Sea and totaling some one thousand four hundred miles in length, the world's largest coral reef system encompasses a mosaic of two thousand nine hundred individual reefs and nine hundred islands. [3] The Earth's largest structure that is built entirely by billions of living organisms known as coral polyps; American astronauts often report that they can see it during their missions to outer space. But all this advance knowledge did not prepare anyone on the team for what they were about to see.

The next morning — as the ECO-Truth team motored out to the reef on an eight-passenger dive boat — the dive captain, Oceanographer

Chaim Guyiere, gathered everyone for a discussion. "Good day, folks, I think you all know what our plans are for today. Your experience will, unfortunately, be much different than yesterday's trip. We will be diving into a section of the reef that has been impacted by ocean warming and acidification; bleaching our precious coral structures and leaving them lifeless. The devastation that you are about to see is so thorough that it will take your breath away — especially compared to the bounteous beauty you enjoyed yesterday. OK, let's all hit the water and we can talk again afterward."

With that — using the traditional back flip method of exiting the boat — eight scuba divers entered the water in quick succession. After she submerged and swan down a few strokes, Sunny was aghast at what she saw. Her vividly colorful dream from yesterday had become a nightmare of destruction and death. Turning in all directions, she saw only bleached white coral spires supporting ghoulish gray masses of dead organisms.

After less than ten minutes of trying to find something, just anything, alive, Sunny couldn't take it anymore, and swam back up toward the surface. Emerging from the water, she was not surprised to find that all the other divers were also either back at the surface or already back in the boat. No one with any ounce of humanity could possibly stand to look at such a biological wasteland for very long.

After the divers had regathered, sitting along the boat's gunwales, Chaim Guyiere asked another question. "So, what did everyone think about today's swim — just remember, please don't shoot the messenger?"

"Ugh… it was just so much more horrible than I ever imagined," shot back ECO-Truth Marine Biologist Marianne Pruitt, holding her head in utter dismay. "Can you please give us some details about how on earth this has happened?"

"Of course, Marianne, here in a nutshell is what is going on," replied Chaim. "One-quarter of the CO_2 released by burning fossil fuels doesn't stay in our atmosphere — but instead goes into our oceans. When the excess CO_2 dissolves in saltwater, two important things happen. First, the pH of the water drops — making it more acidic. Then, the increasingly acidic seawater binds up carbonate ions, making them less available to organisms. This, in turn, causes the populations of many our most important sea-dwelling creatures — like corals, crabs, lobsters, clams, oysters, and sea urchins — to rapidly decline, since they don't have the carbonate ions they need, to build their skeletons and shells."

"OK, I get the basic idea", replied ECO-Truth Oceanographer Michael Morris, stroking his neatly trimmed beard, flecked with gray and white, "but why is this so devastating to our coral reef ecosystems?"

"As I'm sure you all know, oceanic coral reefs are the biotic equivalent of our land-based rainforests," explained Chaim. "They support an incredible biodiversity — providing shelter for everything in the oceanic food chain from larvae and zooplankton at the base to the alpha predators like the orca whales and great white sharks at the top. If the rate of coral loss exceeds the rate at which they can rebuild, then the coral reefs — which are also critical for the protection of coastlines across tropical and subtropical parts of the world — will disappear altogether. This, in turn, has staggering repercussions for closely associated coastal ecosystems like mangrove swamps and seagrass beds. Of course, the final and ultimate impact is on the millions of humans who depend on the oceans for their way of life and food supplies."

"Oh wow, that's sounds really terrible", lamented Sunny. "Exactly how much trouble are we in right now?"

"OK, since you've asked, there's really no delicate way to put this," Chaim replied, slowly shaking his head. "If we don't get control of the climate crisis before 2030, the entire Great Barrier Reef — as well as all of the other coral reefs on Earth — will be gone by the year 2050. I'm sorry to have to end your visit on such a sour note, but unfortunately, I'm afraid that's where things now stand."

As the dive boat motored the two hours back to Queensland, all of the ECO-Truthers just sat, staring out at the passing Pacific in stunned silence. A world without coral reefs was just too unthinkable for words.

A GUT-WRENCHING FILM

The 2017 Netflix documentary film, '*Chasing Coral*', presents all the sad details about the plight of Earth's coral reefs. This production is superbly done by Emmy-award winning filmmaker Jeff Orlowski. But — if you decide to watch it — make sure you're ready to have your heart broken, and also have a box of tissues handy. You will definitely need them, because the film is even more gut-wrenching than the documentary '*Chasing Ice*', which Orlowski also produced and directed.

Attending COP-21

While the ECO-Truth teams were diligently trying to expand the national coffers of climate crisis solvers and biodiversity loss preventers, Sunny and Shiloh were busily making plans to attend what they hoped would be the biggest event in the history of the climate crisis movement. The 21st Conference of the Parties (COP-21) on Climate Change was scheduled for November twenty-ninth through December eleventh, 2015, at the Le Bourget Conference Center in the suburbs north of Paris, France.

Upon their arrival in Paris, Sunny and Shiloh were relieved to see firsthand the profound resiliency of Parisians in overcoming and going about their typically enthusiastic lifestyles in the wake of the horrific terrorist attacks — which had occurred just over two weeks prior — leaving one hundred and thirty people dead and scores more injured. While there was certainly plenty of extra security around, anyone who had not been aware of what happened on that terrible night would have believed that the glorious 'City of Lights' was functioning as normal.

As the twins made their way through the conference's massive exhibit halls, they were pleased to find the that the overall mood was very upbeat — both exciting and spirit lifting. The booths from countries all over the world featured a wealth of information, as well as technology, hands-on demonstrations, colorful speakers, educational brochures, and bucketsful of give-away souvenirs.

A festival of international cuisine, music, and people wearing the clothing of their native countries swirled all around the fascinating array of exhibitor's booths. In almost all cases, the exhibitors were incredibly positive, clearly demonstrating their beliefs that by working together as one, we can solve the looming climate crisis before it passes 'the point of no return'.

Unfortunately, Sunny and Shiloh could not give the same glowing review about the results of the meeting of more than one hundred and ninety heads of state from around the world. While a significant milestone did occur when all of the parties in attendance, for the first time in the two-decade history of the COP process, signed an international treaty, called the 'Paris Accord'.

But in the minds of most activists, scientists, and attendees, the tenets of the 'Paris Accord' simply did not go nearly far enough to make a significant dent in solving the worldwide climate crisis. This was vividly driven home with a mass rally and march, led by many prominent climate crisis activists down the Champs-Elysees to the Arc de Triomphe that took place immediately after the agreement was signed on December twelfth.

During their long flight home, Sunny and Shiloh had plenty of time to discuss the results of COP-21. They both agreed that the conference's achievements simply didn't measure up to what was actually needed. For starters, the Paris Accord reaffirmed the goal of limiting global temperature increase to 'well below' two degrees centigrade. But — in the twins' opinion — this was the ultimate in 'waffle language'. The signatory countries were given unnecessary wiggle room that allowed them to get by with only doing the minimum necessary to officially 'abide by' the agreement.

Based on the findings being produced by their ECO-Truth teams, Sunny and Shiloh knew that the maximum worldwide temperature increase absolutely had be limited to less than two degrees centigrade. As verified by almost every climate scientist in the world, a greater than two degree centigrade global temperature increase would have dramatic short-term impacts on the livelihoods of millions of people living in coastal environments all over the world. Plus, over the long-term, this unacceptable temperature rise would severely affect the quality of all future generations of humans living on Earth.

On the next workday after they got home, Sunny and Shiloh called the ECO-Truth teams into the conference room and briefed them on their trip. Their message was short, succinct and to the point.

Although they were pleased by the enthusiasm and positivity demonstrated by the COP-21 attendees, they were completely mystified by the fact that the world's leaders could not agree on any substantive actions. While they were not privileged to the conference's actual proceedings, the twins could only surmise that — in general — no one was really taking the issue very seriously. They simply did not understand how such a lack of interest in the midst of such an ever-burgeoning existential crisis could really be happening.

Taking Stock of Their Heroes

Throughout most of 2016, ECO-Truth's Climate and Biodiversity Teams concentrated on reviewing their findings and updating events associated with their dual worldwide crises. Driven by their strong-willed team leaders Phil Nevin and Aubrey Shuster, the two groups decided to wrap up their research before the end of the year. Doing so would give them a few months to plan their agenda for the new federal administration that would be taking office on January twentieth, 2017.

To a person, the ECO-Truth staffers were certain that — on that soon-to-be heralded date — they would be celebrating the all-too-long-in-coming election of the first female president of the United States, Hillary Rodham Clinton. Little could they have imagined — at the time — how completely wrong they were going to be.

As the end of the year drew closer and closer, Sunny and Shiloh booked a conference room for September fifteenth, 2016, on the University of California at San Diego (UCSD) campus — three miles north of their offices in La Jolla. They wanted their crack teams of professional scientists to be able to meet together unfettered — without any outside distractions. The twins were most interested in what their proteges had found out about the current crop of power players in the climate crisis movement.

When the day of the ECO-Truth Climate Crisis Symposium arrived, Phil Nevin — serving as moderator — called on his team's co-leader, Evelyn Durnst, to start the discussion.

"Thank you so much, Phil," began Evelyn. "Now, I hope everyone is raring to get into this. Sorry to start things off on a maudlin note, but I think — no, I hope — that you all realize we're literally dealing with matters of life and death here — at least as far as the future livability of our planet goes.

"After a detailed review of who's doing what right now — especially when it comes to the climate crisis — one thing in particular really struck me," continued Evelyn. "The people who have been at this the longest — those who have dedicated their lives to finding solutions — seem to be burning out. And that's just such a shame."

Marine Biologist Sam Oswell agreed, "Yes, I'm afraid you're exactly right, Evelyn. Take former Vice President Al Gore — he's been trying to get the world to pay attention to climate change since 1976 when he was a freshman congressman. Way back then — more than four decades ago — he started proposing bills that would authorize taking federal action to stem the flow of Greenhouse Gases (GHG) into our atmosphere."

"Wow, I had no idea that Mr. Gore has been involved with the climate crisis for that long," marveled Evelyn.

"Yes, and since then, he's presented his amazing and eye-opening documentary — 'An Inconvenient Truth' — more than one thousand times — all over the world, mind you," added Meteorologist Spaulding Sykes, "and still it's like nobody is listening."

"I just don't know how people keep their noses to the grindstone in this situation," replied Sam Oswell, "but Mr. Gore keeps hanging in there. He's now traveling across the globe presenting his sequel to 'An Inconvenient Truth' — he's simply amazing!"

"All right, that was a great start," said Evelyn, giving a thumbs up to the group. "Now, who else has someone to discuss?"

Several other hands shot up immediately, and Evelyn called on GPS Coordinator, Branch Claybo in the back of the room.

Branch removed his horn-rimmed glasses and rubbed his chin stubble before speaking in his pronounced southern drawl. "Well, ya'll know that I've been doing a lot of reading lately about Bill McKibben. To me, he's the superman of climate crisis heroes because of all he's done during the past thirty years."

"How do you mean, Branch?" asked CADD Specialist Stella Carini. "I've certainly heard his name enough, but I'm just not that familiar with his work. Please enlighten me."

"Certainly, Stella, ah'm happy to," replied Branch, glib as always. "Right now, Bill is one of our foremost environmental activists as well as a best-selling author. In fact, he started writing books warning about climate change before anybody had even heard the words. His first book,

'*The End of Nature*' — published in 1989, was considered the first extensive documentation on the potential disastrous effects of global warming."

"Hmm… very interesting," replied Stella. "So, what else has Mr. McKibben done to lead the climate change movement?"

"Quite a bit, actually," responded Branch, "I believe it was 2007 when he started a nationwide environmental campaign that he called '*Step It Up*'. The organization's primary goal was convincing the U.S. Congress to take action on climate change. Under the '*Step It Up*' banner, McKibben organized hundreds of rallies in cities and towns all across the country."

"So, how did that work out for him?" queried Stella.

"Very well," elaborated Branch, "if I remember correctly, '*Step It Up*' used a battle cry that went something like, 'We must curb our carbon emissions by eighty percent by the Year 2050.' The *eighty percent by 2050* catch phrase spread like wildfire. Before long, the '*Step It Up*' campaign had the unified support of a wide variety of environmental, student, and religious organizations."

At this point, Phil Nevin interrupted Branch to ask, "What about '*350.org*'? Isn't that also McKibben's doing?"

"Why yes sir… yes, it is," replied Branch, gesturing toward Phil. "I was just leading into that. Bill essentially spun '*Step It Up*' into a new climate action campaign that he called '*350.org*'. He drew the name from the now famous warning by Dr. James Hansen — made more than thirty years ago — about atmospheric CO_2 readings in excess of 350 ppm being a world-wide danger zone. Let's see now, according to my notes, *350.org* — since it started — has coordinated some five thousand demonstrations in more than one hundred and eighty countries."

At this point, Shiloh chimed in. "You all remember what a thrill it was this past summer when a *350.org* rally came to San Diego — we all turned out in full force. Even actors Mark Ruffalo and Leonardo DiCaprio came down from Hollywood to lead the charge. But then afterwards, we all agreed that the lack of media attention was appalling. It was almost like nobody even cared about this existential crisis that was now enveloping our planet. It's no wonder that Mr. McKibben is so frustrated."

"You've got that right, boss," responded Branch, "I remember that — as we were marching on that day — there was a lot of discussion about all the great work Bill was doing. To a person, we realized that this man had devoted his life to securing the long-term health of our planet. But to what end? Mr. McKibben represents exactly why we must do everything we can to get the fight against the climate emergency off dead center and out into the mainstream of human thought and action!"

"Excellent analysis, Branch. I agree wholeheartedly," concluded Evelyn. "Now how about some female climate change heroes. I know there are several who are making some significant contributions right now."

Several hands went up and Evelyn selected Recreation Specialist, Jessica Wainwright, "I have a definite favorite in this category and her name is Naomi Klein. She's both smart as a whip and cool as a cucumber."

"Oh, yes," replied Evelyn. "I think we have all heard about Ms. Klein. Please tell us why you like her so much."

"Well, for starters," continued Jessica, "she's really great at thinking 'outside the box'. Her primary thesis is that we need to 'trash can' capitalism and come up with a new strategy that is more equitable to all Americans — especially our minority and indigenous populations. How many of you have read her best-selling book, 'This Changes Everything'?"

At least three quarters of the attendees raised their hands.

"Ah... good," smiled Jessica as she gazed around the room, "then you know that Ms. Klein wants us all to care less about economic output — on all levels — and more about each other and protecting our planet for future generations. She summarizes this belief as 'growing the caring economy and shrinking the careless one'. What a concept — right?"

"But I've heard a lot of people say Ms. Klein's viewpoints are too radical for where we are right now," remarked Economist Wallace Longmire. "Are we really ready to completely do away with our capitalistic society?"

"Yes, that's a very good point, Wallace," acknowledged Jessica, "but I think Ms. Klein is really just emphasizing that we need to initiate a major shift in out thought processes. We first have to completely eliminate the wrong-headed notion that humans have the right and duty to dominate nature in favor of the almighty dollar. We must accept the fact that we are just part of the natural world and — as such — are responsible for working to protect all of its components, instead of just human wealth."

"So how do these beliefs translate to the climate crisis?" asked Aubrey Shuster.

"Quite simply, Ms. Klein believes that a shift to renewable energy will make us understand our place in nature. As she emphasizes — while doing this, we should study how indigenous peoples built their cultures around respecting earth and working in harmony with its rhythms and cycles. Let me check my notes for her exact quote. Ah, yes… here it is. As Ms. Klein so succinctly summarizes it, 'If we continue to base our society on non-renewables, at some point we will fail to renew ourselves'. I think that really covers her philosophy — in a nutshell!"

"Extremely well put, Jessica. Ms. Klein is certainly one of our best thinkers — especially when it comes to living in harmony with nature," concluded Evelyn. "So, how about another female hero?"

Geophysicist Ariel Hantu — sitting near the back of the room — was the next to raise her hand. Evelyn was glad to see Ariel's hand up; she was normally very quiet and hesitant to participate in group activities like this.

"Hi, Evelyn," began Ariel carefully drawing out her words, "I really like what another woman — Harvard Professor Naomi Oreskes — has done for the concept of 'speaking truth to power'. I believe that her book, 'The Merchants of Doubt,' has provided the biggest boost for inspiring people to say, 'No — that's just not right, and you all should really be ashamed of yourself for lying that way.' I know her words have really helped me to take a stand and defend the science when it's called for."

"Oh, you're so right on — as usual, Ariel," complimented Evelyn. "What else can you tell us about Dr Oreskes?"

"Quite a bit, actually," smiled Ariel, "I just read Merchants this past weekend — for the third time! What most impresses me about Professor Oreskes is her courage in taking on the pseudo climate scientists who are making themselves rich by lying for money. As she points out in her book, the scientists who are now contradicting the findings of climate

547

experts are the same ones who — decades ago — lied for the tobacco companies that smoking was not harmful to our health and for the chemical companies that hydrofluorocarbons weren't making holes in our ozone layer."

"Oh really — I had not made those connections," chimed in Spaulding Sykes, "do you know for sure these are true?"

"Oh, yes, absolutely — they're all true and extremely well documented," countered Ariel. "As both a scientist and historian, Professor Oreskes has conducted an in-depth analysis of the role dissent has played in the scientific method. Her climate change studies — including more than one thousand peer-reviewed reports — led her to conclude that there was not a single valid rebuttal of the IPCC's reports that climate change is real, and that humans are causing it. I wrote down a quote she had about that. Let's see… here it is… 'My finding ignited a firestorm. I started getting hate mail. Suddenly, I was a hero to the left because I was supporting Al Gore and a demon to the right because I was now part of the conspiracy to bring down capitalism.'"

"Incredible — the pseudo-scientists' tactics actually amounted to a *fait accompli*," railed Climatologist Sven Jorgessen, wincing in agony, "for twenty-five years they have been hornswoggling us all with pig excrement!"

"Yes, I'm afraid that's true. Since before 1990 — this same group of doubt-mongering quacks has been getting rich off their various disinformation schemes," continued Ariel, "but thanks to Professor Oreskes their litany of lies was finally exposed in '*Merchants of Doubt*'. Once she discovered the truth, she didn't back down from calling them out for running organized and well-financed — but pseudo-professional campaigns — designed solely to create confusion and doubt."

"Now, that is quite a story indeed," lauded Evelyn, "thank you so much for telling us about it. I think many people — myself included — don't realize how much we owe to Professor Oreskes for risking her career — and actually her life — to expose the seamy underbelly of the scientific process!"

A smattering of applause mixed with a few huzzahs buzzed around the room as Evelyn turned her emceeing duties over to Phil.

Social Scientist Macy Hermage next took the microphone. "Hello everyone… there's one very important person that we haven't talked about yet. And that person is actually a whole group of people. Here's what I mean. So far, we've only talked about the cliched 'members of the choir'. What about all the people on the other side of the fence — the climate deniers, if you will. How do we reach out to them?"

"Yes, that's an extremely valid point, Macy," responded Phil, "how, in fact, do we get this done? Does anybody have any ideas?"

Anthropologist Angel Guadaluppa, sitting in the middle of the room, quickly raised his hand, "I think I have a good answer for this… and it's actually not that complicated. We need to approach people through their religious beliefs. Every mainstream religion has a mandate to care for creation. I believe that tying the climate crisis to this reverence for stewardship will win us many converts."

"Ah, nicely put, Angel," replied Phil. "Who can talk about someone who is doing this?"

Hands immediately started waving throughout the room.

Smiling broadly at the response, Phil paused to enjoy the show of support then selected, Community Organizer, Jaimie Henderson. "Oh wow, this is such a key issue — reaching out to the other side. I don't know anyone who is doing it better right now than Episcopal Reverend Sally Bingham, and she's based right here in California. Back in 1998, Reverend Bingham founded her Interfaith Power & Light (IPL) Campaign in San Francisco. Her mission was to show the world that the faith community in the United States is fully committed to cutting emissions and creating jobs — while saving money at the same time."

"Oh, yes, I'm familiar with Reverend Bingham," remarked Stella Carini, "but you know, when I first heard about IPL, I thought it was some new type of power company!"

Pointing at Stella and smiling, Jaimie continued, "Actually, my good friend, in some ways it is. You see the people who join IPL are, of course, staunchly faith-based. But thanks to the good reverend's teachings, they are also just as adamant about being powerful caretakers of God's creation. This means that they care deeply about solving both our climate and our biodiversity crises. Today, IPL has affiliates in forty states with a total of eighteen thousand congregations. Now, that's what I call making a difference!"

"Amazing Jaimie — you're so right," exhorted Phil, "If we could all pull off something even close to what Reverend Bingham has done, just imagine where we would be. It's certainly great to know about her for inspiration. Now — how about someone else — anything similar to Jaimie's story?"

"Yes, I've got something that I think is just as uplifting as what reverend Bingham is doing," offered Journalist Annisette Rochambeau. "And it involves pulling support from an even more extreme source — the evangelical church."

"OK, that sounds really interesting, Annisette," remarked Phil, "let's hear what you've got."

"I just read about this — let me see if I can remember correctly," began Annissette. "There's a Professor of Atmospheric Science down in Texas. I believe that she's at Texas A & M… or maybe it's Texas Tech. Yes, it's actually Texas Tech and her name is Katherine Hayhoe. Now, here's the really interesting part. Professor Hayhoe is also a devout Evangelical Christian. In fact, her husband is the rector of the church she attends."

"All right, I get your intrigue here," rejoined Phil, "we have a person who is both a science-based climate professional and what would normally be an adamant climate denier. So, how's that working out?"

"Well, I'm delighted to tell all of you that everything is working out terrifically," replied Annissette, "I know for a fact that Professor Hayhoe is actually a model climate activist. I've heard her speak a few times — both in person and on television. Her message is clear, concise, and unwavering. She's a staunch supporter of the science behind human-caused climate change and the immediate need for the world to do something about it."

"All right — you go, girl," exclaimed Oceanographer Sylvia Pucelli, speaking from the front row. "That's absolutely the up-front way we have to get our message across to the other side. And it sounds like Professor Hayhoe is the perfect person to do this."

"Yes, she absolutely is," continued Annissette. "In fact, her book entitled, 'A Climate for Change: Global Warming Facts for Faith-Based Decisions', has been praised by religious leaders as well as fact-based scientists and environmental activists. She even goes so far as to say that we need to put a price on carbon that will make it prohibitively expensive to burn fossil fuels."

The last part of Annissette's commentary drew a hearty round of supporting applause from the assembled ECO-Truthers, prompting Phil to respond. "All righty then — score one for the good guys! So, let's keep it rolling — what else to we have in this vein?"

"How about the penultimate, Phil?" shouted Geologist Adam Henfrotto from the front of the room.

"OK, Adam, I'll bite," replied Phil cautiously, knowing Adam's well-earned reputation as a prankster. "What have you got?"

"Oh — I dunno whether it's actually that good," smirked Adam, "it's just about The Pope!"

After the roll of laughter died down, Phil stared right at Adam, "All right, I know I'm probably going to regret saying this, but let's hear it. Just remember — if it's a joke — you have to keep it clean, we're recording!"

"Oh, no, I'd never kid around when it comes to something like this," chided Adam. "Just think about it. When it comes to religious authorities on Earth, it's difficult to go beyond the Pontiff of the Roman Catholic Church. How many practicing Catholics do we have — at least a billion worldwide, right? That's more people than any country in the world, except for India and China!"

"Yeah... so a significant percentage of the world's population is Catholic. But what does that have to do with our climate crisis?" asked Organic Chemist Simon Principis.

"Come on, buddy, you're forgetting the environmental encyclical that Pope Francis delivered in 2015," chortled Adam, displaying his ability to charm even while chastising. "Remember, he really beat us all up — figuratively speaking at least. He said the climate crisis was the result of apathy, the reckless pursuit of profits, excessive faith in technology, and political shortsightedness. He also told us that the people we are most harming are the world's most vulnerable and poorest. And that, for the most part, these folks didn't have anything to do with causing the problem in the first place. That's a multiple major ouch — right?"

"Yes, that's pretty brutally candid language, Adam," replied Simon, "but how do we know the Pope's remarks will really make a difference?"

"Listen, man," rejoined Adam, "I'm an Italian Catholic and — while I may not go to mass as often as I should — believe you me, when The Pope speaks, I listen!"

"Point well taken, Adam," concluded Phil. "I think we can all agree that having The Pope take a personal stand on the climate crisis gets a lot of attention world-wide. In fact, we need to figure out how to do a lot more reaching out to the multitudes like that!"

"With the conference drawing to a close," Phil walked up to the podium again. "If I may, I'd like to talk about one final climate change hero who is living and working right here in California. He's Stanford Professor Mark Jacobson, and the interactive model he invented called 'The Solutions Project' (TSP) may very well be the biggest breakthrough in the history of climate change. How many of you have heard about TSP?"

Phil was ecstatic when he saw every hand in the room go up.

"That's just fantastic," continued Phil, "although I'm hardly surprised that you all know about this. I'd be more surprised if you didn't."

"Yes, it's difficult to imagine that anyone who is paying attention doesn't know about TSP," interjected Aubrey Shuster. "Even those of us on the biodiversity side of the fence. But please, go on, Phil."

"OK, thanks for that positive feedback, Aubrey. Let me see now," continued Phil, referring to his notes, "in 2011, Professor Jacobson — along with banker Marco Krapels, filmmaker Josh Fox, and actor Mark Ruffalo — founded TSP as a nonprofit organization. Their mission was to help guide the world toward one hundred percent renewable energy. And they defined renewable energy as wind power, water (hydroelectric, wave/tidal, and geothermal) power, and solar power — conveniently abbreviated as WWS."

"So, how has TSP performed so far?" asked Wildlife Ecologist, Murphy Dequito-Dunn, seated in the middle of the room.

"Actually, quite well," proclaimed Phil again looking at his notes. "Professor Jacobson has proven that the switch to renewables is already economically and technologically viable. In the process, he has debunked the dual myths that we lack sufficient storage capacity to provide sustained reliable energy, and that fossil fuels are cheaper than renewable energy sources. As a result, TSP now provides a plan that would convert all fifty states to one hundred percent renewables by 2050. Their studies also confirm that an interim eighty to eighty-five percent conversion rate by 2030 is entirely possible and achievable."

"Wow — that's incredible, Phil," exclaimed GIS Specialist Ernesto 'Bear' Bellagio — his three-hundred-and-fifty-pound bulk rocking the room as he burst up from his seat. "This is exactly what we need — where can we find this information?"

"Take it easy there, partner," chuckled Phil, fully understanding Bear's ebullient nature, "remember we're only renting this room — we don't want to have to pay for its restoration."

After the laughter died down, Phil continued, "Bear's question is actually quite good. Now that the research is finished, the true value of TSP's work is in widespread information dissemination. In their '50 States — 50 Plans Initiative', TSP has created detailed infographics for each state in the United States and for many other countries as well. Each set of information summarizes the theoretically best renewable energy combinations. TSP's website provides an interactive map that allows users to manipulate this information to clearly demonstrate each state's and each nation's individual plans."

Glancing at his watch, Phil noticed that is was almost six, and realized it was time to end the conference, "Hey, folks, it's getting late. I know you all feel like I do. We could easily sit here talking about this stuff all night — it's just that important. But let's save the rest for another day. It's time for us all to grab some grub, hit the sack, and come up fresh tomorrow morning to go back at it again. Thanks to you all for your rapt attention and enthusiastic participation. Now, good night and travel safely."

The next day, the conference's summary memo concluded with this statement: "Through all of the research study results — involving detailed reviews and assessments of well over one thousand documents — compiled by the ECO-Truth Climate Team, one finding stands on a pinnacle above all the rest. For all future ECO-Truth presentations on the climate crisis, the findings of 'The Solutions Project' (www.thesolutionsproject.org) should always be prominently emphasized."

The week after the symposium, the ECO-Truth Climate Team got busy and finalized their Climate Crisis Guidebook (CCG). They included all the information they had gathered — conducting field trips and interviews — over the past seven years. When they finished, both Sunny and Shiloh praised their CCG as an environmental protection 'bible' and a literary 'work of art'. Unfortunately — per the usual response — no one in the 'outside world' seemed to care.

The CCG was essentially ignored, even though, at only ten dollars a copy, the ECO-Truth staffers were practically giving the document away. While this lack of success with sales of the CCG cast a temporary pall over the ECO-Truth Climate Team, it just made Sunny and Shiloh even more resolute that they were going to somehow, someway, finally make the world wake up and pay attention.

And boy, did they ever do exactly that!

BOOK TWENTY-ONE
Countering Environmental Backlash

Forming RAP — Speaking Truth to Power

With the unbelievably unexpected election of Donald J. Trump on November third, 2016, Shiloh Childers-Knoski and Sunny Childers-Nevin both knew that their aggressive environmental agenda was in big trouble. From the time Trump took office, it was clear that his administration would be the antithesis of environmental support and concern — meaning that there would be none of either. Because of this, the twins needed to come up with a radical new strategy for countering Trump's tactics during the next four years.

As soon as the election results were certified as official, Shiloh and Sunny announced that they were forming a new non-profit organization, called the Resist and Persist Foundation — or 'RAP' for short — to counter Trump's anti-conservation agenda. They also told their staff that, since RAP was going to be a subsidiary of ECO-Truth, they could all expect to be routinely assigned to RAP's activities.

At first, RAP's primary goal was correcting the environmental and conservation lies and half-truths that were constantly coming out of Trump's White House. To accomplish this, the twins opened an office on North Capitol Street in Washington, DC. They also purchased a three-bedroom apartment a few blocks away, so that their RAP'ers could maintain a permanent presence — functioning as powerful Congressional lobbyists.

Once everything was set up, the Capitol Hill RAP'ers spent most of their DC time in the hallways and offices of Congress — aggressively pushing for the advancement of their dual campaigns against the climate crisis and biodiversity loss. In an effort to help ensure that Trump would not win a second term, the RAP contingent also kept track of all the untruths he told.

During Trump's first year in office, the RAP'ers tallied a total of more than one thousand outright lies. Sadly, Trump had no compunction about the damage his ever-burgeoning discourse of deceit was inflicting on the natural world — especially on both the climate crisis and biodiversity loss. As the RAP'ers kept telling every Senator and Congressman they could corner, our Nation's 'reality show president' was actually incapable of telling the truth.

The RAP Forum Hits the Mark

Less than two years after its beginning, the RAP team of crafty and creative scientists had cajoled a significant backlash against the Trump administration's attacks on our Nation's diligently crafted bulwark of environmental laws and regulations. Buoyed by this success, Sunny and Shiloh decided that the time was right to hold a national forum, emphasizing solutions to the dual global threats posed by the climate crisis and biodiversity loss.

Eschewing any concerns about expense, Sunny and Shiloh went 'all in' on producing a precedent-setting event. First, they booked the one thousand-seat Andrew Mellon Auditorium in downtown Washington for the second Saturday in September 2019. Then, they sent hand-written invitations to premiere scientists from all over the U.S. — many of whom had international reputations for their work in the climate and biodiversity arenas. The twins believed that few of these astute minds would turn down the opportunity to be a part of such a long overdue nationwide forum.

The overwhelming response they received proved Sunny and Shiloh were right beyond their wildest dreams. By July first, 2019, the ECO-Truth/RAP Event Team had registered fifty of the country's foremost scientists — representing thirty-two states. Plus, the forum was completely sold out, with two hundred and fifty more people on a waiting list.

On September fifteenth, 2019 — as her proud parents, Abbey and Horace Childers, watched from their seats in the first row of the Mellon Auditorium — Shiloh began the ECO-Truth/RAP National Forum by heartily greeting everyone in attendance. She then got the proceedings underway: "I think we are all here for the same purpose. How can we successfully solve the two greatest environmental threats that we have ever faced — the climate emergency and biodiversity loss?" After posing this question, Shiloh smiled confidently as she watched hundreds of arms shoot up all at once.

The first person Shiloh recognized, was Dr. Richard Larcher, a wildlife researcher at the Pacific Northwest Office of the Environmental Protection Agency in Portland, Oregon. Stretching his lanky frame as he stood to his full six-foot-four height, Dr. Larcher offered this, "Let me start these proceedings off by saying that I think it is high time to mobilize the silent majority of independent thinkers in this country. We need to break down the wall of lies and innuendo that is blockading us from reality. My fellow scientists… it is now time for us to speak truth to power!" The booming round of applause that followed Dr Larcher's opening remark let Shiloh and Sunny immediately know that they had really hit the mark with this event.

The next commenter — Professor William Hale of Hollins College in Roanoke, Virginia — continued the plea for bringing the Nation back to a well-grounded reality. "We must bring scientific facts — not guesswork — back to the forefront of everything we are doing. Only by following the science will we be able to solve both our climate emergency and biodiversity loss conundrums within the short time frame we now have left. We can't wait around folks; we must get this done — and we must do it right away!" A wave of applause again flowed across the audience.

"OK, everyone, we hear you loud and clear," said Sunny, now holding her microphone in the center of the audience. "I think we're all on the same page. But how about some specific solutions. As consultants and lobbyists, we're here to learn from you folks. Please tell us what our RAP Team can do — right now — to lead the national charge for change. Let's start with the Climate Crisis."

For the next three hours, the audience tossed the climate crisis around like a beach ball at a Boston Red Sox game. Problems here. Solutions there. Questions all around about whether anything can really work within the next ten years. Shiloh and Sunny entertained all sorts of ideas about expeditious and judicious climate solutions. But — oddly enough — the single comment that best summarized the overall discussion came from a most unexpected source.

Dressed in flowing colors from head to toe, the speaker introduced herself. "Hola mis amigos, my name is Emilia Estrada and I'm from

Cusco — an ancient city located high in the Andes Mountains of southeastern Peru. My first cousin — I can't tell you his name — is... how you call it... a petroleum explorer, who works for a big oil company and lives in southwest Texas. He has asked me to come here today to read this statement for him for two reasons. First, his English is not so good, and second, he wants to keep his job and not get — you know — deported."

A murmur of knowing chatter rippled around the room.

Pausing to compose herself, Emilia continued, "You see — my cousin — he has a very good-paying job. For the past five years, he has been finding places — mostly out in the open countryside — for his company to drill... I believe they call them... fracking wells. The more he does this work, the more he knows it is a ridiculous idea. The ugly wells are now all over everywhere where he lives. The land is being ruined. The wild animals are dying. The drinking wells of his neighbors are being poisoned. And all of the fossil gas that is produced is put into a pipeline. Then it all goes to El Paso where it is loaded onto ships and sent to other countries. It is not even being used in your own country.

"My cousin — he knows why this is happening," continued Emilia, now red-faced and wiping her brow with a tissue, "it is because his oil company is just plain greedy. They don't care about helping people in this country. They just want to see how much money they can make.

"But — of course — my cousin can't do anything himself to stop this. He needs to make a living, support his family, and stay in this country. So, he's asking all of you to stop it for him. He wants you to do whatever it takes to get rid of Big Oil. Make them switch to building windmills and solar fields — not oil rigs and fracking roads. This will make many new jobs all around your country. And, as my cousin says, it will be like scoring a football goal for everyone — including me!"

"Oooh, that's very well said," replied Sunny — taking back the microphone. "Thank you both so much — Emilia, and your cousin, wherever he is. Let me assure you that transitioning away from fossil fuels and into renewables is at the very top of our list. We believe we have some excellent ways to get this done. Right now, they're in our back pockets, but don't be surprised if you soon see some very big changes in how we run this country. Your comments today have added to our confidence that these changes will be most welcomed — not just in the United States, but across the globe."

The discussion in the auditorium next turned to biodiversity loss. Speaker Walter Radcliffe — the National Audubon Society's Chief Biologist — provided the perfect summary when he strode up to the on-stage podium. Playing his role to the hilt, Walter was all decked out in a tweed hat, plaid vest, and cargo pants with a pair of Swarovski binoculars hanging from his neck and a Sibley Bird Guide tucked into his breast pocket. "Hi there, everyone. As you might have guessed, I'm a pretty serious birder — not a birdwatcher, mind you. And I'm here to tell you that what we're all doing to our planet is making me very unhappy.

"At the Audubon Society,' continued Walter, "our studies are showing that human activity now threatens the very existence of more than half of North America's bird species. That includes a total of more than three billion — yes that's with a 'b' — birds! If we don't start fixing this right away — before we know it — we may be living in a world without any birdsong. Now isn't that a scary thought? So, here's what we need to do. We have to start protecting all of our wild species — not just birds — that are in any sort of jeopardy. This means not only taking care of the animals themselves, but also identifying and preserving the living spaces — the key habitats, if you will — they need to survive."

As soon as he had finished talking, Shiloh walked up beside Walter at the podium. "Thank you so much, you have just perfectly described how our RAP Team is addressing the biodiversity loss issue. And I absolutely love the way you staged your presentation. Only you could have pulled this off so successfully!"

The forum next turned their attention to ways to improve the U.S. agricultural industry which has been shown to be our single biggest generator of climate-harming greenhouse gases. After another two hours of back-and-forth discussion, Shiloh invited Cordelia Angusthum — Assistant Director of the Rodale Institute of Emmaus, Pennsylvania — on stage for a summary.

As she walked up to the podium, Cordelia's polished features and impeccable dress belied her history as a career hands-on, down-in-the dirt agronomist. "For those of you who know me best, you realize that I much prefer to be — like the world's best farmers — always outstanding in my field." Cordelia paused to let those who caught her pun enjoy the moment, then continued. "In all seriousness, folks, we have to reverse this trend of letting mega-scale, agri-businesses take over our farming industry. We must remember our roots. Just like the railroads were our Nation's backbone, small farms and ranches were our historic life blood. They paved the way for our coast-to-coast human spread and settlement. They formed the original economic basis for our society. And now, we are just standing by — watching them get swallowed up by commercial conglomerates that have no concerns beyond their own profit margins."

Cordelia stepped back from the podium and gazed around the room. She could tell that her 'tough love' speech was resonating with most of the conference attendees.

Deftly moving back to the microphone, Cordelia asked, "So what do we need to do about this? Well, we first need to change course and go back to our old ways of doing things. We need to do whatever it takes to break-up the conglomerates and then also subsidize small farmers so that they can stay in business.

"Next, we need to convince everyone who is farming that Regenerative Agriculture — or 'RA' — is the way of the future," continued Cordelia. "We must get the majority of farmers in this country to stop tilling their soil, quit using synthetic pesticides, and let free-range domestic animals be the primary source of crop fertilization. Going back to these 'old school' practices will simultaneously preserve topsoil fertility, biological diversity, and carbon sequestration, while minimizing the potential for soil erosion caused by both wind and water. In other words, making the transition to RA will be a huge benefit in helping us all harness the climate crisis."

With that, Cordelia again stepped away from the podium, allowing Shiloh back to the microphone. "Wow, Cordelia, I don't know how anyone could have said it better than you just did. Thank you so much for that. And — for those of you who are wondering — our ECO-Truth/RAP teams are also working on a legislative plank that pretty much addresses everything Ms. Angusthum just described. So, everyone, please stay tuned."

Looking back into the audience, Shiloh pointed at Sunny who was holding the microphone near the back of the auditorium. "All right, folks

563

— we're almost ready to put a wrap on these proceedings. Does anyone have anything else they want to add?"

Recognizing someone in the back row, Sunny passed along her microphone. "Thanks for allowing me the last word here today, Sunny," said a jovial looking fellow, wearing a blue blazer topped off by a stylish fedora. "My name is Henry Herndon and I'm a Public Policy Specialist located in the America's heartland town of Kearney, Nebraska. Fitting with my background and expertise, I want to emphasize the old adage that 'all politics is local'. Our mission to solve the climate crisis must start at the local grassroots level and then build into a mighty groundswell that spreads across states, regions, and finally the nation. But we must begin now. According to everyone in the know, we have just ten years left to get this right!"

"Yes, yes, yes," repeated Sunny, "I could not agree with you more, sir."

Taking back the microphone from the stage, Shiloh concluded the conference. "Thank you all so much for coming today. Please stay safe. And — let me assure you all — we will stay in touch as we work toward all the solutions we talked about today."

Taking The Message to the People

With the conclusion of their first forum, Sunny and Shiloh knew that the seeds of ECO-Truth/RAP's grassroots movement had been sown on very fertile ground. During the next few months, the twins organized local RAP chapters throughout southern California and the DC Metro Area.

They emphasized their mobilization efforts on the young — ages forty-five or less. This was not because they were prejudiced against older citizens, but because they knew that serious climate crisis and biodiversity loss progress would only occur when the fears of the young have overwhelmed the rationalizations of the old.

Either Shiloh or Sunny were featured speakers at each of RAP's succeeding monthly rallies, occurring in both San Diego and Washington, DC. The majority of these RAP rallies targeted the offices of federal legislators — both Republican and Democratic — Senators and Congressmen. Their RAP memberships fully understood that successfully dealing with the climate emergency required a melding of massive, ground-up grassroots support with strong, top-down federal leadership.

Since the climate crisis embers were now brightly glowing just below America's political surface, the RAP Movement soon ignited a furious fire throughout the Nation. By the end of January 2020, monthly chapter meetings and rallies were taking place in every state. Thanks to the diligence of Shiloh and Sunny, the climate and biodiversity crises were now headline news on every journalistic and social media platform in the country.

Shiloh and Sunny realized that this wildfire of public awareness they had sparked was a very important step — but just the first step. They knew that they next had to pull together a powerful political machine — featuring both Democrats and also as many Republicans as they could muster. In other words, they wanted to carve the ECO-Truth/RAP message about combating both the climate emergency and biodiversity loss into two permanent planks in both the Democratic and the Republican Party Platforms.

All of ECO-Truth/RAP's presentations were specifically tailored to get their messages across to organizations who weren't already 'members of the choir'. The staffers wanted to reach as many climate deniers and 'fence-sitting' folks as they could. This meant they were primarily pitching their programs to organizations filled with conservative Republicans — including Kiwanis Clubs, Rotary Clubs, Chambers of Commerce, Development Boards, Planning Districts, and evangelical churches.

The ECO-Truth/RAP staff's other primary target involved organizations who didn't have either the personal desire or financial wherewithal to worry about the climate crisis or biodiversity loss. These latter groups mainly consisted of socially and financially disenfranchised people who were being hit hardest by these issues — despite having minimal responsibility for their creation. Based on their past experience, the ECO-Truth/RAP teams knew that the best way to reach these folks was through local citizens' organizations and civic groups which typically held their monthly meetings in urban churches, community centers, and other places with strong ties to disadvantaged minorities.

BOOK TWENTY-TWO
But Something Else Is Needed

The Twins Take a Stand

On the glorious November 2020 morning after the election of President Joe Biden and Vice President Kamala Harris, Shiloh Childers-Nkosi sauntered into Sunny Childers-Nevin's office, closed the door, and sat down so forcefully that she spilled some of her caramel latte onto the office's white shag carpet.

"Hey there, careful with the expensive threads," warned Sunny in mock anger. "What the heck's wrong with you, anyway?"

"Oh, sorry," said Shiloh, daubing drops of coffee off the chair cushion. "You know I think our staff does an absolutely amazing job. During the extremely troublesome past four years, they've covered all the bases we asked them to — and then some!"

"Yeah, OK, I definitely agree," replied Sunny, "so — if that's the case — exactly what is your problem?"

"You know we're still missing something here," remarked Shiloh, "and, unfortunately, it's not just us — I think it's the whole world."

"Hmm — very interesting attitude, Shi, my dear," chided Sunny, "so tell me more."

"OK, you asked for it," Shiloh responded, shifting to the edge of her chair. "I'm just sick and tired of — what seems like every day — hearing about some new fossil fuel disaster and knowing that no one anywhere is seriously doing anything about it."

"Yeah, I certainly get your point, Sis," replied Sunny, pointing her Sharpie at Shiloh. "I dug up some information yesterday. I believe it was from the Yale Climate Center. Their surveys found that only eleven media sources in the U.S. mentioned climate change at all last year. And — what's worse — less than 50% of the people in our country believe that the climate crisis is real. That's even though scientists like us have been banging our heads against the wall — trying to get people to pay attention for almost twenty years now."

"Yes, that's exactly my point, Sun!" Shiloh exclaimed angrily.

"Remember the movie, '*Network*' — well, I'm now mad as hell and I'm just not going to take it anymore!"

"OK, now you've got me all fired up too," yelled Sunny, thrusting her fist in the air, "let's start fixing things right now. With the new administration, the front door is suddenly wide open!

"I hear that, Sis," replied Shiloh, flashing the OK sign, "and — while I know you're going to think this is just plain crazy talk — I now know exactly what we have to do!"

"Uh oh, you know I never like it when you preface something that way," cautioned Sunny, switching her hand to a flat and level slow down motion. "OK — let's hear it, but please be gentle."

"I'm afraid there's no gentle way to put this," Shiloh retorted, "we just have to take down Big Oil!"

"Ah, what a relief — so it's as simple as that," mocked Sunny wiping her furrowed brow. "And you're wrong — I don't think this is crazy. I actually now know that you have completely lost all your marbles!"

"No… no, Sis — my plan is actually quite solid. Just hear me out," pleaded Shiloh.

"OK, go — but is it all right if I walk out as soon as I think you've reached the edge of the cliff?" queried Sunny. "I really hate to witness self-assisted suicide!"

"Gee — thanks for your whole-hearted support here." retorted Shiloh. "Listen, many powerful people believe — with good reason — that the fossil fuel industry is on its last legs and may be completely gone in as little as five years."

"Yeah, I've also heard that's the case," replied Sunny, "but exactly how does getting rid of the elephant in the room solve the climate crisis?"

"There you go, Sun, right on top of things — as usual," chuckled Shiloh flashing a wry smile at her twin.

"OK, I'll bite — what am I on top of?" bristled Sunny, now starting to lose her patience.

"Now I can see you want some answers — so I'll get right to my main point," replied Shiloh. "While Big Oil may be on the way out, the corporate giants — the money people — that run these things aren't going away. Just remember that, when push comes to shove, these are still 'energy companies'. They're way too savvy to just give up, fold their tents, and walk off into the sunset."

"All right, so what are they going to do?" responded Sunny, "Where in the world are you going with this?"

"So here's the thing," explained Shiloh, "these deep pocket mega-companies have seen the handwriting on the wall for quite some time — some, like Exxon-Mobil, for more than thirty years. They've known all along, that dead dinosaurs can't run the planet forever. They realized that a shift away from fossil fuels was going to come at some point. And — right now — they know it's just a matter of how and when it happens."

"Yes… yes," enjoined Sunny, now picking up on her twin's train of thought, "please continue!"

"Because they knew what was coming, the energy giants are already prepared to pivot away from oil and gas production and move — big time — into renewable sources," explained Shiloh. "They just aren't going to make this transition until they are forced to."

"Aha, I get it now," replied Sunny, the light bulb clearly going off in her head. "All we have to do is convince these fossil fuel conglomerates that the time for converting to renewables is ASAP."

"Correctamundo, Sis," exclaimed Shiloh — again fist-pumping the air. "If we can get this done, the retooled energy industry will provide all the financial and people-power resources we need to lead our charge into the *Renewables Revolution* — the next phase in human occupation of Planet Earth!"

"Easy there, Sis — don't have a coronary," replied Sunny. "So, how do we start — are we going to run for office or something?"

"Wow, there it is again — that twin thing," exclaimed Shiloh. "As a matter of fact, that's exactly what we're going to do. And with Mom and Dad's help added to our superior scientific staff, we'll have all the expertise, financial support, and political clout we need to make this happen… I can't wait to get started!"

With that, Shiloh hit the intercom switch and told all the ECO-Truth/RAP staffers to meet in the office conference room in fifteen minutes.

Acquiring Political Clout

Once everyone was comfortably settled in the conference room, Shiloh strode to the microphone and started speaking. "Now you all know that — most times — I don't need this thing. My voice carries just fine, thank you. But today, I want to make sure everyone hears me loud and clear. While it's not my intent to further berate the fossil fuel industry and the U.S. government, I believe it's our professional duty to emphasize that coal, oil, and natural gas extraction and production have always been — and will always continue to be — among the world's most dangerous activities. Every minute of every day, fossil fuel workers are handling volatile materials that could blow up in their faces. From coalmine explosions in the Appalachian Mountains, to oil spills on the California Coast, train wrecks in the Canadian outback, and tap water infernos in Pennsylvania, another fossil fuel disaster is always just an errant spark away from happening."

"In my opinion," continued Shiloh, "effective solutions to climate change and biodiversity loss can result in only one way. From now on, our path forward must be based on positive, proactive progress. Achieving this will require de-emphasis of social and political infighting so that we can all pull together toward achieving one set of common goals. Our national leaders must all come together in agreement and work as a team to accomplish results that will provide long-term solutions and benefits for our planet."

"The two major environmental crises — global warming and biodiversity loss — currently facing Earth's human population may seem overwhelming to many people. This sense of impending, irresolvable doom breeds, in turn, hopelessness and indifference. The prevailing attitude can be summarized as 'Why bother doing anything when it won't make any difference anyway?'

"But we must rid ourselves of this current shroud of hopelessness and plant national seeds of hopefulness. This will give us the energy and motivation we need to create the massive groundswells of public support that we must have to force our national leaders to take immediate, tough actions and find realistic solutions before it's too late."

"These actions must include mandating widespread conversions to renewable energy sources, stopping approvals of new fossil-fuel extractions, imposing heavy fees on existing fossil-fuel generators, and passing new laws and regulations that provide nationwide protection for our most vulnerable wildlife species as well as their habitats and migratory pathways."

"In conclusion, I firmly believe that the time is ripe for solutions to both the climate and biodiversity-loss crises. These solutions must be precipitated by the hopeful and forceful voices of the masses. We must speak together as one to express our desire to make a difference for all future generations."

With a gentle sweep of her outstretched arm, Shiloh pointed at the room full of her trusted employees and concluded her impassioned remarks, "This is why that — today — I'm asking all of you to lead the charge in electing Sunny and me to the halls of Congress in Washington, DC. Please mark November fourth, 2020, on your calendars as the day we decided to change the world.

"During the next two years, we are all going to have two primary jobs. For you folks on the Climate Team, I will be your candidate for California's Junior Senator while the Biodiversity Team will be supporting candidate Sunny for the US House from California's fifty-second District. So… my friends and fellow superheroes… what do you think?"

For a full thirty seconds, the entire room was so quiet you could hear a pin drop. Then everyone rose in unison, bursting into raucous applause as they stood. Soon the applause turned to vigorous chants of… 'Shiloh, Shiloh, Shiloh'… and… 'Sunny, Sunny, Sunny'.

After about two minutes, Shiloh held up her hand — asking for quiet — and said, "Well I think you are all obviously on board, so let's get after it." More chants of 'Shiloh' and 'Sunny' stayed with the ECO-Truth/RAP staffers as they filed out of the conference room and back to their offices.

From the day they started, the political campaigns of Shiloh and Sunny worked like a charm. Operating through their now well-established nationwide networks of ECO-Truth and RAP Foundation offices, the twins built political powerhouses in an amazingly short period of time.

Owing in large part to the diligent, dedicated work of their ECO-Truth and RAP staffs, both the climate emergency and biodiversity loss crises were now 'front burner' political issues. This allowed Shiloh and Sunny to feature their nationwide reputations in these two arenas as the primary planks in their campaigns for the House and the Senate. This — coupled with the generous financial and political support from their super successful parents — meant that both twins easily won their respective seats on Capitol Hill during the 2022 mid-term elections. Then on January twentieth, 2023, Shiloh and Sunny were officially sworn in as federal legislators working on Capitol Hill in Washington, DC.

Each of the twin's rapid ascents into the world of politics was enhanced by the progressive governing that was now spreading throughout Capitol Hill. This welcome freshet of change was like a roiling mountain rivulet, cascading down a scree slope during the first warm week of spring. Just the very presence of new esteemed and respected leaders was doing wonders for restoring the positive spirit and humble honesty of Washington, DC.

Though Shiloh and Sunny were still relatively young, they were both quite astute about how DC worked. Their education curricula placed a strong emphasis on reality training. Plus, they had been very well coached by their parents on the whims and nuances of the federal legislative process.

Both twins knew that getting things done on Capitol Hill placed a premium on the 'three p's — presence, persistence, and perseverance'. This was especially important when it came to the pervasive issues of climate change and biodiversity loss.

In order to accomplish their goals, the twins also knew they had to constantly speak 'truth to power' on Capitol Hill. Their Congressional staffs were regularly putting in seventy-hour work weeks — helping them in preparing essential climate emergency and biodiversity loss bills for legislative review in both chambers.

When the 2023 legislative session began in earnest, Sunny and Shiloh both knew that they had done absolutely everything they could.

They fully believed that — owing to the supreme dedication and work ethic of their staffs coupled with the liberal shifts in the Nation's electorate — the time was ripe for passing legislation that would solve both of our Nation's existential environmental crises.

But never in their wildest dreams could they have imagined how right they were about to be!

Building a Powerful Legislative Mandate

As the 2023 legislative session progressed, Representative Sunny Childers-Nevin and Senator Shiloh Childers-Nkosi — demonstrating loyalty to their 2022 campaign promises — successfully promulgated and then quickly pushed through three pieces of landmark environmental legislation that would be forever cast in bronze in the annals of U.S. environmental movement. Specifically structured to end Big Oil's dominance, the most auspicious of their legislative efforts was HR 7667; the *2023 Climate Crisis Resolution and Recovery Act.*

The first challenge to passage of their so-called '*Climate Crisis Act (CCA)*' was convincing their Capitol Hill colleagues to end all subsidies for the fossil fuel industry and then transfer these monies to support the burgeoning renewable energy sector. But this turned out to be a relatively easy sell, given the widespread speculation — including everyone from the Wall Street Journal to the British Financial Times and the National Audubon Society — that the fossil fuel giants were the last hangers-on in a rapidly vanishing industry.

The next step was a quite a bit trickier. To accomplish this, the twins organized a joint session of Congress with the goal of mandating a carbon fee on all Greenhouse Gas (GHG) producers and emitters. According to the resolution they presented, the revenue generated by this 'carbon fee' would be dispersed in the following manner. Each year, the first 70% would be given to any companies — both existing and start-ups with proven track records — that dedicated time and materials to development of new renewable energy sources, expansion of existing renewable energy sources, or both. The remaining 30% would then be evenly distributed to all U.S. citizens as 'relief payments' for both the trials and tribulations suffered from the COVID pandemics, plus the ongoing onslaught of problems associated with the climate crisis. Their proposal also stipulated that these payment percentages could be adjusted in future years — depending on the annual needs of the renewable energy industry and the American public.

Finally, their bill stipulated payment of three trillion dollars in subsidies to U.S. automobile manufacturers for their production of electric vehicles (EVs). By including this action, Shiloh and Sunny reminded their House and Senate colleagues that — in 2021 — General Motors was worth less than one-tenth as much as Tesla Corporation even though GM was selling five times as many cars. It was this stock market disparity that drove GM to transition many of its production lines throughout the country to EVs.

THE CLIMATE CRISIS ACT SHOWS QUICK RESULTS

In achieving strong support for HR 7667, Shiloh and Sunny emphasized that including a large infusion of cash for electric vehicle (EV) production would soon end production of gasoline-powered vehicles and they were oh so right! On July seventh, 2024, the last gasoline-powered vehicle — fittingly a Ford Mustang — rolled off an assembly line in Detroit, Michigan. The U.S. conversion to all new EVs was now complete — more than six years earlier than even the most optimistic proponents had predicted.

In the final analysis, the U.S. auto industry's switch to production of EVs only, the elimination of subsidies, and the severe financial pinch now being applied by the 'carbon fee' proved too much of a 'cross to bear' for the fossil fuel industry. On August first, 2024 — led by Exxon-Mobile and Chevron — Big Oil announced that they were now shuttering most of their coal, natural gas, and oil operations for good.

But — in making this joint announcement — the former fossil fuel giants also strongly emphasized that they were not going out of business. Quite the contrary — just as Shiloh and Sunny had predicted — they were rapidly restructuring themselves as renewable energy companies. Plus, lo and behold, it just so happened that their plans for making these transitions were already in place and — according to an industry spokesperson — 'this had been the case for many years'.

As part of their announcement, the rebranded energy companies miraculously presented 'new plans' that showed a nationwide phalanx of wind farms and solar arrays. Plus — where it was possible — these plans detailed the conversion of existing power grids to service their renewable energy sources. And — where this was not possible — they showed retooling the existing grids, or building new grids to accomplish the same purpose.

While the next piece of Shiloh and Sunny's 2023 legislative achievement wasn't as exciting as their CCA — for all of our Nation's non-human residents — it was even more important. HR 7668 — the *2023 Biodiversity Protection Act (BPA)* — once and for all rebuked the draconian notion of 'man's required dominion over nature'. Instead, this bill honored the belief of esteemed Harvard Professor Emeritus and Father of Biodiversity E.O. Wilson that 'every time we lose a species to extinction, we are sacrificing something that may have provided human society with untold medical or sociological benefits'.

In other words, there is no such thing as an insignificant species. And — because of this — Americans need to treat each species on Earth as being worthy of human protection. With this in mind, the twins structured their BPA to mandate permanent protection for all plant and wildlife species listed as either 'threatened' or 'endangered' under the 1973 Endangered Species Act. Their bill also required specific field identification of and permanent preservation for all 'critical habitats' that are associated with both of these categories of 'listed species'.

The final piece of legislation that Shiloh and Sunny tackled in 2023 involved something that most people didn't associate with either the climate crisis or biodiversity loss. Yet, it was the biggest issue of concern for long-term human health and survival in the world. In a single word, this key issue was 'food' — or more specifically — the process of producing food.

Based on all the climate crisis literature they had reviewed, and the interviews their ECO-Truth/RAP teams had conducted with both agricultural specialists and farm managers across the nation, Shiloh and Sunny knew that current agriculture practices — including everything from growing corn to raising chickens and beef cattle — were the world's biggest generators of climate-harming greenhouse gases. And — because of this — transforming our food and agriculture systems had to be a central component of solving our climate crisis. Based on everything they now knew, the twins fully believed that their HR 7669 — *the 2023 Regenerative Agriculture Act (RAA)* — would provide this desired transformation.

For RAA to work nationally, Shiloh and Sunny knew their bill had to mandate major changes in the way agriculture was currently being practiced in the U.S. So, HR 7669 specified ending billion-dollar giveaways to large-scale agricultural conglomerates — otherwise known as 'Big Ag'. Instead, their act focused future subsidies on farms that feature conservation practices which lead to carbon sequestration and better soil biological structure. The way the twins figured it — over the long-term — their bill would level the playing field for small farmers. In turn; fair, local, and regional food systems — ones that ensure good-paying jobs and healthy food for everyone — would be established.

After all was said and done, Shiloh and Sunny had achieved a Guinness Book of World Records 'first' for their 2023 legislative agenda. Working cooperatively 'across the aisles', they passed more legislation than any other freshman team in the history of the U.S. Congress.

Now, the next step in their collective agenda was convincing the rest of the world to follow their lead.

BOOK TWENTY-THREE
Completing the Circle

Taking Their Message to the World

Now that they were comfortably ensconced in the pantheon of Capitol Hill, Senator Shiloh Childers-Nkosi and Representative Sunny Childers-Nevin received a seemingly endless barrage of offers to speak at venues throughout the Nation. They accepted as many as they could fit into their complex schedules — truly lamenting the many opportunities they had to turn down. Then came the invitation the twins had passionately been seeking from the first day they started ECO-Truth — seventeen years ago.

On September eighth, 2023, Shiloh answered the phone in her Senate Office and heard the following:

"Hi, Senator Childers-Nkosi, this is Juanita LeGrom. I'm the Administrative Assistant for United Nations (UN) Secretary General Dr. Montclave Oranifor. We would be delighted if you and your sister could address our General Assembly in New York City one month from now — on October seventh."

For the first-time in her life, Shiloh was rendered completely speechless. After more than a minute — with Ms. LeGrom repeatedly asking "Senator Childers-Nkosi, are you there, are you OK?" — Shiloh finally composed herself and, very calmly, replied, "Why yes, Ms. LeGrom, I think we should be able to fit that into our schedules."

After politely thanking Ms. LeGrom, Shiloh could no longer constrain herself. She hit the speed dial button for Sunny's office and — before her sister could speak, she screamed, "Sunny — get over here… you'll never guess who just invited us to speak!"

For Sunny and Shiloh, October seventh, 2023 could not arrive soon enough. Working with Ms. LeGrom, they planned it so that Shiloh would present a brief opening statement. Then the rest of their hour-long session would be an open forum discussion, during which the twins would lead a Q & A on their climate emergency and biodiversity loss initiatives.

Since the bulk of their ECO-Truth and RAP Foundation's work had been conducted in the U.S., the twins wanted to understand — firsthand — how the rest of the world felt about these dual environmental crises. Knowing their session before the UN General Assembly would be simulcast to their peers — sitting in a Joint Session of Congress — Shiloh and Sunny had the perfect opportunity to accomplish this goal.

When the day finally arrived — buoyed by the hearty round of applause she received when she was introduced by Secretary General Oranifor — Shiloh began with this 'tough love' introductory message: "Folks, I'm not here to mince words or talk about 'maybe', 'could be', 'sometime soon', or 'perhaps in the future'. No, I'm here to tell you that the climate emergency is already fully upon us. And it's hitting us all with the force of an unrelenting Cat 5 Hurricane that has already made landfall and is devastating everything it touches — both natural and man-made.

"Put succinctly", continued Shiloh, "this means that we no longer have the luxury of taking our time and planning for fifty, twenty-five, or even ten years in the future. No — if we don't start taking significant actions right away, we'll be too late. While no one knows for sure what the future holds, I firmly believe that — if we continue to sit idly by and watch our planet deteriorate — by as soon as 2030, we may no longer recognize the planet we live on. Yes — because of this climate emergency — our world is really changing that fast."

With this dire warning now squarely in front of the UN delegates, Shiloh provided this elaboration, "Because of a physical phenomenon known as synergy, this whole ghastly process is continually feeding on itself and getting exponentially bigger and stronger with every hour that passes. To return to my hurricane analogy, the climate emergency is just like a swirling maelstrom gliding across roiling, warm seas. Every mile it moves, it gains strength and power and when it finally gets to its target everything in its path explodes into tiny fragments. With that, I would like to address any questions you may have."

At least fifty hands shot up immediately — an impressive display of enthusiasm that let Shiloh know her message of urgency had been fully received.

Taking over for Shiloh, Sunny first pointed to Stephanie Klammer; an Environmental Administrator from Denmark. Stridently flipping her golden hair and swirling her stylish dress, Professor Klammer squinched her steely eyes and pursed her lips as she looked directly at the podium and accusingly asked, "Why — as the presumed leader of the free world — does the United States have such a bleak record in accepting the validity of and doing anything substantial about either the climate crisis or the biodiversity emergency?"

Summoning as much tact as she could, Sunny provided this rejoinder to Professor Klammer, "You are quite right, ma'am. For the past several decades, the major obstacle to making substantive progress in battling the climate and biodiversity emergencies in the United States has been public reticence. But now I take extreme pride in announcing that the U.S. Congress has finally amended their heretofore staunchly recalcitrant attitudes about both crises.

"I strongly encourage you all to take a close look at our HR 7667 — the 2023 Climate Crisis Resolution and Recovery Act and HR 7668 — the Biodiversity Recovery Act," continued Sunny. "We passed both of these bills into law just this year. When Shiloh and I wrote these bills, we were considering solutions for not just the U.S., but for the world as a whole. It's our paramount hope that all of the Nations attending this assembly will use both HR 7667 and HR 7668 as models for the expeditious promulgation of your own climate crisis and biodiversity protection legislation."

Next, Sunny selected the raised hand of Avoute Shotar — the Ambassador of the Environment from Bangladesh. Looking resplendent and statuesque in his ceremonial robes, Mr. Shotar's broad, handsome face shriveled to a grimace as he remarked, "Because of the climate emergency, the entire three-river delta region of my country is being swallowed whole. The people living there are losing their ability to grow food for their own families. They have nothing to eat and nowhere to go. What are they supposed to do now?"

"Well, Mr. Shotar, let me start by saying how much we empathize with the desperation of your people," responded Sunny, "but I'm glad you brought up this ongoing catastrophe in southern Bangladesh, because it epitomizes a situation that we should all be scrutinizing immediately."

"We are already undergoing an extreme event that verifies —

beyond the shadow of a doubt — that the climate emergency is decimating huge segments of the world-wide human population," continued Sunny. "This event is a world-wide food crisis.

"At first analysis, we may not be able to directly correlate droughts and famine with the climate crisis. But think about it. These human population shattering events are — in fact — directly tied to our exponentially-changing climate. Each severe shift in precipitation patterns relates correspondingly to losses of agricultural land and food production areas."

"We have seen recent signs of this occurring right here in the United States. The severe drought of 2015 wiped out much of the agricultural production in California's Central Valley. But — right now — climate related food crises are occurring most frequently in many of the most disrespected Nations on Earth — such as Bangladesh. Because of this, these countries aren't getting the attention they deserve in terms of being the bellwethers of our climate emergency."

"Yes, your summary certainly grasps the urgency of our situation," Mr. Shotar responded in frustration, "but you aren't giving me any answers. Right now, every day — as we are speaking — thousands of my country's families are packing their meager belongings and leaving their flooded and sinking homelands. Worst of all, they don't have any idea where they are going. Our capital, Dhaka, cannot absorb any more migrants. The city is experiencing a population explosion of unprecedented proportions. Within a few short years, Dhaka's population has increased from four million to fifteen million people. The city's people already live in 'shanty-towns' with no running water or toilet facilities. There is no longer any room to fit more people in amid the steaming, narrow pathways of this plywood-and-corrugated-tin sea of urban humanity."

Sunny realized that Mr. Shotar was on a roll, providing a first-hand description of the hardships and horrors of the climate emergency much better than she ever could. So, she decided to let him continue. And did he ever!

"As the sea continues to rise," Mr. Shotar continued, "millions of Bangladeshis will be displaced — without any place to go within their own country. Desperate to find a home for their families, their legions will flow toward our border with India. The leaders of India's government have publicly voiced their acceptance of migrants from Bangladesh — but only if they are Hindu. India's leftist politicians, express distress over this tendentious policy, but it is not likely to change. The stipulation is rooted in a long-standing Indian discrimination against Muslims. And Bangladesh's population is more than ninety percent Muslim."

"So, what is going to happen when thousands of Bangladeshi Muslims descend on India looking for a fresh start?", further lamented Mr. Shokar. "This kind of pressure cooker environment is primed for intensive upheaval. There is a direct correlation between resource scarcity and conflict — which history has shown is often followed by an explosion of violence. Will the result of this tension at India's borders be a massive slaughter of men, women, and children at the hands of India's border guards and supporting military troops? Or will violent fighting bring tremendous losses of life on both sides of the border? It's all almost too disturbing to even contemplate."

Fully commiserating with Mr. Shotar's shocking summary, Sunny drew a deep breath to regain her composure and continued, "Mr. Shotar, your potential conclusion to Bangladesh's food crisis is both breathtaking and mind-numbingly harrowing. But let me assure you, I now firmly believe that the dramatic, world-wide food shortages and famines being caused by our climate emergency are exactly what is needed to finally get the world's attention and start demanding answers — not concepts or plans — but definitive, actionable solutions. We must now start paying attention to the droughts, famines, and food shortages that are ravaging so many of Earth's human inhabitants. Absolutely nothing could be more indicative of a crisis than taking away the food that sustains human bodies — especially those of innocent children."

Flailing her arms for extra emphasis as she spoke, Sunny continued, "Mr. Shotar, let me take your unimaginable scenario one step further. Only this time, we are talking about an unprecedented event that has already happened — several years ago, in fact. Consider this question: Take away a human population's food and what will happen. If they can't grow or somehow find more food for their families, are they just going to sit around and starve to death? No — they will become desperate, just as is happening right now in Bangladesh."

"Of necessity, they will do anything in their power to find food to again be able to feed their families," continued Sunny. "This includes mass migrations, regional instability, and — ultimately — widespread revolution. This has already happened in several places. Just ask the people of Syria about what happened because of their authoritarian president!"

"In summary," concluded Sunny, "I think that most of you in this esteemed chamber now believe that the climate emergency is real. So, there's no need to provide any more gruesome truth of what has already happened and what is — most likely — about to happen next. For the rest of our session, I want to have an in-depth, interactive discussion with you about what we — as members of the United Nations — see as the most logical, realistic, near-term solutions to this world-wide climate crisis. I am anticipating a lively debate which will help us refine and polish our ideas and — hopefully — also come up with some new approaches. So — if you've been wanting to express your feelings about the climate and biodiversity crises — now is the time to do so. Successfully fending off this scourge requires us all working together. Not just as Americans, or as Africans, or as Asians but as one world of citizens — united as brothers and sisters — working together to save the Earth as we currently know it."

"So — all right — here we go", exclaimed Sunny — simultaneously jumping toward the audience to make sure everyone was paying attention. "As we have just promulgated in our national climate and biodiversity bills, Shiloh and I firmly believe that the first and most immediately impactful step we can take is legislating a 'carbon fee' on each and every entity involved with producing, processing, and emitting CO_2 emissions throughout the world."

As soon as these words were spoken, a bevy of hands shot up throughout the UN's Assembly Hall. Maintaining the interactivity that Sunny had just promised, Shiloh recognized Athena Mazron — a Resource Conservation Specialist from the tiny country of Lichtenstein.

Young and vibrant with a feathery air and wispy voice, Ms. Mazron stated a question that Shiloh fully expected and knew would immediately be on the mind of most folks in the assembled delegation, "But won't the fossil fuel companies just pass the added cost of these fees along to their customers by raising prices accordingly?"

"Ah yes — that's an excellent question," posited Shiloh confidently, "but in our HR 7667, we included a regulatory provision that prevents this from happening. You just have to hope that the legislatures in your home countries will have the steeled wills it will take to withstand the fury of the fossil fuel industry. Because — as Sunny and I have already experienced — they will fight any 'carbon fee' legislation with their guns blazing. It will certainly become like a stare-down contest in which the person — or, in this case, the nation — that blinks first, loses. But we are confident that a majority of each nation's law-makers will now have enough sense of urgency about this situation to see that it gets done!"

Since many hands were still extended throughout the audience, Shiloh took another question from Alexi Shocovitch, Executive Director of Latvia's Agency of Environmental Economics. Immaculately attired with a neatly-trimmed handlebar moustache framing his thin face, Mr. Shocovitch spoke slowly in broken, but clearly understandable English, "The revenues generated by the recently legislated 'carbon fees' — of which you speak — will be massive. Where will all this money go?"

Shiloh couldn't have been happier with Director Shocovitch's question. It was exactly what she wanted to talk about next. "I'm so glad you asked me this, Mr. Shocovitch," she replied, "this is the best part of our 'carbon fee' process. Again — as it is written into our legislation — the monies generated will be used in two ways.

"Initially, the majority of these carbon fee revenues will be paid to firms involved in renewable energy research, development, and infrastructure construction. Then the remaining monies will be dispersed to the American public — in the form of 'relief bonuses' paid directly to each adult household. So — in the final analysis — our HR 7667 provides the ultimate 'win-win scenario!'"

Next, Shiloh called on Luella Manuello — Director of Peru's Office of Natural Resources Management and Conservation. Walking up to the microphone in a colorful native print dress, Ms. Manuello tightly focused her handsome facial features on Shiloh and asked, "Managing and overseeing the collecting and dispersing of these carbon fee revenues will be a monumental task. Please tell me how you plan on doing this."

"OK — that's another perfect question", responded Shiloh excitedly. She was also fully expecting this question and — accordingly — had a ready answer. "As prescribed in HR 7667, we will do this by creating a new federal agency — the Department of Energy and Resiliency Solutions. If you'll notice, this new agency's acronym is DOERS — a perfect description of how — by working together — we will be able to get this accomplished!"

Next, Shiloh continued explaining her DOERS idea. "While establishing a brand-new government agency — from the ground up — will not be easy, it is also not unprecedented. In fact, the United States did the same thing more than one hundred years ago. And we did it to resolve a situation that was even more dire than our current climate crisis. Back then, two new federal agencies — the Bureau of Reclamation in the western U.S. and the Tennessee Valley Authority in the east — were created specifically to accommodate the basic needs for life — namely water, food, and energy — of tens of millions of U.S. citizens. Yes — the environmental impacts of constructing some of the world's most massive dams, reservoirs, and irrigation facilities were immense. But — at the time — the human needs that were being met by many of these new facilities were even more pressing than our current need for establishing a nationwide grid of renewable energy facilities."

After Shiloh finished talking, Sunny took the podium again and said, "Shiloh and I are concluding our presentation here today by asking you to schedule a Special UN Climate Solutions Forum. And we need to do this as soon as possible to keep the ball rolling on everything we have just discussed today. That's why we suggest scheduling this Climate Solutions Forum for this coming December at the Le Bourget Conference Center in the suburbs north of Paris. We believe that returning to the same location where COP-21 was held eight years ago will provide a special incentive for finalizing the agreement that was started there — but never officially ratified. We know this is an extremely tight time frame. But with the amazing power of the collective forces assembled herein, Shiloh and I have no doubt that we can and will get this done!"

"We believe that all attending countries now have a much better understanding of the problem we all face," continued Sunny. "Ideally — at the conclusion of this next Climate Solutions Forum — each country will officially commit to and fully ratify definitive emission reduction numbers that will pave the way for keeping the global temperature rise at less than 2.0 degrees centigrade. Since Sunny and I now have a strong foothold in both U.S. Congressional branches, we will lead the world effort in finally achieving this essential goal."

Capitalizing on the strength of Sunny's idea, Shiloh moved to the podium and asked, "So, how many of you will support holding a repeat version of the Paris Climate Change Conference — let's call it RENEW-1?" To the delight of both Shiloh and Sunny, almost every one of the attending UN delegates raised their hand. Plus, they did so while getting up out of their seats and enthusiastically applauding. Reveling in the audience's quick response, both Shiloh and Sunny politely stepped out from behind the podium and slowly raised their arms above their heads in a simultaneous gesture of thanks and celebration.

With that, Secretary General Oranifor took the podium and remarked, "Well, that's about as excited as I've ever seen you folks. Based on your unanimous approval, we will move forward — posthaste — with scheduling RENEW-1 for December eleventh to eighteenth, 2023, in Paris, France. I will tell our Program Coordinator to stay in touch with everyone in attendance while this is happening. Finally, let me again thank both Shiloh and Sunny for coming here today and giving us all so much hope about solving these two most worrisome problems. May God bless you both and may God bless all our efforts, as we proceed ahead to this momentous occasion."

Establishing the RENEW-1 Accord

With a mandate from the United Nations now secured, Shiloh and Sunny couldn't wait to get back to Capitol Hill and start pressuring Congress to actively support what they were now calling '*RENEW-1—The Second Chance Paris Climate Accord*'.

On October fifteenth, 2023 — assuming her role as the lead proponent — Sunny stepped up to the podium before the specially-called emergency Joint Session of Congress, "Good morning, ladies and gentlemen, I really appreciate your time today in letting me speak to you about a critically important matter."

"Just as global warming must be addressed as non-partisan here in the U.S., it must also be viewed as apolitical in the rest of the world," continued Sunny. "Global solutions will be forthcoming when the world accepts the precept that the climate emergency is a universal crisis that will severely affect every country and every person on Earth. This will not happen unless we successfully work together to find and implement immediate solutions. Again, thank you all for your kind attention and understanding. And please know that we can't wait on this issue. We absolutely must get started right away."

Picking up her cue from Sunny, Shiloh walked over to the podium and made the pitch, "Congressional colleagues, we have asked you here today to receive your blessings for a matter of worldwide urgency. First — for those of you who may not know it — the United Nations has already approved our proposal for a *Second Chance Paris Climate Accord* to be held this coming December eleventh to eighteenth at the Le Bourget Conference Center, north of Paris. Most of you likely remember that this is the same location as the 2015 Paris Climate Accord. But instead of calling this a 'do over', we are calling it RENEW-1, a chance to get things right the second time around. And — since we already have the near unanimous approval of the UN — we fully expect that this will be accomplished. So, now, let's find out how many of you will join us in getting this done?"

In response to Shiloh's beseeching request, both the Senate Majority Leader and the Speaker of the House requested roll call votes. The final tallies were:

- Senate — 60 Ayes, 38 Nays, 2 Abstentions
- House — 324 Ayes / 107 Nays / 4 Abstentions

Once they were outside of the House chamber, Sunny and Shiloh looked at each other, smiled broadly, breathed huge sighs of relief, and bumped fists — complete with the 'let it rain' final movement. They were off to Paris again — and this time they would make sure that total success did not slip through the world's fingers.

A Triumphant Return

As the days for their return trip to Paris drew closer and closer, Shiloh and Sunny could hardly contain their enthusiasm. Having very full legislative agendas — plus being very active on several key Congressional Committees — helped them both stay focused on their work.

But the dates December eleventh to eighteenth, 2023, were always there — lingering in their minds no matter what they were doing. They were both convinced that *RENEW-1 — The Second Chance Paris Climate Accord* — would be, and likely would forever remain, the most important thing they would do in their lives. They both knew that — if everything went the way they hoped — the world's tormented battles with both the climate emergency and biodiversity crisis would finally be on definitive pathways toward world-wide resolution.

When the evening for their departure finally arrived, Sunny and Shiloh loaded into a White House limousine for the drive to Andrews Air Force Base in Maryland. Once there, they boarded Air Force Two — along with the rest of the U.S. delegation. As is typical on most flights to Europe, Air Force Two left Andrews AFB at precisely 6.30 p.m. — allowing their cadre of high-powered passengers to — ostensibly — catch six hours of 'shut-eye' before arriving at Orly Field in Paris, just as the sun was rising.

Of course, both Sunny and Shiloh didn't sleep a wink during the plane flight. They spent the whole trip busily preparing their presentation plus quietly hobnobbing with everyone else who wasn't sleeping.

When Air Force Two landed in Paris, an honor guard of black Range Rovers — all with their blue emergency lights spinning — was there to pick the U.S. delegation up and whisk them off to their suites at the Relais & Chateaux Hotel Splendide Royal Paris. Somewhat embarrassed by their luxurious accommodations, the twins confidently believed that the out-sized carbon footprints of their trip would be fully mitigated by what they expected to accomplish during the conference.

Once in their rooms, Shiloh and Sunny were able to rest for a few hours of sleep before heading off to the Le Bourget Conference Center. Arriving at the facility in the northeastern suburbs of Paris, the twins were first greeted by a forty-by-forty-foot twirling marquee featuring these words:

WELCOME WORLD DELEGATES TO RENEW-1
Shiloh and Sunny—The Stage Is Now Yours!

Clearly moved by this awe-inspiring yet resolute greeting, the twins walked in and took their center-stage seats in stunned silence. They now knew — without a doubt — that they were about to embark on a new chapter in world history.

On the morning of December seventeenth, 2023 — RENEW-1's final full day — after once again being introduced by UN Secretary General Montclave Oranifor — Shiloh walked to the dais and began reading her carefully-crafted speech. "Good morning, esteemed world delegates, I feel immensely honored to be able to speak with you again about two subjects that are most dear to my heart — global warming and biodiversity loss.

"In the United States, our environmental movement has gone through several significant phases. Starting with the 'Radical 60s', we moved — in succession — through the 'Regulatory 70s', the 'Backlash 80s', the 'Complacent 90s', and the 'Hopeless 2000s'. From the viewpoint of both global warming and biodiversity loss, we are now in the midst of what will — hopefully — become known as the 'Solution 2020s'".

"Solving the world's existential crises of global warming and biodiversity loss will require de-emphasizing social and religious infighting among cultures and countries in favor of electing international leaders who come together in thought, word, and spirit with one common purpose — ensuring the long-term quality of life for all of Earth's future generations."

"The major environmental crises currently facing Earth's human populations — Global Warming, the Sixth Extinction, and

Overpopulation — often seem overwhelming to the majority of people. This sense of impending, irresolvable doom breeds — in kind — hopelessness and indifference."

"But now — going forward — we must supplant this prevailing shroud of hopelessness with a worldwide seed of hopefulness. This mindset change will help all of Earth's people create the massive groundswells of public support that we need to force our countries' leaders to take immediate and strident actions and find realistic solutions. These actions must include mandating widespread conversions to renewable energy sources, stopping approvals of new fossil fuel extractions, and levying heavy fees on existing fossil fuel generators."

"We must also understand that global warming and biodiversity loss are problems that are affecting all of humanity — without regard to class, socioeconomic status, religious persuasion, political affiliation, age, or ethnicity. Folks, all of us — worldwide — are truly in this together."

"As I'm sure all of you know, COP-21 was held at this very same location from November thirty-first through December fourteenth, 2015. At the conference's conclusion, the majority of the world's countries agreed to sign a treaty — now called '*The Paris Climate Accord*'. In some ways, this was a landmark event. For the first time in the history of the COP meetings, more than one hundred and ninety countries all agreed that fossil fuels were not the way forward."

"Unfortunately, most activists — and even many attending nations — believed that the *2015 Paris Accord* did not really amount to much. For one thing, most countries provided little specificity in defining their greenhouse gas (GHG) emission reduction targets. For example, there was limited mention of exactly how and when these GHG emission reductions would be achieved."

"So, today, we are offering, for your approval, a new resolution — *The RENEW-1 — The Second Chance Paris Climate Accord* — that will eliminate the previous agreement's shortcomings. I am quite confident that your ratification of this document — as it is currently written — will stop the global temperature rise in its tracks and truly stave off the devastating, long-term impacts of both the climate crisis and the ongoing loss of Earth's biodiversity."

"First and foremost, this new resolution specifies that the collective targets for the annual *Nationally Determined Contributions (NDCs)* of each country's emission reduction plans must be structured to permanently keep the global temperature rise at less than 2.0 degrees centigrade. Next, each country must present a precise suite of solutions demonstrating how their annual *NDCs* are going to be achieved. This will allow all of the participating nations to take into account each other's inputs — sharing information about what works and what doesn't work, and which technologies hold promise for the future."

"Finally, each country's *Individual Climate Agreement (ICA)* must be a 'living document' that can be revisited and revised on an annual basis. This will allow each participating nation to annually account for their climate impacts in a global analysis, and — as needed — ratchet up their emission reduction *NDCs* in honest and fair manners that are reviewed and approved by all other attending nations."

"In conclusion, I firmly believe that the time is now right for approval of *RENEW-1 — The Second Chance Paris Climate Accord*. We must find global warming and biodiversity loss solutions that are not precipitated by responses to future calamitous events but are — instead — driven by the current hopeful and forceful elicitations of the masses, voicing their desire to make a difference for all future generations."

With that, Shiloh stepped from behind the dais, held her arms out invitingly, and concluded, "So, now — my esteemed colleagues — will you please join me in making history by approving this new UN resolution? Working together as one, we can get this done for the preservation of our planet!"

As the assembled delegates stood in unison and applauded their support, Secretary General Oranifor replaced Shiloh at the dais. After letting the applause continue on for several minutes, he smiled at both Sunny and Shiloh then called for the vote that unanimously approved *RENEW-1—The Second Chance Paris Climate Accord.*

The Accord Heard Around the World

On the evening of December eighteenth, 2023, two Australian Aborigine stockmen — Minjarra and Yarran — are lying back against their bedrolls and enjoying their after-dinner cups of tea. A roaring fire is crackling just beyond their boot-shod feet as they discuss grazing conditions on their beloved rangeland. Befitting the onset of summer in the central Outback, a hot, sultry day has slowly turned into a lovely warm evening.

Suddenly, Minjarra receives an alert signal on his iPad. Casually reaching for his device, he begins reading the message's text. Then — suddenly very excited — he blurts out to his cattle-wrangling friend, "Well guv'ner — would you look at this. Those twin politician gals from the U.S. have just ram-rodded through a binding United Nations resolution that will solve both of our worldwide environmental crises — global warming and biodiversity loss. Maybe now we won't have to endure any more of those gol'dern massive, raging wildfires that have been destroying our native backcountry for the past ten years."

Smiling contentedly as he stretched out his warming legs, Yarran replied, "You know, it seems like in order to solve these problems we've had to *'come full circle'* — harking back to the beliefs of our forefathers."

"How do you mean that, mate?" responded Minjarra — quaffing the last few drops of his bed-time tea.

"Well, you know that way back when our ancient ancestors were the only folks running around out here in the Outback," explained Yarran, "they instinctively understood that — in order to survive — they had to get along with the natural world. In fact — as I understand it — just about every part of Earth had native peoples that believed this same thing. Then, somehow — as humans supposedly evolved and got smarter — we actually just got dumber and started believing that we didn't need to worry about caring about other living things."

"Oh, yeah, I get what you're saying now," responded Minjarra, vigorously nodding his head. "We just decided we could do whatever the bloody heck we wanted, and the rest of nature would just follow along — right?"

"Exactly," emphasized Yarran, pointing his teacup at Minjarra, "except it seems like we've now figured out that that was exactly the wrong way to be doing things. Maybe we've finally come the full way around — inserting ourselves back into nature's *circle of life*. Let's just hope that — from now on — we can keep it that way!"

"Amen to that, brother, I certainly hope so. Sleep well, my friend," replied Minjarra as he tucked himself down into his woolen blanket.

"Indeed, good night, my friend," said Yarran.

Then, as both native Australians slipped off into a comfortable sleep, the still crackling embers seemed to add, "And good on you, Representative Sunny Childers-Nevin and Senator Shiloh Childers-Nkosi. You're both now on your way to accomplishing your life's ambition — saving Planet Earth!"

An 80-Year Retrospective

It's Earth Day 2050 — exactly eighty years since the first one — and everything is now looking pretty good for our planet. Sunny Childers-Nevin and Shiloh Childers-Nkosi are sitting on Shiloh's outdoor patio overlooking the sweeping seascape of the Pacific Ocean. After being the featured guests in several celebratory rallies all over San Diego County, they are now enjoying a sumptuous catered dinner with their husbands, four children and five grandchildren.

While the desserts — toll house pie topped with vanilla ice cream — are being served, Naomi, Sunny's daughter, stands to make a toast. Raising her glass, Naomi begins, "I know we all realize the significance of today. Just thirty years ago, we had no idea what the future quality of life on Earth for humans would be. But now — thanks in large part to the unyielding efforts of Mom and Aunt Shiloh — all of our planet's above-ground fossil fuels have long since gone the way of the dinosaurs from which they came."

"We all now live in a global electric society — totally powered by renewable energy sources. Because of this, we have become a '*zero-carbon emissions*' world. Global warming has been permanently capped at less than 2.0 degrees centigrade. Plus, our biodiversity loss rate has been reduced significantly through a combination of climate crisis control and more diligent protection of our rare species and their associated critical habitats."

"Okay," continued Naomi, "now for the fun part. Shiloh Childers-Nkosi and Sunny Childers-Nevin — will you both please stand. While I understand that no award can ever surpass the Presidential Medal of Freedom you each received from the U.S. President in 2032, we believe that what we are about to show you will keep us in your minds forever."

With that, Shiloh's son — Zane Jr. — stepped over to an easel and pulled off its cover. Underneath was a beautifully finished color portrait featuring Shiloh and Sunny in the middle of a group of twenty very officious-looking people. Everyone in the photo had clasped hands with the person standing next to them, and now they all had their hands raised above their heads. The elegant teakwood frame included a golden plaque engraved with the words:

SENATOR SHILOH CHILDERS-NKOSI &
REPRESENTATIVE SUNNY CHILDERS-NEVIN
TODAY WE THANK YOU FOR SAVING OUR WORLD!
THE UNITED NATIONS GENERAL ASSEMBLY
PLUS, YOUR LOVING AND LOYAL FAMILY
DECEMBER 18, 2023

Tears began streaming down the faces of both Sunny & Shiloh as they stood staring at the photo. With everyone at the table buzzing about the award's remarkable message, Zane Jr. said, "Well — obviously we have successfully pulled this off. I don't think either of you were even aware that this photo existed. We've been secretly holding onto it now for twenty-seven years. We were saving it for just this moment. We dearly love you both and sincerely appreciate all you have done — both for us and for the world as a whole."

After dessert was finished, everyone positioned their chairs in a line to watch the sunset — and Mother Nature did not disappoint. The scattered cloudbank had left just enough gap at the waterline to allow the sun's brilliant orangish-pink rays to penetrate through. For a full fifteen minutes, the sky — from horizon-to-horizon — was ablaze with color.

After the natural light show was finished, Shiloh stood, turned and faced the group, and said, "Wow, what a perfect ending to a perfect day. We are so lucky to still be living in this natural world that we all know and love."

EPILOGUE

In the overall history of human life here on Earth, we have never faced more broad-based and existential environmental threats than those posed by the climate crisis and biodiversity loss. On a geologic timescale, we are accelerating toward our own oblivion at laser-focused warp speed. Right now — every day — the world is adding more layers of atmospheric pollution and species disintegration to the enveloping shroud that may eventually doom our own species (*Homo sapiens*) to extinction.

These twin towers of environmental degradation are not something that might become a problem in the future — maybe by 2100, or 2050, or 2030. They are problems right now, and they're getting worse every day that we sit by and pretend that nothing is really happening.

But here is the good news. The climate crisis and biodiversity loss do not have to remain problems. In fact — if we focus and work together — both of these conundrums can be well on their way to full resolution in less than ten years.

If we play our cards right, we can use the perpetual, inextinguishable energy of Earth — the sun's glorious rays, the wind's constant breezes, and the water's endless waves — to work for us all. And, in the process, we'll leave the polluting fossil fuels right where they belong — buried in the ground, never to see the light of day.

Think about it: Renewable energy here on Earth is abundant and omnipresent. Each time you go outside, you see and feel it everywhere. It's like an endless symphony written by a master composer and played by a world-class orchestra. The golden rays of streaming sunlight are the strings — always there, maintaining the basic rhythm of the interwoven movements. The wind provides the percussion — rising from gentle whispering breezes of the snare drum to the bold resounding gusts of the tympani. Then moving water blends in with the woodwinds and the brass — transitioning from gently lapping melodic notes of the flute to lazy ripples of an oboe's dulcet tones and concluding with rolling waves of trumpet blasts.

We are now right on the cusp of what will be the *Renewables Revolution* — providing a mighty parallel to the Industrial Revolution. The Industrial Revolution resulted in the transformation of our nation from a rural agrarian society to an urban, manufacturing society. Now we are about to transform ourselves again — from a hard-edged, fossil-fuel driven economy, to a softer-sided renewable energy world.

This transformation from fossil fuels to renewable energy is already possible. *The Solutions Project (www.thesolutionsproject.org)* lays out immediate plans for converting each of our states — plus many countries — from fossil fuels to renewable resources. And we can accomplish this at the same time as we create numerous new industries in the wind, solar, and water power sector.

In fact — right now — 'Big Oil' has the wherewithal to lead the transformation from fossil fuels to renewable energy. They know it's coming — they've known this for more than thirty years! They're already planning for the transition. They just want to delay things as long as possible because — in the short term — they will take a financial hit. But — in the long run — they will actually make more money from renewables than they are currently making from fossil fuel production and processing. The sooner we can make the fossil fuel giants make the switch, the better off we'll all be. Over the short term, the mighty impetus created by nationwide conversion to renewable energy will bolster every sector of our economy. As the old adage goes: "A rising tide lifts all boats."

This renewable energy boom will create millions of new jobs — leading to increased financial security for everyone. Now that's a *win-win scenario* we can all live with. Plus, our children, grandchildren, and all future generations will look back and be forever grateful to us for being proactive in tackling and resolving the current climate crisis and biodiversity dilemmas.

So, now the decision is in our hands. The issue is about preserving the existing quality and character of the human species here on Earth. Will we '*come full circle*' and decide to make the changes that will save our ice sheets, tundra, oceans, coral reefs, rain forests, and polar bears? Or will we just watch while our world slides into oblivion — at least for *Homo sapiens*?

REFERENCES

Abbey, Edward. *Desert Solitaire*. University of Arizona Press. 1988.

Abbey, Edward. *The Monkey Wrench Gang*. Dream Garden Press. 1985.

Cameron, James et al. *Years of Living Dangerously*. Showtime Networks Inc. 2014.

Carson, Rachel. *Silent Spring*. Mariner Books, Anniversary Edition. 2002.

Carson, Rachel. *The Edge of the Sea*. Houghton Mifflin Co., First Edition. 1956.

Carson, Rachel. *The Sea Around Us*. Oxford University Press, 3rd Edition. 2018.

Carson, Rachel. *Under the Sea Wind*. Dutton Adult, 50th Anniversary Edition. 1991.

Douglas, Marjory Stoneman. *The Everglades: River of Grass*. Pineapple Press, 3rd Edition. 2021.

Gore, Al. *An Inconvenient Truth*. Viking Books, Revised Edition, 2007.

Hayhoe, Katharine. *A Climate for Change*. FaithWords, 1st Edition. 2009.

Hiaasen, Carl. *Team Rodent: How Disney Devours the World*. Ballantine Books. 2010.

Kitchell, Mark. *A Fierce Green Fire—The Battle for a Living Planet*.

Documentary Film, American Masters, PBS. 2014.

Klein, Naomi. *This Changes Everything.* Simon & Schuster, 1st Edition. 2014.

Kline, Benjamin. *First Along the River.* Rowman & Littlefield Publishers, Fifth Edition. 2022.

Kolbert, Elizabeth. *The Sixth Extinction.* Henry Holt and Co., 1st Edition. 2014.

Leopold, Aldo. *A Sand County Almanac (The Land Ethic).* Oxford University Press, Illustrated Edition. 2001.

Marshall, Robert "Bob". *The Problem of the Wilderness. The Scientific Monthly*, Vol. 30, No. 2. 1930.

McKibben, Bill. *The End of Nature.* Random House Trade Paperbacks. 2006.

McPhee, John. *Encounters with the Archdruid.* Farrar, Straus and Giroux, First Edition. 1971.

Oreskes, Naomi. *Merchants of Doubt.* Bloomsbury Publishing, Reprint Edition. 2011.

Orlowski, J. *Chasing Coral.* NETFLIX. 2017.

Orlowski, J. *Chasing Ice.* Submarine Deluxe. 2012.

Peterson, Roger Tory. *Field Guide to the Birds of North America.* Mariner Books, 2nd Edition. 2020.

Peterson, Roger Tory. *Birds Over America.* Dodd, Mead & Company, 1st Edition. 1948.

Porter, Elliot. *The Place No One Knew*. Gibbs Smith Publisher, Commemorative Edition. 2000.

Rawlings, Marjorie Kinnan. *The Yearling*. Atheneum Books for Young Readers, Reissue Edition. 2013.

Thoreau, Henry David. *Walden and Civil Disobedience*. Barnes & Noble Classics, 1st Edition. 2004.

Wister, Owen. *The Virginian*. Digireads.com Publishing. 2017.

World Wildlife Fund. *Living Plant Report 2014*. September 30, 2014.

CPSIA information can be obtained
at www.ICGtesting.com
Printed in the USA
LVHW102355150922
728494LV00006B/195

9 781800 745681